Copyright © 2024 by Fanny Lee Savage

All rights reserved.

No portion of this book may be reproduced in any form without written permission from the publisher or author, except as permitted by U.S. copyright law.

This book is a work of fiction. Any references to historical events, real people, or real places are used fictitiously. Other names, characters, places, and events are products of the author's imagination, and any resemblance to actual events or places or persons, living or dead is entirely coincidental.

Cover design by Savage by Design

For all you filthy girls (and boys) who fantasize about being chased through the woods by four masked men.
And getting caught.

Content Warning

Oh boy. Where do I start?

This is the second book in a six book, dark romance series. All the main characters are between the ages of 25 and 35.

If you're here, that means you've read *Prey*, so you know what to expect spice wise. When I released Book 1 in this series, I warned everyone the themes would grow darker as the story progressed. What I didn't expect was how fast we'd end up wading through murky waters.

In this book (and future books) please know that when I say dark romance, I mean themes. These boys are various shades of tragically beautiful gray, waving around red flags like a welcome sign. This is a why-choose MMMFFM dark romance, with multiple POV. Meaning pretty much EVERYONE touches each other and we get to read from the perspective of various characters throughout the books. If that's not your thing, that's okay.

Just like in *Prey*, things grow darker as this story moves forward. If you can stomach that these characters will be enduring some pretty horrible things within these pages, and the rest of the books, than proceed.

For a complete list of content, please visit my website.
Themes:

Dark, mafia, friends to lovers, enemies to lovers, bi-awakening, why-choose, military, boarding school, trauma bonding, captive, forbidden, forced proximity, masked men

Contents:

Detailed graphic sexual content, including extremely thorough scenes with two-, three-, and six-person encounters and BDSM themes.

For more info please see my site.

Playlist

Stephen Sanchez - The Other Side
David Kushner - Skin and Bones
Smashing Pumpkins – Disarm
Hozier - Why Would You Be Loved
Shaya Zamora – No Love For A Sinner
SYML - Howling
Shaya Zamora – Pretty Little Devil
mehro - exploding
BANNERS - Perfectly Broke
Nine Inch Nails - Something I Can Never Have
Thirty Seconds To Mars - A Beautiful Lie
Lusaint - Wicked Game (Cover)
3 Doors Down - She Don't Want The World
Lana Del Rey – Cinnamon Girl
Sleep Token - Take Me Back To Eden
SYML – Body
SYML – Symmetry (Dark Version)
Camylio - Running
Abe Parker – Numb
Stephen Sanchez - Howling at Wolves
Isak Danielson - Power
Birdy - Surrender
Bad Omens - The Death of Peace of Mind
Badflower – Mother Mary

FANNY LEE SAVAGE

Glossary

Otets – Father: Russian
Syn – Son: Russian
Soldat – Soldier: Russian
Mo Leannan – Sweetheart: Scottish Gaelic
Madadh-ruadh – Red Fox: Scottish Gaelic

Chapter 1

STRIKER

16 Years Ago , December, Age 14

My first memory is of darkness.

Then the darkness bled away, and bright lights illuminated faces I didn't recognize and places I didn't understand. After that, *he* came, and I was thrust into a bone chilling cold and a different kind of darkness. A darkness where light couldn't bleed in through cracks under the door. A dark so black, so cold, I knew that I'd go to sleep again if I allowed it.

Despite the biting cold that surrounded me, I held onto reality, feeling its icy fingers dig into my skin, creeping beneath my ribcage and robbing me of my breath.

I stayed in that darkness for so long, I feared I'd never come out.

But then I did.

The only memories of who I was before here are shadowy, blank spaces. Just a hollow emptiness and angry pain in my throat and belly. Flickering memories of falling asleep and waking up surrounded by people I'd never seen before. Of fear. Terror.

I don't have any memories of a mother before the darkness other than flashes of a gold bracelet tinkling like little bells around a thin wrist. I know it's her. My mother. How, I'm not sure. Some deep-rooted feeling that lives in my gut, I suppose.

Sometimes, I'll flash on a pretty bracelet and a wave of fear and sadness envelops me. But then I remember the delicate gold chains wrapped around the gypsy's waists at the market. I always enjoyed going to town, watching the gold bells and charms clang together as they walked by. Back when he allowed us to leave the school when we were boys. But we don't go to the market anymore.

Not since we turned of age.

I was five years old when Fallon brought me here, which seems odd that I don't remember my birth mother's face or have memories that aren't black waves of nightmarish terror. Five is old enough to remember your mother. But I was told my mother was a whore and didn't have time to raise a boy, so maybe that's why. She was too busy spreading her legs to earn money so she could shoot poison into her veins.

I remember Fallon telling me this when he sat me down on the icy floor in the cold room. I also remember thinking it was odd anyone wanted to put poison in their veins. When I said that, he told me it was because she was a stupid whore.

"Do you want to be like your mother?"

I didn't like the look in his eyes, so I said, "No."

"I'm your father now," he said, standing over me so that I had to look way, way up to see his face. The way he said each word was strange, like he had sand in his mouth, and couldn't pronounce the words right. "Do you understand?"

I nodded. But he didn't seem to like that I only nodded, so I told him, "*Si.*"

"Do you want to be strong like your *otets*?"

I wasn't sure what an *otets* was, but I figured it was something he called himself. I looked at his long legs, his broad shoulders, his short black hair and eyes the color of water. He looked big and mean. The way I thought fathers should look according to what little I knew about them. I'd never had one before. But I liked the idea of him being mine, even if his face was stern and I had yet to be rewarded with a smile.

"*Si, otets.*"

Then he shut the door, and I was alone.

And cold. For a long, long time.

When the coldness or blackness tries to creep back into my mind, I remind myself I am no longer that boy sitting in that room desperate for a stranger to be my father since my mother didn't want me. I'm a soldier.

At least I will be when I complete this part of my training.

"Striker!"

My name whips across the rooftop as harsh as the wind over the platform where we stand in formation, snapping me back to the present.

I straighten my spine, tightening my fists, blinking to focus my mind. I was floating again. My eyes find my *otets*. My father—Commander Fallon—as he insists we call him when we are in training. His brow quirks, but he says nothing.

The biting chill in the air reminds me of that first day here, and maybe that's why I'm flooded with memories. It's also probably because we are here so he can teach us a lesson. Much like that first cold day when he left me in the empty room with nothing but a thin sweater to keep me warm.

"Your enemies will use your weakness as a weapon," Fallon says, his voice barely audible over the roar of wind as he paces back and forth, back and forth, in front of us. "Weakness is a betrayal to your brothers. Do you understand, my sons?"

"Sir, yes, sir!" We shout in unison like we are one voice. One person. One unit. That's what he's teaching us. To be a deadly force capable of moving as one. A collection of perfect soldiers.

"Viper!" he shouts, turning on his heel to face us. His voice doesn't have that guttural, gravelly accent like Commander Maxim, but it's just as deadly. His usually stoic face flashes with something we all recognize as Fallon scans the line, looking for any flaw in our formation. Father keeps it shielded, but sometimes it slips out from under the mask he wears and cruelty shows its ugly face.

His cold, steely gaze lands on Viper to my right, and my jaw tenses. I think we all stop breathing as Fallon steps forward.

We all know what's coming. We've been here before.

"Step forward, *soldat*," Fallon says, raising a black leather gloved hand to beckon my brother forward.

My insides twist uncomfortably, but it's not like when we don't get food as punishment. It's that sensation in the pit of my stomach, a gnawing that reminds me of fear.

But I can't let the fear touch me. Fallon will try to beat it from me again if I so much as flinch. Not wanting to rile him, I push all my emotions down. Down further until I feel nothing but the coldness inside and out. Coldness like in that room, but I know now I can handle it.

I'm going to be a soldier.

Another gust whips across the rooftop, slashing us to the bone. My fingers ache from the cold, frozen in my leather gloves. I want to unclench my fists and stretch my fingers, but Commander Maxim will disapprove if I make the slightest movement.

Gritting my teeth, I keep my hands fisted at my sides, my arms rigid both from the freezing winter wind and from standing in formation for so long as I watch Viper step forward. His black boots scrape over the concrete, but then he stills, straightening his spine, keeping his chin level and eyes straight ahead, focusing on the open stretch of barren landscape around the school. Just as we've been taught. He's a good *soldat*.

To my left, Breaker shifts. My instincts scream to tell him to stop moving. If Fallon sees any hint of unease, it won't just be Viper up on the platform, it will be all of us taking turns.

Though we probably deserve it.

"Viper," Fallon says, stepping up close to the broad chested boy I've called my brother for the last nine years. Fallon's at least a head taller than my brother, but nowhere near as large. At sixteen, only two years older than me, Viper is bulky. Built like a tank, Fallon often says, as a good soldier should be. "Remind your brothers what makes a good soldier."

"Loyalty," Viper barks out. "Courage. Duty. Honor. Discipline. Respect."

Fallon steps back, clasping his hands behind his back as his icy eyes move over Viper. My stomach does that gross flip thing again. "And tell me, my *syn*, is there honor in theft?"

Viper squares his shoulders against a blast of cold air. "Sir, no. sir!"

"Is there honor in telling lies?"

"Sir, no, sir!"

"Tell me, Viper." Fallon's stony gaze hones in on Viper's face. "Are these considered weaknesses?"

"Sir, yes, sir!"

Those clear eyes land on me, making my gut twist, but he continues to speak to Viper. "As a soldier, we must protect our brothers at all costs, correct?"

It's barely noticeable, and I hope I'm the only one to hear it when Viper stutters, "S-Sir, yes, sir."

His pale eyes keep me pinned in place, memories of another day on this rooftop making my heart pick up pace as he says, "We do not say or do anything that may threaten our brothers, correct?"

Viper gives the correct response, keeping his chin high, but we all see the tension in the set of his jaw.

Breaking me free of his penetrating gaze, Fallon takes a large step back and Commander Maxim steps forward, an evil smirk shining on his pale, wide face. The sunlight catches on the smooth white scar that runs from his forehead, under the eyepatch, and travels down his cheek to his chin. He told us once that a giant crocodile tried to cut off the left side of his face, but he gutted him before he could. The way his remaining right eye gleams darkly as he motions to the platform behind him reminds me he's vicious enough to take down a crocodile.

There's only a slight hesitation as Viper steps forward. My stomach cramps, the bread I shoved down last night threatening to come up. Viper steps up on the platform, turning to face Commander, his back to the thick wooden pole at the center of the raised concrete circle.

"Remove your clothes," Fallon commands.

A ripple of unease moves through our line. It's deep winter and bitter cold with the wind ripping across the top of the school. He'll fucking freeze to death up here, so exposed.

With his mouth set into a thin line, Viper strips his clothes, folding his black peacoat, sweater, and fatigues neatly at the edge of the platform, then placing his black beanie and gloves on top, before resuming position.

"Face the pillar," Fallon says.

We all watch in complete silence as Viper presents his bare back to the Commander who wraps the thick leather straps around Viper's wrists, then cranks the chain fed through the loop at the top of the pole until Viper's arms are above his head. Viper widens his stance, but then goes still. Another gust of bitter wind sweeps over the platform, and a shiver moves through his shoulders, his breath puffing out, wrapping around the pole in a fine mist.

Turning back to us, Fallon walks our line, stopping in front of each one of my brothers, inspecting our uniforms. There aren't many of us left. Twelve in total now. We lost a brother this past spring. Us newer students, like Breaker and I, only joined in with the other *soldats* this past year. Viper the year before. Reaper and my other brothers have been in combat training for several years since they're older, and have moved up in ranks. Reaper, Hunter, and Seeker are the oldest of our regime, and have their first mission next year.

When Fallon reaches the end of the line, he motions for Reaper to step out of formation. Out of the corner of my eye, I catch Reaper's sleek back hair, so similar to Fallon's, as he steps up to our *otets*.

"*Soldat*," Fallon says, eyes still scanning over our line. "Can you tell your brothers why we are out in this cold, freezing our asses off?"

Reaper spins tightly, facing us, fists at his sides. I marvel at his grace. But then everything Reaper does is smooth, graceful like the ballerina's Father talks about sometimes.

"We have a thief in this school," Reaper shouts, his voice rough from cold and trying to be heard over the roar of wind. He's usually quiet. Reserved. It always shocks me when he takes command of our training.

"Is thievery in our motto?" Fallon asks.

"*Sir, no, sir!*" we all shout.

"Reaper, tell your brothers what we do to thieves."

"We cut off their hands."

Fallon watches our line, waiting for a reaction. When he gets none, he says, "But a good soldier needs both his hands, does he not?"

We don't hesitate. "*Sir, yes sir!*"

Fallon eyes us. "Someone crept into the kitchen last night and stole a loaf of bread." He scans all of us, looking for signs of guilt. Of course we give none. "When we steal from our school, we're taking from our own pockets." He's silent for a heartbeat. "Did I teach my soldiers to steal?"

"*Sir, no sir.*"

"Didn't we learn that stealing is a sin? That it is a dishonor to ourselves? To our brothers? To our school and all I have taught you?"

We all shout our response, even as my stomach roils. Next to me, Breaker shifts and I resist the urge to stomp on his foot. He'll give himself away. He'll give us all away.

In front of us, another violent tremor racks Viper's body as the wind gusts over the platform, his knees buckling slightly.

"Have we not learned that our actions have consequences? That if something happens to one of us, it happens to all of us? You, my sons, are a unit. Of one mind. One body. When one of you steals…" his voice trails off, but he doesn't have to say it.

We all pay the price.

His gaze lands on Breaker, and my chest tightens.

I think we all knew, even last night as we shoved buttered bits of bread into our mouths, we were going to suffer our *otets's* wrath, but I guess we're not cruel enough to have thought this up.

Yet.

Not cruel enough yet, but Fallon is trying to cure us of that.

"Breaker," Fallon says. "Step forward, *syn*."

My jaw tightens. The urge to grip Breaker's thin shoulder and pull him behind me is so strong, I nearly do it, but Reaper catches my eye and gives me a slight shake of his head. He doesn't have to say the words for them to ring in my head.

No. Do not stop our otets. *It'll be worse than this if you do.*

I swallow the bile in my throat and watch as the reedy boy next to me steps from formation.

As much as I want to blame Breaker for his inability to follow orders, we're here because we all ate that fucking bread. But if he hadn't been so.... so *himself*, Father wouldn't have put him in solitary with only a metal bucket of water. Then Breaker wouldn't have starved for two days as punishment. And Viper never would have snuck into the kitchen last night and stole that loaf of bread when he found Breaker clutching his stomach and crying about being hungry after Fallon released him.

Stupid kid. Both of them. Viper has a soft spot for Breaker. He always has. But Viper is reckless, and we are all hungry, all the time, so when he brought the loaf back along with a plate of fresh butter, of course we all ate it. Even Reaper. Even Hunter. Our other brothers too.

But now, it's Viper who's going to pay for all our sins.

When he's directly in front of Fallon, Breaker squares his shoulders and looks up at our *otets*. That urge returns. He's only two years younger than me, but he's shorter. Skinnier. Breaker is just a kid, barely any muscle, whose voice cracks whenever he gets excited.

Fallon crosses his hands behind his back, looking down at Breaker. "Remove your belt."

We all watch his hands tremble as Breaker unbuttons his peacoat and removes the belt, fumbling at first because of his thick gloves. The wind carries away the slip of leather sliding out of the loops, but we all know exactly what it sounds like. We've all gotten the belt before.

Just not quite like this.

"You are good at breaking rules. Breaking formation. Breaking *things*," Fallon says. "Let's see how good you are at breaking a thief's skin."

Goosebumps raise on my arms. The back of my neck. Reaper makes a sound in his throat, but doesn't move otherwise.

"Seven lashes," Fallon says, adjusting the black beanie on Breaker's shaved head. His clear eyes scan our line. "From all of you."

I bite my lip, trying to stop my body from trembling but I don't think it's from the cold. My gaze slides to Viper, who's full out shaking now and I'm scared he may go into hypothermia before he can receive our punishment.

Clenching his jaw, Breaker walks up to stand next to Commander. My brother's profile is almost jarring against the unforgiving winter landscape, his deep skin a contrast to the pale blue sky and glittering snow.

With black brows knitted tightly, he draws the belt back, and it lands with a sickening *thwack* across pale skin. Viper's spine straightens, then goes slack, but he doesn't make a sound. Not even after Breaker does it again and a bright red welt forms.

"Harder," Fallon orders.

Breaker lands another strike across Viper's fair skin and his knees buckle as a clean, thin line of red forms, then slowly slips down his back.

"Good boy," Fallon says. "Only three strikes and his skin is already broken." Father turns, his ice eyes landing on us one at a time, when he instructs, "Harder."

By the time the fifth hit has landed, my eyes blur, so I focus on the white line of the horizon, my gut twisting. I know I'm going to have to remove my belt too when Breaker is done. The last thing I want is to take the belt to my brother.

I grit my teeth at the thought, letting my gaze drift.

A bird calls from overhead, its shadow passing over the platform. What I wouldn't give to leap from this rooftop and fly. Escape. Go anywhere other than here. Float away like the fluffy white seeds of the dandelions that bloom in the spring when the snow melts, and we can go outside the school and feel the warm sun on our skin.

A hand lands on my shoulder. I jerk back to the present and find his black eyes.

"Stay here, brother," Reaper says quietly. "What will happen to the rest of us if you float away?"

Chapter 2

DELILAH

The cold is the first thing I feel when my eyes blink open. It cuts through the sleeve of my shirt, moving like acid under my skin. My exposed legs break out in goosebumps, and a shiver shakes my body, making me draw my legs up.

Awareness peels back in layers and I notice four things at once: My hands are still bound behind my back, I'm lying on a hard surface, and the thin material still covers my head, leaving me in blackness.

And my feet are bare.

A violent rush of memories floods my mind, hitting me like a tidal wave.

The terror. My father forced to his knees. His rage. Clyde. Cora's terrified screams. Gunshots ringing in my ears. Blood pooling at my feet.

And then, them.

Him.

My heart pounds against my ribcage as the fog in my head lifts. My breathing becomes ragged, panic needling its way into my mind. I breathe out slowly through my mouth. Inhale through my nose. Focus on my body.

My limbs feel weighed down, thick, my head heavy, a dull ache pounding between my temples like I have a terrible hangover. I force myself to stay still and take a minute to assess the situation once I get my breathing under control.

"Cora," I whisper.

Nothing.

Where is Cora?

Nausea ripples in my belly and I turn my face, pressing my head to the floor to calm it.

They took us. The men we fucked last night—wait. How long has it been? The way my bladder screams for release tells me it's been many hours, but I don't think it's been longer than that. Right? I'd have pissed myself if I had been out any longer.

The memory of a pinch of pain—a needle in my arm—as Striker's hard command to remain still, floods my mind.

They drugged me.

Us.

Cora? Where the fuck is Cora? Where the fuck am *I*?

I swallow the panic rising in my throat, gritting my teeth, forcing the scream to stay in my mouth. Panicking won't give me answers, and I need answers. I refuse to succumb to the fear clawing in my head.

Take a breath. Another. Be still and listen. Assess before you react.

My father's voice echoes in my mind, and I breathe deeply, trying to slow the rising fear. When I have myself in control, I remain still and listen.

Other than my rapid heartbeat and my breathing, I hear nothing. Absolutely nothing. I only know I'm indoors and not outside because of the hard, solid floor underneath me. The air is still. No rustling of leaves, no sounds of animals.

Wait. There is a sound. Distant. The faint crashing of waves against a shore breaks the quiet. I'm near water. An ocean.

That means I'm at least close to home.

Without moving too much, I test the bonds when I remember the slick grating sound and the cutting pain as the zip tie they used to keep me from thrashing around, tightened on my wrists. There's no way I can break them.

I squeeze my eyes shut, trying to piece together the last few moments before they drugged me. I remember the sound of van doors opening, then being slammed shut. The rattle of containers as the vehicle lurched forward. A horn honking and someone outside the van cursing. The last thing I remember was hearing Cora's quiet cries before I felt the pinch in my arm. Then nothing.

Until right now.

My shoulder aches, like I've been lying in one position for too long. How long?

Why?

I shift slightly, but my body is still sluggish from whatever they injected me with. Adjusting my weight, I use my fingers to feel the floor. It's rough, lined with thin grooves like a wood floor, but worn, not polished. I inhale deeply through my nose, but all I can detect is a faint musty scent that tells me little. It doesn't smell dank, or like mildew, so that means I'm some place dry. That at least I know. Basements are damp so at least I'm not underground.

Which would be terrible. But that's what happens when people are kidnapped.

My father's words fill my head.

Did he send you?

He's doing this.

He's come to collect.

My stomach sours.

And I'm here for revenge.

That was the last thing Reaper said before Striker covered my head and dragged me away. That simple statement confirms my fears. Someone is using Cora and me to collect on a debt.

Hope spreads through my chest. That means there is a way out of this. My father will stop at nothing to save Cora and me, even if it means paying an exorbitant ransom or unleashing his wrath upon whoever is behind this. I can almost feel Rune's rage burning inside me, urging me to hold on because he will come for us. He will find us. My father will make them suffer. He'll use any means necessary to track us down and kill whoever is behind this.

They *will* find us.

Clyde will burn the fucking world down to get Cora and me back. He may already be on his way here, frothing at the mouth to exact revenge on the people who took us.

But who?

Who had these guys take us?

And who the fuck are these guys?

The way they stormed the lobby and took out the guards means they're trained. And trained well. Their fatigues and masks were no costumes the other night in the club. Their code names and efficiency screams of military training. Soldiers of some sort, but not like the ones Rune or my father's associates employ. These guys possess too much skill to be regular security detail or henchmen. They were too brutal. Everything they did was precise. Planned.

Including the way they fucked us.

My stomach roils and I curl in on myself, drawing my knees up to my chest. I clench my teeth, trying to keep the burning rage from erupting as my emotions spiral. This shouldn't feel so devastating, but it does. The betrayal cuts into me deep, a sharp blade slicing through my chest, leaving behind a searing ache.

How could they have planned to ambush us like this? Last night, they had the chance to strike. Instead, they chose to bide their time, deceiving us so brutally by gaining our trust enough that we willingly spread our legs. Then, they waited for the perfect moment to take us.

In front of my father.

"Fuck!" I scream through clenched teeth. *Fucking assholes.* They waited on purpose. The men wanted my father to see us taken away from him. They wanted him to *know* we'd fucked them. Reaper's sick words slam into me and I think I may actually vomit.

A tear threatens to break loose, but I cannot lose control. "Assholes," I murmur through clenched teeth. "Fucking *assholes.*"

"Rather unladylike of you."

I scream, jerking so violently that my legs kick out. His familiar voice curls around my neck the way his hand had. I suck in air, trying to calm my breathing. I didn't even hear him nearby.

"Then again, the way you choked on my cock wasn't becoming of a lady."

"Fuck you," I seethe.

"Oh, don't worry, Princess, you will." Striker's boots scrape over the wood floor as he steps closer. "If I remember correctly, you really liked my cum sliding down your throat."

I clench my hands into fists, nails biting into my palms to keep from responding. That's what he wants and I refuse to give him the satisfaction.

I hear more shuffling and then the scent of earth and something else I can't place hits my nose. Something slightly acidic but sweet. Like a cleaner. I didn't detect it before, so he's moved closer, or came into the room without making a sound. Now, I hear the faint sound of leather creaking and sense him close. Too close and immediately that bubbling panic tries to return, but I shove it down.

"If you're a good girl, I'll untie you and you can have my cock again."

I bite back another useless retort. It won't do any good to let him get me riled. That's all he's trying to do. Get under my skin. Everything they've done to us has been a mind-fuck.

I open my mouth to ask where Cora is, but stop myself. I cannot let them know she's important. Men like them will use this information against me. I know because it's exactly what my father taught me to do. Exploit any and every weakness.

"I have to pee," I say instead.

Nothing.

"Hope you have a mop," I say, my throat tightening, cheeks flaming that he may actually let me soil myself. "Because I'm about to piss all over the floor unless you let me use the bathroom."

A hand lands on my arm, and my entire body jerks before I freeze, fear tingling in my arms and hands. My heart skips in my chest as his hand slides down and he grabs my wrists, yanking them up. I'm forced onto my stomach, pain shooting through my arms. His knee presses into my back between my shoulder blades, and an instant later, my hands are free, but the weight of his knee doesn't go away. My hands fly out, palms pressing to the cold wood, my chin hitting the floor as my blood pulses, sending sensation back to my limbs.

"You're going to cooperate," Striker says, his velvety voice right next to my ear, making my pulse quicken oddly. "When we tell you to do something, you're going to listen. You will not fight us, scream, or cause any problems."

His gloved hand slips under my chin, and my head jerks back, breath rushing out. My eyelids flutter in the hood's darkness as fear laces its way down my spine. My bladder contracts, and I squeeze my eyes shut, trying not to piss myself.

"Do you understand, Princess?"

I nod, and the weight of his knee is lifted.

"This will be easier if you don't fight us."

The fabric over my head rips off, and I gasp as the sudden cold hits my face, my eyes scanning the space frantically. A door clicks quietly closed behind me, and I raise to my hands and knees, taking in the sight, arms tingling with pins.

The room's dim, barely lit by small incandescent sconces on the wall. The large room has wood floors, and tall ceilings with ornate crown molding, the paint chipped and cracked in places. Faded wallpaper covers the top half of the walls, peeling off at the corners, some long strips completely gone. Decorative wood wainscoting covers the lower half, reminding me of an old estate.

My legs wobble as I stand. Pain throbs in my temples and I tilt, dizzy as blood rushes to my arms and legs. I scan the space, rubbing my forearms, as my gaze lands on a massive bed at the far end, resting on a rusted metal frame with a scrolled ironwork head and footboard. A small vanity with a chair sits at the other end of the room. Next to it, a massive armoire made from heavy, dark wood.

I spin to find a door, slightly ajar.

Please be a bathroom.

Rushing forward, I nearly melt with relief when I see the vintage claw-foot tub and clear shower curtain, the sink, and toilet. After I relieve myself noting the stacks of toilet paper and feminine supplies lining the counter, I slowly walk back out to the room.

My eyes land on the heavy floor to ceiling curtains and I dart forward, tossing them back, revealing a massive window. I press my hands to the glass as the landscape slowly reveals itself with the rising sun. My belly sinks. My knees hit the floor, hands sliding down the paned glass squares.

"Where the fuck am I?" I whisper as fear slips through me.

Below, a lawn sprawls out for several yards before falling off abruptly at a short craggy cliff. Waves crash on jagged rocks lining the empty shore, stretching for miles along the coast, smoothing out in some places. The sea stretches out beyond that, nothing but fading stars and a burning sun hung over an endless ocean.

Chapter 3

Striker

Large monitors line the wall, the starkly lit blue and gray images flooding the room with an eerie light. The screen that holds my attention shows the tiny figure lying on the floor of the last room in the west wing. She's not moved in hours and my stomach cramps, worry making me doubt the dosage of the injection I gave her.

Did I give her too much? She's so small. They both are, but the tiny, sweet flower curled into a ball on the floor has me more concerned.

Cora woke up several hours ago, crying a little at first before working herself into a frenzy. Then she screamed for Delilah a few times, her voice cracking as she got more and more upset. When no one came, she went back to crying and now…

Nothing.

She's not made a sound in a long time.

A slithering sensation snakes through my gut. I don't like this, even if it's necessary. I keep reminding myself that we have to do this, but it doesn't dissolve the black, tarry feeling.

Reaper says we're not leaving her like this for long. He said we're not leaving them like we were that first day at the school, but it's been several hours, and even he's becoming uncomfortable with watching their fear, though he'd never admit it.

When Delilah woke, we watched her lie still for a beat too long. My mind started racing with doubts. I gave in to the impulse when Reaper left the room and went to untie her. Although he said nothing when he saw our Princess walking around the room, I could feel his anger as if it were a living thing. But Reaper refuses to untie Cora just yet. Even though she's remained dangerously still for the last hour. He insists if we leave her a little longer, she'll crack faster.

But still nothing.

My eyes snap to Delilah's screen. She's back to pacing the room. She spent a good thirty minutes screaming, banging on the door with frantic desperation before finally giving up. After she searched the room, clearly looking for a means of escape, she sat on the bed for a while, staring at her hands and rubbing the red marks on her wrists. Now she's muttering to herself as she slowly paces at the end of the bed.

It doesn't take long for isolation to create fear. You place someone in a dark room, leave them alone, and pretty soon they'll do anything to be let out. It's human nature. We're social animals. Not meant to be by ourselves or locked in a room with nothing but our thoughts.

But we're still animals. And a caged animal is easier to control.

We would know. My brothers' and I all endured a similar introduction into the school. Although Fallon called it lessons, he trained us far more brutally than what Reaper has planned for our girls.

Fallon left us alone. Cold. Scared of the endless darkness in the room he locked us in, our minds warped by an intense fear that slithered into the deepest parts of the mind, creating nightmares. I know the feeling of being so scared that you think you might die from it. That your heart may give well before your will to live.

By the time Fallon retrieved us days later, we were so thankful to be rescued it didn't matter our savior was the one who put us there. We would do anything to keep from returning to that black, lonely cold room, starved and freezing, not knowing if or when we would ever escape.

Delilah swipes at her cheek and I remind myself this is necessary. We need them to cooperate and we have little time. Reaper thinks Delilah's abrasive personality, her hard exterior, and the things she's learned from Rune will make it harder for her to submit.

He thinks the weakest link will be Cora. That she'll break easier. Faster. Beg to be released, doing anything we ask. Reaper believes she'll be the easiest of the two to break and bend to our will, but after watching her for hours, it's clear. She may very well be the strongest one out of the two.

"I don't like this," Breaker says from next to me, snapping my attention over to him. He can't seem to sit still. He's been pacing behind us as we watch the screens, a feral, agitated energy pouring from him like waves of smoke, so thick it's setting my teeth on edge.

"They belong to Rune," Reaper says from behind me. He places his hands on the back of my chair as he watches Cora on the screen.

The statement carries a layer of contempt. His level of hatred toward Delilah concerns me, and I want to remind him she's not Rune but keep the words tucked behind my teeth.

Rune brought this upon himself.

And her.

But when we decided that we'd take Delilah, I don't think any of us were prepared to feel this... uncomfortable.

"No," Viper says slowly, gaze darting between me and Breaker. "*Delilah* is his blood. Cora is..." He cuts off, gaze returning to the screen.

What is Cora to Rune Gavin? On the outside, she's his adopted daughter. She's the child of his murdered friends and business partners. She's something else too that none of us have yet to voice. Or maybe it's that we don't want to.

We've been watching the two for a long time. We know the girl's routines. They differ little from one another, except for Cora meeting with Rune either at his office or his mansion several times a week, but most nights she's out with various men, while Delilah stays home alone.

Since her divorce from that slimy little fucker, Delilah's become a recluse, rarely leaving her home. We didn't want to risk cameras or listening devices being discovered. Our source told us Rune is a paranoid motherfucker, constantly having his men scan for devices, so we had to settle on old-fashioned surveillance.

Maybe this is the cause of that gross, oily feeling in the pit of my stomach. The reason Breaker is so upset. We've watched them for too long.

We gave them *pet names* for fucks sake.

The speakers amplifying the sound from the monitor zoomed in on Cora cracks and we all turn to look at the screen at the same time. My eyes land on her slight frame. Her body tenses, her legs bending. A dark stain pools on the wood floor under her hip.

I close my eyes, lowering my head. This doesn't feel like it was supposed to. This bitter taste isn't anything like the revenge we had planned.

"God damn it," Breaker hisses.

Viper's fist hits the desk holding all our masks and gloves and the equipment for the cameras, and we all jerk back, shocked. His blue-green eyes land on Reaper at my back. "This has to stop."

My gaze moves back to the screen. To the fiery woman we made feel secure enough to allow us to pleasure her, who is now curled into a ball, laying in a puddle of her own piss after we betrayed her and stole her from the only life she's ever known.

I'd think she'd be doing something. Screaming. Crying. Not this blank, empty body lying on the floor, not even fighting her restraints. She isn't moving. Not trying to inch away from the puddle of urine. She's...

She's *resigned*. Already admitting her defeat.

My hands grip the armrest of my chair as rage rushes through me, coloring the world red for an instant. I breathe in deeply and out through my mouth, tamping down the darkness that's constantly threatening to break free.

There's only one way to achieve that level of defeat in a person. Someone has brutalized her before, far worse than this, and the suspicions we've all had may have just been confirmed.

"*Reaper*." The name slips past Viper's lips as a plea.

"We can't fucking do this to her," Breaker snaps. "I'm untying her."

"Breaker," Reaper barks out his name as an order, his mouth twisting in anger. His dark eyes flash dangerously. "If you go into that room, you are violating a direct order."

Breaker's brows furrow. "So fucking what, Reap? This isn't the school."

"We have *orders*," Reaper says, his tone lowering on the last word. "Orders we cannot ignore."

"Orders, you broke the second you took *her*," Viper says.

Breaker steps forward, his chest inches from Reaper, both men's jaws popping with tension. They are almost the same height, but Reaper bests us all. In size. In strength. Endurance. In every way that matters.

"It has to be done," Reaper reminds him, eyes like pools of black ice. A slick smile slides up the corner of his mouth. "You of all people know how brutal a breaking can be."

Breaker's eyes fall.

Breaker got his name for a reason. He is the breaker of rules. Of codes. Of things.

Of men.

Viper's tense laugh tears through the room as my brothers relax. I hate it when those two butt heads. Breaker has always, *always,* been headstrong, going up against orders whenever they don't sit well with him, so I'm glad when he rolls his head on his shoulders, easing the tension from his neck, though he grinds his teeth. I want to tell him I don't agree with these orders either, but, well...

It's too late now. Even if I don't like what we're doing to these girls, we all agreed to this.

"Breaking is never pretty," Reaper says, as he takes a step backward. Reap's black gaze flickers to the monitor. "But it's necessary."

I jump as Breaker's fist goes through the plaster, breath *whooshing* out of me in surprise.

Breaker's clear blue eyes narrow on Reaper. "Necessary? Doing what we had done to us, scaring the shit out of two innocent women, is necessary? Leaving them in isolation? What next? Will we starve them? Beat them? Tell me Reaper, at what point does necessary become your cruel fun?"

"You knew what this mission entailed when you agreed to it," Reaper growls. Lunging forward, his finger lands on the center of Breaker's chest. "You agreed this was the only way, just like the rest of us."

Breaker shakes his head, casting his eyes down. We all agreed to this before we knew their bodies. Before we knew what they tasted like. Before we heard them moan and the feral sounds they made as we made them come.

"He's right," Viper says quietly, and we all turn our attention to him. He points to the screen with Cora in the center. "But this one? She's innocent."

Reaper barks out a laugh that reminds me of our *otets*. "Innocent? We've watched her for a long time. Cora is hardly innocent."

"We watched her, yes, and we all know she..." Breaker trails off. He pinches the bridge of his nose, eyes moving back to the screen. She still hasn't moved.

"Rune Gavin raised her," Reaper says. He points to the monitor. "Which means she's manipulative and cunning. This is the only way to get what we need from her."

"There are better ways to get their cooperation," Breaker says. "We don't have to terrify them to get what we need."

"And suddenly Breaker has a conscience," Reaper says brutally. "Is it because your cum was still inside her when we took her? Since when does coming in a woman make you care for their well-being?"

Breaker's palm slams against the door frame. He's wound up so tight, I fear he may lash out at Reaper.

"There are other ways," he says again. His eyes focus on the screen behind Reaper for a moment, then bounces between us all. "We agreed to do this, but not with her. She's not even supposed to be here."

"He's right, Reap. She's just a girl," Viper says quietly.

Reap laughs. "She's hardly just a girl. She's a sly little Vixen, remember?"

I watch her still form on the screen, a gross, slick feeling roiling in my gut, remembering the day we saw her leave Rune's office. "Ever consider she was made that way?"

Reaper's gaze locks on the screen. "We're all made."

"I'm going in there."

"Don't even think it, Breaker," Reaper snarls as Breaker takes a step back defiantly, almost daring our brother to stop him.

Breaker shakes his head as he backs out of the room. "I will not allow this part, Reap. We don't have to be cruel to get what we want."

I expect Reaper to go after him and drag him back to talk some sense into him, but he doesn't. Instead, he sits in the chair next to me, and leans forward, forearms on his thighs, his eyes on the screen. Despite what he says, he doesn't like this any more than the rest of us.

I think he may like it even less.

Reaper isn't as cold as he pretends. Like the rest of us, he was made that way, but he's lying about Cora and he knows it. We all do. The many months we spent watching them gave us insight into their lives and Cora's life wasn't easy. She's had it hard with little control of her fate, despite being raised by Rune in wealth. She's still been surrounded by powerful, cruel men and if what we suspect is true...

She's had even less control over her body.

"Fucking idiot," Reaper says, but there's no anger in his voice. He may think we have to treat them brutally, but we all know he doesn't want to.

We saw how he acted last night. Cora's sweetness enchanted him as much as the rest of us. He was verging on the edge of utter madness with Princess the entire night, barely able to restrain himself. We see now how he's been in and out of the room, coming in to stare at the monitors, watching Delilah closely, then leaving again only to come back and do the same thing. He's never been like this with a target before and we've done this dozens of times. Held targets for days in fact. Watched them break or forced them by any means until we could retrieve the information we needed. Or we just kept them alive until the price was paid. Then we either released them or disposed of them. Whichever we were paid to do.

But we all know this time is different.

This time, they are ours to do with as we please.

Those are our direct orders.

To make her, *them*, ours, and by the time we're done with them, they'll do anything and everything we ask.

"You catch more flies with honey, Reap." Viper stands and leaves the room, following Breaker.

Several minutes later, the door to Cora's room cracks open and Breaker and Viper walk in. They must have fucking run to get to her so quickly.

"They're going to regret this," Reaper says, eyeing the screen.

I don't tell him I think we're *all* going to regret this, maybe him most of all.

Chapter 4

CORA

Blackness tries to invade my mind, memories threatening to break loose. I know I'm not *there*, but that same fear tangles in my belly, making me want to claw free of this room.

I'm here, I tell myself. *I'm not back there.*

The problem is, I don't know where *here* is.

I just know they took us.

Delly. God, where's Delly?

The thought of them hurting her sends fiery rage through my bones. I've done so many fucked up things to protect her. All to make sure she never found out what Rune is really like, and now he's pissed off the wrong person. I've done so *many* fucked up things just trying to survive him, and I'm *so* tired of surviving.

Life has been cruel sometimes, and I'm sick of making the best of my situation.

My parents died, murdered when I was ten, and instead of giving me to a family who may have loved me, I was handed over to Rune, the man responsible for ending my parent's life. Handed over like a doll to do with as he wished.

And did he ever.

He's made me as much as he's destroyed me. Treating me just like he did his own daughter until one day something snapped in his head, and things were different. He was different. I was different. I look just like my mother, and I think he hated that so much it twisted his affection for me into something cruel.

Fucking *Papa*. My gut twists. The sick bastard got what he's wanted all along. To tear me up, and now I'm fucked. Because of him, I'm in a room, laying in my piss, bound and cold as hell. And angry.

God, I'm angry.

I have adapted to every single shitty thing thrown my way. Dead parents? Okay. I have a new father. New father wants to shove his dick into my barely eighteen-year-old mouth, then punch his cum from between my lips until I was sure my teeth may break? Not great, but I adjusted. I knew there was no escaping him after those first few times he forced me, so I made myself more appealing, hoping he would hurt me less. It worked. Papa now likes that I willingly spread my legs and fall to my knees like the whore he says my mother was. Not fighting the orgasms my body wants, even if they unfold inside me creased with pain.

Not fighting him.

Now, his meanness only comes out in bursts instead of a torrential downpour. He never cared that I cried, or that he hurt me as he fucked me over his desk, but he cared I kept my mouth shut and I have. I was his good girl. His dirty little secret and I never breathed a word. Not even Clyde knows the depths of Rune's sick love for me. And his love has already caused me so much harm, I shouldn't be surprised that I'm here.

The four men I let pleasure me last night have taken us and it's all Rune's fault. How? I'm not sure yet, but things tend to reveal themselves when they're ready. And people love to talk about why they do the things they do. I have a feeling if I wait it out and survive long enough, they'll reveal why they took us.

I just have to do as they ask until then.

I've been lying awake in this cold room long enough to know I'm in a house that is somewhere near the ocean. The distant sound of waves crashing are too loud to be a lake, and it's cold as fuck in here, so that means we're further north.

Delly. She must be so scared and worried. She's always been protective of me and not knowing if I'm okay is going to eat her alive. But she's smart. She will remember what Rune said when they took us, and figure out this is some sort of revenge plot to get Rune to pay up. Which means they won't hurt us.

Or at least we won't be killed.

I think.

The creak of the door opening freezes my spiraling thoughts. Heat travels down from my cheeks to my chest. Even though I knew I'd have to face them, sitting in a puddle of my pee wasn't what I had envisioned. Me screaming and fighting my way out of here, rescuing Delly, and getting back home has played repeatedly in my mind, but not this.

God, I wish Clyde had trained me to be a badass like he always said he would when I was a little girl with dark nightmares.

"Little Red." His voice makes my nipples tighten. Yet another thing to blame Rune for. My fucked up brain mixing terror with pleasure. Not like this situation is helping. Fucking me roughly last night, then killing Rune's security detail before they kidnapped us, is fucking with my mental stability.

Breaker steps closer, his boots scraping on the floor as he comes to a stop near my head. Last night, his boots never came off. Nor his pants or his shirt. An odd thought to have, but those should have been red flags. Then again, I sail toward red flags like a lost ship, desperate for the safety of land, not caring about the color of danger flashing in my eyes as long as I may, just may, be safe. If even for a while.

But I should have known. Should have sensed something. Even if I ignore warning signs, I still feel them, see them. And men not disrobing to fuck us was a sign that something wasn't right. Most men, at least all the men I've fucked over the years, are in such a hurry to ram their dick in you they fling off their clothes, discarding pants and shirts in rapid fire succession.

Not these guys. No. They kept everything on, exposing only the parts needed to perform. Every other inch was clothed. The bits of flesh I saw told me nothing. We, Delly and I, were spread open, vulnerable, naked for them, so they could use us in every way.

"Little Red?" This time my stomach clenches at the name he called me as he fucked me. "Please be okay," he whispers, like he's talking to himself more than me, and I clench my teeth to stop from snapping at him. If he wanted me to be okay, he shouldn't have done this, but the ache in his voice is confusing, so I remain quiet. His tone says one thing, but I need to see his eyes to tell if this desperate, slightly scared sound catching in his throat is real or another game they're playing.

Breaker's hand slides under my head, so gently that I squeeze my eyes shut. The hood covering my head is removed, and I inhale a breath of cold air.

"Is she okay?" Viper's voice comes from behind me.

My cheeks burn, making me wish I could sink into the cold floor. I'm dirty, stinking of fear, covered in pee, and bound like an animal in front of the men I fucked. I can't help feeling mortified. They're the ones who have done this to me, yet I hate they are seeing me like this. Weak.

Last night, I was treated like a slutty goddess. Right now, I'm a broken whore, lying in a pool of cold urine, so scared I'm having to clench my jaw to keep terrified whimpers from escaping my throat as dark memories try to take over my present nightmare.

The plastic digging into my bound wrists at my back suddenly snaps. My hands fall to the floor. My shoulders ache, and pain lances through my arms as I shift onto my back. I bring my hands up, wincing at the sharp pains shooting through my shoulders to rub my wrists.

"Let's get you fixed up," Viper says.

My eyes blink open, and the first thing I see are eyes the color of winter. Then I see the familiar skull mask covering his head. My gaze travels down to the same black shirt clinging to his muscled chest he wore last night. The same black fatigues. It's a uniform.

They are soldiers and they don't want to be identified.

My instincts scream to lash out, hit him, and flee, but logically, I know it's pointless. I'm short and soft in all the wrong places. They are huge. Strong. Powerful.

Deciding that remaining still in my puddle is the best option for now, I let my eyes drift past Breaker to the room, taking in the dusty yellow light of a bedside lamp, the enormous bed and the worn...everything. *Everything* is in a state of decay that makes me think of a horror house. Plaster missing in places, wallpaper torn off in large sheets in some sections, but bubbling and clinging like damaged skin to a wound in others. Rusted posts on the metal bedframe and a worn chair by a vast fireplace, the dark mouth yawning open and cold.

My eyes bounce back to Breaker next to me. "Where's Delilah?" I ask before I can stop myself.

Viper lowers himself to a crouch. I shrink back a little, not sure how to react to his proximity. He's kidnapped me. Bound me. Yet I had him in my mouth last night.

My gaze moves to Breaker, crouched by my head. His hand is still cradling my head, his warm thumb caressing my cheek. He's not wearing his gloves. A quick glance at Viper tells me he isn't either. A strange satisfaction settles in my belly. There's something more personal about having them touch me flesh to flesh instead of using gloved hands to force me. It makes me wonder if that concerned glint in their eyes is real. If maybe they feel bad for doing this.

But that's a dangerous thought. I have to remember we're playing a game. They told us last night, and we were too stupid to hear it.

They're the hunters and we're the prey.

And they've caught us, so I better be careful.

Saying nothing else, Breaker leans down further and scoops me up into his arms. My first thought is that my pee soaked skirt is going to dirty his clean smelling shirt, but I swallow the words, reminding myself it's his fault I was drugged and couldn't hold my bladder any longer.

Breaker's long legs eat up the space as he carries me to an open door at the far end of the room. Viper reaches around and switches on a light. I blink at the brightness, taking in the sight of the bathroom and vintage fixtures and tub. Still not speaking, Breaker tugs at the buttons on my shirt. When it registers that he intends to get me naked, I slap his hand away.

"Don't fucking touch me," I snap, forgetting to be scared.

"You're covered in piss, pretty Vixen," Viper says, crossing his arms and leaning against the vanity next to me. He's still too close. "Would you rather we tied you back up and let you lie in your piss a little longer?"

My cheeks flame, my eyes narrowing on his skull mask, the fangs reminding me of the scrape of his teeth over my clit as he ate up my cum soaked pussy. My eyes fall, too many images flashing in my mind, mixing up toxically with shame, making it too hard to look at him.

"I didn't think so," Viper says, stepping back so he's next to Breaker. The two men together in the small space remind me I'm not in a position to argue. They could do whatever they wanted to me, and there's no one here to stop them.

Bad things don't happen to Rune's daughter. They never have. Only me.

"What do you want?" I ask, sucking in a breath as I eye the two men blocking the door. My escape. My freedom.

But was I really free to begin with?

Rune kept me in a pretty cage, fed luxuries, but bound and gagged by his disgusting hatred for the people who killed his wife.

"Nothing you alone can give us," Breaker says, but the way his eyes travel down my body tells me that's not entirely true. He remembers the shape of my hips, the heat between my thighs. Just as I remember the way he feels moving inside me. He breaks eye contact and glances at Viper, then back at me, and tugs at the buttons on my blouse. "Let's get you cleaned up."

I bite my lip and let him unbutton the shirt, resisting shooing his hands away to do it myself. Over the years, I've learned that being sweet means men tend to be nicer. Most of the time. So I let him drag my shirt over my shoulders, let his thumbs skim down my arms as he slides the fabric down. It falls to the floor with a whisper. My skirt is next. It sticks to my hips and I clench my jaw, keeping my humiliated tears behind the lids, but one slips out and I wipe it away, furious with myself for this stupid weakness. That I *care* I'm in this state in front of the men who made me this way. The pitiful state *they* put me in.

When I'm left in just my black underwear, white bra, and torn nylons, they both step back. It's cold as fuck, and my nipples tighten, my wet underwear like a sheet of ice against my skin, making goosebumps prick all over my body. My arms wrap around my waist as a shiver wracks my shoulders, eyes falling to my feet on the black and white chipped tile floor.

My big toe sticks through the nylon. Dark, rusty brown stains smear the rips around my knees. Bile hits my throat like acid and I suck in a breath.

I'm covered in Manuel's blood.

The room tilts.

"Fuck, she's about to pass out."

My hand grips the vanity.

"Deep breaths, Little Red."

My eyes shoot up to Breaker. "You really think a little blood's going to make me pass out?" I snarl. "I'm a fucking woman. We're born in it, bathe in it, and fucking *live* in it."

Viper lets out a low whistle. "Damn she's spicy." He uncrosses his arms making me look his way. "Might want to turn it down a few notches, Vixen. I'd love a reason to take a belt to that plump ass."

I *feel* the color drain from my face.

Breaker steps closer, like he's going to touch me, but stops, letting his hands remain at his sides. Viper walks past me to the porcelain tub and turns the knob. Pipes groan and water sputters out, dark and dirty at first, then runs clear. He plugs the drain with an old rubber stopper and that's when I see the shampoo and body wash bottles.

The same ones I use at home.

Another tremor starts in my shoulders, but this one isn't from the cold.

Viper's hand lands on my hip, and his thumb hooks the waistband of my nylons. My hand flies out, and I slap him away. His dark chuckle sends heat to my core, making it feel slick as I step back, not liking that my body remembers the way they touched me.

"Fucking creep," I snarl, my back hitting the icy wall and I press myself to it, hating how scared I am, but for all the wrong reasons. Some primal part of my brain knows they won't hurt me, but I've never been one to take the chance that a man will keep to his usual behavior. They're animals, after all. Some are more wild than others. "You have a piss fetish?"

Breaker's loud crack of laughter makes my shoulders jolt. The two men exchange a look, and Viper shoots forward, moving so fast that I'm suddenly trapped between his massive body and the cracked plaster at my back. My heart thunders in my chest. He's so close I know he can feel it beating against him. His hand wraps around my neck and I gasp, my fingers gripping his, trying to pry them off, but he squeezes slightly harder.

"You going to force yourself on me now?" Hatred leaks out with my words.

"Force?" Viper lowers his masked face close to mine. "Did we force you to spread your legs for us the other night?"

Another tremor moves down my spine at the memory, and it's not entirely unpleasant. I bite my lip to keep from saying anything else that might provoke him considering he just threatened me with a belt.

"No, little Vixen, we didn't." His grip tightens. "You gave us permission to fuck you."

"Past tense," I snarl. Me and my stupid mouth can't seem to stop talking. "I wouldn't spread open for you even if you begged to lap up this piss between my legs."

I swear he smiles under his mask. "That's not how it works. You're ours now. You belong to all of us. And I'll fuck you with dried piss on your legs, my brother's cum sliding down your thighs, and my hand over your mouth to muffle your screams as I lick your sweet tears from those pretty cheeks."

My breath rushes from my lungs.

"And you'll love every minute because your hot little cunt knows you belong to us. You have been ours longer than you realize." He steps back and I suck in air, my hand replacing where his had just been.

Viper backs away to the door, his eyes never leaving mine, then turns and stalks out, leaving me alone with Breaker.

My fingers rub the heated skin on my neck, my mind rushing with the lurid images he just planted.

"You have clean clothes in the armoire," Breaker says. He gestures to the bath filling behind me. "Get cleaned up and change. We'll bring you something to eat soon."

As he turns to leave, Breaker pauses, placing his hand on the frame, looking at me over his shoulder. In the bright light, I can see him clearly. His eyes are a pale blue, a stark contrast to the deep warm shade of skin peeking out around his mask. His broad shoulders and chest take up the entire doorway and his head almost reaches the top of the door frame.

He's fucking *huge*.

A reminder of his strength and the danger he carries under his skin.

"I'm sorry, Little Red," he whispers, and my skin flushes with a familiar heat. I wish he'd not call me that. My body likes it too much.

"Sorry?" I ask, biting the word out. "For what part? Lying as you fucked me? Killing men I've known for years because they were protecting me, scaring the daylights out of me and my family, or kidnapping me?"

His eyes scan me from head to toe, softening as they travel down my legs, then back up my torso and stopping at my face. "I'm not sorry for taking you, but I am sorry you're caught in the middle."

He turns to leave and I'm left standing in a cold bathroom in wet underwear, my heart pounding erratically, like a bird trapped in a metal cage. Trapped, and scared because this fluttering in my chest isn't exactly fear anymore.

No man has ever looked at me the way he does. The way they do. No man has ever been sorry for hurting me, no matter how much they've insisted. Not for raising his voice or scaring me. For being mean.

For being a man.

I'm going to have to be careful. Because this is worse than Rune. Worse because the look in Breaker's eyes tells me he means it. But like he said, I'm trapped in the middle of what appears to be yet another war, but this time? I refuse to be another casualty.

Chapter 5

STRIKER

Sitting alone in a room is my worst nightmare. As I watch the girls, I'm reminded of that first day at the school when Fallon left me alone in the cold room.

I had wondered when I heard the lock sliding into place why the doctors and nurses, all the people scurrying about, had made me wake up if they were just going to send me to another dark room. Why put tubes in my arms they said were medicine? Why stick me with needles they said would make me strong again? Then take me to a warm place with other girls and boys when they had planned all along to give me to a man who locked me up again. Why feed me? I had thought when the first pangs of hunger started, I was just going to go back to sleep with a hungry belly and tears on my cheeks.

When Father finally opened the door, I remember him staring at my arms with a strange expression on his face. He'd pointed to the marks and asked, "Why did you do that?"

I had looked down at the bloody streaks, the deep gouges from my nails raking over my flesh and said, "So I wouldn't go to sleep."

It wasn't until after Father retrieved me I learned I was at a school and expected to sit for my lessons with who I was told were my brothers. I'd never had a brother, but I liked that I suddenly had fifteen. I'd never been to school either, but somehow knew what it was. A room where boys and girls sat and were given crayons and papers and learned to read and write. Again, I wasn't sure where this knowledge came from, only that I had it, so it must have been something I learned in those shadowy years before I was brought to the school. Before the darkness.

After Fallon cleaned me up, giving me a cold bath in a metal tub, scrubbing my nails and fingers clean with white bar soap and a coarse brush, he put creams and bandages on my arms and dressed me in gray pants and a dark gray button-down shirt with a pressed collar, then gave me a plate of food.

My new father watched me take every bite, reminding me to eat slowly, using words I didn't understand now and then. But it didn't matter. I was so hungry, so glad to be out of that room before I fell back asleep, that I did everything he asked. Then when I had cleared the plate, he said, using the same words as me, "My sons are smart. But we all must learn to communicate. Every day, you will be instructed and every day I expect progress."

Strange how the mind remembers things. I can't remember my mother's face, even to this day, but I can picture sitting in the large open cafeteria, with rusted metal tables and chairs, walls with peeling mossy-green paint. How Fallon had seemed so large and strong. Handsome, with his black hair and pale eyes, and the pressed three-piece suit. At five years old, I didn't know what a three-piece suit was, nor did I understand that the school was located in a prison until I was much older.

My favorite class was language. Besides my strict education with my brothers in those stark classrooms, and the weapons lessons from Fallon later on, all my education came from the school's staff and the old black and white movies Cook used to watch in the kitchen. All my memories from younger years are corrupted by my mind now and the things I've learned in life. A five-year-old wouldn't know about a three-piece suit, but now every time I think of back then, or another memory surfaces, my older mind replaces the blank information with everything I know now.

Viper once told me it was the same with him. That he seemed to just know some things without knowing how he knew. He was young like me when he was brought to the school and said he remembered the day I joined in on our language lessons vividly. Mostly though, he told me he remembers so clearly because I looked similar to Reaper, tanned skin and dark hair, so different from him and our other brothers. And that I had yet to get a name. I was just "brother" until my skills were discovered.

It wasn't until I saw Breaker I understood what he meant.

A loud bang brings my attention back to the present. I lean in, focusing on the screen showing Delilah's room, but all I can see is her back. We placed several cameras high in the crown molding so we can switch angles if need be. Viper wanted one in the bathrooms, but thankfully Reaper argued that there was nothing in there that they could use to harm themselves or us other than the razors we provided for them to shave their legs.

Shifting, I roll the chair closer to the row of monitors and punch the keys on the keyboard to switch cameras. Delilah's angry scowl comes into view as she stares at the drawer at her feet, undergarments scattered across the floor.

Did she pull it from the armoire on purpose?

The question barely has time to form in my head when she reaches into the armoire and pulls out another. Thick socks spill onto the wood floor and she drops the drawer with a thud next to the other one. She kicks the bundles of socks around like she's looking for something, then after a minute, grabs several hangers holding her dresses and tosses them to the floor. Then does it again.

"What is she doing?" Breaker asks from behind me.

I glance at my watch. He's not due to relieve me from my watch for another hour, but like the rest of us, he can't seem to stay away. Reaper is the worst one. Constantly in here, watching them obsessively. Breaker seems to focus more on Cora, but right now, his entire attention is on Delilah.

"I'm not sure," I tell him as he sits next to me and crosses his arms. We've been wearing our uniforms, and always have our masks nearby just in case, but I have to say I miss seeing his skin and the bold tribal tattoos on his arms. My eyes raise to find him staring at me instead of the camera. Averting my gaze, I say, "She looks like she's searching for something."

"Probably a weapon," Viper says as he walks into the room and takes the chair on my other side.

I resist rolling my eyes. We are supposed to be taking shifts watching them, but it seems sleep and taking any time away is impossible. Then again, these two have been inseparable since Breaker's first day in the classroom.

We all saw Breaker when he first arrived, but didn't see him again for several years after Father brought him out of the cold room. I had always wondered what happened to the skinny toddler with a fat belly and sunken cheeks. He looked nothing like my other brothers, with deep skin and black curls that shot out from his head in tight coils. I remember when our *otets* brought him to class shortly after Breaker turned five, he'd shaved his curls, which made me sad. He was a pretty little boy, and I figured maybe that's why Father shaved him bald. So no one would mistake him for a girl.

Viper took to him immediately. Breaker was smarter than most of us and already spoke some English, but not like Viper, whose coarse accent made the words impossible to understand. I struggled the most with English, so they would sit with me after lights out and teach me how to pronounce words. Of course, I learned all the dirty words first.

When it came time for us to learn French, Breaker knew some of that one too, so he helped us all. It wasn't until years later, when we started taking Spanish, that I could help them.

By then, we had eliminated any traces of our accents, except for mine, which only surfaced when I got angry and raised my voice. But that only happened a few times and when it did, Teacher would rap my knuckles with the thick wooden ruler like the old sour-faced nun at the large church in the village did when we didn't pay attention at Sunday school. I had bruises on my hands for years, but I learned eventually to articulate and enunciate each word carefully. We all did.

Fallon once said when I asked him the purpose of learning so many languages and making sure we had no accents, was because his future soldiers needed to blend in and not be identifiable. I didn't understand then. But I do now.

"God, she's so fucking beautiful," Viper says from next to me. At first, I assume he's referring to Cora, but his gaze is fixed on Delilah.

We all watch as she tears drawers from the little vanity and feels under the top, searching for something. Probably clues as to where she is. Good luck. We stripped any trace of who we are well before we brought them here. Fallon trained us well. She'll find nothing unless we want her to.

"I'd love to wrap my fingers in that soft black hair and bend her over the bed," Breaker says.

Wouldn't we all? When we received the order, we knew our objective. Take her. Train her. Then we went off the rails.

Now? We willingly went along with Reaper's orders to use them that night, and it's got us all fucked up. And having Cora here has rattled us even more. Reaper may have made the call to bring Cora into this, but we all are keeping her here.

Why he decided to take Cora too, I assumed at first, was because she was important to Rune like Delilah, but now I'm not so sure. Reaper has a way of knowing things. Like he can see the result before anyone else. Maybe he knew, deep down, we wanted Cora too. Or maybe he saw something in her that needed to be plucked free.

My eyes flicker over to Cora's camera as my brothers discuss what they'd like to do to the girls. I hold up my hand and they instantly stop talking.

"What's she doing?" Viper asks, scooting his chair closer.

Cora's on her knees, her hands over her ears like she's trying to block out sound, but the room is deathly quiet.

Breaker leans over me and taps the keys to change the camera. From this angle, we can see her profile. Her eyes are squeezed shut, but her mouth is open. Then I hear it.

It starts out low, like a quiet rumble, then grows louder and louder until it's a high-pitched scream. She stops long enough to suck in a breath and the next scream is even louder, more desperate, broken by a sob. She does it again and again and Breaker's standing up, shoving his chair back as Viper's pushing me out of the way to get to the door.

Behind me, Reaper says, "She has demons darker than ours."

Chapter 6

CORA

You don't discover how loud the silence is until it's all you can hear. I haven't seen them since they brought me a tray of food last night and sat with me until I ate it all. I'm still surprised I could even eat, but I guess some things the body can't deny. Even though I asked questions, they didn't answer any of them and just waited patiently until the bowl of warm soup and the sandwich was gone. Then Breaker and Striker took the tray and left, locking the door with what sounded like a sliding bolt.

Somehow, I slept. Again, the body just wants what it wants. Granted, I was still groggy from being drugged and mentally exhausted from being violently kidnapped. I ended up falling into a deep, dreamless sleep. Now the sun is up and I'm sitting at the end of the bed, trying not to hear the quiet all around me. I've tried to hum, but it just brought back terrible memories, so I had to stop that.

Focusing on the distant crash of waves isn't helping either. I've sung a few songs in my head, but memories flooded my mind, refusing to leave.

Darkness. Sharp pain under my nails. Wet streaks on my face and neck.

The sensations flicker through me, and I can feel the dark memories tickling the back of my mind, scratching, like I did, wanting to break out. The tips of my fingers ache, a phantom pain, and I squeeze my hands into fists, letting the nails bite into my skin to distract myself. It doesn't work. Sitting up, I walk to the window and shove the curtains open. At least it's not dark.

I hate the darkness.

She lives there.

Pressing my face to the cold glass, I try to peer to the left. It's just more house, and a massive ruined garden lined with empty planters and brown patches, broken up by pathways and stone arches on a wide lawn. I think the edges of what may be marshland peek around the side of the window, but I'm not sure. Beyond that, way in the distance, a line of trees cuts across the landscape, wrapping around to the other side of the house. I hear the ocean but it's faint, so it must be far away. It reminds me of the country house my parents took me to some summers, but on a much larger scale.

Rune like's the city, not this endless countryside. From what I can tell of the landscape, we're in the same state, or at least near where we had the country home. Just knowing I'm somewhere near there is making my hands ache. My heart flutters painfully like the bruised wings of a caged bird. I feel caged. I am caged. Locked in a room.

Like what she used to do to me.

My nails cut into my skin again as I try to push down the memories, but they slip through. A flash of blackness. My underwear and pretty dress daddy bought me soaked with piss. Agony in my hands. Splinters of pain cutting through me as I scratched at the door. Blood smearing on my face, mixing with the endless tears as I screamed, raking my nails over the door then my cheeks, trying to break out of my head.

My head was always a far worse place to be trapped than the small closet where she put me.

I'm not there now.

Even if I hear no sounds, I'm in a large room with daylight and a window.

And a locked door.

And the quiet. Except for the memories of my screams breaking through, echoing in my head, haunting in its clarity.

Like I'm screaming now.

Bile rises in my throat, and my knees give. I slide down to the floor, covering my ears, and I'm back there. Her cruel smile, the last thing I saw before she shut the door. The sound of voices and then harsh, heavy breathing. Then nothing. Nothing for so long.

A hand lands on my shoulder and I jerk sideways, my mouth closing as I uncover my ears. I turn to see those beautiful winter eyes. My hands latch on to him, anchoring me to the room.

"Little Red," Breaker says, shoulders heaving like he's been running. "What the fuck is happening inside your head right now?"

"I'm trapped," I breathe, realizing I'm panting and tears stream down my face, my entire body racked with tremors. When I see my hands curled into fists around Breaker's forearms, I drop them, placing them on my thighs to stop the shaking, but it doesn't help. Gulping down air, I say, "I'm not there. I know I'm not here, but I'm trapped. Like she did. I can't get out."

I know I'm not making sense. My words, a jumble of sobs and nonsense.

A shadow passes behind Breaker's eyes and he leans down and scoops me up like he did last night, placing me on the end of the bed. Viper sits next to me, brushing my hair back from my shoulders.

"Who?" Breaker asks gently, crouching down in front of me.

A hysterical giggle bubbles in my throat. I swipe the back of my hand under my nose, suddenly aware I'm talking to the men who have kidnapped me about fearing being locked in a room.

"Where's Delly?" I ask.

The two men exchange a look.

"Can I see her?"

Viper taps his foot and slides his hand over his head, making me wonder what his hair looks like. None of them had hair down there and I wonder what color his hair is. What he looks like.

Breaker stands up, gripping my hand, pulling me from the bed. "Are you hungry?"

My free hand moves to my belly, like I'm testing to see if it hurts from hunger, and confusion swirls in my head. "Papa is going to find you, and when he does, he'll fucking slice your balls off."

I don't know why I called him Papa. It just came out. I fucking hate the name he insists I call him. He's not my father. My father was sweet. Loving. My real father gave me kisses and hugs that didn't hurt. He actually loved me, even if he allowed what she did. He was just scared of her, too.

"Hate to break it to you, Vixen, but your Papa doesn't know how to find you." Viper grabs my arm and yanks me toward the door. "And until we decide otherwise, you'll stay here and cooperate. Now let's go eat."

"I'm not hungry," I snap, jerking away. "I want to see Delly."

"If you want to see Delilah, then you'll listen," Breaker says, placing a hand on the small of my back. "And eating is part of listening."

My eyes gravitate to the window. "Are we going outside?" My heart skitters. "I'm I going to get locked in here again after I eat?"

Breaker's body goes rigid, and he shoots a look at Viper, then to the open doorway.

My eyes dart to the door. Striker's large body fills the space. I step toward him, trying to peer past him to the empty hallway that looks just as neglected and worn as my room. "Are you here to make sure they feed me and lock me away?"

Striker crosses his arms, leaning a shoulder against the doorframe. "Who's Prissy, and why did she shut the door?"

My chest tightens, and I look at the floor. "Yes. I'm hungry."

***

It's cold outside in the garden and Breaker slings a huge wool coat over my shoulders as we step outside. My shoulders are warm, but the cold, dry air slips up my dress and goosebumps break out, but I don't care. I breathe it in, letting it coat my lungs.

Before we left the room, they blindfolded me. Then they took me down a stairwell, and we walked for a long time. I heard doors open and locks clicking and it seemed like forever before we stopped and they removed my blindfold.

I stood next to Viper in the center of a large kitchen with tile floors and old appliances, watching numbly as Breaker made a sandwich. Once I ate the food they gave me, Breaker grabbed my hand and led me to a door located in a mudroom of sorts behind the kitchen, and we're now outside in a little garden with dying herbs and wilted vegetable plants with yellow and brown leaves.

It's hard to tell the scope of the house, other than it's massive. Most of the house is blocked by a tall stone wall, limiting my view. It's more like an old mansion than a house. Like those huge country homes people in old movies would travel to so they could marry off their daughters.

A bird calls from overhead. I lift my face, letting the sun warm my cheeks. The sound of waves is more distant here, again reminding me of the house I went to in the summer with my parents.

"Do you guys live here?" I ask, my eyes closed, my hands gripping the black peacoat to keep it from sliding off. "Or do you just bring your victims here?"

I hear Breaker sigh to my left.

"Do you fuck all the people you kidnap?" I ask, lowering my head to glare at Viper in front of me, who's watching me with an intensity that reminds me of the other night. "Or do you just make them suck you off first?"

His eyes narrow, but he remains quiet. They didn't talk while I ate. Just sat me down and pointed to the sandwich. It was an odd feeling, having three men who saw me naked and made me come standing around me like onyx gargoyles while I took bites of a dry sandwich. But really, all of this is weird.

If Rune doesn't know how to find us, I hope Clyde can figure it out. He's smarter than Rune. And even crazier.

My socks stick to the stones as I walk over to the rows of wooden boxes holding the dying garden. I pinch off a mint leaf and crush it, bringing it to my nose, letting my eyes travel around the enclosed yard.

Striker leans against the doorway of the house, and I feel his eyes travel with me as I walk around. I wonder where the fourth one is, Reaper. Delly was so focused on him. I wonder if he's with her now, making her eat and taking her for a walk outside like a dog.

"So, who's the cook and who's the gardener?" When I don't get a response, not that I expected one, I say, "Or do you all come here and play house together, sucking each other's dicks and—"

My words snap off, teeth clacking together when Viper grips my arm and drags me to him. I crash into his chest, my hands landing on the hard planes of muscles.

"Get one thing straight, little Vixen," he growls. "If you keep sassing off like a brat, there will be consequences."

I keep my voice even, though my insides twist up tight with fear. "Scary Viper," I snarl. "I've seen worse men than you."

Breaker chuckles. "Little Red, there are very few men worse than Viper."

Viper's eyes darken and I swear he smiles under his mask, like Breaker was paying him a compliment. Maybe with these guys he was.

I grind my teeth as his fingers dig sharply into my arm. "Scary men, scary threats," I mock.

"Keep it up and you'll learn quickly how he got his name," Breaker warns.

"Do you always resort to violence?" I ask sweetly, curling my lip into a vicious smile as I glare at Viper. "I thought I was here because you wanted to fuck me while I sucked Breaker off this time."

Viper's other hand snaps up and grips my hair, jerking my head back. My fingers weave into the thick material of his tight shirt. "Next time we fuck you, we'll be taking turns with all our cocks in every tight hole."

I swallow the panic all mixed up with some fucked up form of arousal and say, "Sounds like fun, boys. Do I get Striker in my ass or my mouth? I never got to taste him."

"Your pretty cunt," Striker says from the steps. "Then your mouth."

"Good hygiene practice. We don't want to do ass to mouth." I wink, my heart fluttering with nerves, pressing my breasts to Viper's large body. He growls, tossing me off and I stumble back. My eyes land on Breaker. "Gives me something to look forward to while I'm waiting for Rune to gather his army and hunt you down."

I spin on my heel, my socks catching on the white rocks, and stalk toward the door with my head high. I shove past Striker and walk to the center of the kitchen, feeling him follow.

When he ties the blindfold, I know Delly is okay. It's obvious they will not hurt us. They wouldn't be so concerned with feeding me and taking me outside, much less storming into the room when I was overcome with memories if they planned to cut off body parts and send them to Rune.

As Striker shuts the bedroom door behind me, I really hope that the last part is true.

And I really, really hope Delly is okay because they looked dead serious about there being a next time.

Chapter 7

Delilah

The first day I'm here, I scream and pound on the door. Pace the room. Kick at the tray of food and the pretty glass pitcher of water that magically appeared by the locked door while I was sleeping. Then regret it because I'm hungry and the tap water from the bathroom faucet tastes metallic and old.

The second day, I know better, so I keep quiet and tear the room apart looking for any clues as to where I am. I find nothing and I'm left with the armoire drawers and their contents scattered around the room. The flowery vintage dresses and silky nightgowns all over the floor. All the bedding, a soft white coverlet and clean sheets, in a lump near the window.

Day three, I clean up my mess because it's obvious I'm not going anywhere and I'm bored out of my mind, sick of trying to figure out what they want. Worried my father may not know where to look for us.

On day four, I shut the bathroom door and hyperventilate, but not a single tear escapes. Even as the hopelessness consumes my every thought, I can't cry. All my tears dried up and withered like dead flowers that one awful day my mother was taken from me. Just like any hope I've clung to that my father may find us. When I can breathe again, I leave the bathroom and sleep the rest of the day.

By day five, I'm staring out the window, lost in thought. Hoping Zane isn't dragging the company under in my absence or messing up the ledgers Cora and I kept.

Or just being Zane and trying to convince my father to buy another hotel chain from Snyder.... or whatever it was we actually bought. The sum Cora and I had to distribute and hide was astronomical for a chain of hotels.

On day six, I steep in my anger.

Several times a day, I tell myself that my father is coming. Clyde is coming. They have to. Someone, anyone, is coming to get us and return us home. Alive.

Even stupid, annoying Zane would be a welcome sight. He'd love the opportunity to be the hero.

By day seven, I'm boiling. A current of anger coursing through me as my mind spins, searching for answers, anything logical to hold on to while I wait for my father and Clyde.

Anger is easier to feel than fear.

Seven days is a long time to be alone, locked in a room with just your thoughts to keep you company. Seven whole days since Striker untied me. Seven days of pacing this room, suppressing the terror building inside my chest, squeezing my lungs. I don't know where Cora is or if she's safe. If they untied her too and left her to her own thoughts, like they have me. If she's in a room somewhere in this huge house, pacing back and forth, waiting for whatever comes next. If she's scared like I am.

If she's dead.

My sleep is erratic, and I'm only able to get a few hours at a time. At least I think it's that long. Since I have no way of telling the time, I can only guess at the number of hours that pass. I'm lost without my phone and my watch. The two items I relied on so heavily every day.

I only think it's been seven days based on the number of times I've seen the sunset and the number of times a tray of food has appeared while I was in the bathroom taking one of my quick, freezing cold showers. Every time I step into the shower, my heart races, stomach churning with black, oily fear. I had never thought about how vulnerable a person is in the shower before. But then again, I never had a reason to.

I've also never had a reason to care so much about how many days have passed. As I watch the sunrise on this seventh day, I place my hand on the cold glass, wishing they'd just let me see Cora. Outside my prison window, vivid splashes of orange wipe away the purply night and smattering of stars remaining in the sky as the bright sun rises over the water. It's so breathtakingly beautiful, my heart pangs for home.

At least we're still on the east coast.

The view outside my window has told me nothing beyond that the enormous house sits back from the short cliffs, with open greenery along the coast. At night, there are no other lights nearby, nor the pale halo of light pollution in the dark sky indicating a city close to here.

I keep calling it a house, but it's really a vast mansion. Some late 18th century monstrosity, with massive wings jutting off to my room's right and left, gables with ornate spindles, and a gothic feeling that reminds me of something a French vampire would inhabit.

During the day, I can't see any movement in other windows, but at night there are a few flickers of lights in the wing to my left and I think that might be where Cora is being held.

At least that's what I hope.

I've tried signaling at night, opening and closing the curtains in some mangled form of morse code, thinking if it is her, then she must be looking out the window trying to find me too. But I never see anything.

The massive windows don't open and no matter how hard I've tried, I can't unlock the door to my room. I gave up once I realized it was a sliding lock on the outside. So I'm forced to sit and wait. Pick at the food on the platter they leave—hunks of hard cheese, dried fruits, crackers, and bread with a glass and a crystal pitcher of water—and then wait again.

Today, though, that is going to change. Whatever game they are playing, keeping Cora and me separated, keeping me isolated, is working and I'm going stir crazy, ready to get out of this room at any cost.

That's why I have a plan. I know they have a camera on me in the bedroom. I hope not in the bathroom, because they only bring the tray of food while I'm in the shower or sleeping. The first time I came from the bathroom and found the tray on the floor by the door, I figured they were watching me. Then when I woke to find it replaced with fresh bits of food, it was confirmed.

They're keeping me as a prisoner, but like all prisons, I'm being watched.

Heavy footsteps fall outside the bedroom and stop. Through the crack at the bottom of the door, I can see his shadow standing on the other side. I know it's him. It's like my body can sense his nearness. My heart jackhammers in my chest, even though he does this several times a day and I already know what to expect. There's a part of me that fears he'll slide the lock back and come in. But he again just stands outside the door saying nothing.

The first time, I screamed and pounded on the door, giving in to my fear and desperation, only to be ignored. I won't do it again.

Just as suspected, after a few minutes, Reaper turns and leaves.

It's part of the mind-fuck.

That's why I'm about to fuck with them.

My forehead hits the window panel, my breath fogging up the glass. It's cold, bitter cold, but I found cable knit sweaters in the armoire my first day here, along with the old vintage dresses and simple cotton bras and underwear. Some fluffy socks and a pair of brown leather boots with long laces.

"You could at least light the fire when you sneak in here next time, Striker," I say, not turning from the window. I don't know if they can hear me through the camera, but I've been talking to them for days. At first I remained silent, refusing to give them the satisfaction that whatever they are trying to accomplish is getting under my skin, but at this point, who cares? If I don't talk, hear my voice out loud, I'm going to go insane.

"If you're going to kill me, can we just get on with it?" I ask. "I'm so tired of being in this room."

My stomach rumbles with hunger, and I lower my hand from the glass to touch my belly. My appetite is gone, even if my body wants the nourishment. I can hardly stomach any more than a few bites at a time. My nerves are too rattled. .

With all this time I've had to think, I have figured out a few things. When I first woke, I knew they were some sort of soldiers. Professionals, tasked with taking Cora and me.

But, too many days have passed with no sign of my father. If we're being held for ransom, whatever the asking price for Cora and me to be returned safely may be too high for my father to get easily. He'd have to sell shares, hotel chains, and clubs if they're asking for maybe hundreds of millions. My father is loaded, but it's all tied up in real estate. It would take time to gather that much money. He'd have to liquidate all his assets if the price was steep. That would take a while.

Like maybe a few days.

And we're already on day seven.

The second thing I realized is that my father knows *exactly* who took us, or rather who hired the four to take us, which complicates matters. This means it's personal, which could be why the ransom may be high and why Reaper said he was seeking revenge. Whoever has a grudge against my father, and that could be literally anyone, is more than likely going to make him sweat.

That means my father may not have been told what he needs to pay just yet. If that's the case, my father must be losing his mind.

A sliver of delight moves through me at the thought my father probably grabbed Dave and interrogated him in a fit of rage and fear to see if he has any connection to whoever took us.

The one time I acted out when I was a teenager, he sent Clyde to retrieve me. I had gone out on a date, something I wasn't allowed to do, and we'd parked at the beach to make out, but then Clyde appeared. He'd dragged the boy from the back of the car and beat the shit out of him. I stood there and watched, learning as much of a lesson as that boy whose name I can't even remember. I wasn't to be touched.

And so I was careful after that. Then Dave came along and I knew he'd be safe if he touched me.

Now though? The cheating asshole's probably black and blue and I can't say I'm upset about it.

Zane's handsome face flashes through my mind. I wonder if Rune questioned him. He's been with Rune Corporations for years, but only stepped up, working directly under my father around five years ago. My father trusts him, but not like he does Dave.

I wonder if Zane's covered in bruises too. Probably not. He's good at playing the game and more than likely is helping Rune tear through his staff, looking for anyone who might be involved.

Another possibility why my father has yet to come for us is that they haven't contacted him. At all. Once that thought crossed my mind, I had to shut it down because that could only mean one thing. We were being used as tools to get my father to cooperate.

That means we're expendable.

And once that thought took root, it grew thorns and snagged in my mind, and now I know we have to escape. I have to get out of this room, find Cora, and get help. Even if I have no idea where I am, and can only see the ocean spread out before me.

My mind flashes with the image of Manuel on the floor. I squeeze my eyes shut. These guys are murderers. Reaper killed my father's guard in cold blood to get us. I know for a fact he'd not hesitate to kill us if that's what was wanted. We *have* to escape.

I shift, the cold metal fork I tucked in my sock poking into my skin, a reminder that I have a plan and it will work.

It has to.

Turning, I lean my back against the large paned window, keeping my eyes cast down to the rough wood floor. I think I know where the camera is located, but I'm not positive. I took a chance my second day here and slipped the small fork under my blankets when I sat down on the bed to eat from the tray.

My eyes drift up, right to the corner where I think it's located, and say, "Or turn up the fucking heat. You're aware I'm a south Florida girl, it's November, and cold as fuck in here, right?" I lift my thick cardigan. "And this isn't doing the job."

Cold seeps through the sweater as I press my back to the glass, my gaze traveling to the chair by the vanity. It's small, but made of solid wood, with the armrests covered in a worn blue velvet. Like the ones in those dramatic costume movies where the woman sits to brush her hair as she slowly goes insane. Like how I feel right now. Crazy. Driven to madness by isolation, the constant nagging of fear, and the freezing cold of the room I can't escape.

My feet pad softly over the floor, the thin dress whispering around my shins. I stop next to the chair and inspect it. Then lift the arm to check its weight. It's heavy, but not too heavy to lift.

Chapter 8

STRIKER

19 Years Ago, June, Age 11

"Again."

My finger instinctively pulls back on the trigger. The target ripples milliseconds later, leaving a perfect circular hole dead center of the black ring.

"Again," Fallon instructs.

I take another shot, this time aiming for the target's head and landing it with precision. My eyes move to Fallon.

"Good." His gaze flicks to Maxim standing behind me. "He never misses, does he?"

"No," Maxim confirms. "Not once."

That's not true. I missed once, but it was on purpose.

Next to me, our brother, Sniper, shifts. The two of us lie on the rooftop platform, legs spread out behind us, rifles aimed at the target positioned several yards away in the center of the field. The sun beats down, turning the day unusually warm, making my uniform stick to my skin.

I hate feeling dirty. Any sweat or stink or grime on my skin reminds me of the darkness.

Grinding my teeth, I push the thoughts away, forcing myself to focus.

Lowering my head again, I look through the scope and click the rifle a degree left and ten down, until I center the soft red poppy in the crosshairs. With a shallow breath, I wait for the wind to die down. The second it does, I pull the trigger. The dirt explodes behind the flower, red petals bursting away like blood.

"Impressive," Father says, crouching down next to me, his hand landing heavily on my shoulder. My heart picks up pace. Whenever he touches us, it hurts, and my body screams with alarm. But then he squeezes my shoulder and stands. "You're doing well, my son."

I've spent the last six years in the school, nameless. Viper was named early on, his entire personality earning his name. Sniper received his name last year when we began training with firearms, but Fallon says he has yet to see my skills.

As I stand up, I catch a glimpse of Sniper's scowl. He has plain features, with a flat face, like someone pressed his nose into a wall and it stayed that way. The sunlight catches his dull brown hair, shaved close to his scalp, reminding me of dead grass in winter. He may be the same age as Viper, but he's shorter and skinnier. Though he's capable of being just as mean.

"Not bad for a boy who cries at night," Sniper whispers so only I can hear. Something cruel glints in his mouse brown eyes. "Maybe you should go to the other school. Go train to be a ballerina since you cry like a little girl."

I clench my jaw, trying to push past the red haze clouding my vision. "I'd rather be a ballerina than a skinny little shit with buck teeth."

Sniper's arm arches towards me with a clenched fist, but I see it coming and easily dodge out of the way, avoiding his weak punch. He stumbles, but regains his balance quickly.

He's a shit fighter. Everyone knows it.

A low growl rumbles from him before he swings again, but I expected the move and duck, hooking my arm around his chest and taking him to the ground.

"Stop," Maxim growls, and we both freeze.

"Fucking asshole said I have buck teeth," Sniper snaps, still struggling under my grip. But I keep him pinned to the concrete with my knee on his chest.

Commander Maxim strides forward, hands planted on his hips, sun glinting off his silky eye patch. "Because you do." He chuckles at the wounded scowl on Sniper's face, his laughter echoing through the air, earning him a sharp glare from Fallon.

I suppress my own laugh, but it gets choked off as Maxim fists our collars and hauls us to our feet. I smooth my gray school uniform, swallowing a curse when I see dirt staining my shirt. We're supposed to go with Teacher to the village for Sunday school, but Maxim insisted on showing Fallon how well Sniper and I have been doing with the firearms portion of our weapons training program.

"Pushing buttons again, I see," Fallon says, eyeing me. His piercing gaze shifts toward Sniper, lingering for a moment, before moving back my way. "Haven't we learned that testing boundaries leads to trouble?"

I want to tell him that Sniper started it, but I clamp my mouth shut. All that will do is piss Fallon off. We're a unit. What one does we all do. If I tattle, I'm tattling on myself. If I act out of line, my brother's pay the price with me. It's rare for us to be singled out and disciplined individually, although it happens, as I've learned one too many times. I'm well acquainted with Fallon's belt and solitary.

"Sniper," Fallon says, adjusting the collar of my brother's shirt. "How should I punish a boy who can't keep his mouth closed?"

A cruel glint flares in Sniper's eyes as he assesses me. He's just thirteen, but sometimes his viciousness makes him seem so much older.

"Ten whips with the belt," Sniper says, satisfaction making his lip curl.

Hatred burns through my chest like acid, making me tense. We have always clashed as far back as I can remember. Sniper resents that I do better in classes, am faster at learning weapons, and quicker on my feet. He hates that I can always hit the target, like him, but with better accuracy. And almost every single time. Almost because I deliberately missed that one time, so Sniper wouldn't look bad after earning his name.

I bite my tongue, glaring at his plain face, regretting being so nice. I should have his name. Part of me wants to lunge forward and smash my fist into his smirk. Knock his teeth loose and keep hitting until he chokes on his blood. But then I'd be giving into my baser instincts and Fallon teaches us we must never do that. Control over bodies and minds is more important than revenge.

"A fitting lesson." Fallon nods. He unbuttons his charcoal suit jacket, lifting the silky vest to reach for his belt buckle. The slick sound makes my stomach drop. Icy eyes land on Sniper. "Remove your shirt and turn around."

Sniper's brows knit and his eyes dart to me. "Go on, do it," he snarls.

"You, Sniper," Fallon says. He holds out the belt for me. "Striker here will teach this lesson today."

Striker.

My heart hammers upon hearing the name, a flutter of excitement blooming in my chest, but then darkness seeps in as his last few words settle. Before I can think, I'm shaking my head and backing away, my stomach knotting up grossly. I couldn't ever imagine hurting one of my brothers. Even if I don't like him.

"No?" Fallon asks, eyes narrowing. "Shouldn't he be punished for testing you?"

I shake my head, remembering to add a respectful, "No, sir." But my nerves cause my words to stutter, so I clear my throat and repeat myself before adding, "Because I was pushing his limits, too."

Fallon nods, and I think I see a flash of approval pass over his face, but I'm not sure. "Very well. Then you both will learn today." Father's glare intensifies as he turns to me. "Striker, remove your shirt."

Without hesitation, I obey, folding my shirt, placing it neatly on the platform before I present my back. When the first lash lands, I flinch but bite back any sounds of pain. The skin over my back stings with each strike, but I force myself to focus on a distant target. Another hit lands and I can't help but think about my name.

Striker.

After waiting six years for a name, it seems fitting that today it's received with a lashing blow. The next strike lands on my lower back and I clench my teeth, breathing through the burning sensation. My father isn't being as harsh as he usually is with our lesson today, which I am grateful for. Sniper could not handle it if this were any worse. He's never been good at learning. Not in classes. Not with Father. He's usually the one that's kissing ass to avoid notice, so he's rarely been at the end of Father's belt.

When my lesson is complete, I turn and pick up my shirt, not allowing myself to wince as my skin tightens from the movement. I know there will be welts for the next several hours, but at least it won't be days. And I'm glad we're going to Sunday school so I can sit in a cool room and not have to continue sweating out in this heat with red marks stinging my back.

"Sniper," Fallon says, and I glance sideways at my brother.

"No," Sniper says with a quick jerk of his head.

The blood drains from my face, pooling at my feet like tarry oil. It's one thing to refuse to carry out lessons on our brothers—we'd all rather take the punishment alongside each other than be the one holding the belt. But to outright refuse Fallon's lesson is an entirely different matter.

"No?" Father's voice drops dangerously low. Fear tingles my hands, the sensation making me gather them into tight fists. I glance again in Sniper's direction to see if he's lost his mind. Obviously he has, because he shakes his head again.

Father signals for Commander Maxim, who strides forward and grabs Sniper by his shoulders with his large, meaty hand. I've always hated his hands. They're hairy and scarred with burns.

Fallon smooths his palm down the front of his gray suit vest. "It seems my son has forgotten his place." His arm lifts, arching back.

My heart stutters.

When the hit lands, it slices brutally through Sniper's cheek, and I gasp, closing my eyes. Another sickening thwack follows seconds later. My breath bursts free, but I gather it back in, blinking my eyes open.

Father's arm arches back again. I shift my gaze to just over his shoulder.

Another hit lands. Then another, and Sniper screams. I suck in a breath as his scream cuts through my mind, old memories of another scream filtering through my head.

The terrified cry of a little boy sitting in darkness.

The scream stops abruptly, but the lashes keep coming.

I don't think I like my name anymore.

My focus shifts to the row of trees blocking the village from view. In the winter months, the leaves fall, leaving the branches naked, and we can see the smoke rising from distant chimneys over the tree line. But I like the summer months better when the trees have bright green leaves. I like the trees. I like the red flowers and the green grass. The birds that fly overhead and how the sun turns the sky a dark purple before it sinks below the horizon. How after it rains, the entire school smells like damp earth and clean water. How puddles form in the training yard and we have to jump over them so we don't get our boots wet on the way to classes.

During the warm months, if we've had good behavior all week, we get to go to the village market with Cook. I like the market too. We get to see girls. Viper likes to tug at the braids of the schoolgirls in line at the vendors. He really likes the older women who wear the pretty dresses and the fancy gypsies with bells on their ankles and chains around their waists, their clothes a rainbow of colors.

In the village, Cook will give us little coins and paper bills and we can buy sweets. I love the shaved ice and Viper likes the heavy cakes with white frosting. If Breaker comes, he will always buy the sweet candy from the gypsy wagons. Sometimes Reaper and Hunter come too, and they buy bottles of vodka from the old man that makes it in his barn. They sneak the alcohol into school under their uniforms and later drink straight from the bottle after lights out. Even us younger ones will get to take a few shots. Hunter thinks it's funny when Viper gets drunk. He gets friendly, telling everyone he loves them and always wants to play cards.

"Striker!"

My body jolts violently back to the present. My gaze lands on Fallon, his tall frame slowly bleeding into focus. His brows knit and I wonder how many times he's said my new name.

"Where did you go, son?"

"To town," I say, then realize I've not actually left, so I just lied and need to correct myself. "I was thinking about the village."

He nods and his eyes slip down. He gestures to the boy on the ground, but I don't look. I know better. "Take him to the infirmary," Fallon tells Commander.

Sniper doesn't make a sound as Commander pulls his limp body up. I keep my eyes trained on Fallon, so I don't have to see.

"You did well," Father says. His long fingers trail over my cheek then he pets my head. "When you return from church, we'll continue your training."

My stomach churns with slickness, hating myself that his praise makes me smile.

"Go to your quarters and change, my *syn*," Fallon says, dragging his thumb over my cheek again.

I look down at my chest. Long lines, like finger streaks of red, slash across my clean shirt. Unease crawls over my skin, skittering down my spine, stabbing through my back and burrowing in my gut like tiny venomous spiders. My hand shakes as I lift it, lightly touching a scarlet smear. It's thin, dark, and still warm. Sticky like the sweat on my back.

The need to be out of my clothes slams into my chest. I need to bathe. Now. Remove these clothes and sweat and sticky red off my skin.

Fallon wipes my cheek again, his finger coming away with a smear of red. He wipes it on his thigh and I notice the scarlet splashes smattering his pants.

Blood, silly boy, I hear Maxim say in my head. *All that red is blood.*

No. Striker. My name is Striker.

And that's Sniper's blood.

Bile rises in my throat, but I bite back the urge to vomit. My vision moves in and out of focus like the old projector Cook sets up in the cafeteria on Friday nights.

"Give your clothes to Maxim," Fallon instructs, patting my cheek. The sharp slap centers me, my vision returning to normal.

"Yes, sir," I say, squaring my shoulders and shoving the rising wave of horror down. Further until I feel nothing.

Father nods in approval like he can see the blackness that was trying to drown me recede. I watch his back, my mind blank, as he leaves, before returning to my room to change.

After Maxim retrieves my clothes, I pretend I don't see him walking toward the incinerator.

When we return from Sunday school later that afternoon, I find Maxim talking to Fallon in the yard. I dart behind the bleachers, crouching low, careful not to dirty my pants.

"Some dogs just can't be tamed," Commander says. "It's easier just to put them down."

Later that night, Viper tells me that Sniper didn't make the cut, and they removed him from the school. There's just thirteen of us now.

Viper pats my back, saying my name over and over and I'm reminded of the strikes to Sniper. I feel now like my name came at his expense.

Maybe I should have missed. Maybe I should have shot more to the left or not shown off at all.

But Viper said Sniper just didn't make the cut, so maybe it's not my fault he was whipped and then removed from the school. In the end, it doesn't matter.

I'm Striker.

STRIKER

I hit my target every time. I'm fast and smart and even though I'm prone to outbursts, I control it better than anyone here.

My gaze drifts to my brother with pale eyes the color of ice and beautiful, deep skin. I hope when he's named he isn't left wishing it was different.

Chapter 9

CORA

"Viper, can you at least acknowledge you hear me talking?"

He doesn't answer. He doesn't look at me. Of course he doesn't. Ever since that first day here, none of them have spoken to me. It's like they're worried that if they speak, important information will slip out and I'll know where I am, who they are, and what is happening.

They don't have to worry about that. I'm clueless. The only thing I know is Clyde and Rune haven't come for us. Viper told me they don't know how to find us. At first I figured it was a scare tactic, but now I'm starting to believe him.

Viper adjusts his weight, his eyes on the cards in his hands. We've established a boring routine of them taking me down to the kitchen, watching me eat, and letting me outside. We do this three times a day, Striker usually the one to retrieve me, and even Reaper once, though I'm glad I haven't seen him again. He's too dark. His black eyes too intense.

In the evenings after I'm led from the garden back to my room, either Viper or Breaker will stay and play silent Gin Rummy, or Texas Hold'em until I'm yawning and then they leave.

Today is day seven and I'm so sick of cards, of them not talking to me, and of not knowing what is happening that I want to scream.

When I first woke up, I worried they'd torture us. Force us into depraved sexual acts and beat us. Keep us chained like animals. I never once worried I'd die of sheer fucking boredom.

Viper places a card down and takes another, acting like I didn't just ask a question.

"Is she okay?" I ask for the third time today. "Do you play cards with her too?"

Nothing.

"Rune used to play cards with Delly and me when we were kids."

Viper's eyes slide up to my face.

"He'd always let us win."

Pretty blue-green eyes dip down to his cards. I didn't notice in the club how his eyes are the color of the Mediterranean sea. I did, however, notice that night, just as I do now, how absolutely massive he is.

He's leaned up against the metal headboard, his enormous body taking up what feels like half the bed. I'm at the end of the mattress, my back pressed to the railing of the footboard, my dress tucked under me. Even though they won't let me out past the kitchen or the garden, made threats that sound more like promises, and won't let me see Delly, I'm not scared. Not really. Not like when they took us.

I watched them kill Rune's guards, but after that first day here, I don't feel like they'd hurt us that way. Maybe it's the way Viper and Breaker look at me. Or the way they touched us that night. Roughly, their hands demanding, but never pushing. Never forcing.

I could just be hanging on to a sliver of hope, but I don't think so. I'm good at detecting the bad in people, having witnessed enough evil first hand to know when a man isn't what he pretends to be.

And Viper, Breaker, Striker, they don't feel bad.

Reaper though... he's something entirely different.

"How did you guys get the nicknames?" I ask, remembering Breaker saying he was given the name as I shift, crossing my legs. Viper's gaze locks on to my exposed thigh. My stomach flips.

Ripping his gaze from me forcefully, he adjusts his weight, and that's when I notice it. The prominent outline of his dick straining against the thick fabric of his pants. Between my thighs pulses. I swallow, averting my eyes, but he catches me looking and

I detect the subtle movement under his mask that tells me he's smirking.

"Let me guess," I say, blinking away the memory of that gigantic cock in my mouth. Of his hands on me, in me, pleasuring me in ways I've never experienced before. "You guys wrote down the stupidest code names from video games and pulled them from a hat. You got last pick."

His eyes narrow.

"And lost."

Before I can move away, he's shot forward, on his knees in front of me, his hand at my throat. My cards fall to the bed, scattering like dry leaves. Thick fingers dig into my pulse, making my heart stutter. I swallow the whimper his harsh grip creates, though not just from shock.

I lift my chin. "So you got your dumb name because you're quick." Now I smirk. I've been testing him for days now, tossing around subtle insults, seeing what sort of reaction I get from them. Breaker is level-headed. Striker is so calm, it's weird. But Viper? He reacts to *everything*. "How clever."

His fingers tighten at my throat. "I got it because I'm mean."

I grip his gloved hand, nails scraping across the coarse material. "How *original*."

Viper chuckles, and even though he doesn't let go, I relax hearing the coarse sound. Still gripping me by the throat with one large hand, he drags me with him as he sits back and I'm forced to my hands and knees. My breath huffs from me, my pussy throbbing.

God, I'm fucked up.

"Cruel. Cunning. Fast." His grip tightens a little more, my breath catching on the pressure. "Vicious. Spiteful."

"You're describing the man who raised me," I manage to say. "Am I supposed to be scared?"

The mention of Rune creates a ripple of darkness behind his eyes, but he lets me go. I sit back on my heels, resisting the urge to rub at my neck.

"Rune plays at being powerful," Viper says, tossing his thick legs over the edge of the bed and standing, adjusting his hard dick as his gaze slips over my body. "You were raised by a weak man who thinks power is in controlling others."

I laugh, looking around the room. "Because keeping me locked up isn't controlling me?"

He leans in, resting his palms on the bed, the skull face and its fanged mouth so close to mine I can feel his warm breath on my lips. "I don't think anyone controls you, but *you.*"

My belly dips. If only he knew how wrong he was.

"I've been controlled since I was born," I say, leaning forward so my mouth is almost brushing his. "I've just learned how to reduce how much of my power is *stolen.*"

"Power isn't stolen." The coarse material of his gloved hand lands on the side of my neck, almost tenderly, his thumb brushing along my jawline. I tilt my head to look into his eyes. My pulse skips when I see the softness in them. "Power is created."

His thumb skims over my bottom lip and there's a part of me that wishes he'd take his gloves off again. I enjoy watching his large hands with the pale dusting of freckles across the backs, and how his long fingers flip the cards. I really like how they touch me.

Closing my eyes, I shut the thoughts down and lean back, kneeling in the center of the bed. "Power is created by taking consent. By inciting fear." I lock my eyes with his. "So tell me, *Viper,* whose power are you creating by locking me in this room? Yours or mine?"

He cocks his head to the side, inspecting me. "You think power and control are the same thing," he says, letting his gaze drag down to my knees peeking out from under my dress. "Stealing control differs from earning the privilege of being given it. That's where the power lies, little Vixen. Earning over taking."

My brows knit.

"You, sly fox, know Rune Gavin like no other, don't you?"

My heart skips, my stomach instantly clenching. *Does he know? It's impossible.* No one knows what Rune has done to me.

What I've allowed.

Maybe he's right. I stole some of my power back from Rune the second I changed the way he used me. I created something new with his control over me, influencing how much it affected me, but I'm still helpless. Rune's still stealing bits of me every time he touches me.

But I may give him chunks of my soul, yet he's never going to earn the privilege of my heart.

"You know every detail of his life," Viper says, and relief makes me dizzy, glad they don't know the details of my relationship with Rune. "You know exactly what he's like, who he's pissed off, and why someone would want to make him suffer."

Now my belly is churning for an entirely different reason. "So you'll hurt Delly and me to hurt Rune." It's not a question.

"There are many ways to hurt someone," Viper says, slowly removing his gloves one at a time and placing them on the mattress. Lifting a knee, he places it on the edge of the bed. It dips under his weight and he crawls forward until his masked face is near mine again. "Without ever breaking the skin."

I swallow, my pulse skyrocketing as he dips his head to brush his nose along my jaw, breathing in deeply through the material of his mask. "Does this hurting involve broken bones? Or necks?"

His dark chuckle in my ear sends a zing through my core and I back away, but land on my ass. He uses both his hands to part my legs and crawls forward, the heat of his skin sending a confusing pulse to my core.

Slowly he moves forward, leaning me back until he's hovering over me, laid out between my thighs, hands bracketing either side of my head. My heart's racing so fast I can barely breathe, and when his dick presses to me, I gasp loudly, my back arching off the bed at the contact.

"Our pretty little Vixen thinks we're going to hurt her," he says, and I don't know if he's talking to me or himself. "Does that scare you?"

I tilt my hips, his dick hitting right at my clit, and he hisses. A smile curls my lip. "It seems to turn *you* on. Does scaring women half your size get you all hot and bothered, big and bad, *Viper*?"

He widens his legs, forcing my thighs open more. "I love lapping up fear pouring from pretty pink lips. And you like the fear, don't you? If I were to slip my fingers inside your panties, I'd find you wet, wouldn't I?"

I clamp my mouth shut as he grinds into me again, not wanting to give him the satisfaction that he's right. I'm turned on and I hate myself right now.

Bending his elbows, he dips down closer. "You want me," he whispers. "My cock shoved down your throat again, don't you, little Vixen?"

I bite my lip, despising how my body responds so eagerly to him. "So like a man." I smirk. "Always blaming the woman for your desire. You can't even admit that you'd love to lick Breaker's cum from my pussy again."

His palm flattens to my cheek, turning my face to the side, pushing it into the mattress. His masked mouth presses to my jaw, his hot breath fanning over me through the thin material, making a wet heat pool between my legs.

Shit, he's fast.

"I have no problem admitting I'd love to fuck that pretty mouth again," he rasps. "Love to eat your pink cunt, hear your sweet little cries. Taste Breaker and you on my tongue."

His dick grinds into me, and I whimper, my hips tilting to meet him. It's like I've lost all control over my body. It's just doing what it wants. And it wants him.

"But you have to earn my cock," he whispers. "You have to prove you can be trusted before we give you what your needy little pussy craves."

His hand slides to my throat as he leans back on his heels. The feeling of his rough fingertips skimming over my hot flesh sends a fluttering through my entire body. He's so much bigger than me he can still hold me by my neck and kneel between my legs. Viper's gaze flickers down my body, his chest heaving, his hungry gaze stopping between my thighs spread open to where the dress has slid up, exposing my cotton underwear.

The intent is clear as his eyes slip up from between my legs to my face. My pussy throbs, wanting him to touch me as much as I don't want him to. Viper slides the back of his fingers delicately along my inner thigh and I can't help but shiver as my fingers and toes curl into the blankets. Other than the tremor moving through me, I don't move. Not even when he rips the fabric of my underwear aside, tearing the thin cotton, exposing me to him. Not when he slides his thumb over my opening and groans at the slickness he finds there.

"Fuck," he grates. When he does it again, my hips involuntarily lift from the mattress to meet his hand. His fingers around my throat tighten and push down, keeping my shoulders pinned to the bed. "What a good little slut you are, all flushed and wet."

He lets the torn fabric go, fumbling with his belt. The metal buckle *clinks* as he undoes it, then pops the button of his pants. My heart hammers as he frees himself. My mouth opens, but he releases my neck and shoves three fingers past my lips to grip my jaw. I gag as his fingers hit my throat, eyes watering.

His brutal grip sends sparks flying through my veins, my body lighting up at his familiar taste. Slightly salty. Clean. Masculine.

"You crave me and hate me," he rasps, slipping his length over my pussy, using the silky head to rub my clit. My fingers grip the blankets, nails scraping the fabric. "Crave my cock and hate that you want me to fuck you."

With his fingers in my mouth, I can't tell him to stop, much less form words. When he slaps my clit with his dick, I don't think I want him to. Viper shoves his fingers deeper and I choke on a gag. A tear slips from the corner of my eyes and pools in my ear. He slaps my clit with the head of his cock again and I moan around his fingers.

Viper's fingers slip from my mouth and he drags the wetness down to my throat, letting his fingers trail lightly over the hollow of my neck to the top of my breasts. "Look at how desperate you are. Your pussy is dripping for me to fuck you rough. Hard. Like I fucked your mouth."

My breath heaves from my lungs when he slaps my clit again. My eyes dip to where our bodies slick over one another. The sight of his dick slipping over my clit and then slapping the flesh sends a shivering heat through my belly, my body arching to meet him of its own accord. "Fuck you."

He shakes his head, making quiet *tsking* sounds, his large hand slipping a slow, lazy stroke along his cock. "You wish I would. Fuck you. You crave it. Even as you scream and curse me, you want my cock deep inside you. I think you like that edge of desperation."

Another slap of his length to my clit and a furious whimper escapes, my legs opening further.

"You want my cock in your ass, Breaker's enormous dick in your pussy, stretching you until you think we may split you apart."

"Maybe I want to watch your ass get taken," I rasp. He slaps my pussy again and I curl into myself, hands fisted in the bedding as I clench my teeth to keep my moan trapped in my mouth.

"Filthy little thing, aren't you?" he growls, his hand stroking hard as he slaps my clit again and again. Pleasure builds in my lower belly, and I want to rub myself against him, but I keep my hands at my sides, desperately clutching onto a sliver of sanity.

The muscles in his arm tighten under his tight shirt as he strokes himself, working up a steady rhythm, breaking it a few times to slap my clit with his dick, sending heat and confusion through me each time. I keep my legs open, watching him masturbate, gripping the bed and eating up the sight of this enormous man pleasuring himself over my throbbing pussy. Resisting the feral need to tilt my hips higher so he can slip into me.

My entire body screams for more, my pulse thundering in my ears. My jaw pops from trying to keep the desperate sounds in my mouth, but I fail and a few slip out, making his rough strokes and hard slaps come faster.

Soon he exhales roughly, and warmth hits my clit. I clench my teeth as he groans, the familiar sound sending fiery sparks through my belly. Viper rubs his dick and his cum all over my pussy, throwing his head back as his orgasm fades.

He's so fucking sexy, it's infuriating. All thick muscles and broad chest heaving as his breathing slows. Strong hands I crave between my legs again. Beautiful eyes that fall back to my face, igniting like sparklers at whatever he sees in my expression. Even his black mask with the fanged skull is sexy as hell, making me want to sink my teeth into his jawline.

I remember the auburn stubble and how it felt rubbing into my skin. That's the problem with this entire situation. I remember too much.

He tucks himself back into his pants as he slides off the bed. "Now our pretty little Vixen has my cum like she wants." Not bothering to buckle the belt, he grabs his gloves and walks from the room, shutting the door and locking it behind him.

My fingers unfurl and I raise up on one elbow, looking down at the mess he left on me. With one finger, I touch the wet heat on my clit and groan, letting my legs fall open. I do it again, closing my eyes, picturing him kneeling before me, stroking himself. When I slip my fingers covered in his cum into me, I don't care the others may be watching.

In fact, I think I may like it.

Chapter 10

STRIKER

My cock's so hard, but if I try to readjust myself, they both will notice.

On the screen in front of us, Viper throws his head back, hips thrusting, stroking his cock as he comes all over Cora's perfect bare pussy. Her words ring in the room like the echo of a bell.

Watch your ass get taken.

My cock jerks and I shift uncomfortably. I didn't touch her that night. My sole focus was on our Princess, but I'd love to now. Rub my face all over her slick pussy, even with Viper's cum sticking to her.

With Breaker in her ass.

Or maybe in Viper's.

I might like that idea more than I want to admit.

To my right, Breaker groans and grips the hard length of his dick through the material of his pants. For a second, my mind fills with the image of his long, deft fingers slipping down my abs to grip me just as hard. His pale eyes move to me and I look away, trying to blink away the image.

He has never hid his excitement at the sight of Viper with a woman. They don't hide their attraction the nights we share a pretty cunt. And the night with our Princess and Little Flower has left us all in a strange place. Being so close to them, wanting to touch them, fuck them, taste them, has been fucking torture.

As the day's progress, I think we've all been aware of what we're doing. Watching them too much. Thinking about them too much. Talking about them constantly.

With Viper and Breaker sitting with Cora for several hours a day, this was bound to happen. I don't think it's a surprise it was Viper. His lack of control is part of who he is.

"Jesus," Reaper says, watching with us as Viper walks from the room and Cora slips her fingers between her thighs. "She may very well..." his voice trails off when he looks at me. Something about my expression makes his lip curl upward at the corner.

He didn't need to finish his sentence. *She may very well ruin us.* I agree wholeheartedly.

I drag my gaze from him back to the screen, trying to ignore the heated energy coming from Breaker next to me and the knowing look from Reaper.

"Is she...?" Breaker asks, his breath huffing out. My gaze darts to him, only to find him squeezing his cock again. He glances my way and catches my laser sharp focus on his hand. Our eyes meet and I look away.

Again.

Her quiet moan fills the room and we all watch as she fucks herself with cum soaked fingers. We should probably look away but...

"Fuck, she's so beautiful," Breaker says. "She knows we're watching."

"She does," Reaper agrees, leaning back in his chair as he watches her. "And she likes the thought."

Another delicate moan fills the room. I can't rip my eyes off her. The way her breasts move under her pretty floral dress as she slips her fingers in and out. Her other hand moving from her clit up to her breasts, squeezing her nipples through the material and then back down again to slide over her clit. The way her silky hair fans across the bed, a splash of vibrant red over the white covers. How her creamy thighs spread wider as she gets closer to her release and her head tilts back.

"Oh, shit." Viper's voice cuts through the room and I turn long enough to see him leaning against the door frame, his pants and belt still undone. He must have run to get back here so fast. "What a naughty thing she is."

"What was that about, Viper?" Reaper asks, not taking his eyes off the screen.

"A reminder," Viper says. "That she wants us."

Her soft cry shivers through the room as she comes undone, legs curling around her hands. As her orgasm fades, her thighs part and splay open. She lies on the bed, her arms sprawled at the side as she stares at the ceiling, unmoving.

"She doesn't need a reminder," Reaper says, leaning forward, his dark eyes moving between the two women on different screens. "What she needs is a little more fear and less spitfire."

Cora groans, covering her face with both hands, and rolls to her side, her back to the camera.

"I think she's plenty scared," I say. "She talks big, but underneath it all, she's a terrified little girl."

Reaper looks over at me, quirking a brow. "Does that look like terror to you?"

I meet his eyes. "It looks like a woman trying to survive."

His jaw ticks. Reaper doesn't like being wrong, and I think he may be wrong about Cora. She may be more like us than he thinks, just forged from something far different.

"When do we let her see Delilah?" Breaker asks, leaning back in his seat and crossing his arms. The faint scent of the soap he favors hits my nose. It reminds me of the the woods. Crisp. Clean. He shifts again, widening his legs.

I know we've been trapped here too long already, because I find every minor thing he does so fucking…. fascinating.

"It's been a week," Viper adds.

"It's too soon," Reaper says. "Give it a little longer and you'll see I'm right."

"So we just keep her locked in her room?" Viper snaps. "Keep her from her best friend to prove what?"

Reaper raises a dark brow and rips his eyes from the monitor to look at Viper. "She's still our—"

"What, Reaper?" Viper asks sharply. Breaker shifts and meets my eyes. *Yeah*, I agree silently. *I've never seen Viper like this either.* "She's our what? Prisoner?"

"Ours," he says. "Not just yours."

"Ours," Breaker grates, watching the camera as Cora stands and walks to the bathroom. His tone carries such possessive heat, I begin to wonder at what point we decided they were ours.

Because it's starting to feel like we made them ours before that night in the club.

Maybe they have been ours this entire time and we just never voiced it.

"It's not like I fucked her, and it's not like she wasn't willing."

Breaker shakes his head, a disapproving growl building in his throat. "We all agreed not to touch them yet. We *all* agreed to wait."

Yeah. We did. Doesn't mean we like it, but it's too soon. We need their trust before we move forward.

"Next time you want to get off, Viper," Reaper says, leaning back in his seat, spreading his legs and locking his eyes on

Viper. He lifts his chin in Breaker's direction. "You know where to go."

Viper's gaze flickers over to Breaker, crossing his arms over his chest. Breaker's jaw pops, his gaze slipping from Viper's face to the unbuttoned pants as he unfolds himself from the small chair. Taking a step toward him, Breaker cocks his head to the side, the open appreciation as he licks his lips and eyes Viper, making Reaper and I raise our brows as we exchange a look.

Viper opens his mouth and to everyone's surprise Breaker shoves four fingers past Viper's lips, hooking his thumb under his chin and yanking him forward. Their chests crash together. Viper's eyes somehow go wide and narrow all at once as his hands clamp down around Breaker's neck.

"That's right. You know where to go when you want to come." Breaker leans down, dragging his tongue over Viper's top lip. "You come to me, like a good boy."

My balls tighten, and I lean forward, resting my hands on my knees, breath catching in my chest, unable to tear my eyes away. With all the kinky shit we've done, I have never once seen their mouths brush. Breaker has never attempted, hasn't even come close to trying to kiss Viper. It's never been this...

Intimate.

Or fucking erotic.

With his fingers still buried into his mouth, Breaker shoves Viper back against the doorframe, his massive body pressing into Viper's shorter frame. He thrusts his hips, grinding his cock into

Viper's belt. My eyes slip down and I can't seem to look away from the enormous bulge in Breaker's pants and the way Viper thrusts his hips aggressively back into him.

"I know my good boy likes my cock shoved down his throat and my hand on his dick." He brushes his lips to Viper's ear and whispers loud enough that we all hear, "And when you think no one's looking, when no one could hear, you would love to moan like my little whore when I fuck your ass again."

With an angry roar, Viper shoves Breaker away, his cheeks heating in rage.

Breaker laughs, stumbling back, his eyes gleaming dangerously. What they do behind closed doors is not something we talk about. It doesn't matter that we know.

"Fuck you, man," Viper hisses, shoving again at Breaker's chest. "Just fuck you!"

Breaker smirks, gripping his hard cock and shakes it tauntingly. When Viper shoves him again, Reaper barks out, "Enough!"

Chest heaving, and Viper noticeably hard, the two men back away from each other, Breaker grinning and Viper scowling.

"We are a unit," Reaper says with a sigh. "We are brothers. What one does, we all do."

"So I can go jerk off all over them too?" Breaker asks. "Because my balls hurt right now."

Before Reaper can respond, a loud scraping noise cracks out from the camera on Delilah, making him clamp his mouth shut and lean forward. We all stop and inch closer to the screen, focusing on her tiny body dragging a chair across the room.

"What is she doing?" Breaker asks, gripping the back of a chair and leaning in closer.

"Probably something destructive," I say, watching as she has to stop for a minute to catch her breath. She's not eating enough, or drinking enough, and she looks like she's lost weight.

"Isolation twists your mind," Reaper says, finger tapping at the keyboard to change cameras. "You, Breaker, know more than anyone how being left alone makes you go crazy."

Next to me, I feel Breaker's chuckle when his arm brushes mine. I glance over to find him watching my face. When he winks, I look away.

He spent enough time in isolation. He knows exactly what she's feeling right now. Chaotic. Not talking to anyone, no contact with any other living creature, draws things out of the mind that should be left hidden. Funny how the mind creates chaos when nothing else is present.

It takes her a few minutes, but she finally gets the chair near the window. The chair isn't large, but it's solid wood. Someone of her size—she's barely two inches taller than our Little Flower—not eating properly the last seven days means she's weak.

Seemingly satisfied with the chair's location, Delilah flops down and stares out the window for a few minutes, chest heaving as she catches her breath. All I want to do is to march in there and force food down her throat until she's gained the few pounds she's lost and that hollowed out look leaves her eyes.

After a few minutes, she stands upright and turns to face the chair.

Reaper slowly stands, resting his knuckles on the desk, eyes narrowing.

Bending over, she grips the arms and tugs. The chair leaves the ground, then drops.

"She wouldn't," Breaker says, awe in his tone.

Reaper reaches for his mask, fisting it, the black lines of his tattoos harsh against the white knuckled grip on his mask. Rage paints his features dark, slashing his eyes with violence.

She does it again, managing to lift the chair in the air. Then we all watch as she swings, aiming for the window.

Chapter 11

Delilah

The door bursts open, slamming into the plaster wall, the sound reverberating through the room like a thunder clap. I lose my grip on the chair and it falls with a loud crack and skids to a stop next to the window.

His massive body fills the entire doorway, nothing but a black shadow, chest heaving, like some dark, demonic creature. I stumble back, terror gripping my throat with sharp claws, raking down, cutting into my chest, stealing my breath. My back hits the heavy curtains, gaze locked on the mask with the melting face and the piercing black eyes that stare at me with murderous intent.

I was right. They are watching my every move.

And they aren't far away.

"You've got my attention," he growls. "But I think you may regret it."

Reaper prowls forward, movements graceful, his long legs eating up the space between us. I shrink back, ill prepared for the level of hatred rattling out of him in heavy breaths as he stalks toward me.

A tendril of fear slithers up my spine, coiling around my neck. My eyes dart to the open door, my heart beating wildly. Before he's across the room, I leap toward the bed, using the blankets to help pull myself over it, eyes locked on the open door. When I land, my socks slip, but I grip the mattress and remain upright. Behind me, Reaper grates out a low rumbling growl, and before I can take another step, he lunges in front of me, blocking the door. My ass lands back on the mattress, dread pooling like ice in my belly.

Fuck, he's furious.

"What was your plan, Kitten?" he snarls, inching closer as I scramble back on the bed, reaching for the fork in my sock. "Break the window and *jump*?"

With an angry roar, he lunges forward and I raise the fork, moving solely on instinct and aiming for his neck. Onyx eyes gleam as he latches on to my wrist, twisting my arm, forcing it behind me. I scream as pain shoots through my shoulder, my grip loosening. The fork clatters to the floor at our feet. Reaper releases my wrist as I spin to stop the agony in my arm. His hand clamps over my mouth, his other arm locking around my waist, dragging me back against his solid chest. My head slams back into his shoulder, my teeth hitting my bottom lip under his large palm, covering half my face.

"Stabbing?" The word scrapes out, laced with fury, the deep guttural sound shivering through my body. "You're going to have to do better than a fucking *fork*."

Heart hammering, I reach up behind me, my fingers seeking his eye sockets. He growls when my index finger digs into the corner of his eye, then rakes down his cheek, catching the fabric of his mask. My figures curl around the cutout and I tug. Forced to release my mouth, he grips my arm, but his mask rips from his head and falls to the floor. He releases me, grasping my hair by the roots and shoves me forward so violently my shins slam into the metal bed frame as he throws me face down across the bed. His massive hand pushes my face down into the mattress as he hooks his other arm around my elbow, then grips my free arm, pinning both to my spine. Reaper falls forward, hips keeping me in place, his chest heaving with ragged breaths against my back.

"Naughty, naughty little kitten," he grates.

Tucking my chin, I suck in air, my hair sliding down around my face in slashes, obscuring my vision. I can't see him behind me, but feel every solid muscle, his huge male frame trapping me.

"Get off!" I scream, bucking my hips to push him off, but he's too big. If anything, my movements drive his...

My entire body stills, every single nerve ending snapping to focus right where his dick presses into my ass crack. Slick heat floods my core. He's so hard I can feel every inch of him straining against his pants through my flimsy dress. My body lights up, skin sizzling with awareness, remembering him like this. Taking me from behind. Taking my pleasure for himself until it no longer belonged to me.

Until *I* didn't belong to me anymore.

A low, raspy sound slips from him with a rush of air, brushing against my flesh like he's remembering too. For a second we remain still, sucking in lungfuls, the air popping with electricity. I'm breathing so hard moisture makes the blanket stick to my face, each ragged inhale sucking strands of my hair into my mouth.

I squeeze my eyes shut, hating how my body betrays me. How I can feel every inch of him, his cruel grip in my hair and his arm looped around my elbows, locking me in place.

How I like the weight of him on top of me.

"Get off me," I say again, but it sounds like a plea instead of a demand. He sucks in sharply when I squirm, my ass digging into him again. I clench my teeth. Between my legs throbs, and I choke on all the rage singeing my chest. He did this to me. Confused my body. Confused my mind. *They* did this. Unfurled something inside me, then used it to cut me open.

"What were you going to do once you broke that window?" Reaper whispers, his lips brushing the flesh of my ear. Woodsy smoke and male flood my senses. "*Run?*"

He somehow makes the single word sound like a threat.

"You were going to leave your friend?"

"Never," I hiss, arching my back, but it just drives his dick into me harder.

"Then what?" he asks. "*Save* her?" He presses my head further down into the mattress, mashing my face to the blanket. "Did you plan to fight your way through us with your little fork? Then what, Kitten? Tell me what you hoped to achieve with this little stunt?"

When I struggle, gasping for air, he eases his grip. I suck in a breath and say, "It fucking got you in here."

He stills, but his weight doesn't leave. For a second I regret my words, thinking that I've pissed him off so much he may hurt me, but then he says, "Negative attention isn't always good attention. I should punish you for being such a brat."

"Fuck you," I seethe, unable to control myself. Not my best response, but it's all my scrambled brain comes up with.

"Oh, Kitten," he rasps. "I'm not going to fuck you again until you're weeping, begging, and crawling toward me on hands and knees, your pretty pink pussy so wet, it's dripping down your thighs."

The hand pinning my head to the bed leaves, and lands next to my face, long fingers splayed out, but I don't dare move. Between the strands of my hair fanning my face, I see tanned skin covered in black ink with slashes of faded red. Roses and skulls with black vines twisting around them. My heart slams in my chest, aware I'm seeing a part of him. Something he's kept hidden until right now because I forced him.

I can't help but wonder how many people his hands have killed.

I don't linger on why that thought sends a dark shiver down my spine to my core. His hand leaves and Reaper shifts at my backside. I hear the recognizable clink of a belt coming undone and disbelief washes through me.

"I thought you guys didn't force," I say, hating how dread makes my voice crack.

He doesn't answer. I cry out, when he repositions himself as he brings my wrists together and warm leather slips around them. The moment I realize what he's doing, I choke on a scream, jerking in his grasp, trying to break free.

His heavy weight returns, dick once again digging into me. "Stop," he growls in my ear.

I still, not wanting to give him the satisfaction of knowing I'm terrified. My father's name has caged me, yes, but it provided a level of protection no one ever dared cross. My body has never been touched without my consent, if anything I've craved attention. Craved being touched, craved being desired and wanted.

"I should spank your ass raw." There's something in his voice that makes me freeze. Something raw and jagged. Like sand slipping through broken teeth. "Then spank that pretty pussy until you come for me."

I bite my lip, the images he just planted, taking over all thoughts.

Reaper loosens his grip on the belt looped around my wrists, and I feel his hand land on my waist. My breath sucks in when it slips down, his fingers dipping into my dress, feeling the curve of my hips, then sliding lower to my thigh. Gathering the thin fabric, he lifts my dress slowly, the silk slipping over my skin until it's bunched at my waist and my ass is exposed. A warm, calloused hand glides over my hip and he squeezes it roughly. Possessively.

I bite my lip to stop the sound I want to make from slipping out. My breath rattles from my lungs on a slow exhale as his warm fingers dig into my skin. I don't know what I was expecting. I knew damn well that escaping was going to be impossible, but wanted one of them in here. I want answers.

"Why do you want revenge on my father?" I ask, tensing, waiting for his harsh words or his rough hands, but he gives me neither.

Nails dig into my flesh for a second, then leave. "He took something important from me."

So they took something important from Rune. Me. Cora.

"What?" I ask "What did he take?"

I'm not stupid enough to think he'll tell me, but I am surprised when he lets go of my arms. I'm even more shocked when I feel both his hands drag down my outer thighs, fingertips skittering along my skin delicately like butterfly wings. The softness of his touch sends a slick heat between my legs and my heart picks up pace. He didn't touch me like this before. He didn't really touch me at all.

I curl my fingers around the leather belt binding my wrists, needing something to hold on to as I sense him kneeling behind me, his hot breath fanning over my cold flesh. His hands, his breath, feel like fire lancing over my flesh.

Reaper's fucked me, come inside me, but never really touched me. The way his hands slip up my thigh, lightly moving over my ass, feels more intimate than when he was fucking me over the back of that couch.

His fingers outline the dimples in my lower back so gently, my breathing stops entirely.

The need to see him, know what his eyes look like as he touches me this way, if that brutal gleam has left, if they're a softer black like satin sheets or still hard as ice, makes me want to sit up, but I know if I try he'll pin me back down and whatever this is, whatever gentleness he's feeding me will stop. And I don't know if I want it to.

When he hooks a finger under the waistband of my panties, I clench my jaw to stop a whimper from escaping. Then he gathers the material in a fist and yanks up, tugging it between my ass cheeks. I cry out at the sting, at his sudden roughness, of the feeling of the fabric drawn tightly over my pussy.

"Are you wet for me, little Kitten?" he rasps. "I know your pussy remembers me."

Then there's warm flesh and hot breaths on my skin, and his nose slides down my ass crack. I gasp at the intrusion and then grit my teeth as he yanks me up higher, forcing me on my tiptoes. Reaper's fist presses harder into my lower back, my hips angling upward for him. His nose dips lower and I feel him press it into the fabric outlining my pussy. And then he breathes in deeply.

My chest heats, my hands releasing the leather and splaying out at the sensation of his nose on me. Of him gathering my scent into his chest. Everything in me pulses as he rubs his nose over me again, like he's savoring the wetness and smell and heat of my cunt.

"Fucking pervert," I bite out, even as I tilt my hips to meet him, silently cursing my body and the fabric that's keeping us separated.

"I am," he rasps. "And so are you. You're soaked."

I cry out when he presses his mouth to my pussy, a low groan escaping him with a hot breath. His teeth scrape over me. Then he bites. I hiss at the sting of pain, mixed with feral pleasure that bite zings through me.

"I need you to be a good girl," he grates out, forehead hitting my ass, rocking side to side, his breath fanning over my heated flesh. "I'm not a nice man, Kitten. And I have a long memory. If you cross me, I'll make you pay."

The gravelly way he says it makes me believe him. Reaper stands, letting my underwear go, and backs away. I arch my back, pressing my face further into the mattress, fighting the urge to turn my head to look at him. If I do, I could identify him, and I know they'd never allow that.

He undoes the belt, slowly unwrapping it from around my wrists. "Next time you seek my attention, be prepared for the consequences."

Gripping the edge of the bed, I slide to my knees as the door clicks shut. I spin, my eyes landing on the doorknob, waiting for the grating sound of the lock sliding into place.

But it never comes.

Chapter 12

STRIKER

15 Years Ago, September, Age 15

"Hurry!" Viper whispers, looking over his shoulder.

"If you shut the fuck up, I can," Breaker hisses back, angling the butter-knife he stole at breakfast just right, and the door pops open. The sound rings down the dark, empty hall as loud as a gunshot, and we all turn to look.

"We're clear," I say, shoving at Breaker's back and pushing him into the office. Viper follows behind and spins to shut the door with a quiet click, then leans against the glass, chest heaving.

"Fuck," he says, panting like he's just run the circuit, but all we've done is creep down the hall and break into Father's office.

Maybe I should be panting and freaking out too, but nothing much seems to faze me anymore.

Then again, Fallon has made sure of that. Emotions are a weakness.

I glance at my watch and set the timer, giving us ten minutes. We are due for our midnight training with Commander soon and if we're even a second late, we'll all be punished.

Out of all the schooling and training, I hate the midnight run the most. With Reaper, Hunter, and Seeker gone for the final test, Maxim has been meaner. Sometimes I think I would rather be a dancer like the ballerinas I hear Fallon talk about sometimes. But then the way he speaks about them, maybe I don't want to be a dancer. Their bodies don't belong to them. Not after they are fully trained. At least I get to keep my body to myself, even if it's bruised and beaten.

I point to the ornate wood desk at the center of the room. "Viper, you search the desk. Breaker, you look in the filing cabinet by the window." I move to the large bookcase lined with thick leather-bound volumes and remove a large bound file folder held together with elastic. "I'll search for the files here."

"We're so dead if he catches us," Viper says, eyes locked on the door as he slips behind our *otets's* desk and begins rummaging through the drawers.

"Commander won't catch us if you hurry," Breaker says, cleanly popping the lock on the cabinet. He glances over his shoulder at me, the beam of light from his flashlight on the top of the cabinet a white slash across his face. "What color did Cook say the file was?"

I close the ledger and place it back on the shelf. "Red." At least I hope that's what he said. Cook could have said dead files, but hopefully it was red or we'll never find what we're looking for.

"I think I got it," Breaker says, spinning and holding up a weathered, thick file. He rushes to the desk, opening the folder. When I step over to inspect the top page, my heart jumps.

When I overheard Cook and the Commander talking last week, I thought it was impossible. But as I stare at the first page, Breaker's toddler face staring back at me, I know now it's true.

Our Father has a file on us all, containing our histories. Where we came from and possibly even our real names. Not the names he gave us.

"Fuck, man," Viper whispers, glancing up at Breaker, the flashlight lighting up only his chin. "You're from France."

Breaker picks up the pages held together with a paperclip, staring at the picture of the little boy with thick curls puffed around his head and gaunt cheeks. It makes sense he knew some French words. Some part of his brain must have remembered the language even though he was so young.

"And my mother died while giving birth," he says, thumbing through the pages. "She was fifteen. Raped."

She was the age I am now. My stomach dips as our eyes lock. His mouth turns down into a frown as he breaks eye contact and flips the page. "I was placed into foster care for three years before I came here."

Three. The small boy who Fallon placed in the cold room was only three years old.

Goosebumps break out on my arms as I watch Viper grab the next few pages. I catch the picture of one of our old brother's who's no longer with us. He holds up the first stack for us to see. A large red mark slashes across the top page stamped with the word DECEASED across the top. Nausea churns in my gut as Viper flips through the rest of the stacks.

This is what I needed to know.

We lost another brother last week. Whenever we've lost a brother over the years, Fallon has always told us he didn't make the cut and was removed from the school. That the person who he removed wasn't strong enough and didn't have enough grit to graduate with his brothers. Being removed from the school is feared more than Fallon's punishments. The thought that we may not have what it takes to stay with our brothers pushed us harder. No one wants to be removed.

No one wants to leave the others behind to go out into a world we know so little about.

In the last month alone, Fallon removed two of our brothers and when I overheard the Commander telling Cook, we lost another one, Cook responded with, "Another red mark in the red file."

"Holy fuck," Viper whispers, holding up a stack of papers. "I'm from Scotland."

Breaker rolls his eyes, still reading his papers. "No shit."

Viper frowns and says, "He didn't list my mother and father. Says I came from an orphanage, but I already knew that."

"Satan's spawn," Breaker says. "Like I've been saying." He stumbles back, smirking as Viper shoves his shoulder.

"Strike, here." Viper slides a stack of papers across the desk toward me.

I grip the edge of the desk and clamp my eyes closed before I can see the top page and the little square picture in the corner. The thought of learning about my past, filling in the blank spaces of my parentage, sends a shiver of dread down my spine.

Seems this is the only thing that can get under my skin.

But then that's why he's been so hard on us. We have to be as hard as stone. He wants us prepared for graduation. But when Fallon informed our group that we lost another brother last week, our strongest one, I was suspicious. I'd seen him the day before, his body so battered and bruised it had looked like he'd been beaten with something far harsher than father's leather belt. He'd gone to the infirmary and two days later our *otets* told us he was removed from the school.

We're down to just six now.

It reminded me so much of that day on the rooftop; I had to know the truth.

STRIKER

Reaper refused to talk about what happened in training that day, how Raid ended up black and blue, deep gouges slicing his face. Hunter wouldn't talk either and when I asked Seeker, he clamped his lips shut and walked away.

And I've been worried ever since. Now with the three gone, it's just been us Viper, Breaker, and me here. Fallon left shortly after them, traveling to oversee the order for supplies. This was the only opportunity we were going to get to find out what happened. Cook usually drinks his vodka after he serves us our last meal and we know we won't see him again. It's just Commander and Teacher here until Father gets back, but that's not until next week.

Or until Reaper and our other brothers return.

Which I hope will be soon.

"Broken ribs and a punctured lung," Breaker says, reading over the files. He places the papers down and I see his face. The brother who never made it out of the infirmary. "Broken neck." Breaker flips the papers to the next one. "Cracked skull." He lowers the papers and casts me a strange look that almost gets eaten by the surrounding darkness, but the flashlight glints off his pale eyes and I catch his flinch before he says, "Multiple lacerations."

My brows knit as I realize he's reading off how each of our brothers died. I lean over to see who's file he's looking at when my eyes land on a small pale face with plain features.

My stomach churns.

Sniper.

"It's not your fault," Breaker says.

But it is my fault.

He died that day. All because I showed off. Sniper died because I refused to be the one holding the belt. If I had been the one to deliver his punishment, I wouldn't have hurt him. He'd still be alive. If I had just done what was asked of me, Sniper would still be here.

I shake my head, trying to rid myself of the memory of that day, swallowing past the lump in my throat. There's not enough time to wallow. I glance at my watch. Five minutes. I grab the next stack of papers, recognizing the first set of soldiers that were sent out for graduation when I first arrived at the school eleven years ago and never returned.

Flipping through the file, bile sours the back of my throat when my eyes land on the small typed letters. My gaze lifts to my brothers. "Drowning."

My heart picks up pace, thinking of Reaper and Hunter out in the wilderness.

"Shit," Viper hisses, no doubt thinking about Reaper and Hunter too. About us. How we'll be the next group to go out for the final test before graduation.

"They'll all come back," Breaker says quietly, but I'm not so sure.

Because the longer they're out there, the more likely they'll end up with a red mark across their files.

We've watched Reaper and Hunter train together for the last month, preparing for the week in the wild. Seeker has always been a bit of a loner and refused to train with them. I was surprised Reaper even offered. He and Hunter are always together, training, eating, and at the range. But then, Hunter is the only one Reaper lets touch him. It's only ever just Hunter wrapping an arm over his shoulder or playfully patting him on the back, and Reaper always smiles when our brother teases him. It's the only time I see him smile.

If something happened to Reaper, to Hunter...

I shake my head, tossing the thought loose and focus on the wooden desk, the smooth top gleaming in the slant of light from Breaker's flashlight. Fallon and his fancy desk. His fancy clothes. His sleek hair combed back over his head, making him look severe. He's all we've ever known, and he's been slowly killing us all.

"Are you going to look?" Breaker asks, eyeing the door, then my stack of papers. "Do you want me to look for you?"

I shake my head and slide the papers toward me. My gaze lands on the picture of the little boy with warm brown hair and golden skin. Eyes so big, he looks like he's in shock. Like someone just pinched him before they took the picture. At five I was small, the background showing my height and weight like an old prison picture. Fitting, I guess.

I look further down to the names listed. "Mother Isabelle Pena. Father unknown," I read aloud. "My mother was a receptionist at a dental office but was laid off, then she worked nights..." my voice trails off and I read the rest in silence.

My mother worked the streets at night, and was found dead in a hotel room from an overdose. I was found in a closet, half dead.

I slam the papers down, not wanting to read anymore.

Darkness creeps into the corner of my vision. It slips up my back, tingling my scalp, trying to take me back to that black place.

A closet.

Did she put me in there? Did I go in there and get trapped?

My head swirls and I grip the glossy desk before I pass out, the shadowy images of lost memories trying to cut through reality. I suck in air and look up at the dark ceiling, trying to center my thoughts.

Fallon was right. My mother was a drug addict who sold her body to put poison in her veins.

"Look at this," Viper hisses. Something in his voice makes me drop my chin to look at him. With wide eyes, he slides two stacks of papers toward us and taps them both. Reaper and Hunter's boyish faces look back at me.

Breaker leans in and reads the list of names and dates with me.

"Holy shit," Breaker says, meeting my eyes.

We all knew. It's obvious when you look at them, but having it clearly stated, typed on a sheet of paper washes away any doubts we may have had.

"Do you think they know?" Breaker asks, picking up Reaper's paper. "Do you think he told them?"

I shake my head. There's no way Fallon would have told them.

I grab all the files and place them back into the folder, snapping it closed before stalking over to the cabinet and shoving it back in.

"No," I say when I turn to look at my brothers. "And we won't ever speak of this again."

No one can ever know the truth.

Reaper most of all.

Chapter 13

STRIKER

Reaper has been in a foul mood all night. Part of me wants to tell him to go rub one out, or just convince her to fuck him already, but I think his dark mood is more about *him* than her.

Having them here is bringing up the past.

I think we all thought that when we took them, knowing Rune was sitting at home, sick with fear, it would fix that broken piece within us, but instead, it feels like we're being cracked open even more.

Reaper has become obsessive. Walking around and muttering to himself like some Poe character slowly losing his mind. He's usually focused, in control of himself during a job, but he's unraveling more and more as the days go on.

STRIKER

It's only been seven days since we took them and at the rate he's going, he's going to come unhinged by next week. On top of it, Viper and Breaker are spending too much time with Cora. Viper losing control and nearly fucking Cora is proof. I may be the only one keeping my shit together, but then I usually am.

Until I don't.

My eyes travel back to the screens as I rub my temples. My head hurts. Like I have any room to talk. I've been staring at these cameras just as much. The entire room reeks of male. A mixture of sweat and soap. I glance at Breaker's spare mask next to Vipers. The room smells like them.

I rub my eyes, leaning in to get a better look at Cora. She's sleeping, curled into a little ball in the center of the bed, all lights in the room on, the fire flickering in the background. On the other screen, Delilah is still laying across the top of the bed, face down, knees on the floor where Reaper left her about thirty minutes ago.

I haven't seen him since I watched him on the monitors stalking from the mansion, the front door slamming so hard it popped back open. I debate going and closing it, but figure he'll be back soon enough. Although, if Princess goes exploring, she may decide to run.

My cock thickens at the thought. What fun that would be.

A light whimper grabs my attention and I focus on Cora and turn up the volume. She shifts, curling into an even smaller ball and squeaks another little whimpering sound of distress.

She's dreaming.

Or having a nightmare.

After hearing her scream like that the first night, we've all been keeping a close eye on her. She's somehow stronger than Princess in many ways, but also more fragile in so many others. Like leaded glass, some pieces of her tightly bound with metal, less breakable, but other parts paper mache thin.

She whimpers again and murmurs that same name she was screaming. Prissy. We've watched the girls for a long time, dug into their pasts, and have never come across anyone named Prissy.

When she whimpers again, I grab my mask and stand. If she screams again, Breaker and Viper are too far away to hear her, and Reaper is gone to walk off his rage or to the carriage house to work out. I'm the only one in the house, but from the look of things, Delilah won't be a problem anymore tonight. After Reaper, I highly doubt she'll leave her room, even though he left it unlocked. Something we decided she was ready for.

We need to earn her trust and she knows now that we will not hurt her, even if she acts out. Now she needs to learn to follow rules and the only way to do that is to give her a choice to break them.

Shutting the door behind me, I take the cellar stairs two at a time and unlock the door leading to the kitchen. Locking it behind me, I walk through the series of rooms to the foyer, double checking that the adjoining rooms are locked as I pass each one in case she ventures out. Viper is terrible at locking doors behind him, so I always check. When I reach the foyer, I shut the front door, cursing under my breath, and continue on to the west wing of the house, the furthest away.

When we bought the mansion, we only ever planned to use it as a base. It's in a perfect location, secluded, sitting on hundreds of acres overlooking the ocean. A person can scream for hours and no one will ever hear them. Perfect for what we needed, but we never used it. It's just sat, for years, untouched.

Until now.

It takes a few minutes, but when I reach the stairwell leading up to her room, her desperate scream tears through me like a knife.

"Shit," I snap and break into a run.

Chapter 14

CORA

I bolt upright as a scream tears from my throat, throwing my arms out to catch myself. A sharp pang of pain cuts through my hands. I bring them up expecting to find the nails cracked, half gone, the fingertips bleeding like they were when I scratched at the door, but it's just another phantom pain.

I'm not there. I'm here. Trapped in *this* room.

Panic bubbles up, sticking in my throat. Just as I suck in air, reminding myself that even though I'm locked in this room, I'm safe, the door bursts open and Striker stalks in. When he sees me sitting upright, he pauses, eyes scanning my body like he's looking for damage.

He won't find any on my skin. It's all in my head.

"Nightmare?" he asks when he sees I'm unharmed, reaching behind him to shut the door. I notice he doesn't lock it. None of them do when they come in. I guess they know there's no escaping them. It's pointless for me to even try.

I swallow the unease gumming up my mouth, glad to see one of them because it means I'm no longer locked in. "Yes," I say, surprising myself at my honesty. I must be so relieved not to be alone that I don't care who's keeping me company.

Striker leans against the door, his mask slightly skewed like he put it on in a hurry. "A reoccurring nightmare?"

I gesture around the room with a sweep of my arm. "Every fucking day is a nightmare."

If I could see his mouth, I'd bet he frowns.

"The dream, Little Flower," Striker says. "Is it the same dream?"

I nod, warmth blooming in my chest at the sweet name, watching as he walks across the room and stands at the end of the bed. He's wearing the same uniform they always wear, but this one's a little different. His long-sleeved black shirt is looser and his fatigues a tad tighter on his thighs. He's got an amazing body like the rest of them, just not quite as largely built as Viper or Reaper. He grips the metal bed rail, and I notice he's not wearing his gloves. The knuckles under his warmly tanned skin turn white as he grips the bar with his large hands. I wonder what those long, delicate fingers would feel like sliding between my thighs as he called me a little flower again.

"About Prissy?"

My eyes dart up to meet his, my curiosity dying at the mention of her name. "How do you know my mother's name?"

The skin around his golden eyes creases like he's confused. "Was Prissy your mother's nickname?"

"It's what they called her," I say, not sure why I'm telling him. Maybe it's because his eyes look so warm. Like firelight on a summer night. "When they came to visit."

"Who?" Striker asks, moving around to the end of the bed to sit.

"The men," I say before I can think. I shake my head. *Stupid.* He isn't a fucking therapist. He's my captor. "Don't worry about it."

"If you keep having nightmares, it's something I'm going to worry about."

"I'll try to keep it down," I snark, red flooding my cheeks, fully aware, a little *too,* aware of *him*. "So I don't inconvenience my kidnappers."

His eyes dart away, and when he looks back, his eyes seem harder. "Your mother's name was Caroline. You're named after her grandmother Cora. Your father was Drake. They both died in a car accident when you were ten. Who is Prissy?"

I swallow my shock at the level of details he knows about me, but then again, the shampoo and soap I use at home are sitting in the bathroom along with the brand of tampons I buy, so maybe I shouldn't be. They've done their research.

"My parents didn't die in a car accident," I say. "Rune killed them."

His head cocks to the side, making it look like his skull mask is mocking me. "How do you know?"

"He told me."

Striker takes a deep breath. Blinks a few times. "Why?"

"Why did he tell me, or why did he kill them?"

His hands squeeze his thick thighs. "Both."

"If there's one thing you need to know about Rune Gavin, it's that he's cruel," I say. "Why else would a grown man tell a ten-year-old girl he killed her parents? To keep me in line."

"And why did he kill them?"

"They betrayed him."

"How?"

I shrug, the lie slipping out easily, "I honestly don't know. Does it matter?"

"I guess not," Striker says. "They're still dead, whether or not you know why they were killed."

I nod, leaning on the headboard, smoothing the sheets at my sides. "Did you watch me earlier?"

Striker tenses, then says, "You like being watched."

"And you enjoy watching."

His gaze flickers away for a moment, then lands on the hollow of my neck, moves lower, then up to my eyes. I wonder if he's thinking about that night in the club or maybe me touching myself earlier.

"Do you want to watch me again?" I say with a smirk as I spread my legs, my sleep dress falling open, and pull my underwear aside, revealing my pussy. "Or maybe you want to jerk off on me like Viper did."

Striker's eyes drop to between my legs, not looking away like a decent man would, uncomfortable with the way I'm taunting him, showing myself to him. But then, he's not a decent man, is he? Decent men don't kill guards and kidnap people. I open my mouth to ask him why he thinks he's better than Rune, but I shut it because I already know the answer. He has yet to touch me without my consent.

"Who is Prissy?" he asks again.

"Not one to be derailed, I see." I close my thighs, stretching my legs out, a strange, oily feeling in my gut at his attention, but lack of action. It feels like disappointment, but that would be demented, so I leave the feeling unnamed. "Where's Delly?"

Those golden eyes flicker up to my face. "Somewhere safe."

My shoulders relax. "Can I see her soon?"

"Not yet." His eyes darken, like irritation singes the edges. "Who is Prissy?"

"My mother's men called her Prissy," I say with a sigh. "When they came to visit. I heard all of them call her that. Even Daddy did when they came. They'd say, 'Hello, Ms. Prissy, I'm your bull for tonight.'"

If I could see his face under his mask, I'd bet he blanches.

"And you..." He rocks his head side to side like he's searching for words, or maybe debating, then says, "You witnessed this? Interaction? As a little girl?"

"No," I say, slightly pleased I managed to rattle him. I've not told anyone about the games my parents played before, and I don't know why I'm telling Striker of all people. But he seems upset for me. For that little girl. Maybe that's why I continue. "Prissy put me in the closet and my mother would let me out."

Striker's entire body recoils like I kicked him in the chest and he bolts upright. He moves his hand up, like he's going to run his hand through his hair, but drops it when it slides over his balaclava. His chest rises and falls rapidly, like he's about to hyperventilate, but then he looks up at the ceiling and seems to calm down.

Seems he's not made of stone after all.

"Sick, right?" I say. "She'd shut me in the hall closet whenever they came over. She started it after I came out of my room one night and caught Daddy watching her get fucked on the couch."

"That's disturbing," Striker says, sitting back down on the bed. "How old were you?"

"Six."

His head twitches oddly. I notice he's rubbing his forearms, his fingers kneading into the fabric of his shirt.

"I think being locked in this room is reminding me of that time. Every time I close my eyes, it's like I'm in the closet, trapped and alone," I say, looking down at my hands. A warm tear lands on my wrist and I wipe it away with my thumb, irritated at its appearance. His boots squeak as he stands up again. I glance back over at him. "That's how I feel here. Trapped. Alone."

A shadow passes behind his eyes and he looks away.

"She left me in there once for two days," I say, watching his reaction. When his eyes close and his shoulders bunch, I think that maybe I've hit a nerve. Like maybe he—maybe none of them—are as bad as they want us to think. Or maybe they just draw the line at disturbing stories about children. "She got high and forgot about me, too caught up in her game with her men, I guess."

"Get some sleep," he says, his voice strangled as he suddenly marches to the door. "We'll get you for breakfast after sunrise."

My heart hammers when he reaches for the doorknob. "Striker." He pauses and turns. His eyes look lost when they meet mine. Hollowed out, like my words created a crater inside him. I wonder if he fears the dark too. "Will you sit with me? Until I fall asleep?"

He hesitates, then releases the knob. Instead of sitting at the end of the bed, he takes the chair by the window and folds himself into it, resting his ankle on his knee, his eyes still holding that lost look as he stares blankly out the window.

After a while, he looks back at me, but he still looks vacant. Gone. Not even in the room with me. "My mother was a prostitute." The confession slips out so quietly that I lean forward, unsure I even heard him correctly. "Isabella. She wasn't always one. She was someone's daughter. Someone loved her. She had a little boy. Then she left him when she died of a drug overdose."

"I'm sorry," I whisper, and I'm surprised that I mean it. I'm surprised at the stabbing sensation slicing through my middle. At how his words seem to spill out from him but not unaware. Intentionally. Handing me a heavy secret because he know I can carry its weight.

Because I lived in darkness for a while just like him.

"I was five when she died." His eyes move over to me, and he doesn't look lost anymore. He looks completely present. "I was found in a closet, almost dead."

I wince, an ache forming in my chest that some other child knew about that type of darkness and fear. That deep hunger and what felt like never ending thirst.

For a while we sit in silence and I watch the man who thinks they stole me, not knowing they saved me from a terrible life.

I slip under the blankets and curl onto my side, watching him. "So your mom fucked you up, too."

He nods slightly, more to himself. "Father was worse."

Chapter 15

DELILAH

I WAKE SHIVERING COLD. My eyes travel to the door and nausea ripples in my belly. It's open, showing a bright hallway lined with windows, heavy curtains pulled back revealing the cloudless winter sky. Early morning light casts long lines across the wood floor.

Fucking Striker.

The man makes no sound. I know he's the one who brings the tray of food, always managing to sneak in here without my knowing. Except last night. After Reaper stormed out, I didn't get a tray of food, just an unlocked door and a strangling fear of what it meant.

Heat flames my cheeks, remembering Reaper, his ungloved hands moving over my body. His warning that sounded a little too much like he wished I'd have broken the window.

My stomach churns, another bout of nausea rolling through me, along with a pinch of pain. I clamp my hand over my abdomen and bite my lip. I'm hungry.

The house creaks, and my heart leaps into my throat, my eyes darting back to the open door. I half expect one of them to come leaping into view, but it's just the house settling.

My belly rumbles again. They're going to force me out. Starve me out. Last night I was so scared the unlocked door was a trap that I didn't dare leave the room. Now I know they want me to. Or at least, they are inviting me to leave. Or maybe it's a taunt.

Hungry? Come and get it, if you dare.

Problem is, I *am* hungry. I've barely been eating.

I slide my legs over the edge of the bed, wrapping my oversized sweater tightly around me as I creep toward the door, heart rattling in my chest.

Calm down, Delilah. They are keeping you alive for a reason. Reaper could have hurt you last night, but he...

I mentally swipe the thought away, not letting the memory settle. In the late hours, I spent too much time replaying how he bent me over the bed for it to be healthy. My body thrumming, wanting the feeling of him touching me again, need throbbing my clit to the point I almost touched myself, but I knew they'd be watching.

When I reach the door, I pause, taking a deep breath. Clenching my teeth, I step out into the hall. To my left, the long corridor is lined with more doors, ending with a massive window and a door leading to a balcony. To my right, the hall ends at an enormous set of wooden stairs with marble pillars and iron railings leading up, another set going down. When I see no one, I rush to the row of large windows across from my bedroom door and peer outside.

My entire body stiffens at the sight. I place my hands on the cracked sill, pressing my face to the window, trying to absorb everything I'm seeing.

An open lawn sprawls out for several yards before ending at a line of trees. Right below me are pathways weaving around an old garden lined with pillars and empty pots. I can see what I'm guessing is the main part of the mansion to the right. It's like I've been plucked from the lobby of the modern world and placed down in a vintage photograph of an old French estate.

I need to find Cora.

I rush to the door down the hall from mine, but it's locked. Even though I know she's more than likely not being kept anywhere near me, I check all the rooms lining the hall as I make my way to the staircase. They're all empty or locked, with no sign that anyone has been in them for some time. My gut tells me she's not in this part of the house. For the last week, I've heard no other sounds except for the occasional groan of a pipe. There's no noise at all.

When I reach the end of the hall, I peer up the huge spiral staircase and see a large domed ceiling with a faded mural two floors above. My gaze falls to the staircase that curves down to the landing, and I lean over the railing, but only see more empty space, more pillars, and ornately inlaid wood floors.

My hand lightly slides down the rough railing as I descend, my socked feet making no sound. As my feet hit the bottom step, I stop, leaning forward to peer through the massive doorways flanking the entry. On one side looks like a formal living room, but furnished with only a few settees and a table with no lamp. The other side is possibly a library or study of some sort. In front of me is a huge double door with large floor to ceiling windows on either side, sunlight like a gauzy mist pouring in through the milky white leaded glass.

My belly flutters and I leap off the step and run to the door, skidding to a stop as I grip the knob and pull. It groans as it swings open and a blast of frigid air nearly steals my breath.

"I wouldn't run if I were you."

My scream catches in my throat, my hand flying to my mouth as I spin, the dregs of my cry echoing in the large, empty space. Striker leans against the doorframe leading to the sitting room, arms crossed over his broad chest. He looks exactly as I remembered him. Skull mask with the scar over the eye. Tight black shirt and fatigues that hug his muscular legs. Black gloves and belt.

I swallow, pressing my hand harder to my throat, but that only makes me remember the way he did, and my belly dips.

"Where's Cora?"

No answer.

My chest heats, anger flaring like firecrackers, my fists curling at my sides. Now that I'm standing here with him, the rage at what they've done to us breaks free and I have to bite my lip to keep from screaming. From lunging forward and punching my fist into his fucking jaw, hidden behind a fucking mask, like a coward.

His brown eyes move from my mouth up to my eyes. That night with them, they looked dark in the dim light, but now I can see they are lighter than I thought. Gold, woven with amber flecks, like a lion. Or a wolf. My cheeks heat, remembering the way he looked at me as I sucked his dick.

The way his gaze drags over me right now tells me he's thinking the same thing, those gold eyes slipping over every inch, making it feel like he's seeing under my clothes, remembering the shape of my breasts and the curve of my hips.

"If you want to keep the privilege of leaving your room, you won't try to run," he says finally.

I have no response because I can't even try to escape until I find Cora.

He uncrosses his arms and steps toward me. Instinctively, I step back. Striker moves forward, darting toward me, and I back away even more, but he grips my arms and tugs me to him before my foot can pass over the threshold. Shoving me aside, he slams the door shut, glass rattling, then turns to face me. Up this close, I'm reminded of how crazy big he is. Muscles and chest and height.

How very male he is.

I clear my throat, his words from a moment ago finally settling in my head. "Privilege?"

I swear he smiles. "If you try to run, we will catch you."

We. Them. All *four* of them.

"There are terrible creatures out there." Striker steps forward. My feet move of their own accord, my left foot sliding back to keep him from closing the few inches separating us. "Bears. Wolves. Dangerous things."

"There are terrible things in *here*," I say, but it comes out shaky.

His right arm shoots out so fast, I gasp, then he's gripping the back of my neck, dragging me to him. My hands land on his warm chest and I realize my entire body is shaking from the cold. Fear. *Him*.

"It would be wise for you to remember that." He lowers his head until his masked mouth is next to my ear. "Promise me you won't try to run."

I inhale sharply as his grip on my neck tightens, making everything down low clench.

"Do you know what happens to naughty girls who try to run?" Striker shifts so his leg moves between my thighs, the long dress sliding up my calves. His thigh hits the space that's aching from his nearness. "They are caught and tied up. Wrists bound so tight it'll make your pussy wet."

At some point, his other hand slid around my back and I'm now pressed flush against him, feeling every inhale. Butterflies dance in my belly as his fingers dig into the small of my back. His nose presses to my hair and he inhales slowly. The same way he did in the club. I wish I would stop flashing on the memories of him. Of how he felt. How he made me feel. The feel of his lips, pulling, eating, sucking at my clit. The way the fingers pressed to the small of my back felt moving inside me. How badly I craved him. All of them.

"Then," he whispers, his voice breathy, like he's struggling to get enough air into his lungs. "Once you're dripping wet and begging for our attention, you'll be punished."

The way my clit throbs tells me I spent way too long alone in that room.

I bite my lip, trying to keep the question in my mouth, but I fail and ask, "You get off on threats?"

"I get off on teaching a particular bratty Princess to behave. Maybe you'll get the belt until your pretty ass is raw and red. Whatever we want to do to you, you'll endure." He leans back and his eyes catch mine. "Be a good girl and stay inside where it's safe."

He releases me. I stumble back. The cold hits me everywhere. I wrap my arms around my chest. As if on cue, my stomach rumbles.

His gaze drops to my belly and his shoulders rise and fall as he takes a deep, exasperated breath. "You've not been eating properly."

"I wonder if it has anything to do with being held hostage," I say, sarcasm dripping from my words.

Striker snatches my wrist. I attempt to jerk away, but he grips me tighter, tugging me through the large entryway toward the back of the house. My heart leaps, hope blooming that maybe he's taking me to Cora.

"Where is she?" I ask, my eyes darting in every direction, taking in not only the stunning sight of the old mansion, but where we are going, trying to remember the route we're taking. "Will you please tell me if she's safe?"

Striker stops suddenly and turns to face me, dropping my hand. We're outside a vast room with a black grand piano and an empty table holding a lamp. Like the rest of the house, it's old, worn, but still clean.

His gold eyes land on my face. They look softer than just a few minutes ago and I wonder if saying please is what made him turn nice. I wish I could see his face.

No. I take that back. If I see his face, that means I'm dead. They'll never let me go if I can identify them.

"She's safe," he says and turns, continuing to walk to the back of the mansion. "Follow me."

Relief floods my entire body, making the tension in my shoulders ease. I don't know why I believe him, but I do.

"When do I get to see her?" I ask, rushing to keep up with his long strides. "Can I see her now?"

"Do not ask me again."

"Striker."

He spins, tension apparent in how his shoulders stiffen. "Do not ask me again, Princess. You'll only anger me."

"Why are we here?" I ask instead. "Ransom? Did you take us to get my father…" my voice trails off, remembering Reaper's words. "What did Reaper mean when he said my father took something from him?"

Without answering, Striker grips my arm again and pulls me along. Instead of asking anymore questions he obviously will not answer, I focus on absorbing the details of the mansion, my father's lesson flashing through my mind.

Don't be distracted by flashy clothes and money. You want to see what's underneath the facade. That's how you outsmart them.

The mansion is massive. Old. Reminding me of those huge gilded mansions from the late 1800s. The house is not really in decay, but sitting dormant. Unused. Unloved. Like a museum capturing a fraction in time but allowed to rust and collect dust. The lack of furniture or other decor and the fact the place isn't maintained makes me wonder again about ransom, but then Reaper said revenge.

But my father said collect.

My head swims, trying to piece everything together. We reach a large dining room and I freeze in the doorway.

"Hello, Tiny Thing."

My entire body jerks at the sound of the voice behind me and I stumble into Striker, who catches me by the waist.

"Your little tantrum got you what you wanted," Breaker says, moving around me to stand next to Viper, who leans against a huge wooden dining table. Striker shoves me ahead of him into the room.

That's when I see him.

Reaper. And he looks furious.

Chapter 16

Delilah

It's like he poisoned my body against me. The way it just reacts to him makes me wonder what the fuck he did to me that night in the club.

Onyx eyes rake up and down me, as invasive as his hands and mouth were last night.

"If you pull that stunt again, I'll lock you in the basement where there are no windows to break," Reaper says, pushing off the wall at the back of the room but he stops in the center of the dining room next to the long table. Even several feet away, he feels like he's invading my space. "Then you'll just freeze to death and you won't be a problem anymore."

"I'm about to freeze to death in my room," I snark.

"You really think after your attempt to break a window, we're going to trust you with a fire in your room?" Viper laughs. "You'd try to burn the whole house down to escape."

He's not wrong.

"This place has radiators." My smile is coated with venom. "I'm sure between all of you, there is enough brain power to get them up and running."

Breaker chuckles.

"Again," Reaper says, large, stupidly sexy shoulders tensing. "When you decide to stop tearing your room apart looking for weapons and I know you won't try to somehow use the radiator to murder us, I'll adjust the boiler so you have heat."

I narrow my eyes. "You're an asshole."

"I've been called worse, Kitten." Reaper points to the table. "Now sit down."

Next to me, Breaker pulls out a chair and settles down. He pats his lap in invitation.

Yeah. I don't think so.

Before I can voice the thought, he tugs me onto his lap. I cry out a surprised peep, and land awkwardly, my hands flying out to catch myself with the edge of the table.

"Now it's time to eat," Viper says, and that's when I notice my usual tray laden with food sitting in the center of the table. "Be a good girl and listen to Reaper."

Breaker's arm wraps around my middle, and he adjusts me on his lap, pressing my back to his solid, warm chest. I sit upright, my fingers curling into the tabletop, my spine ramrod straight. This is the first time I've been close to any of them and my heart hammers, feeling his long fingers dig into my hip, squeezing me like he can't help himself. Like maybe he's constantly flooded with memories of that night, too.

"Hands on the table," Reaper says, leaning over to drag the tray of food toward him as he moves closer, stopping so he's towering over me, his belt level with my eyes.

Shit. He's big. Everything about him is large. The thought sends heat shivering through my belly, pulling my lip down in annoyance.

My eyes lift from the black metallic buckle up to his black eyes. Something flickers behind them. Anger. Disdain. Something else, some other emotion I can't place. He shifts, his thumb hooking on the belt. My gaze snags on his long fingers, and the dark ink on the back of his hand. He's not wearing his gloves again. I focus on his bare hand, and that's when I notice it.

He's hard.

They *both* are.

My entire body goes rigid. I grip the table and try to pull myself up, something fluttering weirdly, low in my belly, as Breaker's thick cock digs into my butt. Reaper's hand slams down on my shoulder, keeping me in place.

"Stay," he growls.

I grind my teeth, glaring up at him, knuckles turning white as I try to keep from shoving them both away and refusing to listen. But I'm not sure what they'll do if I try to move. The angry stare I'm getting from Reaper right now tells me it's pointless to fight them. There's four of them and one of me.

They're going to win.

Behind me, Breaker grunts from the pressure of my ass on his hard dick when I shift again, trying to avoid sitting on his erection, but that's just impossible. I remember vividly what he looked like as he fucked Cora.

A chair scrapes across the wood floor, breaking the tension as Striker sits to our right. Reaper's hand drops from my shoulder and he places it flat on the table. He taps on the wood top with one finger, and my eyes track his movements, drawn to the tattoos. I caught a glimpse of his tanned flesh and the ink over the back of his hands last night, but now I see the skull's below his knuckles on each finger, the one on his index finger slashed over with a red mark, and the intricate details of the flowers and vines snaking up to his wrist and disappearing under the shirtsleeve.

"Hope you're hungry, Sweetheart," Viper says, lowering his large frame into a chair across the table from us.

Reaper taps the tabletop again. My eyes snap to his hand. "Hands on the table, palms flat," he says, and that's when I notice the wooden ruler, like the old ones used in schools, laying on the table next to his hand.

My brows knit, but I place my hands on the cool surface, palms flat, fingers splayed out.

"Good girl," Breaker says and I feel his praise rumble through my back.

Reaper picks up a block of cheese and holds it up. "Open."

"I don't think so," I snap when I realize his plan. "I can feed myself."

Shifting, I lift my hands, but before I can pull them away, Reaper snatches the ruler and slaps it across my fingers.

"What the fuck!" I pull my hands back, pressing my fingers to my mouth, glaring up at him.

"Hands on the table," Striker says and I turn to look at him. He's dead serious, not even phased by the fact Reaper just rapped my knuckles with a fucking ruler. Like this is normal. He cocks his head to the side as he taps the tabletop. "Listen."

"Fucking psychos," I mumble. Hesitantly, I lay my hands back down, watching the ruler in Reaper's hand for any signs of movement. Breaker's hips tilt, and his huge cock digs into my backside, letting me know he very much likes me sitting here. Or maybe he likes the entire situation.

"Good girl," Viper praises when my hands are flat on the table.

Reaper holds up the cheese again, and I turn my head.

"I can *fucking* feed myself."

With a low growl, Reaper lurches forward, his black eyes flashing dangerously, and grips my cheeks, squeezing hard enough to force my lips apart. "When I can trust you with a fork, you'll get the privilege of feeding yourself. Now open."

I attempt to jerk away, but his grip just tightens painfully. When I move to lift my hands to fight him off, I remember the sharp smack of the ruler and keep them in place. Before I can protest further, he shoves the bit of cheese in my mouth and covers my lips, releasing his grip on my face just enough for him to snap my jaw shut like I'm a dog getting a pill.

"Chew and swallow," he orders, a dark edge in his voice.

Shit. I *really* pissed him off last night.

As I chew, he picks up the ruler again, daring me to lift my hands. I leave them flat on the surface, knowing he'd love the excuse to smack my knuckles again. After I swallow, I open my mouth to show him, making Viper chuckle.

"Such a brat," Reaper says and picks up another bite. My eyes drop to the bulge in his pants as he taps the food on my bottom lip. This time, though, I open. He shoves it roughly into my mouth, like he can't stop his hatred of me from spilling out. I smile sweetly as I chew, making his black glare turn deadly.

I'm not stupid. The sick gleam in his eye tells me he'll hold me down and force the food in my mouth if I continue to fight, but that doesn't mean I will sit quietly and let him bully me. He warned me not to push him too far and from the intense gleam in his eye, I believe he's capable of hurting me, maybe even would love the chance, but last night taught me one thing.

He remembers me just as much as I remember him.

Chewing, I eye him. I know I should be terrified of him, of all of them, but I'm not. I've grown up around dangerous men.

Men who've murdered people. Men like the ones who shot my mother. If Reaper didn't hurt me after I nearly broke the window in the room, then I know I'm at least physically safe.

Maybe not mentally.

Hell, maybe I'm *not* entirely physically safe. They may want me alive, but that doesn't mean they can't or won't harm me.

He killed my father's guards in cold blood, after all.

My heart falls to my stomach. Manuel. He was a good man, a good bodyguard, and a dedicated soldier for my father.

The food sticks in my throat as I swallow. Curling my fingers into the wood table, I ask Reaper, "Do you even feel any remorse?"

"No," is Reaper's response.

"About what?" is what Striker asks, and the other two remain quiet.

With a scowl, I lock eyes with Reaper, his skull mask taunting me, just as he did when he punished me with the ruler. "For killing Manuel."

"I've killed many people, Kitten," Reaper says, shoving another piece of cheese past my lips hard enough that my head hits Breaker's chin. "I need you to clarify."

"I'd known him half of my life," I say. "The man you shot in the head has been my father's security guard since I was twelve years old."

"That's a sad story," Reaper says. "He did his job well until he didn't."

I clench my teeth, fighting the sudden sting of tears, and shove down the memory of his blank eyes as he bled at my feet.

Like he can sense my distress, Breaker's large hand lands on my thigh and he rubs it up and down over my dress. The move's weirdly comforting and I settle back into him, watching Reaper pick up more food from the tray.

"Open." He shoves another bit of food into my mouth. Reaper repeats the movement, feeding me little bites at a time, his movements turning less and less rough, until the tray is almost clear while Viper, sits quietly, his arms on the tabletop across from us, greenish-blue eyes watching my mouth with an almost perverse interest, while Breaker's hand moves up and down my thigh, or brushes my arm, and Striker sits silently beside us.

Having their focus on me makes my belly flutter, but I recognize the sensation. It's not just nerves making me squirm. It's arousal.

God, they fucked me up.

Reaper was right. I'm not sure I actually *want* their attention now that I have it.

But I don't think I *don't* want it either.

Keeping my hands on the table, I lean back against Breaker and shake my head when Reaper offers a hunk of bread. "I'm full."

"You eat until the food is gone," Reaper says, and there's a warning in his voice. "You're not eating enough and you've lost weight."

Breaker's arm tightens around my middle, his hand flexing on my hip. He's *still* hard. "Come on, Tiny Thing, you need to eat more."

"Fattening up your prize pig?" I snarl, too aware of their closeness, their excitement, their *everything*, yet unable to control my mouth. My father told me it would be my undoing and I think right now he may be right. "Is that what you guys have planned? Sell me off to the highest bidder since my father's not coming through with the money?"

I bite my lip, regretting the words as soon as they slip past my lips. A tear threatens to break free and I furiously swipe my eye with my shoulder, keeping my palms flat. I focus on the tray of food, anger at myself making my cheeks heat.

Damn them.

I haven't allowed myself to feel for days and the first time I admit to myself I'm scared my father won't pay, or can't come to get me, is in front of all of them, which just infuriates me further. I can not let them see any weakness. It's obvious they'll use it against me.

My fingers curl into the wood, nails scraping. "He's going to kill you all when he comes to get me."

"Your father doesn't know where you are, Sweetheart," Viper offers, leaning forward to scoot the tray closer to me. "He can't get you if he doesn't know where to look."

"It's hard to find someone when you take them hundreds of miles away," I snap, faintly aware that I've opened my mouth, allowing Reaper to slip more food past my lips.

"How do you know you are hundreds of miles away?" Striker asks.

I swallow and accept another dried piece of fruit from Reaper before looking at Striker. "The landscape. It looks like the land around my father's lodge. And there are no palm trees and white sand."

He just nods, glancing at Reaper.

So I was right. I knew I was, but had held on to the silly hope that maybe Florida suddenly had craggy cliffs. If Cora and I were simply being held until my father paid, we'd be close to him. Not sitting in a crumbling mansion hundreds, possibly even as much as a thousand miles away.

No one says anything for a few minutes and I eat until the food is gone and I feel like I'm going to explode. Satisfied, Reaper removes the tray and Viper hands me a bottle of water, leaning against the table, looking down at me in Breaker's lap. I'm so full I can't fit any more in my stomach, so I stuff it into the pocket of my sweater for later.

"What now?" I ask. "Are you guys going to strip me and bathe me too? Don't trust me with a comb or brush? There are razors in my bathroom that I could use to make a shank."

Viper laughs, brushing a strand of hair off my face. The move is intimate. Familiar. *Because we are*, I remind myself.

"If that's a concern, maybe we should bathe you," Striker says, and I swear he's smiling under the mask.

"Or with you," Breaker says, his words soft in my ear, his hips tilting to remind me of his erection.

Not like I need it. If anything, I'm a bit *too* aware of him.

I jump up, turning to glare at him, as his hands slip away, trying to ignore the heat flaring between my thighs. "You'd have to take your stupid masks off for that. And being you can't even fuck without them on, I don't think I need to worry about you joining me."

"You need to worry about adjusting your tone," Striker says, voice dropping low. "Be a good little hostage and go back to your room before you piss one of us off and that rude mouth earns you a lesson."

My lip curls into a wicked grin. "You sure enjoyed my rude mouth before."

Breaker sighs, stroking my thigh. "Tiny Thing, behave."

Jerking back, I hit the table, a primal part of my brain lighting up, acutely aware of their proximity, their hands, their large sexy muscles that my body sings for like a starved siren.

"Go back upstairs and rest," Breaker says, standing up. I suck in a breath. How I forgot how intimidatingly sexy he is seems stupid on my part now that he's right in front of me, touching me with gentle hands.

My gaze falls to his chest, my mind flashing with the memory of his abs and sweat slicked flesh. When he hooks a finger under my chin, tilting my head back, I grip the table behind me, trying to control my breathing.

Pale blue eyes drop to my mouth. Breaker's thumb swipes at my bottom lip, igniting flames under my flesh. "Run along, sweet girl, before we change our minds and tie you to this table and teach you a lesson."

Shit. That shouldn't sound so enticing.

Yeah. I definitely don't need any more reminders of how large and infuriatingly sexy he is. And I certainly don't need a lesson from them.

My body remembers just fine on its own.

Breaker steps back, letting me slip past. Their eyes bore into my back as I walk from the room. It feels like they can see under my flesh, to my blood burning in my veins, shining with heat from their words.

With my head high, I keep my eyes on the door and walk out, part of me wondering if I'm going to be fed like that for every meal.

Chapter 17

STRIKER

Sleep evades me tonight. My mind fills with thoughts of Delilah's pretty mouth as Reaper fed her. Thoughts of maybe now she'll regain some weight that we're making her sit and eat. With thoughts of Cora's sad eyes and pretty taunting smile. But then the sweetness of their faces gets slashed out, cut sharply from my mind's eye and another face flashes before me.

I know it's my mother.

Some primal instinct that remembers her now. Warm brown eyes like mine. Bronzed skin. Long deep umber hair that curled around her cheeks. Then it's blackness. The stink of piss and feces. Phantom pangs of hunger, clawing in my belly like ghosts.

Watching our Princess eat floods my entire chest with delight. I think it does for all of us. We were all so hungry all the time. It's easy to control boys when you withhold food. That's one thing Reaper didn't want them to feel. That stark, painful gnawing like we felt in the cold room. In solitary. Like I felt for who knows how many days in the darkness where my mother left me.

It may be because of Cora and how open she was with me that my mind now flashes on the woman whose face has evaded me my entire life. Whose addiction drove her to an early death and left a little boy half alive only to be handed over to a man whose own addiction to cruelty and control would rip him apart so he could form a new person.

Sometimes I wonder if that's what Reaper intends to do with Delilah. Rip her to shreds until he can mold her into something new. Someone capable of accepting the truth.

Her father is an evil man. Far worse than our *otets*.

Although we all agreed to take Delilah, and ultimately Cora, I don't think we ever discussed exactly how we'd get their cooperation. We just blindly followed Reaper, as we tend to do. He knows us. Knows what's best. He's taken care of us, protected us, most of our lives. I can't even count the number of times he accepted a punishment for Breaker. Viper. Telling Fallon it was he who broke a rule, or didn't follow a command.

Fallon's techniques to train us were harsh, too harsh to be humane, but effective. We learned quickly that if we did as he asked, we were rewarded. If we didn't, we were disciplined. Fallon always used food, along with another form of punishment. Starving a young boy is a quick way to get them to behave. Reaper was always hungry growing up. Hell, we all were. I think that's why he insists on feeding her. As much as he says she's Rune's blood, deserving of his punishment, he can't stand the thought of anyone being hungry.

I think that's why he can't bring himself to be as cruel as Fallon. Reaper remembers what it's like in the cold room. To be scared. Confused. To be given snippets of praise, then words that cut so deep, you're bleeding with shame.

Reward and praise

Humiliate and degrade.

Those, along with consistency, are effective tools when you need someone to follow your orders. When you need someone to *fear* you enough to follow your every command. But we don't want them to fear us. Which is why we're finding it harder and harder to train Delilah as we were.

We need her trust in order for her to *want* to follow us into the war we're about to wage.

The thought of our Princess learning about her father sends a sick shiver of excitement through me, but it twists up grossly with the dread that pools in my gut. When she finds out...

It may very well destroy her.

Cora's already learned hard lessons. She's been torn apart and cracked open, and if what we suspect is true, it's been many times. She already knows it's in her best interest to follow along with us. Her trust on the other hand? That's something we have to earn, not demand.

My stomach lurches, remembering her blank expression as she talked about her mother. Yeah. Our Little Flower has already been crushed by her parents. The only things she needs now are safety and security.

Delilah as well. She may have lived a carefully protected life, but Rune still trapped her.

My chest squeezes and I rub at the ache, wondering if the entire world is filled with such darkness or if we were just the unlucky ones, born into it.

Glancing toward the far end of the room, the moonlight washes across the floor, and I can make out the small figurine on the dresser. I rub absently at my chest again. Fuck. Sometimes when I remember, I feel the black, empty cavity in my chest just as acutely as the day it formed.

Rune Gavin has to pay for his sins. All of them.

Scooting back on the bed, I lean my head against the worn wood. A low groan from the room next door makes me still. Another gravelly sound makes my cock grow thick, picturing Breaker bent over Viper's back, slamming into him. I tap my head to the headboard again and again in frustration, envious they have an outlet.

They don't talk about the nights they spend together. I've only witnessed Viper dropping to his knees, accepting Breaker into his mouth during and sometimes after we've shared a woman. Reaper and I have never brought up the sounds of them together later on, because if they were doing it in secret, then they didn't want us to know. Hearing the two together now is surprising. But maybe it shouldn't be. The women have been torturing us for days.

Their proximity is making us do crazy things. We all crave them again. We've spent too many hours watching them on the cameras. I know that same gnawing hunger to taste them, claws at Reaper, Viper, and Breaker just as brutally as it does me. That the same desperate feeling to own every minute of their day, absorb their every thought, smell them, touch them drives my brothers to madness like me.

They've quickly turned from a mission into an obsession and we all feel the danger lurking in that.

As soon as I hear the loud bang and the door slamming shut, I quickly jump out of bed. Reaching for my pants, I slip them on as I make my way to the door. Reaper is on duty tonight, watching over the girls, and he's not alerted us, so I know it's not about them. As I open the door, Viper's muffled growl carries down the hall.

Fucking idiots. They know we have to be quiet. We may be two floors above Delilah, but it's still possible to hear sounds in this old empty mansion.

I stalk down the hall but stop mid-stride when I see a very naked Breaker pinning a naked Viper to the wall, his forearm at his throat. He's leaning over him, crowding his space, his hard cock pressed up against Viper's stomach.

Crossing my arms, I lean against the door frame, waiting for Viper to snap, letting my gaze slide lower to Breaker's bare ass. I've seen his ass plenty of times, but I don't know if I've ever noticed how tight and perfectly shaped it is. How…

Shit.

Blinking, I grip my biceps, refocusing back on Viper's red face. He's so angry that if Breaker pushes him any further, I'll have to break them apart. I usually do when Breaker crosses a line.

Both men glance my way. I lift a brow.

Breaker lets his arm drop and as soon as it's at his side, Viper shoves him backward, slamming him into the far wall, pinning him the way Breaker had him. Breaker's hard dick slips over Viper's stomach and my eyes drop.

I suck in a lungful. "Can you guys keep it down? I'm trying to sleep," I say, already bored with them.

"This fucking asshole here doesn't know how to listen," Breaker spits out. He's not fighting Viper's iron grip, but he's not backing down either.

"I thought you were a good boy, Vipe." I don't know why I say it. It just comes out. Maybe because I'm tired. Maybe because we're all bored. Possibly because we're all on edge and we all feel it. This slippery sensation that feels like we're all teetering on the edge of a cliff and any small thing will send us over.

Viper's attention snaps over to me, and he's rushing forward, muscles tense, and slams his hand around my neck, shoving me back until I'm pressed against the door. I'm so shocked, Viper and I don't clash often, that a sharp laugh slips free. Viper's face contorts with rage. Pulling back a fist, he slams into the wood next to my head.

"Fucking asshole," he grates. "You want to make fun of me? Maybe you should look in the mirror."

"Maybe you should back the fuck off," I snarl, trying to keep from reacting. I clench my teeth, sucking in a breath, but his arm at my throat presses harder. I fist my hands at my sides. "*Now*, Viper."

When he doesn't back down, Breaker places his hand on his shoulder, trying to pull him back.

Viper snarls. "You don't think we don't notice?" His voice drops, low and throaty. "We see how you watch. You'd love my mouth on your cock. Breaker fucking your face." He punches his hips forward and his dick grinds into mine. "You'd love to taste me, wouldn't you? Swallow all my cum as you fucked Breaker's ass."

"I said back off."

"Viper," Breaker says quietly, again trying to pull him away.

Viper leans in, his mouth next to my ear, and a shiver of awareness runs through me. Every sensation suddenly snaps into focus, and I feel everything all over. His hard cock digging into my thigh, rubbing against my thickness in my pants. His warm chest slipping over mine, the fine hair brushing my nipple. Taste his warm, minty breath.

We've fucked women at the same time, two in her cunt, but this... this feels more invasive, more demanding of my senses than any of those moments when our hands brushed or our dicks slipped inside a warm pussy. My cock grows hard, and he smiles.

"Just admit it already, Strike," Viper says, pressing into me harder. His lips brush my ear and my pulse rushes, drowning out every sound other than his rough breaths. "You would love me to be your good boy. Or maybe you'd be mine."

That red flash of anger returns and I fling him off, grabbing his face with one hand, then kick his feet from under him. He goes down, hard on his back. I move to straddle him, fist formed, arm already pulled back, but Breaker grabs my wrist and yanks me back, wrapping an arm around my shoulders, dragging me to my feet.

I glare down at Viper as he stands, somehow with dignity and grace for a naked man that was just tossed to the ground. But he always gets up even when he should stay down. Like right now.

When I try to snap my head back, seeking to connect with Breaker's face, he stops me by slamming his palm to the back of my head.

"Fucking stop," Breaker snarls, shaking me until I stop fighting. "Just fucking stop."

"I think I hit a nerve," Viper says, eyes narrowing.

When I stop fighting, I instantly notice Breaker's dick pressing into my lower back. Hard, slippery with pre-cum. My dick throbs and I suck in a breath, wishing I had enough control to stop my body from responding.

"Do I need to grab the lube so you guys can work this out?" Reaper's voice from behind us makes us all freeze.

Breaker releases his grip and eyes me as he lets me go, waiting to see if I'm going to lunge at Viper again. I give him a nod and his shoulders relax.

Reaper stops next to me, and slowly takes in the scene, his eyes sliding up and down Viper, then Breaker, then slipping over to me. "Lover's spat?"

"Fuck off," the three of us say at once.

The corner of Reap's mouth lifts. "If you three are done here, we have more important matters to attend to." His eyes gleam, lit up with that dark light we all recognize. "I think Kitten wants to play."

Chapter 18

Delilah

*S*HARDS OF RUBY GEMS *lie scattered at my feet, glistening in the moonlight. I reach down to pick up a broken piece from the concrete, but my fingers slide through the gems. It's wet. Sticky. Warm.*

Red like blood.

I rub my fingers together, feeling the thick, warm scarlet moisture between my thumb and forefinger.

Blood is thicker than water.

My mother's voice rings in my head. She always used to say that. I never knew what she meant. People aren't bonded by water. We're bonded by blood. Like my mother and me. We're blood. Like my father and me. We're blood too.

Cora.

Maybe she's the water.

My name whispers in my ear. I turn, but no one is there. Wiping my fingers on my dress, I look down and see the pretty lavender dress I wore that night. The night I couldn't save her.

Coldness brushes my ankle and I look down at my feet and see blue sapphires. My mother loved sapphires because they matched her eyes. The sapphires at my feet crack, splinters forming, running in lines from a dark center. They aren't gems at all but eyes. My mother's eyes.

And they aren't rubies at my feet. It's blood.

Everywhere.

Running down the walls, pooling at my feet, dripping down my face like tears.

A scream cracks through my head, clawing at my mind.

I bolt upright, the scream echoing in my head. I can't tell if it's the lingering sound of my scream from my dream or if it was real.

It cuts through me again, far away.

Cora.

My stomach drops. Did I hear Cora screaming? I swing my feet over the edge of the bed and grab my sweater, slipping it on over my silky nightgown as I walk to the window.

Wind howls outside, rattling the panes of glass. The moonlight casts a haunting glow on the ocean below the cliffs, illuminating the crashing waves along the shoreline. The distant scream cuts through the night again and my blood chills.

Without thinking, I run to the open door and cross the hall to peer out the window overlooking the gardens. Other than the empty planters and spindly trees, the garden is empty.

The scream rips through the night again, but this time, it's cut off.

Gathering my sweater around me, I run back to my room to grab my boots before heading for the stairs, but remember, as my foot hits the top step, to be quiet. Moonlight slants across the stairwell from the row of windows that wind down the stairs, turning the cracked and peeling walls ice blue. I creep down, the wooden steps creaking under my weight, trying to control my breathing.

Did they let her out?

Images flood my mind, my overactive brain flooding with terrible scenarios: Cora trying to escape, running and getting lost or worse, hurt by a wild animal. Striker warned me there are dangerous animals out there. What if she's hurt and screaming for help?

I don't know where the men are, or where they spend their time in this giant mansion. Most of the house is blocked off, doors locked, so I don't know what lies beyond the library and the few rooms where they've let me roam.

Halfway down the stairs, I freeze, terror gripping my lungs. Silvery moonlight spills through the opaque leaded glass windows framing either side of the front door, which stands wide open, like someone left in a hurry.

Or fled in fear.

I rush forward and stumble through the door, the frigid night air nearly sucking the breath from my lungs. The cliffs are to my right, a long dirt road a slash of white along the cliffs edge. In the center of the large circular drive sits a broken fountain and beyond that lies the gray tree line below a dark, star studded sky. My toes curl in my boots and I bite my lip, debating.

It may not be her.

Another distant scream breaks through the night like splinters of glass. My fingers curl into my sweater. I cast a look over my shoulder, to the dark, empty foyer, then break into a run.

Every step takes me further from the mansion, Striker's threat echoing in my head. But then the scream slices through the cold air and I pick up the pace, my boots hitting the earth, barely audible on the soft grass.

By the time I reach the tree line, I'm panting, panic scratching at my insides, making each breath scrape in my throat. My step falters and I stop at the edge of the dark woods, pressing my hand to a thick tree trunk, my breaths bursting out in white puffs in the cold night air. Now that I'm here, I hesitate, common sense returning with each ragged lungful. I have no flashlight. No weapon. I don't even know if it's Cora.

What if this is part of some game and they're luring me out here?

The scream cuts through the woods, sending a sliver of terror down my spine. Without even the slightest hesitation, I bolt past the tree line and run toward the sound, using the bright moonlight filtering through the skeletal tree limbs to dodge roots and sticks.

The shrill scream seems to travel further and further away the deeper I get into the woods, moving from my left to my right. It rings out again, this time even farther away.

It's not her. It can't be her.

Freezing, I glance around, realizing I have no idea which direction I came from. I think I went straight, but every time the sound shifted, I changed my path slightly and now I'm turned around. I glance up to the moon, trying to determine east from west, but everything I learned in Girl Scouts flees my brain.

"Fuck," I hiss.

Instead of being murdered by four men in masks for leaving the house, I'm going to die of fucking exposure.

"Delilah!" The distant, terrifying sound of my name being called sends dread up my spine and I stumble forward, catching myself on the exposed roots of a massive tree.

Oh god.

My knees hit the dirt.

"Deli-lah!" he yells again, this time closer, his voice slicing through the night as dangerous as a switchblade.

They know I left the house. They know I disobeyed.

Striker's threat rings in my head again and terror creeps up my throat.

Scrambling backward to a large tree, I kneel between thick, twisted roots, my breath catching in dread, snagging in my throat.

A twig snaps somewhere to my left, and I press my hand to my mouth to suppress my scream.

"We warned you not to run, Kitten," Reaper calls, his voice just far enough away to tell me they must have been close behind me when I ran from the house.

"And now our pretty Princess is in trouble," Striker yells, his voice closer. Too close.

My heart skips in my chest, and I press my hand to my throat like this will somehow slow it down.

He warned me. Striker told me what they'd do if I left the house.

If you try to run, we will catch you.

Do you know what happens to naughty girls who try to run? They are caught and tied up. Wrists bound so tight it'll make your pussy wet.

I'm so fucked.

"I'll make a deal with you," Reaper calls, his deep voice closer than before, but still behind me. "If you can outrun us, we'll go easy on you."

Viper's cruel laughter shivers through me, even closer than Reaper and somewhere to my left. I turn my head, scanning the dark woods, looking for movement but see none. It's just a blue-black night, thin branches bleached white by the moonlight, stretching toward the star-filled sky like boney fingers.

A twig snaps to my left.

My stomach drops. I scramble back onto my ass, pressing myself to the tree, trying to control my breathing.

"Maybe we'll let you get back to the house," Breaker says and my heart flutters when I realize he's somewhere in front of me. "Before we tie you up and punish you."

"What do you say, brothers?" Reaper's voice rings from behind me, like he's just on the other side of the tree I'm pressed against. "Let's make a game out of it."

Leaves crunch, and suddenly he's all I see. A black mass with gleaming eyes. My scream tears from between my lips, but it's cut off when his hand slams over my mouth.

"Pretty little Kitten likes to break rules," Reaper growls, weaving his other hand into my hair and yanking me up onto my knees. Twigs and leaves cut into my bare skin. He drags me forward, making me practically crawl. "Or maybe you wanted us to catch you."

On instinct, I open my mouth and then bite down. Hard. The sharp, coppery tang of blood fills my mouth, but he doesn't remove his hand. He clamps it down harder, using his free hand to secure my head, until my nose is crushed and I can't breathe, his blood smearing on my lips.

"Don't you remember?" he asks cruelly. "I like the pain. *Crave* it."

A scream builds in my throat, but then he drops his hand from my mouth, using it to grip under my arm, dragging me to my feet. I suck in a breath, stumbling against him as I'm forced up, biting down on my lip, cutting through sharply. Coppery blood hits my tongue, mixing his with mine.

His fingers snake into my hair, and he grips it by the roots, shoving me backward. My head hits the tree, but his hand absorbs the impact. His body presses to mine, molding to me, every curve and dip invaded by his hardness. Reaper's thigh slides between mine, pressing to my core, and I gasp at the electric jolt that shoots through me. I squeeze my eyes shut, trying to ignore the way my body thrums with awareness. The way his hard planes feel so right against my soft curves. The way the cold air skates across my heated flesh, and how the heavy sound of our breathing, almost animalistic, creates a primal need to throb between my legs.

I whimper when I feel his thick cock press into my belly.

"Oh, sweet, innocent girl," he grates. There's a hint of something, almost like regret, but I know better. "You don't know what you've done."

My entire body shivers, mostly from the adrenaline and only slightly from the cold. Possibly from the gravelly sound of his voice and the threat hidden in his words which blooms desire in my belly. "Where's Cora?"

His head twitches slightly, letting me know he's surprised by my question. Reaper backs away, his chest heaving, hands lingering, letting strands of hair slip through his fingers as he lets me go. His black eyes in the white skull cut through me, the melting face and stitching something out of a nightmare. He takes another step back, letting his gleaming gaze drag down my body. "I'll give you a head start, Kitten." He lifts his arm, motioning for me to move. "On a count of three."

I shake my head.

"One."

"No." My heart stutters. My palms flatten to the tree.

"Two."

I push off the tree, eyeing him, fear locking my jaw tight.

"Three."

I turn and run.

Chapter 19

Delilah

Fear licks at my heels, my heart hammering faster than I can run. Loud laughter rings out behind me, reminding me that my fear is their fun.

My boot catches on a thick branch and I stumble, catching myself on a spindly tree, but it was enough to slow me down.

"Here, kitty, kitty," Viper calls. "We just want to play, Sweetheart."

My eyes lock on the break in the trees and the little squares of lights shining like yellow beacons from the windows of the mansion. I dig in, sprinting forward, but before I can break free, a hand slams over my mouth, muffling my scream. We stumble forward, bending over, but he keeps his footing. My legs fly out from under me as I'm slammed back to a broad chest, my head hitting hard muscles as a powerful arm wraps around my waist, pinning me to him.

"Naughty Kitten," Reaper rasps in my ear, heavy breaths hitting my flesh like flames. "I caught you."

I kick back but don't have enough force behind it. My heel just grazes his shin, but it's enough that he buckles slightly. My hands fly up and I grab his mask, ripping it away.

Reaper growls, this irritated, animalistic sound, grating through my back as he shoves me forward. My knees hit the dirt, my teeth gnashing together from the impact.

"I didn't run!" I scream under his palm, but my words are cut off as he grips my throat, yanking me back into him, the back of my head hitting his hard length. Fear, and something dark, tangles up in my belly.

"Naughty Kitten, I just caught you running," Reaper growls, fingers digging into my pulse. "Running through the woods, trying to escape."

When he loosens his grip, I jerk away, falling to my hands and knees, small rocks and twigs cutting into my palms.

The slick sound of leather slipping through belt loops makes my blood freeze, my breath *whooshing* from my chest. I look around, my mind tripping over itself, and I see Striker, Viper, and Breaker stalking forward from every direction, wolves coming in for the kill.

They surrounded me. Like hunters closing in on their prey.

"You're going to regret testing me," Reaper says and slams his leather belt over my eyes, drawing it tight at the back of my head. I scream from the shock of his brutality, from being suddenly blindfolded, as he uses the belt to shove me forward. He drops with me, covering my back with his enormous body, until we're both lying in the dirt, my face pressed to the earth under his palm. Reaper digs his hips into my backside, his erection pressing into my ass crack. I try to buck my hips to get him off me, but he's absolutely massive.

"No no, little Kitten," Reaper growls in my ear, grinding my cheek into the dirt. "You've been a brat for days, wanting our attention, and now you have it."

With the belt covering my eyes, all my senses scream, every sound, smell, and taste heightened. I hear as the others approach, their boots cracking over the sticks and dried leaves. Taste the dirt as it slips past my lips. Smell the dry earth under my cheek. Feel his weight, his raw power and how, no matter what I do, there's no escaping.

"I told you not to run," Striker says. Dusty dirt hits my lips. The cracking of his leather boots near my head tells me he's crouching. "Yet you chose to disobey."

"No," I croak out, barely able to form words, my heart's thumping so hard in my throat.

"No?" Striker says, his tone close to mocking. He doesn't even sound like how I remember him. None of them do. "No you didn't run, or no... what Princess? No, don't dirty your pretty nightgown or no don't—"

"Where's Cora?" I scream, the sound bloody and raw. "What did you do to her?"

"Nothing," Breaker says from my right. I suck in a raspy breath as Reaper shifts upright. "Cora is in her room like you should be."

Reaper's hot breath fans over my face as he leans down again. His hips dig harder into my rear and I gasp, breathing leaves and dirt into my mouth. He's so hard he feels rock solid against me. "Why did you run?"

"Answer him," Viper says somewhere to my left. "Didn't we tell you not to run?"

"Fuck you," I manage between gasps, the gritty dirt in my mouth caking my lips. My fingers curl into the earth, nails digging in for purchase, but someone, Reaper I think, grabs my arms and twists them, pinning them to my lower back.

"God, she's spicy," Striker says. "I think she needs to be tamed a little more."

"Fucking perverts," I scream, but I choke on more dirt as I inhale.

Reaper's grip on my wrists tightens, and he wrenches them up higher on my back, sending a sharp pain shooting to my elbows. I bite my sore lip, trying not to cry out from the pain.

My nightgown slips up, slowly sliding up my thighs. Cold air hits my exposed rear. My entire body stills. The entire *world* halts, all sounds fading until there's only the faint chirp of birds, the distant cracking of branches rubbing together, and our ragged breathing.

A hand lands on the back of my thigh. I jerk at the sudden warmth against my flesh.

"Pretty Kitten needs to learn a lesson." Reaper's words crack at the end, scratchy like they're clawing his throat. His heat leaves as he sits upright. "Viper, hold her down."

My heart skips. A choked gasp escapes when his hand slides over my ass cheek, tugging my underwear down some. Another, different, warm hand wipes strands of hair away from my face.

"I fucking went outside and now you're going to hurt me?" I hate the way the last few words catch in my throat. Hate him for sending this awful fear skittering through my body.

"We're going to do something far worse than hurt you, Kitten," Reaper growls. "We're going to *own* you."

I squirm under him, fear and rage flooding my senses.

"We don't hurt helpless creatures," Striker says. "Punish yes. But I promise you we'd never hurt you."

The irony of my situation makes a guttural laugh escape. "You're fucking insane!"

"Hush now, Princess," Striker whispers. "Reaper has a point to make."

I open my mouth to curse him again, to threaten him with the vengeance of my father, but the sharp sting of flesh meeting flesh rings out over my ass cheek and I scream, more from shock than the actual pain. Stinging heat radiates out, spreading from my right butt cheek to my thigh.

"Fucking asshole!" I scream when I realize what he did. "A fucking spanking?"

Another slap to my other ass cheek makes my entire body jerk, my hips digging into the ground, bucking away from the pain.

"Two," Reaper growls. "How many until our little Kitten learns to obey?"

Another, another. Two more in rapid succession, each one making me cry out.

"How many more, Sweetheart?" Viper asks, shifting his grip on my wrists so my arms are up even higher and I'm forced to bend, draw my knees up under me, my ass in the air.

"Fuck y—" My scream gets cut off with another sharp slap to my ass.

"How many?" Reaper's hand lands again. "Ten more?"

Another. Another.

My sob breaks on a growl. My heart hammers. It's not so much the pain as the humiliation. I'm pinned down, four men standing over me, spanking me because I was trying to find my best friend. To fucking save her from god only knows what.

"I wasn't running," I whimper, my ass hurting so badly, I'm squirming, like if I move enough I can outrun the pain.

"You don't leave here," Reaper says. "You're ours."

I shake my head, my forehead grating into the dirt, a red tide of fury making me wish I was stronger so I could get free. Kick him.

Another slap to my ass rips a cry from my throat.

"You don't run," Striker says as another punishing spank lands.

"You belong to us now. You'll listen to us. Be rewarded by us. Get punished by us. Do you understand?"

"I belong to no one," I hiss, regretting my defiant words the second another harder spanking stings my sore ass. Something twists, low in my belly like embers spiraling upward, stained with darkness.

When another slap lands, I buck into it, an explosive heat hitting between my thighs.

"Ours," Reaper says. "You're ours, Kitten. Do you understand?"

I nod, my throat tight, fear making my heart race. Not of another spanking to my sore flesh, but of that dark feeling curling through me.

"Say it, Kitten."

"Yes!" I scream.

"Say you understand."

"I understand," I plead, trying to twist my hips, instinctively trying to avoid another spanking, but there's not another slap to my skin.

Reaper's hand slides over my ass, kneading the tender skin as an arm slips under my hips and I'm hauled up, knees scraping over the dirt until I'm kneeling. Viper adjusts his grip on my wrists, holding them crossed at my back, drawing me against him in a twisted embrace. I drop my head, my forehead hitting his warm chest. I breathe in and out heavily, all my senses crashing together violently. Every nerve ending is lit up brightly so that I'm aware of their every breath. The way Reaper's fingers feel on my ass. How Striker's hand slides along my jawline. Viper's chest moving up and down under my cheek and his grip on my wrists. The faint smell of sweat and soap and earth mixed with a dark, woodsy scent. Breaker's hand running up my back to my neck. The deep intense clawing low in my belly like a gnawing hunger, but for something I can't name.

Reaper's fingers slip down lower, over the fabric of my underwear, right at my core, and he curses under his breath. "She's soaked."

My cheeks flame and I tuck my face into Viper's shirt, inhaling his clean, slightly citrusy scent. *Fuck you* seems to be the only response I'm capable of, but I clamp it behind my teeth and remain silent, refusing to give them the satisfaction of my anger.

A light slap lands on my pussy, making me jolt. I hiss out a breath into Viper's chest. Lightning shoots from my center to the base of my spine.

"Naughty, naughty, Kitten," Reaper rasps. "This pretty pussy is begging for us."

My tongue flickers over the slightly swollen cut where my teeth bit into my bottom lip, out of retorts and... words. I have nothing because he's right. That nagging ache is begging to be soothed.

Striker makes an approving sound in his throat. My heart skitters at the quiet praise. "Did our pretty Princess just need to be put in line? That's what you wanted, isn't it? We warned you what would happen if you ran and you did, anyway."

Reaper slips his hand slightly over the material again and I arch back into his touch, hating his dark chuckle. Hating myself and my body that I can't seem to control. Detesting how a spark of need flies outward, catching fire, and I want him to do it again.

"What a good girl," Striker says, petting my head. "You took your lesson so well, maybe we should reward you."

I lift my head from Viper's chest and bite my lip to keep in an angry growl, wishing Reaper would just do it already. Take me. Fuck me ruthlessly again until this hunger dissipates.

His fingers tap up lightly again and I clench around nothing. He does it again. Then again. "You need to come, don't you?"

An angry, slightly desperate, fully anguished sound slips out, and I press my cheek back to Viper's chest.

My nod's going to send me to hell, but I do it anyway.

"Say it, Sweetheart." Viper's gentle tone fires through my brain as his voice reverberates through my cheek. "We need to hear you say it."

I don't want to say it. Saying it means I want them.

The word clings and claws, grips the inside of my throat, desperate to stay in, but it breaks free on a whimper. "Yes," I whisper, elongating the word as a finger slips over my cheek.

"What a sweet little kitty you are when you want us to please you." Reaper runs a finger along my opening and I feel how wet I am, my panties soaked. He presses hard as he slips a finger over my clit. "You want to come so bad, don't you?"

Fuck.

I nod, burying my face in Viper's chest.

Reaper's growl as he slips over my clit again shoots fire to my core. "Good girl."

My mouth opens, breath rushing out. Viper shifts, his grip tightening. A tear slips down my cheek. He's going to make me say it. "Please."

"Such a sweet little purr," Viper whispers into my hair. "Let's hear it again."

"Please."

He slaps my pussy again. My back arches. A moan slips past. I've lost all control of myself, my body, my mind, and I don't care. I just want him to touch me. Soothe this ache twisting between my thighs, curling like thorny vines in my belly. "Breaker, remove her panties."

I hear the slick sound of a knife leaving its sleeve, feel the cold metal flat against my skin. Then the material is cut away as Striker holds my left leg and Breaker grips my other, spreading me wide.

I don't need help. I do it for them, mindless with need.

Cold air touches my heated flesh. I tilt my hips, straining to get my ass higher, leaning into Viper's solid form, my body begging for more.

The next slap lands viciously, sending a bolt of pure desire through me. My clit stings from the impact and when he does it again, I cry out.

Reaper does it again, working up to a brutal pace. The sting mixes with pleasure, building until I hear myself making low keening sounds, my hips moving to meet his hand. Something dark and primitive claws at my insides, wanting to break free. The sting gets worse, the pleasure gets higher, flaring on my clit with each punishing spank. And this is what it feels like. A punishment for wanting their touch. Another punishment from Reaper for his dark need to touch me.

Viper's solid body moves away, and my hands are released. I fall forward on to my hands and knees in the dirt. Someone's hand slips over my lower back, pressing down so that I'm forced to dip my hips like a cat in heat. A tear slips out, and the belt tightens, my head snapping back.

"Do you want me to kiss you, Princess? Is that why you're whimpering?"

Please. Please. Please, just kiss me. Like you did before. When Reaper was taking my pleasure in the blue tinted room. When you knew I needed softness.

My head's yank back further. Striker's hand clamps around my throat, his mouth enclosing over mine. I open for him, groaning into his mouth as he kisses me with long sloppy sweeps of his tongue. Kissing me savagely, as Breaker pulls my leg, so I'm open wider. As Viper presses my lower back down, keeping me still. As Reaper continues to spank my pussy. They're all doing this. Taking part in this. Willingly sending me over the edge of sanity.

The slaps get harder, faster, all our breaths heavier, until I'm crying, pleasure rippling through me, mixed with the edge of pain. Until that wild feeling breaks free.

When I come, it's as cruel as the slaps on my clit. It cuts through me just as sharply, ripping a scream from deep in my throat. Striker's throaty groan as I continue to whimper against his mouth sounds like he's devouring my demise. Eating my will.

Savoring my ruin.

Because that's what this feels like. Like they are destroying one small piece of me at a time, until I'm nothing but theirs to use, to have.

To control.

Then it's just emptiness. All the hands leave my body and I melt to the ground, forehead pressed into the dry earth. One of them slips the belt from my eyes, but I keep them closed, not wanting to see them.

"Come here, Princess," Striker says. "Let's get you inside."

FANNY LEE SAVAGE

I feel warm hands slipping under my arm and legs and I'm lifted. I press my cheek to his shirt, hiding my face. But I can't hide from the darkness inside my head.

Chapter 20

Delilah

The warm air in my room blasts over my icy skin as Striker carries me through the door and walks us toward the bathroom. He doesn't speak as he flicks on the light and sets me down in front of the bathroom sink. Instead, he fills the tub, not looking my way. The adrenaline of the night leaves my body in little tremors that come and go, so I grip the counter to keep my mind from wandering back to the woods.

"The radiator's fixed?" I ask as he bends over to test the water.

I stare at his mask, the slash over the eye, waiting for him to say something, but he doesn't respond as he walks to me and grips the sleeve of my sweater. He tugs it and I shrug it off. Then he lifts the hem of my ruined nightgown. My eyes dart up to his, but my pulse slows when I don't see that dark edge in them like I've seen before. He gathers the gown around my waist and pulls up. Without a word, I lift my arms so he can slide it over my head. It slips to the floor and my hard nipples brush the front of his shirt.

"When did you fix it?" I ask, my voice a whisper. A light trembling starts in my shoulders, moving down to my legs.

"Reaper did this afternoon."

My eyes flicker away and land on the open door, but I don't see him. I know he's out there, just outside the doorway. Just out of sight. Just out of reach. He must have done it earlier after they fed me and it hadn't had enough time to warm up my room.

I wonder if I would have thought it was Cora screaming if I woke up warm, knowing he'd turned it on for me.

Gripping my bare waist, Striker turns me to face the mirror. His warm brown eyes drop to my hard nipples in the mirror as he backs away. The way his gaze slides over my naked body sends a wave of warmth between my thighs and I think my sanity was left in those dark woods. When his eyes land on my ass, he glances up briefly at me and then slides my hair off my back, over my shoulder. That same hand grips the back of my neck tightly, making me gasp and my pussy clench. Then he releases me, and lightly trails a finger from the back of my neck down my spine to my tailbone, sending a violent tremor through me.

"Your ass is beautiful this color," he whispers. "The perfect shade of sin."

My hands grip the edge of the vanity, heart picking up pace.

"Do you understand now what happens when you don't listen?"

Faintly, I'm aware of my nod, telling both of us I've learned my lesson. I won't leave the house. I'll do as they ask.

"Bend forward and let me see you."

My heart slams once, twice until it's beating so hard it feels like my entire body is shaking with it.

"Good girl," he praises as I lean over the sink, parting my thighs slightly.

My focus shifts from his reflection to my face in the mirror, and I see myself. The streaks of tears through the dirt on my cheeks. The thin cut on my swollen lip. My hair tangled, wild, leaves and twigs stuck in the ends. My eyes wide, but hard. I look untamed. Like some feral creature they plucked from the woods. That's what I feel like inside, too. Uncaged. Unlocked. They pulled something from me, some shadowy thing that lived in my heart and now it's free. Free to be this woman who's bending over the sink, spreading her legs so Striker can see the marks they made and the slickness between my thighs.

I'm still so wet. Needy. That one orgasm was not enough to tame the wild feeling coursing through my limbs. I need more. Want more.

A fleeting thought flashes in my mind. Striker pulling himself free. Driving into me hard. Fast. Deep. Until this tightness in my chest is released and I feel like myself again. Until this feral woman in the mirror quiets her silent scream for more.

"So wet and pretty," Striker says, grabbing my focus. He slowly lowers himself, until he's kneeling, his palms skimming down my thighs to my ankles. "Lift." I raise my foot and he unties the boot and pulls it off, then the other and sets them aside. I gasp, finger's gripping the sink edge, when he grabs both my ass cheeks and spreads me until I'm completely exposed. Air leaves my lungs as he kneads my ass gently, rumbling moans of approval behind me, his thumb skimming over the wetness at my opening, then up to the tightness of my rear. I still, then melt as he presses lightly to the hole there. Warm lips touch my skin. "So beautiful."

I clench my teeth, biting back the need clawing in my belly so I don't whimper at his touch. When he finally lets me go, I relax and turn around to face him as he stands upright. Taking my hand, he leads me to the tub. I sink down into the water, my ass raw and my pussy sore, drawing my knees up to my chest.

He pushes up his sleeves, revealing toned forearms. I stare at the thin white scars running along his skin like tiny claw marks under the dusting of brown hair as he uses the cloth to wash my face, rubbing away the dirt.

"What are those from?"

His eyes drop to his forearm. "From the darkness."

Darkness. Like where she was created. That wild woman in the mirror. I wonder if my time here will leave me with thin white scars. Maybe not on my flesh. Maybe only in places that can't be seen.

"Princess."

My eyes collide with his. I wonder how many times he's said my pet name.

"Why Princess?" I whisper.

"You've lived in a gilded castle with a man who calls himself a king."

"With a man who is creating an empire," I snap, my anger fizzling as fast as it heated my chest.

"Your father is creating something, but it's not an empire," Striker says. "He's a miserable, greedy man who's cruel and depraved."

I let his words sink to the bottom of the water, too heavy for me to deal with right now. I'm already weighed down with too much, including my own thoughts.

"What's your name?" I ask. I don't know why I do. Maybe because they took intimate parts of me and I want something back.

"Striker," he says quietly.

"Just Striker?" I ask.

He drags the cloth over my collarbone, then says, "Just Striker."

"Who were you before you were Striker?"

"I was a boy who lived in darkness," he says.

When he moves the cloth over my lips, my heart skips. Aches. His tenderness has returned, like that night in the club when he was brutally rough, but everything he did to me was edged with a sweet tenderness that made my heart hurt. Made me crave more. Like right now.

"I don't understand," I whisper as he drags the cloth over my shoulder, then down my back. I don't understand any of this. Why I'm here. Why Cora is here. What they're doing.

"You will soon," Striker says and swipes at my cheek. I hadn't realized a tear had slipped out.

"If he's so bad, why don't you just kill him?" I ask. *Or us.*

Striker's hand stills, eyes darting from the cloth to mine.

"If we killed Rune, he'd no longer feel pain."

He'd no longer feel the fear of not knowing where we are. Viper said Rune has no clue where to find us. That's why he hasn't come. If they simply killed my father, Reaper wouldn't be able to draw out his revenge.

"Whatever my father did must have been truly heinous to gain this level of hatred."

"Your father isn't a good man." Striker drops the cloth, his eyes suddenly hard, like he forgot he was supposed to treat me with disdain. Like he forgot he's supposed to hate me.

"You say that but won't tell me what he did," I say, watching as he stands and walks to the door.

Instead of answering, he says, "Wash up. Come down for breakfast after sunrise."

"Striker," I say as he nears the door. "I deserve to know what sin I'm paying for."

He turns to face me. "You will find out when you're ready to know." He glances down at his watch before he turns to leave, but stops.

When his eyes meet mine, I suck in a breath. He barely looks present. Far away. But then he seems to snap back and shakes his head. "You may go out to the front garden, but do not go past the wall. Do not step foot on any ground that doesn't take you right there."

When I hear my bedroom door shut, I sink down into the water and dunk my head.

They don't have to worry about me running again. I'm a fast learner.

And I know now exactly why I'm here.

Chapter 21

STRIKER

THE MOST IMPORTANT LESSONS are always the hardest to learn.

That is what Fallon said, as he locked the door and left us. Or when the belt cracked over our skin for the fifth time that week. Learning anything from Fallon hurt. I don't know if lessons are supposed to, but they always did.

It's amazing what can be learned when you crave affection. Touch. Even if the person touching you is not worthy of yours.

Whenever we were punished, it was earned. There was always a reason behind Father's cruelty, even if we didn't understand it at the time. We learned eventually. Locking us in isolation gave us time to think, reflect, he'd say, so that when we emerged, we'd be different. Stronger for it, both mentally and physically. We knew we could survive three days with only water and our own thoughts. We knew we could handle the belt. The beatings. By the time we were faced with the final test, we knew, too, that we could survive the wilderness.

In order for Delilah to let go of all the false things she's learned in her life, she needs to be broken apart and reconstructed. She now knows that if she stays inside, she'll be safe. I told her as much. She knows if she clears her plate, or doesn't protest, she'll not get the same knuckle cracking lessons we got as children. Delilah knows as long as she follows orders, things will turn out well for her.

And when she can take the consequences of her actions, she'll be rewarded.

She learned a harsh lesson last night. One I was surprised to find she took rather well. Surprised she responded by letting her own darkness seep out. But then Reaper knows what he's doing.

That's why we follow him.

She's so much like him. Maybe that's why he's being so hard on her. He knows what it takes to empty a person. Carve off the misshaped bits. That's what he's doing with our Princess. Carving out the places she keeps hidden until they're empty and we can fill them with the truth about her father. That's the only way she'll be able to handle it. Because when she finds out what her father is really like, she's going to need us to guide her. And we need her trust, her acceptance, before she'll be willing to help us.

I just hope when Reaper tries to crack her open a little more, he doesn't go too far. She's already accepting us, listening. We just need a little longer, but I fear that if he slips off the ledge he's leaning over with her, she'll close herself back up and we won't ever be able to reach her. I worry that his hatred for Rune is bleeding all over her. A little too much. So much so that she may drown in it before we can accomplish our mission.

I fear too that maybe I'm forgetting too often that I'm supposed to hate her. Just a little, so that what we're doing is justified.

But some days...

Some days it's easy to forget she's here for one reason and it isn't to fill that blank space in our hearts.

It's solely to pay Rune Gavin back, and using his daughter is the only way.

The loud slam of the front door cracks through the room. I spin away from the window and look across the library to the entry.

Viper looks up from his book, slipping his mask down over his face. "Is she crazy?"

I catch Breaker's grin before his mask slips down. "Maybe she wants another pussy spanking."

I do the same, adjusting my mask over my eyes as I stalk toward the foyer, but before I can reach the other side of the room, Delilah comes into view. When she sees me, she freezes, and her face flushes pink.

We've been waiting for her to venture out of her room. She never came down for breakfast and we never retrieved her. But we all know her pride will not allow her to hide from us. She just needed time to work up the courage to face us after last night.

"Which one of you assholes left the door open?" she asks, pressing her fingers to the hollow of her neck. Her pulse flutters wildly and I want to lean down and press my mouth to the skin and feel it move against my lips. "Resorting to more taunts?"

"Reaper," Viper says, "he never remembers to shut the door."

Her brows knit as she looks at each of us. "He just *forgets*?"

I shrug and back away before I lose my loose grip on my sanity and do something foolish. Like throw her over my knee and spank that sass out of her. Then shove two fingers deep into her until I hear that greedy moan again.

It's obvious after last night, we're too close to the edge. I don't know how long we'll last before we all do what Viper did. Hold them down and force them to take our cocks.

"He was in a hurry," Breaker adds, looking strangely at me. After a few heartbeats, he says, "The door was open last night, wasn't it?"

She bites her bottom lip, tongue gliding over the tiny cut. "I heard screaming. I thought it was Cora and the open door…" her voice trails off, and she shakes her head. "Doesn't matter."

"Foxes," Viper says. She gives him a blank look. "The screams. You heard foxes. It's a mating call."

"You've never heard a fox scream?" Breaker asks, glancing at each of us when her brows raise.

"I'm a city girl, remember?" she says. "I've never even seen a wild animal that wasn't in a zoo."

"You never visited your father's lodge?" I ask, keeping my tone even.

"His boy's club?" She laughs. "God no. I'd rather stay here with you four than be surrounded by those old men and their dusty wives."

Breaker's gaze flicks over to me. I can picture his scowl. Just as we suspected, she knows nothing.

She had screamed that she hadn't run last night. It's clear now she was looking for Cora. Not that it matters. She still left the house, and on top of it put herself in danger by running into the woods. Delilah's been talking to us via the cameras for days. She could have just....

Fuck. I refuse to feel bad. She still has to learn to listen to us. It's for her own good, but she was out there because she must have thought we were hurting Cora.

That thought sends anger snapping down my spine.

I step forward and weave my fingers into her hair, pulling her to me. God. She smells like that shampoo she uses. Woodsy and dark. Like sin.

"You thought we were hurting her." It's not a question. Her hands land on my chest and fuck me if my cock doesn't get instantly hard. My gaze dips to her pink mouth. "After last night, do you really believe she'd scream in pain if we touched her?"

Her entire face turns red, her eyes falling and focusing on the center of my chest.

"Those aren't the screams we want to hear, Princess," I tell her. "So next time you think you hear screaming, it'll only be when Cora comes."

She shoves against my chest and I let her go, watching as she stumbles back and grips the chair Breaker's sitting in. She's so flustered that I smile. I can't wait until we have her. Fully.

She has no idea what she's in for when we do.

She turns her back to me, resting her hands on her hips as she looks at Breaker. "I'm hungry."

Viper chuckles. "Me too, Sweetheart. You going to spread your legs for me to feast?"

"I thought you preferred dick."

His head twitches in that way that tells me to be on alert.

"Wait. I forgot, you only like pussy after it's filled with Breaker's cum."

He shoots up so fast even I can't move quick enough to stop him before he fists her hair and shoves her to her knees. She falls gracefully, like she knew what he'd do before even he did. "You've got a mouth on you," he snarls.

She smirks, daring him to... I'm not even sure *she* knows what she wants. She's figured out we will not hurt her and that may be a dangerous realization because now she's going to test our limits.

God. Reaper's in for it now. I think we all are.

"You sure liked my mouth that night in the club," Delilah says so innocently that Viper's grip tightens even more, making her wince. "Liked it so much you groaned like a fucking pig."

"Jesus," Breaker says, shaking his head as he pulls himself up from the chair. He glances at me, then grabs Delilah from Viper, yanking her up roughly by her arm. She flattens her palm to his chest and looks up at him with a defiant, possibly even a little satisfied, smirk. "You like pushing buttons, but Viper has a hair-trigger temper."

"What's he going to do?" she says. "Fuck my mouth again? Spank me? Give me an orgasm?"

Breaker's gaze darts to me. Yeah. We're fucked.

She spins and marches toward the doorway. When we don't all follow immediately, she turns around, brows going up. "Hungry, remember?" she says, crossing her arms. "You're the freaks who insist on feeding me, so let's go."

"Don't act like you don't like it," Viper says. "You love feeling Breaker's cock against your ass."

"I guess that's one thing we have in common."

My laugh is so loud Viper turns to glare at me.

Shaking his head, Breaker saunters over to her. He hooks a finger under her chin, tilting her head back to look up at him. She's so small next to him, it's almost comical that she has the guts to sass him. "You're going to like it even more when my cock is deep inside your pussy," he says, "and you're swallowing Viper's cum."

Her eyes dart to me. "Where's Striker going to be?" she snarks. "And Reaper? In your ass?"

She spins on her heel as I call after her. "Watch out, Princess, or you'll have your privilege of leaving the house revoked."

I really, really, hope she doesn't try this shit with Reap. He's on the edge, barely hanging on as it is.

She'll regret it if she pushes him too far.

Chapter 22

DELILAH

My heart races as I slide the drawer closed and reach for a bottle of water lined on the counter. I glance over my shoulder, then slowly lift my foot as I watch the door behind me in case one of them walks into the kitchen. I slip the thin steak knife between my thick sock and my boot. The jagged teeth snag on my sock, and I have to readjust it but manage to get it down far enough into my boot so none of them will notice it.

Bending over, I adjust the long laces of the leather combat boots just to be on the safe side. I don't want to get stabbed by the damn thing before I can get to the long hallway that leads to the west wing of the house. It's not like I plan on stabbing anyone with it, least of all myself. I just need something thin enough to pop the locks on the doors that access that part of the mansion.

STRIKER

They have been letting me roam around the last few days, but it's limited to a few rooms, which tells me one thing.

They are keeping Cora in the west wing.

The three men left me alone after we did our feeding ritual that I absolutely refuse to acknowledge I am starting to like, and I went to hide in my room for the rest of the day. When none of them came to get me for dinner, I realized that if I was going to get food, I had to go to them. I wasn't ready to face them again, so I waited until the sky outside my window turned pink and came downstairs.

Striker may have told me I could go outside, but after last night, I'm hesitant to step through the front door, much less venture out to the driveway or past it again. At least not just yet.

It's only been twenty-four hours since my trek through the woods, and whatever they're doing with me is seriously fucking with my head. I've spent the last several hours thinking too long and hard about Reaper's lesson, between my legs throbbing every time I remember my face down in the dirt and my ass in the air. Their hands on me. Reaper.

I wonder if they're doing all this with Cora, too.

I wonder if her smart mouth got her a spanking, and a fucked up reward.

I wonder, too, what will happen if I disobey again.

I close my eyes, sucking in a breath to calm the desire that rushes through me at the thought of them holding me down again.

I'm a mess.

At least I know I am, so maybe that's a plus.

I *need* to find Cora. If my brain is scrambled and I have a hard time separating the men who stormed the lobby, shot Manuel, and kidnapped us, then chased me through the woods with the men who feed me my favorite foods and gave me pretty dresses and boots that look like the ones they wear, I can only imagine how she must feel.

I've always been the logical one, to the point I was told I was cold and distant. Except for the night in the club, Cora's the wild child, driven by her emotions, ready to dive headfirst without checking to make sure the water's deep enough. If I'm feeling confused by being around them, she may very well be to the point of recklessness by now.

That's why I need to break into the other rooms and find her. We're more logical together. We always have been. If we can just find each other, we can figure out what to do next.

Taking one last look around the kitchen, I turn around and scream, my hands flying to my mouth, my bottle of water hitting the floor with a thud and rolling to a stop at his boots.

Viper leans against the doorframe, arms crossed over his massive chest. "What are you up to, Sweetheart?"

I lick my lips, sucking in a breath, my eyes moving from his biceps to the fangs on his skull mask.

His turquoise eyes narrow when I don't answer, and he pushes off the doorframe to stand at his full height. He's not nearly as tall as the other men, but just as powerful. Maybe even more so, with a sculpted, broad chest and thick thighs. I flash back on him in the club, his hand on my jaw as his cock slid in and out of my mouth. I wanted to touch him then, but Reaper and Striker had restrained me.

I want to touch those thighs now.

"Sweetheart?" Viper says, stalking closer. "Your eyes have that glazed look like you get when you come."

He stops in front of me. I take a step back, remembering how rough he can be. I pushed him earlier this afternoon, but the other men were there. I don't know what he'll do if no one is around to stop him.

"Did pretty kitty forget how to speak?" he asks, gaze dropping to my hands.

I clutch at the dress, trying to control my breathing. *He will not hurt me*, I tell myself, but I don't know if I fully trust that. Like Reaper, he has a darker edge to him, though I think his is streaked with something slightly more untamed.

"Don't make me ask again," he says.

I clench my jaw. I will *not* be intimidated by this man. He's nothing compared to my father. Viper is just a large, sexy bully in a stupid mask that is currently trying to use his size to intimidate me into answering.

"I was thirsty," I snap, unfurling my fingers from my dress, and I shove him aside. My hand lands on his thick arm, and damn him for the way it sends heat to my core. Whatever they did to me last night—hell, whatever they did to me in the club—has screwed me up mentally. I toss over my shoulder as I walk away, "Unless there are new rules, the last I checked, I am allowed to drink water without help."

"Don't lie to me, Sweetheart." He grips my arm and spins me around, lowering his head to look into my eyes. This close, I can really see the vibrant color. Light blue, like turquoise gemstones, but woven with emerald green instead of rusted copper threads. My mother had loved the stone, once telling me it was one of the softest gems even though the blue color was created from traces of copper and the greener ones traces of iron.

Viper's eyes are blue and green. Hard and soft.

"Where did you put it?"

I blink, biting my lip, too aware of his closeness and his familiar grip on my arm.

"Answer me, Sweetheart," he says, lowering his voice seductively. "We both know I'd love to give you a spanking."

Jerking in his grip, I snap, "And we both know how much you wish it was Breaker's ass you had your hands on."

His eyes narrow and they no longer look soft or pretty. Viper tilts his head to the side, still holding me still with his gaze. "Where did you put it?"

Damn it. There is no way he saw me take the knife. Even if there are cameras in here, I was careful to hide it when I opened the drawers to peek inside, making it look like I was searching for food or a cup when I went rummaging through the cabinets, looking for a tool.

"Your criminal activities are making you paranoid," I snap and twist out of his grasp, relief flooding me when I feel his fingers slip away and let me go.

The instinct to run eats at my gut, but I push it down as I stalk from the kitchen and head for the front of the house. As I walk past the dining room and the piano room, I can feel him at my heels, following just far enough behind to put me on edge. Just far enough that two, maybe three of his strides could close the distance and he'd be on me.

Right before I reach the foyer, I *feel* him bolt closer. The hairs on the back of my neck stand up, and just as I'm about to break into a run, he slides around me, dips down, digging his huge shoulder into my stomach, and hoists me over his shoulder. My scream echoes through the empty hall.

"Hush, now, Sweetheart," he growls, patting my rear. "If I wanted to hurt you, I would have by now."

"Put me down!" I scream, hitting his back with my fists. Bending my knee, I kick upward, trying to connect with his face, but he clamps his hand down on my thigh to hold me in place.

"Hold still." Viper turns abruptly and stops in a long, dark hallway. I hear the jangle of keys and hear a lock slide, then a door clicks open. Placing my hands on his lower back, I try to shift so I can see behind me, but the angle won't allow it.

"What are you doing?" I ask, panic climbing up my throat.

He doesn't answer. He stops walking and kicks the door closed behind him. I reach for it, trying to grip the rough wood to keep it open or use it to—I don't fucking know—but it slips past my fingers as he carries me into the room.

The last thing I want is to be alone in a room with Viper. I can still hear his cruel laughter cutting through the woods last night.

With panic still climbing higher, I look around the room and realize it's completely empty save for the thick drapes and a huge oriental rug. The only light, the dim purple of dusk, bleeding across the floor through the open drapes. He stops in the center of the room and grips my hips, setting me down in front of him. I back away, feeling like a caged animal, my heart hammering, watching him for any sign of danger.

"What are you doing?" I ask again, eyes darting to his hand as it moves to a sheath at the side of his belt.

That's when I notice the knife.

A hunting knife.

On instinct, I kick, hitting him in his shin and attempt to run past him. Viper grunts but grips me by the back of my neck.

"Fuck, you're a wild little thing," he says, dragging me back, turning me to face him, my chest crashing to his. His eyes gleam dangerously, his gaze dropping to my mouth as I open it, ready to scream. Viper's free hand clamps over my lips and he whispers, "*Shhh*, sweet girl. If you scream, I'll have to gag you."

My knees grow weak at the same moment my clit throbs. I'm aware my response is royally fucked, just as I'm suddenly acutely aware of his dick straining under his pants and pressing into my belly.

"Where did you put it?" he asks quietly, watching my eyes.

"I don't know what you mean," I say, but his hand still covers my mouth, muffling my words.

"You took something from the kitchen."

If his hand wasn't already covering my mouth, I'd clamp my lips shut.

"So where is it?" Viper says, slowly lowering his hand.

Shit. Did one of them see me on camera? Or is he guessing?

Refusing to answer, I remain still as Viper releases his hold and backs away. He's barely visible in the low light, just glowing predatory eyes and a shadowy outline, but I feel like I can breathe again now that a few feet separate us, and suck in a slow breath, resisting the urge to press my thighs together.

"Hand it over, Sweetheart," Viper says, eyes lowering to my chest, then lower between my thighs like he can sense the carnal pulse in my core. "I'll have to search you if you don't."

My heart slams into my ribcage. He *has* to be guessing. If he'd seen me take the knife, he'd go straight for my boot.

He makes a light *tsking* sound when I don't move or speak, then says, "Strip search it is," and steps forward.

Just as his words register, he's dropping, thighs bulging as he dips, gripping my thigh and swinging my body downward, and before I can react, before I can scream, I'm on my back. My hands reach for him as I land, tucking my head into his chest and I grab at him, fisting his shirt, a low squeal slipping out as he shifts and is suddenly between my thighs.

Shit, he's fast, I think the same moment I realize he took me down in a matter of seconds, and is using his larger body to pin me to the ground. He slips the hunting knife from its sheath and a rush of fear makes me dizzy. With his free hand, Viper grips my throat and presses the flat side of the blade to the front of my dress between my breasts.

"Where did you hide it?" he asks, his face just a black blur, his massive form a silhouette against the open curtains behind him. The knife catches the row of buttons on the front of my dress. "Is it here?"

"I don't know what you mean," I say, intending to sound hostile, but fear makes my voice tremble.

"Did you tuck it away under your pretty dress?" he asks, voice husky. I gasp, feeling the slight movement of the knife. He flicks his wrist, and a button flies off. My heart hammers so hard, but I dare not move as he flicks another button, the *pinging* sound of it landing on the wood floor feels like a shotgun ripping through me. "Where did you put it, Sweetheart? Tell me and make this easier on yourself."

When I don't answer, he places the side of the blade along the front of my dress, hooking the neckline with the tip, and tugs. I freeze, terror tingling up my hands, moving up my arms, and locking my jaw. The knife slices cleanly through the thin material. The dress falls open, revealing my cotton bra. He makes a sound in his throat, eating up the sight of my pebbled nipples under the material.

Viper leans back just enough to pull the knife lower, cutting the dress all the way to my waist. As he moves back, my thighs spread wider around him, making me aware of how sexual this position is. Releasing my neck, he adjusts his hold on his knife, angling the blade away from me, then grips the cut material and rips it open. Like the sound and his movement are attached to a string in my flesh, I feel the dress tear open as if he were tearing my skin apart, making my body arch up, shoulders pressing into the rug beneath me.

I'm so stunned, I can barely breathe, much less move, so I lie frozen, gasping for air as his gleaming eyes drink in the sight of my exposed flesh.

"Do you know you whimper when you sleep?" he asks, his voice barely above a whisper. He gently spreads my dress out, laying the fabric open on the floor like torn wings. "You make these little sounds that remind me of when you're about to come."

The mention of me sleeping reminds me they watch me all the time. The reminder of him knowing what I look like as I come makes heat pool between my thighs. His gaze drops to my panties. The way he reacts to me, *reacting to him* feels like he can see that feral creature they created last night hidden under all my layers, and he's beckoning her to him.

And part of me wants to let her out again.

"You made those sounds last night as Reaper spanked your beautiful pussy." Viper lowers the knife and places it on my belly. My stomach dips, fear and cold making my breaths seize. He grips the inside of my thigh, near the seam of my underwear, and I clench my jaw to keep from moving, scared the long blade will cut into my skin. His thumb skims over my panties. I know I'm wet. I feel it dampening the fabric. Now he does, too. He shifts, pressing into me harder, eyes moving over me again. "When you were begging us."

I bite my lip, squeezing my eyes shut, fighting that primal part of me that wants to tilt into his touch.

He slides the back of his hand along my thigh and grips under my calf. He lifts my leg, bracing my ankle on his shoulder. My fingers splay on the cold wood floor. Turning his head, he presses his masked mouth to my inner calf, placing soft kisses on my skin as he slides his covered lips to my ankle.

I freeze when he grips my boot.

"Do you dream of us, Sweetheart?" he whispers. His masked face is in profile, and the light behind him filters through just enough, letting me see the outline of a nose. "All of us between your thighs. Your pussy filled with our cum?"

I swallow, chest heaving.

"But you weren't dreaming of us last night, were you?" he asks. "You have bad dreams, don't you?"

My mind trips over his words. They must have watched me on camera when I woke screaming. Did they see me wake, knowing I had a nightmare and still chase me? Still play a game that ended with me on my hands and knees?

I'm not sure how I feel about them knowing I have nightmares. It makes me feel weak. Vulnerable.

I don't like it.

"You know we watch you," he whispers. "Always. Every second of the day, we know where you are."

Fear slithers down my spine. *He knows*. He's just been toying with me.

With his other hand, Viper unlaces my boot, slowly, methodically loosening one lace at a time until I may pass out from the slick feeling moving through my gut. Then he grips the handle of the steak knife, and rips it free with such force I jerk, the cold blade on my stomach slipping upward.

"You and cutlery," he says, placing another gentle kiss on my inner leg. "If you tried to stab one of us with this, you'd only piss us off."

Except I wasn't planning on stabbing. I just wanted to pop a few locks.

"You'd need something sharper. Something that cuts cleaner so you can press it in deeper." Viper reaches around his back and whips his arm out, gripping a small knife. The blade gleams in the faint light spilling from behind him. He flips the blade, and it closes, then he does it again. When he repeats the movement, I realize he's showing me how the blade quickly pops open. How to hold it. That the knife is meant to be held backward, away from the body, the blade extending outward from the palm, the hilt up by the thumb.

He flicks the knife closed, then glides the back of his fingers across my cheek. "Pretty little girls should be scared when they're trapped in a house with men who want to eat them alive."

My pussy flutters.

"If our sweet girl needs to feel safe, take this. I won't tell them our secret, *mo leannan*." He slips the knife in my boot and re-ties the laces. "Put it under your pillow at night. Then maybe when you have another nightmare, you'll know you're armed and can fight."

Viper drops my leg and grabs his knife on my stomach, re-sheathing it as he stands. He doesn't look back as he walks from the room. I watch his solid back as he walks down the hall, then disappears around the corner.

Gathering my dress, I cover my breasts, sitting upright. Viper was the one that felt more dangerous than the others.

He's also just handed me a tiny piece of safety.

Without the other's knowing.

Chapter 23

Delilah

It's been two days since Viper gave me the knife. I practice whipping the blade out, like he showed me, in the bathroom at night when I take a shower. It's taken me several tries, but I can pull it from my boot and have it at the ready pretty fast. More than likely not fast enough, but Viper is right. I feel safer walking around, knowing I have this tiny knife even if I'm inexperienced with using it.

Viper was the last one I would expect to give me a weapon. But then I felt his softness that night in the club. He just chooses when he lets it free. Like Reaper, Viper is cut from something sharp and cruel, but even he carries around softness and I'm reminded again of Reaper's gentle touch followed by his harsh slap.

I know I'm mentally wrecked when I reach between my thighs as I shower to ease the ache there.

This on top of the fact I now look forward to my meals three times a day, though I tell myself it's because I'm lonely, and not because I like sitting on Breaker's lap, feeling his hard length beneath me. How Viper laughs at my snarky commentary, and how Striker's hand caresses my chin, or he brushes his fingers over my lips as he takes a turn feeding me. I think the only reason I have yet to get a fork or feed myself is simply because they like touching me. Feeding me. Taking care of me in this twisted way. Reaper's been absent from each meal these past two days. I haven't seen him since the woods.

You belong to us now. You'll listen to us. Be rewarded by us. Get punished by us.

My belly flutters. I tuck the book in my hand under my arm as I stop in the foyer to shut the front door, noticing when I do, the latch doesn't catch so I have to shove it closed harder like I did the other day. Maybe he's not leaving it open. Maybe the catch is old and worn. It seemed so careless for a man so in control of everything.

As I pass the large windows overlooking the front of the house, I glance out at the bright cloudless sky and the open stretch of lawn leading to the garden. Yesterday, my first day out of the house, I was able to see the scope of the estate, and know running is futile. The mansion sits back from the rocky little cliffs, surrounded on one side by the dense woods that wrap around most of the property, the other a marshy area that looks like it goes on forever.

Even if I tried, I'd never make it through the marsh. The woods, I know from experience, are dense. I have no idea where we are or how many miles separate us from the nearest town.

Leaving here isn't an option.

So I don't even bother thinking about it. Instead, I do my best to keep my mind busy, which is why I'm so grateful for the library. Curling up with a book is a good escape since an actual escape is out of the question.

When I step through the doorway to the library, I freeze, my entire body flushing with heat.

His back is to me, but his mask is off, letting me see black hair. It's shaved at the sides, the top long enough to be slicked back over his head. The long, thick column of his neck reveals black ink vines snaking up out of his tight black shirt, twisting around more flowers, then climbing up toward his skull.

As Reaper covers his head with his mask, adjusting it as he turns around to face me, I notice the small book in his hand. But then his gaze collides with mine, making my toes curl, and my mind blanks.

His black eyes slide down to my lips, then to my boots and back up again. How is it, every time he looks at me, it's like he's seeing parts I didn't know existed. Like the darker part that craves his hands on me. That got soaking wet as he spanked me. As he completely controlled me.

I clear my throat, desperately wanting to run from his intrusive gaze, but I lift my chin and say, "You left the door open again."

He makes a rumbling sound in his chest, running his thumb over the top of the book as he lowers his hand to his side, staring at me with that intense glare. When his eyes snap back to my face, I'm reminded he kidnapped me. Chased me. Held me down and...

My clit throbs.

I need to go home.

I lick my lips, feeling the little cut that lingers, trying to recenter my scrambled brain. "You have to close the door hard for the latch to catch. Or just lock it."

"Look who suddenly wants me to lock doors," he says, walking lazily toward me. My eyes eat him up, his black pants and long sleeve shirt. The way his pants tug at the crotch. The slow, predatory way he moves. God. Everything he does is arrogant. Graceful. Beautiful. He taps the little book to his thigh, drawing my eyes. "Worried you may be tempted to run again?"

I hate that my face turns red, but I refuse to look away and I refuse to be embarrassed about what he drew out of me. It was just my body responding to the adrenaline.

Except I liked it. A bit too much.

My eyes fall to the floor and I focus on why I'm here. The library is full of the classics and I've been reading Jane Austin each night. Taking a deep breath to calm the heat in my cheeks, I set my eyes on the bookshelves lining the walls, refusing to let him rattle me.

"I think you get off on hurting people," I say, walking around him to get to the shelf to return the book I took last night and pick a new one, all too aware of his closeness. He's still several feet away, but even that's not far enough.

He chuckles darkly. "I think you got off, Kitten. Not me."

I turn, my boot catching on the worn wood floor to glare at him, the little knife tucked between the boot and my sock reminding me I can fight back. Fisting my hands, I resist the urge to lunge at him. I want to rip that mask off and shove it in his arrogant mouth because I know he's smirking. Again.

The words nearly spill out in a scream. That he held me down and forced it out of me, but I bite my lip, remembering how I begged him for it.

"I think," he says, creeping closer, moving between me and the door, "That you liked me being rough with you. I think you liked it so much, you want it again. And again."

Ignoring the zing his words send through me, I inch around him so I'm not so trapped, but he darts in front of me, blocking my exit from the room.

"Then maybe even again. And again. There are four of us willing to please."

"Is that what that was?" I ask. "Pleasing me?"

"Oh, Kitten, the moans you made sounded a lot like pleasure."

"More like anger," I snap, my cheeks flaming again. "I never wanted you to touch me. You're a liar. You said you'd not hurt me."

"I lie?" Reaper bolts forward. My back hits the bookshelf as he braces his arms on either side of me, the leather-bound book hitting the shelf next to my head, trapping me.

This is the first I've been this close to him face to face. He's fucking huge. Not just in size, but sheer muscle. Every encounter I've had with him has been at a distance, or from behind me, where I can't fully see him. Feel him, certainly. Even from Breaker's lap I didn't capture his size, but standing in front of him, pinned to the bookcase with his body, his hands at either side of my head, I am fully aware of how huge he is. My head barely reaches his shoulder.

"I'm not the liar," he says. "You begged me to touch you, Kitten. From your hands and knees with your mouth full of dirt, and your cunt soaking wet, you *begged* me. Just like our perfect needy slut you pretend you don't crave to be."

"I don't crave you," I hiss, heart in my throat.

He dips his head, his mouth near my ear. "I can't wait to drown all those pretty lies with my cum."

"Good luck getting your dick past my teeth."

The asshole laughs. He pushes off the bookshelf and backs away. When he's a few feet from me, I take in a shaky breath, hoping he can't see the way my hands shake or how I press my thighs together to relieve the pressure blooming there.

I point to the small leather-bound book in his hand. "So you're a sadist who reads the bible."

His gaze falls to the book like he forgot he was holding it. He doesn't answer. Instead, he opens to the page marked with the ribbon, running one finger down the thin paper, forcing me to remember that same hand trailing between my legs.

I shove the memory away. "Do you read the bible after masturbating and flog yourself as punishment for your sins?"

"If I flogged myself after every sin, my skin would be flayed open and raw, never able to heal." Reaper flips the page, not bothering to look up as he folds himself into a large wingback chair. "And that would be a masochist. They like pain. Sadists inflict."

"So you're just a sadomasochist."

His eyes flicker up to me then back to the bible. "Such a sweet pet name for me, Kitten."

I glower at him. If I could see his mouth, I know I'd catch his lip pulling up into a grin.

"You seemed to enjoy my tendencies every time you've earned them."

I say nothing because we both know he's right.

"My father always said that every man needs God," Reaper says, flipping the page again. "Whether it be to atone for our sins or beg for his forgiveness at the end."

"You chose forgiveness, I see."

I get that glare he's so good at. Then he presses a finger to the page and reads, "'Out of the eater, something to eat; out of the strong, something sweet.'"

"Samson and Delilah," I say, recognizing the quote easily. My mother was obsessed with the story. The day they took us flashes through my mind. "The text." He flips another page, ignoring me. "You sent me the quote from the movie."

He still doesn't answer and I bite my lip, forcing myself not to ask why. Why send me a text message, quoting my mother's favorite movie right before he took us?

Reaper flips to another page like I'm not even in the room.

I take in a breath, all too aware that I have to tread carefully with men like him. "I was named after Delilah."

His black eyes slide up to mine. "You were named after a traitor. Fitting."

"My mother named me after a woman smart enough to take down the world's strongest man."

"With deceit," Reaper says, snapping the bible closed. He stands and stalks across the room, placing it on the shelf with all the other bibles from various religions. I peel my eyes from his ass to his broad shoulders as he says, "And she wasn't powerful. She was resourceful and greedy."

"Sounds like some *men* I know," I snap.

Reaper turns to face me. "Samson possessed physical strength, that's it. He was morally weak, weak minded, and kept secrets."

"Sounds like someone *else* I know."

I swear he's smirking.

"Is that why you hate me?" I ask. "Because you think I'm a traitorous, deceitful woman?"

I can feel his anger from across the room. Reaper stalks forward, and I stumble back, the intense gleam in his eyes putting me on high alert. My back hits the wall and his hand is at my throat, gripping just under my jaw, forcing me to look up at him.

My body arches into him.

I don't know what they're doing to me. I know this is wicked. Wrong. I'm not supposed to want their hands on me. Want them to touch me. Everywhere. Something was created. A rift was torn open, or a change in the tides occurred and we're being swept out to sea, and I don't think any of us can stop it. Or wants to. But something happened that night in the club, then again in the woods between us all, and I know they feel it. He feels it right now.

"I don't hate you, Kitten," he says so softly that my body melts against him.

"You hate my father."

"I hate your father for what he did."

"So, you're punishing him through me?"

"You're his blood."

My mother's words come to mind. *Blood is thicker than water.*

"But I'm not just him," I say. "I'm also my mother."

Darkness clouds his eyes and his grip loosens on my throat, but he doesn't back away. Reaper leans in a little more and I feel his breath against my lips through his mask. "Blood isn't the only substance that creates family."

Cora's face flashes in my mind.

"Loyalty. Love. Sacrifice. Those are what create a family. And the family we choose is more important than the family you're born into. Rune Gavin is a sick man, Delilah." This time, when he says my name, there isn't any hatred. He says it softly. Almost like my name doesn't burn anymore as it slips past his lips. "You think you know your father, you work for him, but you don't know everything about him. You need to choose wisely."

"What did he do to you?" I ask, fully aware that my hands have moved up and my fingers curl into the fabric of his shirt over his chest.

Reaper's thumb sweeps over my bottom lip and I suck in at the feeling of his skin on mine, so wickedly hot it feels like his heat sinks into me, saturating my blood until my heart's pumping lava through my veins.

"He cut away a piece of me," he whispers.

"So you're going to carve me up and send me back to him in pieces."

"Never." His breath fans over my face and he lowers his head until his forehead touches mine. "We told you we'd never hurt you."

"Being away from him hurts." My heart hammers against his and when he moves, I feel his hard length press to my belly, forcing all my senses to focus on every place we connect. A warm breath fans my face, reminding me of summer nights, smokey liquor, and regrets. "You're trying to get revenge on him, but you're just hurting me, and Cora, too."

His breath heaves from his chest, and his body presses harder into me. I look up into those black eyes and for a second I swear I see something resembling tenderness, but then it's gone and when he lowers his masked mouth near mine, his hungry, desperate gaze makes my fingers curl into the muscles of his chest.

Using his free hand, he lifts his mask just barely. My eyes move to his full lips, drinking in the dark stubble on his chin and the two thin lines slashing down his lips like melting claw marks.

He lowers his mouth and presses his lips to mine.

My eyes grow wide, locking on to his. My pussy clenches.

Gently, he sucks my bottom lip, then tugs it with his teeth. A sharp pain cuts through my lip as he sucks harder. Then even harder.

The thin slice where my teeth bit into my lip feels like it splits open again as he sucks even harder, then releases it with a pop. His hot tongue slips over my lip, then slides between my parted lips. Metal and tangy heat touch my tongue. My fingers unfurl. My core tightens.

My hips tilt into him.

He releases a low growl, then sucks my lip in again, tasting my blood before he releases my mouth with a slick *pop*.

My lashes flutter.

"Can you be a good girl for me?" Reaper asks so low I'm not sure he even spoke for a minute, but I feel the movement against my lips, making my lungs feel like they're about to collapse. "Because I don't know how much longer I can refrain from being every nightmare you've ever had."

His breath against my flesh sends a shivering heat to my core. My fingers splay out over his hard chest, greedily slipping down, feeling the thick planes of his body.

Reaper's mask falls, covering his lips. Black eyes burn into me.

And that's when I hear it.

Her sweet laughter rings out from the foyer and I suck in a breath, my chest expanding and nearly collapsing at the same time.

Reaper hears it too and backs away. I shove past him and run toward the door. My boots slip on the wood floor, my heart hammering, as I rush forward, gripping the doorframe to propel myself forward.

When I see her, framed on either side by the men, a sob catches in my throat and she turns at the sound.

"Delly!" she screams, running forward.

We crash together, arms tangling and drop to our knees as I weave my fingers into her soft curls, pressing my face to her neck.

"You're okay," I say over and over, pulling away to look at her face. My hands move all over her as a painful sob creaks from her throat. I feel her chin. Her cheeks and the tears streaming down them. Her pretty lips and her thin arms. I cup her face, running my thumbs over her perfect cheeks, eating up the sight of her.

"Are you hurt?" I ask, barely able to contain the joy bursting through my chest.

Cora shakes her head, curls falling around her shoulders. "I'm fine. Worried sick about you, but I'm fine." She wraps me in a hug, burying her face in my neck. "Oh god, Delly. You're real, right? You're here?"

I pull her back. "I'm here." I press my lips to her cheek. "I'm here and you're okay."

A fresh sob escapes and I realize it's me. My entire body shakes, trembling as I clutch at her, then press her to me. I'm suddenly aware of everything around us. Her delicate tears, her body molded to mine. Her fingers in my hair. The men before us, Reaper at my back. How her tears feel so warm as I kiss her cheeks again. The terrible aching desperation coursing through me. The need to have her close. Feel her against me. Her realness. Make her feel safe ,and me, too.

I want to absorb her. Mold her to my body and never let her go, so she's never away from me again.

"Delly," my name is a whisper and I nod, knowing she feels this terrible ache too. "Oh god," she chokes out, weaving her fingers into my hair and pulling me close. Her lips press to mine.

My whole body melts. I wrap my arms around her neck and pull her closer, sitting upright to press my chest to hers. She whimpers, angling her head and parting her lips. I sweep my tongue into her mouth, devouring her. Wanting to consume her until she's a part of me and I can't lose her again.

We calm down after a minute and pull away, our breaths ragged.

Her green eyes lift, and I remember Reaper behind me. "Please don't take her again."

My gaze darts to Striker at her back, then Viper and Breaker. They wouldn't dare. A wild rage crashes through me at the thought they may try to take her from me. I'll fucking make them bleed. But they say nothing and back away, leaving us alone.

As Reaper passes by, following them, his hand slides over the top of my head and I feel like I was just given a gift.

And I was.

I got Cora.

And I was given another moment of his gentleness.

Chapter 24

STRIKER

Delilah's sobs wrack her body as she clings desperately to Cora, burying her face in the crook of her neck. A painful, searing ache twists my heart, knowing all too well the pain of missing someone so deeply that it feels like a piece of you has been ripped away. It's like walking through life with an open wound, always throbbing with pain.

I'll never know what it feels like to have that part of me back.

None of us will.

"Delly," Cora whispers, running her fingers through our Princess's hair repeatedly. When her lips press to Delilah's, both women still, hands clutching at one another. Then lips part on an exhale. Delilah's eyes squeeze shut tighter, another tear slipping past. Her fingers tighten on Cora, then suddenly her arms wrap around her and they crash together.

A sharp intake of breath pulls past my lips, taken aback by their explosive reaction. My eyes flicker up to Reaper. He's watching them intently, yet doesn't seem surprised. Even though the mask hides his face from me, I know every detail of his features as if they were my own, and I can picture the stern set of his jaw and the way the muscles in his neck stand out as he clenches his teeth. I can picture his face now and know that he guessed they'd react this way upon being reunited.

Delilah lets out a soft whimper, reminding me of the night in the woods. My heart thunders, watching as the kiss deepens. Turns feral and desperate. Viper shifts next to me and our arms brush. A bolt of awareness shoots straight to my cock.

I close my eyes briefly, trying to calm the thoughts swirling through my head. Of us together again, but this time Delilah and Cora kissing like they are now. Not holding back, not exploring, but desperate for one another.

They break the kiss and stark blue eyes flash up to mine. The lust mixed with fear makes my stomach fall.

As Reaper's fingers slip over her hair, our eyes lock. I see it then. Understanding floods me as I rip my gaze from him, looking back at the girls as I back away and follow my brother's to the back of the house.

He doesn't have to say it. I get it now and I wonder if Breaker and Viper do too.

STRIKER

***

I shove my hands deep into the pockets of my jacket, tucking my chin into the collar. It's cold today, the wind cutting over the path and slicing through my mask. My boots kick the little rocks along the path as I walk to the old carriage-house, where we keep most of our training equipment. Viper wants to turn it into a full gym eventually, which we should have done before coming here. If we're not careful, we're going to get soft from sitting idle.

As I enter, Reaper looks up from the bench, but continues to curl weights when he sees it's just me and not one of the girls. Over on the second bench, Viper's laid back, legs bracketing either side, head under the bar, holding his phone. He glances my way, but goes back to scrolling, no doubt breaking Reaper's no social media rule and watching videos.

"Breaker on watch?" Reaper asks, continuing with his set.

I nod when he looks up at me.

"What were they doing when you left?" Viper asks, tucking his phone into his pocket and reaching for his shirt. My eyes slip up his torso as he stands, landing on the tattoo spread out over his chest. He's built similar to Reaper, but compact. Raw power wrapped in fair skin.

"Huddled together whispering," I tell him.

"Where?" he asks.

I rip my eyes from his zipper, catching his lifted brow. "In Delilah's room."

Viper adjusts his shirt around his waist after he pulls it on. I don't know what the fuck is wrong with me today, but everything he does draws my eye. He snatches up his mask and walks to the door. There's no need to tell us where he's going. We already know.

When the door behind me shuts, I pull off my mask, tucking it into my jacket pocket. "Why?" I ask.

The air's cool in here, but Reaper's bare chest gleams with sweat. He stands up, lifting the gold chain around his neck as he rolls his shoulders. Reaper rocks his head from side to side, loosening the large muscles. His abs ripple, each muscle outlined like an artist drew them, the many tattoos only accentuating the lines of his body.

My gaze lifts and I find his dark eyes watching me watch him. Can he blame me? I don't think there is a single human alive who'd not stare. He's male perfection. I'd have to be dead not to notice him. And it's not like I haven't seen him watching me. Fuck, he stood in the doorway just over a week ago watching me jerk off after the night with the girls.

His onyx gaze feels like it penetrates under my skin, letting him see all the secrets I keep hidden, and for a second, I think he likes what he sees, but he looks away. Maybe he doesn't like whatever he saw mirrored back at him.

"You know why," Reaper says. "They'd have spent the last week plotting to escape if they'd been together."

"That's not what I mean and you know it," I say, following him to the row of shelves where he's left his mask and shirt.

"Why what, Strike? Why take them?"

"Why fuck them before we took them? Why Cora?"

He keeps his back to me, grabbing his water bottle off the shelf and uncapping it. He brings it to his lips but doesn't drink.

I watch his profile as he turns his head slightly. "Why did you want to fuck them in *Rune's* club? There's a reason, a fucking *plan*, behind everything you do. You can't even take a piss without planning it in advance. So explain."

He recaps the bottle and sets it down, grabbing the towel and facing me. "The cameras."

My brows knit.

"What's the first thing you'd do after your loved one was taken from you?" Reaper wipes his chest with a towel. I shift my focus to the stack of weights by his side. "He would retrace their every step leading right up to the moment we took them."

The cameras. Rune would have immediately requested footage of Delilah and Cora in his club. He'd see us take his daughter and Cora into that VIP lounge and stay there. For hours. He'd lose his mind knowing we were all in there fucking his two girls.

We walked right into his club, wearing the same uniforms and instead of stealing them then, we fucking claimed them right under his nose.

"That's the only reason?" I ask, lifting a brow.

Reaper isn't one to run, much less back down, but his eyes drop from my face.

I step closer, forcing him to look at me and acknowledge what I'm saying. He got a taste of Delilah before we ruin her, while she was still innocent. Before she finds out the truth. "Or did you want to know what she felt like before she hated you?"

He doesn't answer, but he doesn't have to.

"Cora," I say. His black eyes dart back to my face. "Why did you insist on Cora?"

I already know why, but I want him to say it. Reaper is a cunning, ruthless killer on his worst day. A manipulative asshole on his best. But he's a fucking liar every day and I'm sick of sitting stagnant while he lies to us and himself.

His jaw pops as he grinds his teeth.

Yeah. I'm going to make you say it out loud.

He pulls his shirt over his head, looking out the grimy window over my shoulder as he tugs the shirt down over his stomach. The silence stretches between us until it snaps and he grabs his mask, hitting the row of weights as he does. They click loudly. His gaze locks on mine. He squares his shoulders like he's preparing himself for his next few words, running his tongue over the thin scars on his bottom lip. "Imagine having your most valued possession taken from you."

My jaw tightens, breath sticking in my throat. I don't have to imagine. Neither one of us does.

"Then, suddenly, it's back," he says. "You can hold it, look at it. What would you do to keep that important thing from ever leaving you again?"

I press my eyes closed, my teeth grinding together like this will stop the stabbing pain from cutting through my chest and clawing up my throat. "I'd do anything."

"Exactly," Reaper says. "Delilah will do anything now."

I shake my head, eyes popping open. I open my mouth to remind him that when he kept them apart for so many days, he created that same scared feeling within them, but I shut my mouth. Princess knew Cora was safe, just as Cora knew Princess was safe. We made damn sure of it.

Maybe he took Cora for this reason. Delilah will more than likely be a little careful with her actions now out of fear, but it's more than that and we *all* know it.

"Why Reap? The fucking truth. Why did you take Cora?"

His hands flex at his sides. "You *know* why."

None of us want to say what we fear, but Reaper's refusing to acknowledge why *he* wanted Cora.

I had thought at first he wanted Cora because we were all so taken with her. That taking her would hurt Rune a bit more, but it's more than that. Reaper wanted Cora not just for us to do with as we please like we've been ordered to do with Delilah, not entirely.

We watched them for so long we all know the unbreakable bond the women share. They'll do anything to protect one another from being hurt. And maybe having them apart has made our lives easier as well as made them a tad more cooperative, but the real reason is he didn't want them to suffer like we did.

He didn't want Delilah alone without the only person who makes her feel loved and safe.

He didn't want Cora's *person* ripped from her.

"You wanted Cora for *her*," I say. "For Delilah. So she'd have her most loved possession. And so Cora wouldn't be scared, left alone, losing sleep, wondering what was happening to her best friend."

He doesn't deny it as he slips his mask over his head and brushes past me hard enough that I stumble back.

"Admit it," I call after him. "You care and you feel *guilty*. If you just fucking admit it, then maybe you—"

The door slams so hard the glass pane rattles. Through the window I watch his black clad form as he stalks back to the house.

I don't know how much longer he can keep denying his obsession with them. *Her*. With this need for revenge on something that is *all* our faults, not just Rune's. It's ripping him in two, making him volatile.

He disappears down the drive and I'm left standing in our homemade gym, wondering when the house of lies he built around his own self deception crumbles, if we're all going to go down with him.

Chapter 25

Delilah

"You had heat?" I ask, tucking the blankets up around my chin. Even though the room is now warmer, there's still a bite in the air. We went to my room after the men left, and have been here ever since, under the blankets, talking about what we endured over the last nine days.

"They kept the fire going for me most nights," Cora says, "But the radiator worked just fine."

Something ugly and green coils like rotten vines in my stomach. Cora, it seems, has been perfectly fine. She even gets to feed herself. Guess she didn't try to stab them with a fork.

"They even got the shampoo right," she says. Her eyes move down to the front of my dress. "And our clothing sizes."

I didn't dwell too much on those details. I figured they have been watching us for a while, planning to take us for some time. It was the fact that they gave us things that made us comfortable that disturbed me the most.

She swipes her thumb over my cheek in a way that heats between my thighs.

"If I had to endure another card game with Viper, I was going to scream," she says, smiling at me so brightly, I tuck my response behind my teeth and don't tell her we never played cards. I was freezing, scared. Lonely.

Although I'm glad she wasn't those things, I still can't help my jealousy that they treated her so differently. I don't understand why, but then she's always been treated sweetly. My father dotes on her, always kissing her cheek, or petting her head like she's a prized pet. Clyde too. He's crazy about her.

They've treated me so differently from her over the years, and as we got older it became clear, they expected me to be harder. Like Rune. Cora's soft light and sweet candy. I'm supposed to be hard stone, unbreakable. Unmoveable.

I wasn't even allowed to mourn my mother. Instead, I was dragged to my feet, my hands still sticky with her blood and told to stop crying.

"Delly?"

My eyes find Cora's.

Her brows knit. "Did Reaper take you outside? For walks?"

My stomach sinks. No. Not fucking walks. No niceness from any of them.

I wonder…

"Did Reaper…." I bite my lip. Not sure how to phrase the question.

"I've barely seen him," she says, her cheeks turning pink. "It's mostly Breaker and Viper and sometimes Striker."

Satisfaction curls in my stomach, but then my gaze lands on the large, black jacket she was carrying, and I wonder which man gave it to her. That slick, gross feeling slips through me again, wishing they'd been nice to me too.

I don't understand why they hate me so much. Why they've left me alone. Why they're treating her so differently.

"I kind of like not having to go to work." She grins. "Or sit in another meeting."

A chuckle slips out at her delighted smile. I smirk. "Or spend so much energy avoiding Zane."

Her laughter loosens something in my chest. I don't miss those things, but I do miss home.

"I'm so glad to see you," Cora says, inching closer. Her toes hit my shin the same moment her thumb traces the cut on my lip. "Why do you think they kept us apart for so long?"

I have asked myself that same question so many times and the only answer I can come up with is, "Control."

Her brows knit, but she nods, understanding. We were easier to control because we were separated.

"Daddy will get us. And Clyde," I tell her, brushing a fiery ringlet from her face. A dark shadow passes over her features. "They will Cora. They'll figure out where we are and come for us."

She nods, but remains silent. When her eyes meet mine, they're filled with tears. "They aren't bad, Delly."

"Who?"

"Them."

Them. Our captors.

"They took us, Cora. They killed Manuel," I whisper, reaching for her hand under the sheets.

She grips mine and scoots closer. "I know they did, but I think Papa did something terrible to them."

He took something from me.

"It's the business, Cora," I say. "You know Daddy and Clyde do what they have to do."

Cora shakes her head. "Most things, though, they don't *have* to do. They *choose* to."

I flip over onto my back, and she slides over, tucking herself against me, resting her head on my shoulder.

"Go to sleep," I whisper, wondering if they'll come get us for breakfast in the morning.

We haven't seen them in hours, and they never came to get us for dinner. I close my eyes, imagining Reaper's black hair and solid body. The brush of his hand over my hair. The feel of his lips on mine. Hard and soft. Pain and pleasure. Striker's warm brown eyes and the way he watches me. Breaker's laughter whenever I make a snarky comment. Viper's slightly feral energy.

They aren't bad. Not entirely.

They aren't good either.

***

Cora's whimper drags me from sleep. I blink at the bright lamplight she insists stays on, and I roll over to find her curled into a ball. Gripping her shoulder, I shake her, but she doesn't wake.

The nightmares began when she was around six. We grew up together, our parents' best friends and business partners, before my father became well known in his circle. After they died and Cora came to live with us, it was usually me who woke her from the nightmares. I'd shake her awake, then climb into bed with her afterwards, holding her as she cried.

She never told me what they were about, just that she dreamed of darkness, and I wonder if anyone held her or woke her up in the last few days. I hope they did.

"Cora," I whisper, trying to ease her out of the dream. Her eyes pop open and a burst of air escapes her lungs. "You're okay," I tell her, brushing hair from her face. "You're with me."

A tear slips from her eye and she flings an arm around my neck and buries her face in my chest, tucking her head under my chin. My heart twists painfully. I hate that she's been so scared. Hate that she has nightmares, and is suffering because this entire situation feels like my fault. I wanted the wild night. I wanted to feel free. I wanted to feel sexy, adventurous, everything my stupid ex never saw me as. It's my father they want revenge on.

"I'm sorry," I say into her hair. "This is all my fault." I feel her shake her head under my chin.

She backs away and tilts her face up, her mouth a breath away from mine as she rests her head on the pillow by me. "This is Rune's fault. He did something terrible. I just know it." Her eyes drop to my mouth. "He's not what you think he is."

An uneasy feeling slithers through my belly. That's exactly what Striker said.

"If Rune Gavin is bad, then so am I," I say, remembering Reaper's words. I'm Rune's blood. He's taught me everything I know. I willingly work for him, for his company. We both do, Cora and I. We cover up whatever he's doing with numbers and lies. He could be selling drugs for all I know. Feeding heroine to mothers and fathers, someone's sister or brother. And I *help* him.

Even though I don't know where his money comes from, Cora and I both know it's from criminal activity. Buying an entire hotel chain cost a hefty sum, but the excess....

I don't ask. I see numbers and hide the figures so the IRS doesn't investigate. When he is granted an enormous sum, like he is once a year, millions that come from nowhere, I have to set up channels to hide it. Cora and I are experts at hiding the money trail, tying them up in real estate sales for exorbitant amounts and over priced hotel fees. Luxury expenses or his favorite—his lodge membership fees.

"Delly," she whispers, bringing my thoughts back to her. Her leg slides over mine, and she hitches it up to my hip, wrapping her thigh over mine and using it to pull me close. "You're nothing like him."

"What's that supposed to mean?"

She shakes her head, scooting even closer so my hand is trapped between our bodies. I'm aware of her nearness and the thin satin of her nightgown. Of her warm skin and how the silky material has slipped up and heat radiates from between her legs. Her green eyes move over my face, then drop again to my lips.

"I missed you," she says, lifting a finger to run it over my lips.

My mind flashes on her mouth pressed to mine, the desperation coursing through me into her. Or maybe it was the other way around. Maybe she fed it to me and I ate every ounce, grateful to have her near me again.

Cora's thumb presses into the center of my lips and I brush the finger on the hand between us along her belly. She makes this tiny sound and tilts her hips. I do it again. She slides her hands into my hair, cupping the back of my neck, inhaling slowly, watching my eyes. Our noses brush and we keep our eyes open as our lips touch. Breaths slip out in a heated rush. I pull my other hand from under the blankets and drag it over her bare arm, letting it slide down further. Over her hip, along her outer thigh. Lower.

Cora's eyelids flutter as I brush my knuckles to her inner thigh. Her breaths hitch delicately when I slide my hand up and feel the heat of her skin.

Our lips press harder together as my thumb glides over her panties, feeling her clit. She releases a little moan and then her hands are moving, and she's rising over me. Pushing me onto my back, capturing my lips in a harsh kiss. Slipping her tongue into my mouth and groaning as she dips it deeper. Toothpaste and sweetness floods my tongue. Something delicate and desperate. As the blankets are tossed aside, she straddles my hips, and my fingers slip under the material of her panties into her wet heat. Our kiss breaks on a gasp and her head's thrown back, the fragile lines of her neck shadowed in the tungsten light and then she's riding my hand.

For a millisecond, I marvel at her tightness. How wet she feels, how slick and delicious my fingers feel slipping in and out as my thumb drags wetness over her sensitive little bud. How she feels like me, all slick and soft and greedy.

"Oh fuck," she whispers, grinding down. "I need you."

My belly flutters. My pussy clenches. An ache deep in my core grates inside against my spine.

With my hand still inside her, she props herself on hands and knees, back arching into my touch like a cat when my thumb rubs harshly into her clit.

"Lift your hips," she whispers, and I immediately obey.

She gathers my nightgown and tugs it until my breasts are exposed. When she captures a hardened nipple between her teeth, I cry out, driving my fingers deeper into her. When she slips my underwear down enough to press her mouth to my lower belly, I gasp. Hot lips trail kisses down to the thin line of hair and she places another soft kiss there.

"Cora," I whimper, my thighs parting, legs falling open. Her fingers dip under my panties, cupping me, then she slides two in to me roughly, her thumb skimming my clit, fucking me with her hand like I am her.

"Ah fuck," she hisses as I pick up speed. Sloppy wet sounds fill the room, both of us fucking each other with a frenzied rush.

Pleasure builds quickly, too quickly, and then erupts from me with a gasp. She follows behind me, her forehead falling to my chest.

We stay like that for a minute, fingers still inside one another, catching our breath. When I pull my hand away, she does the same and sits upright, looking down at the slickness coating her fingers. Green eyes flicker up to mine, then dart away.

I open my mouth to say something, but nothing comes out. Cora glances down again at her hand, then slips off the bed until she's standing next to me, eyes dark, lost. Worried. Before I can tell her, we're both freaked out and scared and confused. I love her. Nothing's changed. That we're okay. She rushes to the bathroom and shuts the door.

Adjusting my nightgown to cover myself, I sit up and stand, walking to the window. My forehead presses to the glass. Something strange roils in my belly, making my chest hurt, but I'm not sure what I'm feeling. We kissed the night we were with them. I watched her get railed by Breaker. She put her hands on me that night but this....

This was just us.

I roll around, keeping my head to the glass and groan. When my eyes dart up, I see the little black hole where the tiny camera's tucked in the crown molding and I remember.

They are watching.

Always.

Heat travels to between my legs, making me jitter with desire. I must be coming unglued if the thought of them watching us turns me on. Grasping my nightgown at the hem, I pull it over my head and let it drop to the floor. My heart flutters, but I set my eyes on the bathroom door.

When I knock, Cora opens it a crack and I see her red eyes and tears on her cheeks, but when she sees me naked, the green flares brightly.

"Come to bed," I say, pushing the door open. I grip her wrist and tug her forward. "You're not allowed to hide from me. You're going to talk to me."

"Okay," she says, allowing me to pull her out of the bathroom.

We stop at the end of the bed and her eyes move up and down my body. Drinking in my curves like I've never seen before. We've seen each other naked plenty of times, but this look she's giving me is different.

It reminds me of the men downstairs. Almost predatory with its hunger.

"I liked what we did with them. When you touched me," I say, my belly dipping from my confession. I never thought I'd say it out loud, but we're not under normal circumstances. "I like kissing you. I loved what we did just now."

She bites her bottom lip, meeting my eyes. "Me too."

"Then why are you crying?"

"I don't know," she says, but looks away, like she does when she's lying or hiding things from me.

I grip the hem of her nightgown. "Take this off."

Her gaze collides with mine. She sucks her bottom lip between her teeth. I want to suck on her lip. Taste her again. The need to do just that makes my movements jerky, but she lets me slip her nightgown over her head, breaths heavier, chest heaving, nipples pebbling.

She's so fucking beautiful. Fair skin with pale freckles along her shoulders and chest. Large breasts that I cup, pinching perfect rosy nipples. Her throat moves as she swallows, then she moans, back arching into my hands. She's removed all the hair between her legs and I can see the pink slit and her clit.

God. It's no wonder men go crazy around her. She's perfect and so pretty it makes my chest ache.

"Lie down and spread your legs," I whisper, gently pushing her down to the bed. She complies as I crawl over her. When she's flat on her back, legs spread wide, I lean in and whisper, "They're watching you."

I realized the other night why they took us. My father has been possessive of me my entire life, never allowing any man to touch me. What better way to get revenge on him than take his two most precious jewels and tarnish them? He has no idea if we're being raped. Being tortured. The not knowing would be enough to force him to do whatever it is they want.

Funny thing though. I think these men are better than that. They may have sexual preferences that are outside the norm, but they certainly aren't violent predators. At least, not with Cora and me. They've proven it every day we've been here. At any point in time, they could have forced themselves on me, or abused me in ways I probably can't imagine. They may be a tad perverse by some standards, but it seems I am as well.

I spread my legs willingly for them, my pussy wet, with my face in the dirt.

Cora's jade eyes dart to the camera. I see the thought spark in her eyes and she grins and whispers back, "Then let's make them regret it."

Chapter 26

STRIKER

15 Years Ago, July, Age 15

It's too hot to be out in the yard, but Reaper insists they need to train more. They only have a few weeks before they leave, so it's understandable he wants them to be prepared. It'll improve their chances of survival. At least for two of them.

This last year has been harder than the previous and several of our brothers haven't made the cut. Fallon's training has taken a dark turn and we're all on edge, so tired by the time we're allowed to sleep that we're out as soon as our heads hit the pillow. Reaper and Hunter and our two other remaining brothers have had it worse. They only have a month before the final test.

They have to prove themselves in the wilderness.

Hunter nudges my shoulder with his, forcing me to tear my eyes from the circle. "Ready to get your ass kicked, shrimp?"

I dig my elbow into his ribs. I'm far from a shrimp. I grew almost three inches this past year and am now an inch taller than Viper, though Fallon keeps saying only Breaker will manage to get as tall as Reaper and Hunter.

"I'm ready to kick your ass," I tell him, returning my gaze to the circle where Reaper fights with Seeker one on one.

Hand to hand combat training is my least favorite, although I am good at it. I'm fast and have even taken Viper down several times.

"Bet you can't take him down." Hunter points to Raid. My eyes move to the large boy sitting on the bleachers at the back of the yard, his blonde hair shaved, gleaming like rabbit fur in the sunlight.

I don't really know him well. He's older, closer to Hunter and Reaper's age, quiet and sits alone a lot, not interacting with us much. Raid never has. He is fast though and stupid strong, with a mean streak that makes Viper seem sweet.

I glance at Hunter. "You know damn well you and Reap are the only ones who *may* be able to take him down. And that's a big maybe."

He winks. "Wanna make a bet?"

I shake my head. "No. You'll lose and look like an asshole with a broken nose in front of everyone."

Hunter's laughter makes my stomach flicker weirdly.

"How about this," he says, turning to face me. His lip curls into a grin as he looks down at me. "If I win, you have to give me your lunch for a week. If he takes me down to the dirt, I'll give you my lunch."

"I don't want your lunch." And I don't want him in the circle with Raid. He turns vicious the second he enters the circle. That's why no one wants to train with him. As big as Hunter is, he's still not as largely built as Raid.

Hunter grips me by the back of my neck. My breathing stops as he squeezes. When he lets me go, he steps forward and points at Raid. "You!" he calls.

Raid's gaze lifts from the circle and lands on Hunter as he approaches. My gut twists when he stops next to the bleachers, and he braces a black boot on the bottom step. I can't hear them, but I see Raid's gaze move from Hunter to the circle.

Reaper and Seeker have stopped sparring and stand with arms crossed listening to whatever Hunter's saying.

Idiot. He's going to get the shit beaten out of him.

Raid stands and stretches, muscles flexing in his chest. Hunter is solid, broad chested, and muscular, but he's got nothing on Raid. Fallon always says Hunter and Reaper are going to be his largest, meanest sons when they're full adults. It's easy to see why, but they're only nineteen.

"Is he crazy?" I turn just as Viper comes up to stand next to me. His auburn hair looks streaked with red in the afternoon light. He doesn't shave his head like Reaper and Hunter and keeps it a little too long. The others tease him, saying he has hair like a girl, but I like it. It reminds me of burning embers or a waterfall of fire curling around his ears. His eyes meet mine. "He's going to get his ass kicked and Reap will have to save him."

Taking a deep breath, I face the circle again, dread climbing up my arms as Hunter and Raid enter the walled-in pit. It rained last night, so it's just mud now, but usually the circle is hard packed dirt that hurts like hell when you land. At least when Raid drops Hunter, the mud will help break his fall.

"Fucking dumbass," Viper says. He sounds like Cook, cursing every chance he gets whenever Father isn't around.

Reaper shakes his head, but hops out of the pit, casting a warning look over his shoulder at Hunter as he walks toward us. If Raid doesn't take him down, Reaper may.

"Reap's pissed," Viper says. "It's a dumb move. They only have a month before the final test and Fallon won't care if he has a broken arm. He'll still make him go."

I nod, catching sight of Breaker entering the yard from our sleeping quarters. Viper waves him over.

"Does he have a death wish?" Breaker asks when he stops next to Viper.

"He's just trying to show off." Viper glances at me, then says to Breaker, "You know he's always trying to get *someone's* attention."

My jaw tightens, my gaze dropping to my boots. I feel my cheeks warm, but I don't want them to notice.

"Leave him alone," Reaper says, catching my expression when he stops next to me and turns to face the circle. "Hunter's ego is bigger than the whole yard. He wants to impress *everyone*."

Viper smirks. "And one person in particular."

A muffled grunt grabs our attention and I look up in time to see Hunter land a punch to Raid's jaw. Wincing, I cross my arms, hope curling in my gut that maybe this will end quickly, before Raid can land too many hits.

Lunging forward, and dipping low, Hunter hooks an arm around Raid's thigh and uses his shoulder to help lift. Raid falls backward and hits the mud with a thud. Dark water splashes up and sprays across Hunter's gray shirt like a smattering of blood. Raid's guttural scream of rage makes my blood freeze. Before Hunter can complete the move, Raid swings his leg, forcing Hunter to lose his grip.

"Shit," Reaper says, already moving forward.

Raid twists from Hunter's grasp and changes positions, hooking him around his waist, bringing both men to their knees. Like he already knows what Raid's trying to do, Hunter releases him and attempts to hook him around his neck. Raid anticipates his movements and grabs Hunter with both arms and lifts. Hunter's feet leave the mud as Raid stands, bringing Hunter up higher and higher.

Then I watch, air leaving my lungs, as he slams him down. Hunter hits the mud with a sickening smack that sends pain through my teeth like it was me hitting the ground. The hiss of pain that leaves him as his head lands makes my eyes blur, then sharpens to focus as red colors the world around me.

The world seems to fade, all color bleeding away until it's just hazy scarlet with Raid in the center. I feel my feet moving. Feel my hands reaching for my belt. Feel the cold metal buckle against my fingers. Hear the leather hissing as it slips from the belt loops. How my boots squelch in the mud as I stalk forward. But then all this noise gets drowned out by the *thump, thump, thump* of my heart beating in my chest, pounding like war drums.

Smooth leather wraps around my hand as I wind the belt over and over, until I know it's the perfect length, the metal buckle dangling from the end. The muscles in my shoulder and arm stretch and ache as I pull back, then release violently as I slam the leather down. The metal hits with a vicious *thwack* and a guttural scream breaks through the sound in my head.

The world snaps back into focus, everything around me vividly outlined. Reaper's on one side, Viper on my other. Breaker at my back.

I do it again, feeling the hit reverberate up my arm. When I release the belt again, a slick satisfaction curls in my gut. Then again, not caring that I recognize the sickening screams as a boy's skin slices open.

Not caring that it's me causing the pain this time.

I want to hurt him.

He hurt Hunter.

My chest heaves, breaths bursting from me almost painfully. The belt lands again, then again and again and there's a part of me that's surprised no one is stopping me. That I'm not stopping myself.

I could if I wanted to.

But I don't.

When it lands again, Raid whimpers, and it jolts through me like a bolt of lightning.

"Striker." Reaper's voice blends in with the whimpers for a second, but I drop my arm, letting the belt uncoil and fall to the mud. "He's had enough."

"Has he?" I ask, turning my head to look at Reaper by my side. "Has he learned his lesson?"

"Please," Raid says, his voice hoarse from screaming. He touches the thin red lines on his cheek, bruises already forming under swollen skin.

"Ah, fuck," Hunter says, sitting up. Mud smears his cheeks and lumps in his hair. His dark eyes meet mine and teeth flash as he smiles. "You're a crazy son of a bitch, Strike."

My heart stutters at seeing his smile. Seeing him sitting up, then pulling himself to his feet.

I glare at him, anger making my stomach roil. "You owe me lunch."

His laughter cuts through me sharply, but my shoulders ease when he hooks an arm around my neck, pulling me to him. We both watch Reaper offer a hand to Raid. He refuses and staggers to his feet, boots sloshing in the mud. He casts me a lethal glare.

"You're lucky Strike here has a good hold on his temper," Hunter says to Raid.

Viper's chuckle breaks through the tension as Raid storms from the yard.

Hunter releases me and grips my shoulders, turning me to face him. I suddenly feel more like myself again. That surge of electric rage fleeing me when his midnight eyes fall to my lips.

"I told you I'd take him down," Hunter says, that smirk returning.

"He fucking nearly cracked your skull," I snap, my heart picking up pace all over again.

"Sometimes I forget you're just a boy," he says, hands slipping up the sides of my neck.

And sometimes I forget he's supposed to be my brother.

Chapter 27

STRIKER

They're teasing us.

They have to be.

"Can you imagine being able to get off like that?" Viper asks, gripping his dick as he leans in and watches the camera. "Consecutively? One right after another?"

I'd feel like we were being invasive, hovering around the monitors with arms crossed, watching them, but they know we can see them. They know we're keeping tabs on them via the many cameras around the mansion. So right now, they're both well aware we're somewhere, watching as Cora spreads Delilah's legs and slides a finger into our Princess.

For the third time this morning.

They spent most of yesterday and all morning in bed, petting each other. I'm not sure what happened between them last night, but whatever it was has led to this. Maybe acceptance or a way to cope with their situation. Possibly a silent agreement to make us all pay for keeping them hostage. For... God I don't fucking know what, but if they keep it up, I don't know how much longer Viper is going to last before he stalks in there and demands he be allowed to join them.

Hell, I don't know how much longer *I'm* going to last before I go in there and force Cora's face between Delilah's thighs until she comes all over her mouth the way she should be.

Considering what we'd like to do to them, their little make-out sessions are tame. Kissing, nibbling of hard, rosy nipples. Fingers sliding into each other, rubbing over their pink cunts. It's innocent and sweet compared to what we'd do to them if we lost control. It wouldn't be this light petting. No delicate little cries. Delilah loves it rough. Hard. I've heard her scream out her release so loud it was like we were tearing apart a wild animal.

Cora's sweet laugh rings out, bringing me back from that night, as Delilah arches her back, squeezing her eyes closed and comes, gripping Cora's wrist to make her stop.

"Do you think a man can die from having a constant hard-on?" Viper asks Breaker.

"You got off this morning, asshole," Breaker says.

"Not with that wet cunt," Viper says, pointing to the screen. He moans and leans back on his heels.

I glance at Breaker, catching his scowl before it evens out, and he focuses back to the screen. Maybe Breaker helped him. *Fuck*, that thought makes my dick even harder.

"Seems she's right," Reaper says from behind us.

We all turn, stepping away from the screens, guiltily.

"About what?" Viper asks, glancing back at the girls. They're both up, pulling on dresses and socks.

Reaper enters the room, mask in hand, and leans on the desk, face illuminated by the glow of the monitors. "About you three being perverts."

"Us?" Viper laughs. He points to the screen. "Those two just performed for us."

"Wait. Us *three*?" Breaker asks, grabbing his mask from the pile on the desk. "You're worse than the three of us combined."

Reaper pushes off the desk, standing upright. His lip curls into a wicked grin. "Never said I wasn't."

Viper picks up his mask and slips it over his head. "Come on. It's time for breakfast."

***

We find the girls out in the garden at the front of the house, both women bundled up in thick sweaters, their little feet tucked into the leather boots we provided for each of them. When Cora spies the three of us, she leans in and says something to Delilah, who spins, a little frown turning her pretty lips down.

STRIKER

Our boots crunch on the white marble chips of the paths we restored last month, the four of us headed toward them in a line. Slowly, we've been renovating the mansion. Viper has been adamant about getting the house in shape, putting in most of the work himself. He has this dream of it being a home. An actual home. Something we've never had. We've only ever lived in hotels or short-term rentals after the school, as we moved from job to job. Nothing permanent. Nothing like what he envisions for us when we complete this mission.

Except, I don't know when or how this one will end.

"Feeding time?" Delilah asks as we surround them. "Come to gather the livestock?"

Cora saunters over to Breaker and Viper. Both men watch her with wolfish intensity. Before she can make a sassy comment or tease Viper more than she already has, I grip Cora's arm and jerk her toward me. She gives out a little squeak of surprise and Breaker's glare should unnerve me, but this is getting out of hand. We're losing control and not only of ourselves, but of them. We've been too scared to hurt Cora more than life already has, that we've been too delicate with her. Because of that, she thinks she can sass us left and right and get away with it.

"Where are you taking her?" Delilah's panicked cry almost makes me let Cora go, but I remember we've been too soft on them. When I don't answer, she marches forward, placing her hand on my chest to stop me from moving. The look I give her makes it drop.

I grip her by the nape of her neck and pull her to me, pushing both girls ahead as I walk them back toward the house.

Viper laughs. "There's the Striker I know."

Neither woman says a single word as I march them through the house and into the dining room where their food sits waiting. Viper darts forward and grabs the chair in front of Cora's plate, pulling it out. I deposit Cora into her seat, then grab the chair across from her, waiting for Breaker to sit before slamming Delilah down into his lap. She grips the table and stares up at me with big blue eyes, like she doesn't know who I am.

Seems she forgot.

I think I did too. We're all so wrapped up in them, in this mission that feels like it's going off the rails as each day passes, I think we're all forgetting our roles.

We took them for revenge.

We control *them*. Not the other way around.

"What a strange form of foreplay," Cora says, scooting her chair closer to the table, her eyes sliding up and down my body with open appreciation.

I exhale an exasperated breath.

"I thought you remembered how rough we play, Baby Girl," Reaper says, dragging Delilah's tray toward him.

"You boys know we like it rough." She winks at me. "I just didn't know Strikey-boy was into domination."

"He's into more than domination," Viper says. His eyes slip over me, making me wonder what he's picturing, that he's giving me such a... *heated* look.

I rip my gaze away, ignoring how that look made my cock thicken and say to Cora, "I'm sure Princess can tell you we're all into unusual forms of foreplay."

Delilah's cheeks turn beet red, but then Reaper shoves a bite of food past her lips and her embarrassment turns to anger, eyes flashing with irritation.

When we do this, he always starts out this way. Like he can't stand the sight of her, but then after a few bites, his movements soften.

"Um, yeah," Cora says, sandwich paused halfway to her mouth as she watches Reaper break off a piece of bread and Delilah opens for him. "Can someone explain what's happening right now?"

Before I can say *power play*, Delilah says, "I tried to stab Reaper with a fork, and now they won't let me feed myself."

Cora's lips press together, eyes dropping to her sandwich.

"Open," Reaper growls, holding up more food.

Delilah's eyes narrow.

"You do this every day?" Cora asks.

I can't tell if it's fascination or confusion in her tone, but she takes a bite of her sandwich and leans back in her seat, chewing as she watches their interaction.

Reap presses the food to Delilah's lips but she doesn't open, her entire body going stiff. The glare she gives him would melt a lesser man.

Sometimes I hate it when Reaper's right. They *are* stronger together.

He was right to keep them apart for so long. Our lives would have been a fucking nightmare if they'd spent this first week here plotting against us and attempting to escape.

Although chasing them *both* down would have been fun.

But keeping them apart meant we could focus on each of them individually. And in turn, they focused on us.

"Open, Kitten," he says again.

"No." She slaps his hand away. Reaper goes motionless. Viper's eyes grow wide. Breaker looks my way, as if making sure I'll intervene.

Reaper grips her cheeks and shoves the food into her mouth. I expect Cora to sit up and scream in outrage, so I'm surprised when she chuckles, picking up her food again.

"This is insane," she says, taking a large bite and smiling as she chews. "You guys realize this, right? This is completely nuts."

It is. We know damn well Delilah won't use any weapon on us. She's not afraid of us or even wants to harm us at this point. Even though Reaper would never admit it, we're only doing this because he was nearly pulling his hair out whenever I retrieved her plates and the food was barely touched.

And because it's an excuse to be near her. Touch her.

God, we're fucked.

Reaper picks up the napkin, wiping his hands. Delilah tracks his every single movement like he's a predator and she just stumbled into his den.

When he leans over and grabs the fork off the tray, handing it to her, her blue eyes dart to me.

Looks like this predator just invited her in.

Reaper, it seems, thinks they're ready.

"Trust me with a fork now?" she asks.

"No," Breaker says, lifting her off his lap to stand. "I'm pretty sure Reaper will never trust you with anything that can be used to stab him, but I doubt you want Cora witnessing what happens when you don't listen."

"What happens?" Cora asks Delilah, eyes wide. She looks at each of us, then up to Reaper. "What happens if we don't listen?"

He tucks a curl behind her ear. "To you, nothing Baby Girl. You'd never try to stab me."

Viper leans forward, crossing his arms over the table, watching in rapt fascination as Reaper picks up Cora's sandwich and tears a piece off, offering it to her. She leans forward, and grips his wrist, enclosing her mouth around his fingers, sucking on the tips as she takes the bite. Reaper runs his thumb over her bottom lip when she backs away, looking up at him with a smirk.

We all pretend we don't notice. Viper suddenly becomes interested in his hands. Breaker situates Princess back in her chair, handing her the fork again, but catches my eye when he passes by.

Seems they haven't been watching the camera's as intently as I have.

Reaper *hates* being touched. The only time he'll allow *anyone* to touch him is during sex. We know better than to even sit too close to him for too long because he'll either end up moving or glare holes through our skin until we're uncomfortable enough to move.

But he lets Delilah touch him *constantly*.

Seems these two women have slipped under his armor.

I don't have to wonder when it happened.

I know the exact date.

***

After the girls eat, Cora goes up to their room and Delilah walks back to the garden. She spent most of the last few days out here, walking around, picking little flowers she leaves in a water glass on the dining room table. Even when it rained a day ago, she stood out here, face to the sky, cold rain pelting her skin. I wonder what she thinks it was washing away.

I stand in the doorway watching her pick flowers, adjusting my mask, wishing I could just take the fucking thing off. But it's too soon.

Everything is too soon. I don't think any of us know what we're doing. Lately, when I'm around them, there's this chaotic thundering in my head and chest, and I know, just know, they feel it too. I can't seem to be more than a few feet from one of them at any given moment. I'm as bad as Reaper, obsessing over them. We all need distance. We're trapped in this house with two defiant, beautiful women we want to fuck, but every day we grow closer and closer to getting what we want is another day we lose sight of our original plan.

We took them, Delilah specifically because the best way to get to Rune was through the only thing he ever loved. The second thing that is. He loved his wife to the point of madness. When she died, when she was shot? He went insane and has never come back.

Even when he tried to rip apart the person responsible for taking her, it didn't heal that place inside him. Instead, it's now just more people with gaping wounds that can never be healed.

Hurting Rune won't make us feel better. Hurting his daughter makes us no better than him.

But turning her against him? Turning Cora? Making them ours?

That will completely ruin him.

Delilah bends down and picks up a red flower, and my heart skips a beat. Sleek black hair falls around her face. It reminds me of Reaper. I can imagine them together again. Hair tangling as she rides him. My hands on her ass, spreading her for me. Viper in her mouth. Or maybe Cora laid out, a perfect picture of Aphrodite in the flesh, taking Breaker as Reaper kisses her pink mouth. But then I remember that possessive flash Princess displayed that night and wonder if she'd even allow him to touch Cora. That's if he even wants to. Something in me thinks maybe he finds her appealing, but not quite like he does our Princess.

My hand slips down and I grip my hard cock, fully aware that I'm falling to pieces as the day's progress. We all are. If this morning is any indication, we're all struggling with their proximity. With waiting until the time is right to show Delilah the truth about her father. But we've been careless. Too soft.

But Reaper seems to think she's ready.

Cora is already there. Breaker was right. She needed a softer hand. She already trusts us enough to know we'd never hurt her. Just the thought of her being harmed makes my stomach sink. Pretty Little Flower. She comes across so delicate. Like the poppies that grew in the fields by the school. But just like them, her frailty is deceiving. She's intoxicating and capable of bringing a man to his knees.

They both are.

As I watch Delilah now, I think Reaper was right in his tactic. She was there that night. I don't know how much she remembers. I doubt much. She was only ten. But trauma has a way of sticking to your memories like an extra layer of skin. It hardens over time, making it difficult to penetrate until no one can slip past and you're just a hard shell. Trusting no one. Not allowing anyone too close. Until you're nothing but concrete skin and bones made of rebar.

Rune has made her into a stone version of himself. And we have yet to crack her open.

When I shift, my movement catches her eye, and she stands upright, holding the flower to her nose. My feet move before I have time to think, boots crunching on the hard packed dirt of the driveway, then whispering across the lawn. As I step under the stone arch of the entrance to the garden, she drops the flower and backs away.

Maybe I shouldn't have been so stern with her this morning. Maybe she needs a softer hand too sometimes.

"Come to manhandle me again?" she asks as I stop in front of her, blue eyes darting to my hard cock, then to my masked face. If she only knew. "Tossing women around seems to be your kink."

"Never," I spit out before I can think. God. My mind is a mess. How can wanting to spank her ass raw and simultaneously want to protect her be normal? Then again, I'm not normal. None of us are. We were made to be brutal. Even the way we care is harsh.

"Or do you need the others before you can—" her words cut off as I grip the back of her neck and pull her forward. She crashes into me, her hands landing on my biceps as I lean down and press my nose to her neck and breathe her in. She smells like spice and sin and everything I shouldn't crave.

Giving in to the primal need, I jerk the row of buttons securing her dress and rip them apart. The *plink* of the little metal buttons hitting the gravel starts a gnawing in my chest. Her gasp sends an electric jolt through me. I turn my head, resting my forehead on her frail collarbone and watch my fingers trail under the torn fabric, over her pale skin down to her bra. Right now, I'm grateful for Viper's fetish with cotton undergarments. It's so thin, I can see the hard rosy nipple straining against the fabric. When my hand catches on the material, I skim over it and cup one breast, pinching her nipple between my thumb and forefinger through the cotton.

The guttural groan she releases reminds me of the night in the woods when she begged us to please her.

I know I need to stop. I know it, but all logic flees as my senses flood with her. Her scent, her warm body pressed to mine. I can almost taste her, like she's imprinted on my mind. Gripping her jaw, I turn her head to the side, giving me better access. She breathes out, hands sliding down to my forearms. I expect her to push me away, but her fingers dig into my shirt and I groan at the feeling as she presses her body to mine.

She's killing me.

"Striker," she whimpers.

I hate my name, but every time she says it, it sounds like a praise.

She presses her face to the side of my mask, whispering my name again, and I feel the single word through the fabric as I pinch her nipple harder. A shuddering moan slips out against my temple.

My mind screams to slam her down and take her. Lift her dress and sink into her wet heat. Right here on the hard stones. So she's marked, skin raw and red, not just by me but by the marble chips at her back and the entire fucking situation we're in.

With my free hand, I skim over her waist and cup her ass. She groans, melting against me. I can't seem to stop myself. Every little sound she makes drives me higher and higher. I tilt my hips, grinding my hard cock into her belly, growing harder when she gasps. I press my face to her neck, hating the mask. I just want to press my skin to hers. Feel her everywhere. Strip our clothes and feel every inch of her flesh against mine. Press my lips to her cheeks. Her nose. Take her mouth and suck on her pouty bottom lip.

"Fuck," I grate out, aware I'm out of control and not caring. I want her so desperately that I don't think even the world ending right now would stop me from tasting her skin.

I suck in a breath, filling my lungs with her scent all over again. I want to drown in it. Bathe in it. Fuck her until I'm drenched in her sweet flavor.

Pressing my mouth to her ear, I say through the mask, "Close your eyes."

Chapter 28

Delilah

"Close your eyes," he orders in a low, gravelly voice that sends shivers down my spine. His thumb and forefinger pinch harder and my body instinctively curves into his, craving to be as close to him as possible.

He mutters out a curse, but doesn't let me go. Doesn't remove his hand or stop touching me. It's like he can't help himself any more than I can ignore the desire that courses through me in his presence. I know I shouldn't want him, any of them, not after what they did, but every fiber of my being craves his touch.

"Princess." The word sounds desperate, like a plea. "Close your eyes."

Without hesitation, I obey, not caring that he's the reason I'm here, ignoring the logical part of my mind that screams at me to resist, to fight back. Shove him off me. Stop him from touching me.

But right now, he sounds like that man in the bathroom, who groaned at the sight of me, who spread me open.

There's a part of me that wants him to do that now.

Force me to my knees. Hold me down.

Force me to admit I want him.

"Keep them closed," he whispers. "Keep your hands still. Promise me, Princess."

"I promise," I say, knowing I'm careening toward ruin, but the way he's touching me makes me want to fall, lose myself completely, and stay here in this fantasy. Where I no longer have to work numbers and hide my father's actions. Where I live in a huge mansion with four men and my best friend and I don't have to be anything or anyone but me.

The woman who likes it rough. Whose heart pounds with excitement at the possibility of danger.

Who desperately wants the man holding her to kiss her like he did that night when she was allowed to be out of control and reckless.

When I feel hot breath brush my skin, my heart leaps. Then warm lips meet my forehead, and I gasp at the shock of his flesh against mine, and I realize he's removed his mask. Arching into him, my skin's suddenly sizzling like a live wire, electric and charged with the thrill of his lips on me again.

"Shit," he hisses. "You feel so good."

Before I can stop myself, I nod. He does.

My breath leaves in a rush as his lips skim down to my cheek, hair tickling my face as he moves lower. The need to open my eyes, lift my hands, and run my fingers all over him is so strong that my fingers curl into his forearms and I squeeze my eyes shut tighter. He must sense it because he grips my hand and tugs it behind my back—a silent reminder to not move. I give him my other hand so he can keep it still because I don't trust myself to keep my word and not touch him.

His lips glide softly over my cheek once more, his chest rising and falling in sync with mine. Desperate for the taste of his mouth, the feel of his lips against mine, I turn my face towards him, but he denies me, pressing his cheek to mine. Rough stubble grazes me gently as his jawline trails along my cheek. A fresh, citrusy scent envelops me, a hint of lemon and clean soap overwhelming my senses as his kisses trail down to my neck. Tenderly brushing my hair aside with his free hand, he moves aside my sweater to place a delicate kiss on my collarbone. He's so much taller than me he curls over me, enveloping me in his warmth and clean smell. I throw my head back, head dizzy, craving his touch, more of his lips.

We don't say anything, we just stand like this, his mouth moving over me, silently taking tiny fragments, particles of me with him every time he removes his mouth from my flesh. But then his warm lips will land some place new, behind my ear, on my jaw, and it feels like he's giving me something back.

"Someday, you'll understand we're what's best for you," Striker whispers into the skin behind my ear. "You'll surrender and give yourself over."

My breath bursts from my lungs. I bite my lip, trying not to open my eyes. Trying not to give into what my body craves. What he knows I already want. Him.

Them.

"That's the day you'll give in and let me make love to you. Let me feel your skin against mine. Feel you wrapped around me so tight as you scream my name," he breathes. "Then you'll be mine—ours—as much as hers."

When he lets me go, I stumble, turning around, squeezing my eyes shut so tightly, tears form, and place my hands on the cold stone archway. My chest deflates when I hear him back away.

That felt a lot like a goodbye.

It's not until I catch my breath and the sound of his boots crunching on the gravel fades that I dare turn around.

Midafternoon light slants across the garden, the shadows of the pillars lining the path straight black lines across his back. I blink, the world and all its colors overly saturated. Like how I feel. Too bright. My hands remembering too much. My skin too hot, too alive.

I watch his back as he crosses the lawn, walks up the stairs, and shuts the front door behind him, wondering if he seeks retaliation like Reaper or if what he wants is something that can't be found in revenge.

Chapter 29

Delilah

It's been almost two weeks since the incident in the garden. I know because I started cutting thin lines into the plaster in the bathroom with my little knife, marking every sunset I've seen. I also know because my cycle came. It had been late based on my estimate, and I cried with relief, not realizing I'd been worried. Then Cora's followed the next day, and we both sent a silent thank you to our past selves for getting the birth control implant.

My ex-husband was so scared to get me pregnant he had me get the implant, used a condom, and pulled out. Reaper's the only man who has ever come in me and I don't think I'll ever forget what he felt like.

We've barely seen them since that day in the garden. Just in passing, in the kitchen or in the foyer. Sometimes I find Reaper in the library, but he gets up and stalks away without a word when I come in, leaving me feeling rejected like a fool.

They stopped feeding me after that first day with Cora, and I find I miss the weird interaction. I miss sitting on Breaker's lap as he runs his large hands up and down my thighs. Reaper's dark glare that always, always ends up looking more hungry than angry. Striker's gentle touch and Viper's laughter.

The few times I've found Viper alone in a hallway, or in the foyer, he'll watch me pass, leaving my skin tingling. There have been a handful of times, late at night I hear music from the large room with the piano, but the door's always locked so I don't know who's playing.

One night I found Cora sitting outside the door, wiping tears from her eyes so I sat down with her and listened to the haunting music, thinking about all the operas my father forced me to attend with him, or the nights I spent with my mother when Rune was gone, cooking for just the two of us while "Ava Maria" played in the background.

I miss her. Growing up, I've often wondered what she would think of me now. Most days, I'm glad she doesn't know me. I don't think she'd be proud of the woman my father created. There's a part of me that's glad she's not here anymore, so she isn't at home right now, sitting up late at night, wondering what is being done to me by these men who took us. Scared that I'm being hurt. I may be glad she's not here to be afraid, but part of me fears she's sitting in heaven, watching me now, shaking her head in disappointment that I walk around this huge mansion, wishing these men, my captors, would talk to me.

I wonder if she'd be disappointed with how Cora and I have survived these past few weeks, turning to each other for comfort.

But it's more than that, isn't it?

"Delly?"

I pause on the staircase, Cora's voice from the foot of the stairs sending panic through me.

Calm down, Delilah. She's not psychic.

I turn to face her. Her brows knit.

"What are you up to?" she asks, her socked foot moving onto the first step. She rarely wears her boots. Then again, she isn't hiding a knife. "You look suspicious."

She knows me too well.

"I'm headed up to the room." Not a complete lie.

Her full lips turn up at the corner. "Want company?"

The seductive tone and the little jut of her hip make me want to rethink my plan, but I shake my head. "Just going to nap."

"Suit yourself," she says, backing away. "I'll be up later."

I wait until she disappears into the library before I continue up the stairs.

We've spent more and more time apart as the days go on. That desperate fear that kept us clinging to one another left when we realized we weren't going to be separated again. So now most days we part ways, coming together in the evenings for dinner.

We eat the food that's set out for us, then go to bed where we continue touching. Kissing. Though each time we come together, it's less and less about making them watch, daring them to cross the line they seem to have drawn, and more about feeling her close. Smelling her skin. Tasting her hungry mouth as she seeks me in the dim light, slipping her small hand between my thighs.

Neither one of us admits we think of them. That we want them to be with us again. Have their fingers sliding into us. Their mouths taking sweet kisses. Or rough ones. I want those too.

I also want to go home, but with each passing day I find I don't mind the quiet. Chaos consumed my days before, my head swimming with numbers. Mornings were meetings and mergers, then long hours spent at the office or sitting with my father as he negotiated another deal I pretended not to listen to. Cora and I, nothing but pretty faces who kept sleazy men distracted while my father took over their lives, turning a blind eye when he gave Clyde an order to remove a threat, or convince someone to sell or pay up.

We knew what that meant, though we never voiced it.

I don't miss it. I miss my father and I miss Clyde, but I have Cora and as each day bleeds into the other, I'm content with just seeing her smiling face.

And the men. Whenever I see one of their masked faces, my heart skips.

Cora likes to go in the little garden off the kitchen and I enjoy walking the paths in the large empty one out front. I spend most of the days out there if I'm not in the library, and I think I've figured out where we are. At least geographically. I have no clue of our exact location, but it's still somewhere on the southern east coast. Being mid November, it's still warm some days, though not humid like back home.

I've never seen a vehicle but the men seem to disappear every day, off to do whatever it is they do. It's strange to suddenly not see them after being forced to be with them so much for several days. I can't help but wonder why all of a sudden they have no interest in their captives. I find myself wishing Viper or Striker would pop up and drag me to the dining room for a meal, and I have to remind myself that they kidnapped us.

I've never been kidnaped before, but this sure isn't what I imagined it would be like. It all feels weirdly domestic. After every meal they set out for us, Cora and I clean up our mess, then part ways to wander around, acutely aware of their absence but their watchful eyes. I know there are cameras around, but I don't think they have the entire place monitored. Some days they seem surprised to find me in parts of the house. Most of the doors are locked, but occasionally I find one open and I go exploring, only to discover it's locked the next day.

I'm tired of the same rooms, the same endless days with no answers.

Today I'm going to find out why we're here and what they plan. There's a reason they took us, and I am determined to find out. So, today I'm going to break into the rooms on the top floor. I know that's where they sleep. It has to be.

Gripping the cold railing, I lean over the staircase and peer down at the first floor, making sure Cora isn't watching. Then I twist my body to glance up at the two floors above. The open staircase reveals a ceiling adorned with an elaborate mural, its colors faded with time. I can make out flowers and maybe naked cherubs, but the paint's flaked off in places. Taking a shaky step, my heart in my throat, I begin to climb.

A few days ago, I finally gathered up enough courage to go to the third floor, but all the doors along the hall were locked. When no one came flying up the stairs to reprimand me, I figured there were no cameras up here.

Right now I really hope so.

By the time I've reached the fourth floor, I'm slightly out of breath and my nerves feel frayed. The hall is like the others, with ornate wall sconces positioned between each door lining the wall, ending at a massive window and a door, leading to a balcony.

The first door in the long, dark hall is locked, but I move further down and stop at the last one on the left. Casting a quick glance over my shoulder, I pull the knife from my boot and ram it between the latch and the frame. It pops easily. Looking over my shoulder, just to make sure Viper or Striker aren't looming behind me, I tap the door. It slowly swings open with a creak, like something in a horror movie, sending tingles to my fingers and toes.

I slip in and shut the door behind me.

I was right. It's one of their rooms.

It's neat and like my room, furnished with just a bed, a dresser, and a large wingback chair. The bed's made, blanket perfectly smooth and tucked at the ends with a military perfection. When I see a row of masks on the chair with the slash over the eye, I know I'm in Striker's room.

Other than the masks, I don't see anything in the room that is remotely personal until my eyes land on a small figurine on the dresser. Walking forward, my boots tap on the rough wood floors, sending my nerves higher, so I slow my movements, trying not to make a sound. I stop in front of the dresser, catching my reflection in the mirror. Besides my tense jaw and flushed cheeks, I look surprisingly well rested for someone being held hostage.

A familiar vibrating sound makes my heart leap into my throat. The *buzz, buzz* of a text notification, vibrates again. Placing the knife on the dresser, I grip the handle on the top drawer and pull. A sleek black phone sits all alone in the center. Without thinking, I pick it up and slide my thumb over the screen. An image of five men all wearing the familiar skull masks and all-black uniforms appears on the lock screen.

It's them. But there's five instead of four, the fifth one's mask much like Breakers, but stitched around the edge like Reaper's.

I swipe the screen again. The lock screen disappears and the thumbprint request pops up. Knowing I don't have any chance of breaking into the phone, I hold the power button down long enough that the icons to power off the phone or make an emergency call pop up.

My thumb hovers over the red icon, but I stop.

Shaking my head, I lower my thumb, but...

My pulse quickens, yet I can't seem to figure out why I'm not hitting the screen and calling for help.

Maybe it's because I know, deep in my gut, the only authorities my father may have contacted are the ones on his payroll. So if I call, it would be on record.

But, if I call, my father will know I'm alive.

Clenching my teeth, I squeeze the phone, but still hesitate.

If I hit to call the police, tell them we'd been taken, they will eventually swarm this place. Guns will be drawn. Clyde will gather a fucking *army* and these men will never, never just hand us over. They will never let themselves get caught, either. The four took so many risks to take Cora and me, and they have a reason. Reaper says revenge, but it has to be something more. Something that would be worth all of this.

Taking us.

Keeping us warm and fed and dressed.

Your father isn't a good man.

Everything they've said spins in my mind. I know he's bad. But what could he have done to warrant all this *effort*?

My eyes slide over to the figurine, and I pick it up, examining the dark wood. It's a crude carving of a wolf, but the wood is smooth, like someone's rubbed away all the rough edges.

When I hear the door open, my breath seizes in my lungs. I spin, clutching the two items to my chest. I catch a glimpse of full lips, high cheekbones, and a delicate nose before I hear growling, and he yanks his mask down.

Striker.

He stalks forward with such malice in his eyes that I drop the phone and say in a rush, "I'm sorry."

His hand darts out, snatching the wolf, brutally yanking it away.

"What the *fuck* are you doing?" he grates, his voice deadly low. He grips the back of my neck, jerking me forward. My hands flatten to his chest to balance myself, completely unprepared for his rage.

"I'm sorry," I say again, but I'm not even sure what I'm sorry for. For coming up here. For breaking into his room. For picking up the phone. For being Rune Gavin's flesh and blood.

His grip tightens on both me and the wolf. Glancing back at the figurine, he somehow looks even angrier than before as he places it delicately on the dresser.

"How did you get in here?" he demands, but then his gaze snags on the knife, eyes widening, then flaring with disbelief. His jaw moves under his mask like he's grinding his teeth, then the phone vibrates and his shoulders go rigid.

Amber eyes snap to me. My blood chills.

Watching my face, he slides a boot back as he steps away, lowering his gaze to the floor. My hands curl into fists, dread clawing into my chest as he stares down at the phone at my feet, completely still. Suddenly, like something in him snaps loose, he springs forward, fingers weaving into my hair, yanking me brutally downward.

I cry out as my knees hit the hard floor, my hands flying up to grip his, my scalp burning from his painful grasp.

"Pick it up!"

Tears spring to my eyes. I try to grip the phone but I'm shaking now, my hands fumbling and it slips from my grasp, clattering to the floor as I say, "I didn't call!"

"Pick it up and fucking call for help," he growls, the pitch black edge to his voice making my heart beat so hard it feels like it may pound right out of my ribcage. Hands trembling, I grab the phone and pull it to my chest. With a growl, he yanks my hair, dragging me to my feet, then shoves me toward the bed. "Don't drop it, Princess. You're going to need help now."

With a forceful shove, Striker pushes me forward. My arms fly out to catch myself, the phone flinging across the mattress.

I tuck my head, turning my face as he slams me down, his palm pressing my head brutally into the mattress. He bends over, chest heaving, eyes dark with rage in his skull mask. In the weeks I've been here and the times I've interacted with him, I've never seen this wild, dangerous energy. He practically vibrates with rage, something cruel rippling under his skin.

"You were fucking *warned*." Striker releases my hair, then tugs up the back of my dress until my ass is exposed. Gripping my underwear, he rips them down my thighs, tugging them off completely and throwing them down next to my head.

"You just can't seem to listen," Striker grates. When I hear the familiar clank of metal, my eyes move to his belt. The sound of leather slipping from the loops sends an odd heat surging to my core. "We have told you the consequences, yet you insist on learning the hard way."

I watch, my heart skittering, as he grips the buckle, then winds the belt around his hand, heat flaring between my thighs at the sight. Biting my lip, I say nothing because he's right. I was warned and here I am. Suffering the consequences for doing exactly what they told me not to.

The leather belt snaps behind me, and then suddenly pain radiates from my left butt cheek to my thigh. I'm so shocked, from the pain, the intense, horrible burn, and the realization he just spanked me with the belt, that my body goes still, air seizing in my lungs.

An animalistic growl vibrates from him, and the belt lands again. My mouth opens, fingers curling into the blanket. It cracks over my flesh again and again, searing heat shooting out like an electric current, radiating down my thighs. Shock holds my breath hostage, keeping me frozen in place.

The belt lands again and pain cuts through me like a knife. The need to cover my ass, lessen the pain almost makes me reach behind me, but I clutch at the bedding and hold on as he spanks me, something pulsing and primal sparking inside my center as

I lie still watching him loom over me. His muscles tighten in his arms and shoulders as he pulls back and lets it land. Thick, muscled legs spread wider, adjusting his stance as the belt cracks down again.

The sweet man from the garden is gone, replaced by this unhinged devil with the scarred face. Something inside me coils up just as tightly as the muscles in his chest and arms, cutting deep into my core as harshly as the belt.

As it lands again, instead of jerking away from the pain, I lean into it and that darkness blooms, unfurling inside me all over again, that feral woman they created breaking free. Liquid heat pools between my thighs and when I arch my back, meeting the punishing pain, the belt lands lower, spanking my pussy with a cutting slap.

Pleasure fires through my clit. I moan, hips arching downward, my body rocking to meet the belt, reaching for that blinding release I felt before.

Then it stops.

Striker lunges forward, and grips my hair, jerking my head back, ruthlessly. He drags the belt around my neck, then yanks. The leather presses into my throat.

"You will not *come*," he hisses into my ear.

Pressure builds in my head from how tightly he's holding the belt. My mind swirls, my body aching, pain radiating all over my ass and thighs, but it's not nearly as bad as the ache between my legs. I rub my ass into his erection despite the sting in my skin, unable to control myself or the lust rushing through me.

"Fuck," he hisses, loosening the belt. I gasp for air. His dick grinds into me. "Greedy girl, better be careful." He yanks the belt. "I'll turn you into my good little slut and you'll regret the day you fucking begged for my cock."

He slaps my ass, and I wince.

Leaning forward, he whispers in my ear. "Beg me, Princess. I dare you. Beg me to spank your pussy. Because you love it, don't you? Love the pain and the pleasure."

I clamp my mouth shut, too scared my denial will sound like the lie it is.

"You'd love for me to shove my cock deep into your tight cunt. Take you. *Force* you. Then you'd get what you wanted and not have to admit that you fucking *crave* me."

Using the belt, Striker pulls me up from the bed. I slide my hand around to feel the skin on my sore ass, expecting to find cuts. It stings like hell, but it's smooth, no broken skin or open wounds.

I adjust my dress until it falls back down, biting my lip as the fabric smooths over my burning flesh. My chin quivers, a rush of confusion and anger making my eyes burn. Confusion at why his violence turns me on. Anger because he's right, I want him. Fury because if he'd just have hurt me, maimed me, flayed my skin, I could hate him. If they'd just be completely cruel, this want snaking through me would finally go away.

"Pick it up," he growls. "Pick up the fucking *phone*."

My hand shakes as I reach for it, the belt barely giving around my neck as I lean forward. He plucks it from my hand the second I stand upright. His grip on the belt tightens for a moment, sending heat to my clit, and I close my eyes, trying to center my thoughts, but Striker tugs at the belt, forcing me to walk in front of him. I stumble as he shoves harder, but he catches my arm, keeping me upright, but doesn't give me much of a chance to regain my footing before he's pushing me to the door.

Fear skitters through my belly. "Where are we going?" I ask, even though I already know.

"I'm taking you to Reaper."

Chapter 30

Delilah

Striker leads me to the dining room, each of my steps laced with a faint pain as my skin on my rear pulls and stretches. By the time we reach the bottom floor, my legs are trembling as much from exertion as from fear, my fingers curled under the leather around my neck like a collar.

"Walk," Striker grates when I pause at the bottom step, nerves getting the best of me. He shoves me forward, forcing me toward the back of the house. My belly flutters, my breath leaving me in a rush when we reach the dining room.

He pushes me through the doorway and my stomach drops.

They're here. All of them.

Reaper leans against the table, arms crossed, exuding arrogance like a perfume. Breaker's in a seat at the table to his left, Viper on the other side.

Heat blooms between my legs, the memory of the woods scorching my body and my cheeks.

I've officially gone over the edge.

Striker tightens his grip and shoves me again. I wince, my fingers trapped between the belt and my throat.

All eyes land on me. I feel like a bad child being delivered to the principal.

Principals. Plural.

A sudden primal urge to run snakes down my legs, but I know it's futile. I'm trapped here, completely at their mercy.

Like right now.

"Where's Cora?" I ask them. She'd be mortified if she walked in and saw the belt around my neck.

Fuck, *I* should be mortified right now.

Reaper cocks his head to the side like he finds my question interesting. "She's been instructed to stay in her room."

What he doesn't say is she's locked in, because there's no way she'd listen.

"What's she done now?" Viper asks Striker as he leads me to the center of the room.

"Broken into my room," Striker says, adjusting the belt at my neck, loosening it enough that I relax slightly, letting my hands fall to my sides.

"How did she get into the room?" Reaper asks, that dark gaze never leaving me.

Striker holds out my little knife. Breakers bark of laughter makes my eyebrows raise. Reaper's glare makes my belly dip. His black eyes move to Viper and Reaper doesn't even have to say anything for his turquoise eyes to drop. He reaches for the knife and pockets it.

Reaper shakes his head, focusing back on me. "I warned you, Kitten, yet here we are." He shoots forward, stopping an inch from me, his hand clamping down around the belt at my neck, thumb digging under my jaw. The breath I was inhaling catches in my throat as he presses into my pulse. "Seems you are determined to test me."

"I didn't use it," I say on a gasp, acutely aware of his heat radiating from his body. How I'm trapped between him and Striker at my back. Too aware of Reaper's bare fingers at my throat again. His skin feels like a lit match to mine, burning me with his anger. With unleashed desire.

Reaper's eyes narrow, and that heated look freezes, turning to black ice.

"The phone," I whisper. "I didn't call anyone."

Those icy eyes dart to Striker behind me.

I feel his exhale move through my back. "She found my phone in the dresser."

The way Reaper's eyes ignite tells me that Striker may be in as much trouble as I am, but then his gaze falls to mine and I know I'm completely fucked.

"What did I tell you?" Reaper says, his voice deadly low. "You are ours. You do not leave here."

I swallow, fear tingling my hands.

"You said, little kitty, you understood you belonged here. To us. Isn't that why you've been such a good girl? Performing for us? Flirting? *Tempting*?"

"I never promised anything," I snap, my face flaming at the mention of Cora and me at night, feeling stupid because I got what I wanted by stripping down and finger fucking her. His attention, *their* attention. But not like this. Not laced with anger.

"Jesus." Breaker huffs out a disbelieving laugh. "I'm going to enjoy this one."

The little I can see around Reaper's eyes creases like he's confused or just as dumbfounded as Breaker sounds.

No. He's fucking smirking.

"Put her on the table."

Striker turns me around, letting the belt slide around my neck until he's holding it closed at my throat. Breaker and Viper move forward to grip my arms. I'm guided back to the table, my head snapping to follow Reaper's movements as he steps aside, allowing them to place me on the table. I wince when my ass lands on the hard surface. Both men bring my arms up, forcing me to lie back, my rear right at the edge, my legs dangling over. The angle hurts my ass like all hell and I wonder if I'm going to have welts.

Reaper steps up and leans over me, taking both my wrists in his one large hand, pinning them to the surface. Striker lets the belt go, but Reaper grasps it, using it to hold me down. My heart thunders. I stare up at his masked jaw above my head, and the outline of his chin.

"Close your eyes," Viper says. My gaze darts to him next to us. He holds up a long silky piece of fabric. Before I can protest, he places it over my eyes and lifts my head to tie it in the back.

It's like the second my eyes are covered, every other sense heightens immediately. Over my pounding heart, I hear them moving around me, pushing chairs away. The belt's released briefly, then Reaper's grip returns. Someone makes a *tsking* sound. I swear I hear a whisper, then a light laugh.

"What are you going to do?" I ask, my voice trembling slightly. They can't spank me like this. Not with my ass on the table. Part of me is relieved since it still hurts, but I'm not sure what they have in store for me as punishment.

A hot breath caresses my cheek. Warm flesh touches my ear. My already pounding heart skips. I feel silky hair fall across my face.

Reaper took his mask off.

"Bad Kitten," Reaper says next to my ear. "What should we do to you?" Hot lips press to my temple. Air bursts from my lungs. "You've been so naughty lately."

My chest tightens. I was expecting his anger. Reaper's usual black rage, but he's so calm, his tone dark yet steady. Not rippling with fury like it does when I piss him off. I'm not sure what it means, but my body ignites as his lips gently graze my cheek.

"Little temptress who can't seem to *behave*." Reaper's voice drops, growing darker. There he is. *Reaper* has come out to play and I know I'm going to regret stepping foot in that room. "You know what you've been doing, filthy girl. Playing with each other's pretty little pussies. Coming so sweetly on her hand, like you don't remember how I tore you apart."

"How you screamed, when my tongue was inside you," Breaker says from my other side.

"How you groaned as you swallowed my cum," Striker says.

"And how you moaned like the perfect pretty little slut around my cock as I fucked your throat," Viper adds.

"My body doesn't belong to you," I snap, tasting the lie on my lips.

"Oh, but it does," Reaper growls. The belt tightens, squeezing my throat. "Every curve. Every inch of flesh. That wet, greedy space between your thighs you let her touch, belongs to us. Every tear and every drop of blood belongs to us."

Striker's voice whispers in my ear, "Your mind, your body, your fucking soul belongs to us."

I jerk against Reaper's tight grasp, rage slashing through me. "I belong to no one," I hiss.

"That's where you're wrong, Princess." A finger brushes over my lips. I taste salt and *him*. Striker. "You've belonged to us since you stepped foot in that club."

"Since the moment I first laid eyes on you," Reaper grates, "You have been *ours*."

"Seems we have a communication problem," Breaker says, and I hear something sliding across the floor. "Maybe instead of telling her she belongs to us, we should show her."

I can't see shit. I'm held to a table by my kidnappers. I've been spanked, forcefully brought to orgasm, and whipped with a belt, but that sentence terrifies me more than anything.

A finger, I don't know whose, slides up my calf to my knee, dragging my dress up. I kick out on instinct, but one of them catches me by the ankle.

"Scared kitty thinks we're going to hurt her," Reaper says. "Didn't we promise we'd never hurt you?"

When I say nothing, a hand grips my jaw and Striker says, "Answer when we speak to you."

"Yes," I say immediately, "but Striker here just proved you're all liars."

"That ass beating wasn't nearly as bad as you deserved," Striker growls.

"I'd have loved to have seen that," Viper says, and I feel my dress being lifted higher. "Did you leave welts?"

"More than likely," Striker says.

Viper's hungry groan creates a flutter low in my belly, the craving from earlier returning.

"Perverts," I snap, aware I might as well be calling myself one too.

"Jesus," Breaker says, "She doesn't know when to stop."

I clench my jaw, keeping my retort behind my teeth. Upstairs, Striker beat my ass red, but it wasn't much worse than the spanking Reaper gave me. That night in the woods, I wasn't hurt. Humiliated, yes, but I've not been hurt at all since they took me. Even then, when they took us, I could have been handled far worse and they may have left me alone and cold, confused, but my body was never harmed. I don't think I've been in any real danger this entire time.

"Do you think that's why we took you?" Reaper asks, a dark edge to his voice. "To torture you. Fuck you and abuse you?"

I shake my head, but when Reaper lightly tugs the belt I stutter out, "N-No."

"Why didn't you use the phone, Tiny Thing?" Breaker asks and his is voice painfully gentle.

Why didn't I call for help? I had the opportunity in my hands, and didn't take it.

Clenching my jaw, I shake my head like this will stop the truth from coming out. I already know why I didn't call for help, even if I don't want to admit it.

I don't want them hurt.

After everything, after watching them kill, after them drugging us, after being left alone, I know deep down they aren't bad like Cora said.

And these men are right, Rune isn't good. He's not even a decent father. He's a power hungry man and I've been trapped by him, forced to perform my tasks like a dedicated daughter. Trained on how to hide his actions. Educated by a cruel man that wants to make me like him. Cold and ruthless, and I'm so desperate for love that I did everything he told me to do. I had no choice. I was born into this life of greed and death and was never allowed the choice to fight my father's rule.

The moment I was born, all my choices were taken. I didn't get to pick my parents. And I didn't get to choose whether or not I did Rune's bidding.

I just did it and told myself I wanted to.

For weeks I've denied the quiet voice in my head that sang with relief. I was free for the first time in my life. Every morning I woke here was another day I wasn't sitting in my empty kitchen, telling myself that I was going to make my father's company even more powerful once I took it over. That when the day came, I could rule over it *my* way. And until then, I was okay with sitting passively while my father and Zane took over another club or chain of hotels, all while working the numbers to hide what was probably a shipment of drugs or something far worse.

Being here meant I wasn't obligated to be my father's protegee. Being here has meant I was unchained even if it's been at the expense of my freedom.

"I didn't want to," I whisper, wanting to turn over, curl into a ball and weep for the woman whose first real choice in life was in the club that night with them. For this stupid ache inside me that's making tears soak into the blindfold because I craved them again. For the nights that I felt Cora's touch and wished it was his. Theirs. Even when I wouldn't admit it to myself, I just wanted to feel that way I felt with them that night. Out of control and worshiped.

"Who do you belong to, Kitten?"

I bite my lip, fighting the sudden rush of tears. "You." Sucking in a breath, I whisper. "All of you."

"That's right, Princess," Striker says. A warm finger slides along my jawline. "You're ours. We don't harm what's ours."

I nod. I think part of me has known the truth. From the moment they took us, I knew they had planned this entire plot against Rune, designing it in a way to make him suffer. I think maybe I've known all along they wanted my mind even more than my body.

"Do you want us, Kitten?"

Reaper's grip tightens on my wrists, reminding me to answer. The word breaks out of me on a sob. "Yes."

Then, there are hands everywhere.

Chapter 31

Delilah

The sensation is overwhelming, my senses flooding with the musky scent of male mixed with shampoo and soap and woodsy cologne. I can feel their warm hands on my skin, calloused fingers, and rough grips. But I can't see them and that creates a desperate, almost primal need to bloom between my thighs.

"Ours," Striker rasps before his mouth claims mine.

The familiar feeling of his skin against mine again makes my chest pang with longing. I clench my hands into fists, aching to reach for him. To feel the outline of his jaw and the hardness of the long muscles in his back.

Hands slip up under my dress, tugging at the hem to expose my thighs. Someone's calloused fingers graze my collarbone, trailing them down my chest to the neckline of my dress. With a forceful tug, the fabric rips open, the sound tearing through me. Hands, maybe the same, maybe different, drag across the thin material of my bra, then move under it, long fingers kneading my breast. When a hot mouth skims over the top of my thigh like a promise, I groan, spreading my legs, waiting for what's coming.

"Viper, Breaker." Reaper's seductive voice breaks through the lust. He's still holding me solidly to the table by my hands and the belt at my neck. Knuckles brush over my cheek and I know it's him. I think I'd know his touch from any other's for the rest of my life. That gentleness is burned into my memory. "Bring her to the edge."

"Lift your hips, Sweetheart," Viper says, voice smooth. I obediently tilt my hips, allowing him to push my dress up slowly, careful not to let the material drag over the sore skin at my rear. Fingers wrap around my thigh, shifting me forward. "Such a good girl for us," he praises. "We knew you wanted us touching you."

"That's why you wanted us to watch," Reaper murmurs in my ear. "You wanted us to come into that room and fuck you."

I nod even though it feels perverse to do so. I did. As much as I wanted Cora's kiss, I wanted them just as desperately. Their hands on me, like they are now. All over. The word tumbles out with a breathy exhale. "Yes."

It's like the single word unleashes something. Not just within me, but them. My legs are lifted and hooked over someone's shoulders, then fingers are moving into me. One at first, then two, then three stretching me deliciously, fingers driving in and out slowly, like they're savoring the feel of me. As one set of fingers slips out, another replaces it.

"So fucking wet already," Viper hisses with appreciation, letting me know it's his hand now, moving into me with a roughness that makes me moan.

A guttural cry escapes my lips as Viper's mouth lands on my clit with a soft kiss. "Oh fuck," I breathe, turning my face toward Reaper, but he shifts, moving just out of reach, making my chest feel like it's going to collapse.

The slick sound of Viper driving his fingers into me fills the room. A hot breath brushes against my inner thigh before his warm lips descend on my wetness, sucking me in. Angling my hips lower, I cry out again when I feel kisses—someone else, Breaker maybe—on my other thigh as Viper's tongue swirls around my clit. Another mouth latches onto my hard nipple, sending heated waves through me. Viper's mouth between my thighs devours me, sucking and licking until I'm straining against Reaper's grasp, driving my pussy harder into that wicked mouth, chasing my release. My back arches off the table, the sting of pain from my sore skin only adding to the pleasure. But just as I feel myself about to trip over the edge, it all stops.

Hands leave. My legs are dropped. Mouths no longer kiss me with hungry intent.

"What are you doing?" My mind splinters in different directions, but before I can make sense of anything, a hand slaps against my pussy and I groan. The feral woman within me awakens once again—hungry and ready for more.

Reaper's voice pierces through the darkness, taunting me. "Pretty little Kitten thinks we're going to let her come."

My breathing slows as I try to process his words.

Let her come.

When the meaning of his statement settles, I jerk my hands, trying to break from his grasp. "Fucking asshole, " I snap, my voice hoarse with frustration.

"We've established that," Reaper responds, shifting to press my hands harder to the table. The belt squeezes, cutting into my skin. To the others, he commands, "Again."

When they all touch me again, I cry out at the shock. It's more brutal this time. Two sets of hands knead my breasts, pinching nipples, while a mouth teases between my legs, but there's a bite to this pleasure. Instead of soft tongue flicks, it's little nibbles and sharp sucks. They bring up my legs by the ankles and brace them on the table's edge, exposing me completely. The belt tightens. A hot tongue slides from my clit to my opening, delving deep inside me. I hear Breaker's groan, drowning out my own. I press my shoulders into the table, hips moving in circles, my breaths shallow as he licks and sucks, devouring me sloppily like he's starved. Like he's been craving this moment since he first tasted me.

Then it stops. The belt loosens.

"Fuck!" I scream, struggling against the grip on my ankles, but it only tightens, keeping me splayed open like a helpless butterfly with its wings pinned down.

"Such a temper," Striker says. I feel fingers—I think his—drag down my body before slipping slowly into me. I choke on a moan. When he withdraws his fingers, he spreads me open and says, "Viper, finger fuck her while Breaker devours this pink cunt."

Viper drives his fingers in roughly. Breaker sucks me into his mouth, wet and soft against Striker's warm fingers. My back arches off the table, a throaty groan breaking free as I spiral toward the edge. Then I'm there. Panting. About to slip over.

"She's too close," Striker says and they all back away.

I'm left teetering on the edge. The sound of my desperate, needy whimpers fills the room along with their heavy breathing, and for a moment I marvel at their self control. My entire body feels like a live wire, coiled up and sparking with heat, ready to spring loose and catch fire. Like I'm about to break free of my skin.

"Again."

This time I swear I feel two tongues, and two sets of fingers as Striker holds me open.

"She's fucking divine," Breaker groans. "You taste so good. I could eat you all night."

"Please," I choke out, writhing against Reaper's firm hold, against the grip on my ankles.

"That's right, Tiny Thing, beg for it."

Fingers slap harshly to my clit. My spine curves, my body drawn tight like a bowstring.

Viper's gravelly moan as he tongues at me roughly, as Reaper tightens the belt around my throat, as fingers slip deep into me, as hands drag over my belly, nearly trips me over, but they seem to sense it and back off.

"Beg me more, Sweetheart," Viper says, letting his tongue drag over my clit. "Tell me how badly you need to come."

Their hands move over me once again, pushing me to the brink but refusing to let me fall over.

This is my punishment. Being driven to the edge repeatedly, only to be yanked back right before I fall over, keeping me precariously close, wishing they'd push me, send me head first into oblivion.

"Please," I whisper, all shame rushing out with my beg. "Please, just let me come."

"So pretty," Reaper whispers, his lips grazing my cheek. Another sob escapes as I turn my face to him, but he backs away, denying me that small bit of closeness. "I love it when you beg. It sounds like defeat."

They continue their cruel game, but instead of begging, I choke on a sob. The pleasure is so intense it's painful. My chest constricts, my mind flashing on images of them over the weeks. An ungloved hand caressing my cheek before handing me the knife. Breaker's gentle touch along my thigh and his masked kiss on my shoulder. Striker's silken lips tasting my skin as the chilly wind carried my moans away from the garden. Reaper's feather-light touch and harsh bite. It all spins in my head, driving me to this point of ecstasy and agony.

The belt tightens and Reaper's lips press to my forehead. I gasp, my body feeling like it's expanding. Like they each have a part of me and are tugging more and more of me free.

When it becomes too much, my feet slipping over the side of the cliff, they stop and an enraged scream tears free, breaking on a sob. My heart aches, bleeds, torn apart, so desperate for something they can't give me. I want to wrap myself in them, smother myself in their embrace until this bone-deep pain, this hideous *need* for things I can't even name, goes away.

"Enough," Striker says, but I barely hear him.

The leather belt around my throat is loosened and removed. When they release my ankles, my legs fall limply, trembling from being tense for so long. Reaper lets go of my wrists and I turn to my side, drawing my knees up, my entire body shaking.

"Come here, Kitten." Reaper's rough voice breaks through my tears, and I feel him scoop me up in his arms. I tuck myself against him, looping my arms weakly around his neck. His scent—musk and male and a hint of smoky cologne—just makes me cry harder.

Reaper carries me across the house and up the stairs. I hear the familiar slide of the bolt, the creak of a door opening, and then Cora's exasperated cry.

"What did you do to her?" she whispers.

The blindfold falls away, but I keep my head tucked into Reaper's chest, just breathing him in. When he lowers me, I cling to him, scared if I let go, he'll take that last piece of me with him.

"Delly." Cora's soft hands gently massage my tense back, sending tremors of pleasure through me.

"Take care of our girl," Reaper says, then the door closes behind me.

Tears stream down my face as I collapse to my knees.

She kneels next to me, asking in a hushed voice, "What the fuck did they do to you?"

My body's spun up tight, needing to unravel. I grip her by the back of her head and forcefully pull her mouth to mine. She gasps at my roughness, but then melts into me as my tongue slips past her lips.

"Please," I beg, desperately needing release.

Cora nods, but she doesn't understand. I need to come. To completely unravel. To shatter until I'm no longer me. I guide her hand between my thighs, and she slips a finger inside as she devours me with a fierce kiss. But it's still not enough. I need more. I need them.

"Please," I choke out and she leans back, breaking our kiss, brushing hair away from my face.

"I have you," she whispers, laying me back on the floor as she pushes up my dress. Feeling raw and exposed, I spread my legs greedily for her, hiking the fabric higher as she thrusts two, then three fingers into me. Tilting my hips to meet her hand, I fist her hair as she leans over to kiss me. When she moves lower and pulls the torn material away from my breast, I cry out at the sting of pain as she takes a nipple between her teeth.

"Fuck," I grit out, writhing under her. "Cora." They brought me to the edge so many times, nothing but violence will satisfy this carnal desire. Only savagery will feed this feral woman within me.

"I know," she whispers, moving even lower, lightly kissing down my belly to between my thighs. She's being too gentle to do me any good, but when her lips press against my clit, she does it hard. Then she sucks me roughly into her mouth and I scream out in pleasure, gripping her hair as I watch her suck me into her pretty mouth. She looks up at me through long lashes, smiling as she sucks again. And again. When she swirls her tongue against my clit, the world explodes violently, my scream cutting through the room. I fall back onto the floor, heart hammering as my orgasm subsides.

"Jesus," she says, slowing her thrusting hand. When my breathing returns to normal and my mind works again, I sit up on my elbows and look at her. Her brows knit at whatever she sees in my face. "What happened?"

I'm ruined. The men who kidnapped us have manipulated my emotions, making me care if they get hurt. We're trapped here, in this old mansion in the middle of nowhere, cut off from reality.

STRIKER

"I don't think we're going home," I finally say, but I don't know what to make of her smile.

Chapter 32

STRIKER

I take the stairs two at a time, my cock so hard I can barely think straight. Viper and Breaker left after we delivered Princess to Cora and Reaper left the house to go only god knows where. Now, I'm alone with my thoughts.

When I reach my room, I crash through the door, slamming it too hard. Leaning against the frame, I attempt to collect my thoughts, but they're scattered, tossing loosely around in my skull. I grip my fucking mask and rip it off, flinging it across the room.

Now that they know we're living above them, I don't care about being quiet. I push from the door, raking my hands through my hair, then sit at the end of my bed. My eyes fall to the wolf figure.

Seeing her hold it. That little piece I have left of him. It sent rage through me. Black as night. Like Rune was in here himself, delicately fondling with corrupt fingers the only shred I have left of him.

She's not Rune.

The thought flashes through me, and I groan, standing up to pace the room, clenching my jaw, remembering her red ass and her delicate groans.

Princess is lucky I have such control and didn't unleash my darkness like I wanted to, so she would feel that burning pain we all felt that day. She's lucky I reined it back in. That before I removed my belt and struck her bare ass, I'd coiled my shadows back tightly, just as tightly as I wrapped the leather around my hand so they only leaked out like whispers instead of black waves that drowned her.

But I should have known better. The night in the woods taught us all. She's desperate to be free of her lifelong restraints. She's so receptive to the darkness that lives inside me, in all of us, that it breaks free around her and I find myself wanting to stain her with it.

Delilah is our payback after all.

But she fucking eats up everything we give her, drinking in every sip of darkness that lives within us, and feeds it back to us until we're the ones starved for more.

She may not be Gavin, but she wasn't supposed to be...

This fucking enticing. This fucking receptive.

This much of a fucking *problem.*

When we decided to make her ours, to make her turn against her father, we never thought that we'd actually feel something for her. She was supposed to be a tool. Something we used to pry him open until he bled all over. We were meant to manipulate her submission, her desire, her entire body, until we owned her. Controlled her. Until she willingly helped us, but now she's snuck into that empty space in my chest and every time I touch her I want more, more, more.

My fist slams into the wall, all this pent up energy turning into aggression. I need to get off.

I stalk to the bathroom and turn the shower on, then strip my shirt and pants. When I'm undressed, I grip my cock in a tight fist. Bringing my hand to my nose, I inhale her sweet scent. I can still smell her hot cunt. Taste her in my mouth.

Fuck.

We intended to punish her, but I think we only succeeded in punishing ourselves. My dick's so hard it hurts.

I grip my length and tug roughly. Not the way she would. Not delicate but hard, with a dry hand. My hips jerk at the punishing grasp. I stroke again, faster, harder. Like Breaker when he grips Viper's cock. I reach around and grab my ass, the way Viper does when Breaker buries his cock deep in his mouth.

"Need some help?"

I jerk into my hand, Viper's voice sending a flare of panic and something else through me. I spin in shock, then realize I'm still holding my dick and turn back around. My eyes meet his in the steamy mirror.

"What the fuck?" I hiss, grabbing the head to try to calm myself. "Did you forget how to knock?"

His eyes drag up and down my body. "Door was open."

"Unlocked doesn't mean open, Viper." My gaze skims over his bare chest to the tattoo in the center, noticing how the bright light overhead outlines every plane of muscle and deepens the shadows under his eyes. Highlights the gleam of sweat on his collarbone.

He shrugs, leaning his large shoulder against the frame. "Breaker's mad at me."

I grit my teeth. *Like I give a shit.* "He's always mad at you."

Viper's eyes flicker down to my ass. "He is."

"Probably because you're an asshole."

He lifts a shoulder again, giving me an absent nod, his eyes moving up from my ass to my back and the tattoo between my shoulder blades. He has the same one on his stupidly sculpted chest. I don't know why he's staring.

"Can you leave?" I snarl, my cock growing even harder with him looking at me like that.

"I could," he says, stepping forward. My spine straightens. "Or I could stay."

Always fucking pushing boundaries. "Go," I snap.

"What If I don't?" He takes another lazy step toward me. Lifting his hand, he places his finger delicately, barely brushing the skin on the back of my neck.

When his finger slides down my spine, my back goes straight, my blood running so hot it scorches my veins, making my skin feel like it's on fire and freezing at the same time. Viper steps in so close, I feel the heat of his body along my bare back. His forehead hits my shoulder, slicking over the sweat gathered from the steamy room. He exhales slowly, breath dampening my already sticky flesh. The finger on my spine drifts to the dimple in my lower back. Presses into the divot. He breathes in. Deep. Taking my scent, my heat, into his chest with a quiet moan.

My hand tightens around my shaft. My thoughts splinter. Shards of images of us over the years—of his heated looks, his mouth around Breaker, the way he throws his head back when he comes—cutting through me.

His full lips skim over the flesh on my shoulder blade. "We both know you want my mouth instead of your hand. You have for a long time."

Desire punches me in the gut and all those splinters weave back together, stealing my breath. I spin, my fingers gripping his throat. "Don't fucking play with me," I snarl, my cock slicking over his stomach.

His hands land on my shoulders, his lip curling into a smirk. "I thought I was the one with the temper."

My fingers tighten, and I shove him back until he slams into the wall. A breath escapes him, fanning my face with mint and lemon as his eyes move to my mouth. Slowly, watching my eyes, the fingers gripping my shoulder loosen and slip lower, down my chest, dragging over my nipple to my stomach. His nails scratch at my abdomen, making my stomach ripple with heat.

"*Viper*," I say, but it sounds like a plea more than a warning.

My jaw pops when his fingers brush below my navel. Then fingers move to the base of my cock. Brush along the top. My chest heaves. His mouth falls open as he slips his fingers around my girth and I buck into his hand, my body lit up, desperate for any touch.

"So needy," he whispers. "Maybe I'll fuck your mouth and make you my good little boy."

Red clouds my vision. Rage tangled with something dark and primitive makes me move before I can think. He grunts when I grip him by the back of the neck and slam him down to his knees.

"Open," I demand, moving on instinct, completely mindless with fury and need.

When he opens, I thrust forward, driving into his mouth, my cock hitting the back of his throat. His head slams into the wall. Viper's arm flails out, but I grip his wrist and pin it above his head as I thrust. He grunts, and the vibration nearly makes me blind as I drive into his mouth deeper, forcing him to take me into his throat. He chokes, eyes watering, looking up at me with such fury, I laugh.

"Good boy," I taunt, punching forward with my hips viciously. "Take me deep. If she can take me all the way, so can you."

He grunts again and his free hand lands on my ass. I grate out this desperate, reedy sound as he grips my ass and forces me even deeper.

"Fuck," I whisper, my shoulders dropping as I drive in again. I pull out and his tongue swirls over my head before he greedily sucks me back into his warm mouth. My head falls forward, resting on the wall as I watch him take me deep. "Yes, just like that."

He does it again, then again, my balls drawing up tight. I release his wrist, weaving my fingers into his thick hair, holding the back of his head, thrusting hard and fast, then hold my dick in his throat until I know he needs air, only easing up when his eyes water. He sucks in a breath through his nose, but sucks me back in.

"Greedy boy," I rasp, absolutely ravenous for his mouth. His tongue skates over my slit and I tighten my grip, letting my nails dig into his scalp. "You want my cock? Take it like a good boy because I'm about to fucking *own* you."

His rumbling groan makes my hips punch forward harder. My dick hits his throat. Keeping him still, I drive deeper until I feel him gag, throat moving. His lashes flutter, hand flexing on my ass.

"That's it, tongue out," I grate, eyes practically rolling to the back of my head. "Choke on my cock, you fucking filthy boy." Viper swallows. "Oh fuck. Take me deep. Fuck yes."

When he taps my ass, I ease up. The grating sound of his zipper makes my abs flutter. Then he frees himself. The sight of his large hand on his thick cock ignites fire in my veins. Viper grips himself tightly, jerking from root to tip with fast, harsh strokes.

"Good boy," I grate, devouring the sight of him. My thumb skates over his jaw, over the spit dripping down his chin, and his lips wrapped around my dick. "So beautiful with my cock in your mouth."

Warmth hits my ankle and his eyes roll back in his head. My spine tingles, the pressure building up so tight that when I drive into his mouth one final time, I hold him to me, throwing my head back, all tension and fury exploding out of me with brilliant heat. His throat moves around my tip as he swallows, making me groan and buck into his mouth deeper as I spill down his throat. My hips move back and forth with jerky movements, riding my release, then I pull away and stumble back to the sink.

Viper falls forward on to his hands, gasping and coughing. He swipes at the saliva dripping down his chin, at my *cum* on his chin. Raising his head, his eyes meet mine and something flares behind the blue color.

My head spins, and panic slams into my chest, clawing at my throat. With shaking hands, I grab my pants and shirt, and stalk past him out into the bedroom, frantically dressing. I grab one of my masks and tug it on. Pants still unzipped, I fling the door open, this wild, dangerous fear chasing me as I take the stairs two at a time. As I fling the front door open and storm past the driveway, then out over the lawn, that panic needles its way into my stomach and I have to stop and bend over. Breathe.

Just breathe.

His face flashes in my mind. I squeeze my eyes shut, but his face is replaced with Viper's and the memory of how he sucked my dick, eyes flashing with the same pent up desire I constantly feel around him. Around Breaker.

Yeah. He was right.

I've wanted him for a long time.

Chapter 33

STRIKER

15 Years Ago, September, Age 15

We're in the training yard when they return. I only know they are back because I hear Cook yelling something to Commander, and the two of them rarely speak. The word "gurney" cracks across the yard, and I lower my rifle, turning to look at Viper next to me.

The way his expression turns to panic tells me he heard it too.

"Please don't be them," Breaker says and I glance his way. He looks scared too. Scared that our brothers wouldn't return. That they wouldn't make it to twenty like so many that came before us.

They've been gone so long, I think we all feared the worst. We've heard the whispers about the wilderness over the years. The set of brothers to go before Reaper, Hunter, and Seeker never returned. They were lost out there. The record's we saw confirmed it.

No. Not lost.

They died.

"Get in formation!" Commander Maxim yells and we scatter, complying with his order as quickly as possible.

In the distance, I hear the familiar grate of the fence sliding back, allowing someone entrance to the front yard. I remember the sound from that first day I arrived, and nearly every day after, as supplies were brought in. The school is an old high security prison that used to house the criminally insane. Men who couldn't be placed with other normal criminals. Men who tore their victims apart. We've all heard the stories.

I always wondered why Fallon chose this place to house the school. But maybe it's fitting. He's turning us more and more every day into cold, hard killers.

"Fuck," Breaker hisses from next to me, drawing the word out so long that I glance at him. He lifts his chin in the direction of the entrance.

My stomach sinks. I don't want to look.

"Get the body on the gurney," Commander says.

The body. I press my eyes closed, fear and a slick sickness making my legs weak. It's always amazed me how people are no longer people when they die. They're just a body. But then that's all that's left. Whatever spark of life that makes us who we are disappears when the mind dies. We become just an empty shell.

"Who is it?" Viper asks, and I realize he's as much of a coward as I am. Neither one of us can look. We don't want to know if Reaper or Hunter has had their life snuffed out. If they are just simply a body now.

"You did well, son," I hear Fallon say. "Was it an accident or a choice?"

When I hear the response, "Choice," my knees buckle at Reaper's voice. Strong but edged with something cruel.

"Your brother was stronger than we gave him credit for," Fallon says, and I feel bile rising in my throat.

No. No. No.

Please don't be Hunter.

If Hunter was the one to go, our unit would never survive. He's the glue that keeps us all together. He's the heart. The soul of us all. The only one who's managed to go into the wilderness with his heart and mind still intact. Not even Reaper has kept all the pieces of himself from being turned hard and cold.

"Seeker will be missed," I hear Reaper say, and my entire body melts with relief. We all knew that one of them wouldn't come back. I should feel bad that we've lost another brother, but I'm so glad it's not Hunter or Reaper that I can't feel bad.

"Hunter, Reaper," Fallon says. "You've returned to us and are ready for your first mission."

My eyes pop open and my head snaps in their direction. They just returned. They just survived the wilderness and they already have a mission?

I watch as Reaper takes the envelope from Fallon. His hand shakes, no doubt from exhaustion, from dehydration. Reaper rarely feels anything beyond rage, so I know it's not fear or something as mild as trepidation. He tears open the envelope and that's when I notice the blood. He's covered in it. The entire front of his uniform is drenched in rust-colored splashes. My eyes fall over the gurney and I see Seeker. His pale face. His empty, unseeing eyes. I have the sudden urge to go over and close them. Like he can read my thoughts, Hunter glances my way and delicately places his mask over our dead brother's eyes. My body relaxes.

"I don't understand," Reaper says, staring down at the paper. "This says—"

"I'm well aware of what it says, son," Fallon barks, his handsome face contorting.

Reaper's spine straightens, and he folds the paper before tucking it back into the envelope. Fallon snatches it and turns to Hunter.

"You both leave tomorrow," he says as he hands the envelope to Hunter.

When Hunter reads the note, his brows furrow and he glances at Reap, his arms falling to his sides. "This is our first mission?" he says, obviously in disbelief.

"We have no sides, my sons," Fallon says. "We go where the money is, and the money is there." He points to the paper hanging limply in Hunter's hand. "It doesn't matter who they are, it only matters if they pay."

"But we just came—"

"Silence!" Fallon shouts, so loud we all freeze. "Did I train you to question me?"

"No, sir," Hunter says.

Fallon spins and glares at Reaper. "Be ready to leave at dawn. Do not miss the flight."

As our Father walks away, Commander tugs at the gurney and wheels Seeker inside toward the infirmary. Reaper and Hunter exchange a look, and as soon as Fallon and Maxim clear the yard, we three shoot forward. Breaker hooks his arm around Hunter's shoulders, pulling him in for a hug as Viper awkwardly pats Reaper on the shoulder. It earns him a dark glare, and he drops his hand.

As I walk forward, Reaper meets my eyes and shakes his head. He's not happy.

"His choice?" I ask, watching Reaper snatch the paper from Hunter's hand and ball it in a fist.

"He chose to be the one," Hunter says.

The one.

Bile churns in my gut. We all know what that means.

Hunter comes to stand next to me and I look up at his dark eyes. He's so tall, just like Reaper. "You really think I'd let that place best me?" Digging into his pocket, he pulls out a little lump of wood, offering it.

My eyes flicker from his open palm to his face, my brows knitting.

"Take it."

I pick up the small figurine, examining it. It's a crude carving of a... "Wolf?" I ask, running my thumb over the curled tail as I watch his lips lift into a grin.

"It's not great, but it's the first thing I've made."

"I like it," I say in a rush. "Did you see wolves?"

Hunter shakes his head. "Just in my dreams."

The wood feels coarse, the edges rough, but I like the way he etched little lines in its tail like fur.

"They're pack animals," he says, voice low. My gaze darts up to his. "They're loyal. Protective. Mean as shit when one of their own is threatened."

At first I think he's describing Reaper, but then I realize he's talking about wolves.

"They hunt in packs. Live in packs."

My fingers enclose on the carving.

"Fuck within their pack."

My hand hesitates as I slip the figurine into my pocket. I lick my lips then say, "And they mate for life."

Hunter nods. "They do." He hooks an arm around my shoulders. Scratches and bruises mar his thick forearms. "Come on. I need some real food. My stomach is eating itself."

"Was it bad?" I ask.

His step falters. "Yeah." But then he pulls me close and chuckles.

"What's so funny?"

Hunter turns to face me. "You were scared for me." I drop my gaze, focusing on the mud caking his boots. My breathing hitches when he shifts, his large hand squeezing the back of my neck, thumb skimming over my pulse. He leans down, so only I can hear, to whisper, "You really think I'd not return to you, little wolf?"

My gaze darts up to meet his. Hunter winks and steps away. I watch his strong back as he stalks across the yard, leaving me with a thundering heart.

Yes. I want to scream. *Yes. I was scared you'd not come back*, but I remain quiet, watching as Viper runs up to him and hooks his arm over his shoulders, pulling him down to press his forehead to his. He says something to Hunter, but Breaker's loud crack of laughter keeps me from hearing.

I may be four years younger than him, not as experienced in life or in other ways like he and Reaper thanks to the girls in the village, but I know what this sinking feeling in my gut means. And I don't want to feel it. I don't want to care too much. About any of them, but Hunter most of all.

"Fucking Christ," Reaper curses, staring down at the paper. I snap my gaze to him, having forgotten he was standing just feet away.

Reaper tosses the paper to the muddy ground and turns toward our quarters. I lean down and pick up the paper, uncurling it, smoothing the wrinkles out so I can read the order.

Center of the page, in small letters, reads one name. I look up at Reaper's back as he walks away. Reaper is cold. Distant. Calculating. So different from all of us. But this?

I don't know if he has it in him to kill a little girl.

Chapter 34

STRIKER

The setting sun at my back washes the ocean in front of me a garish gold, the sky turning purple slashed with pink and yellow as the light fades. The waves crash against the large rocks below, a fine mist dampening my face with cold, salty water. I shove my hands deeper into the pockets of my jacket, turning my face up toward the sky. Now I know why Reaper comes here to think. It's peaceful. A vast open area to spill out the disaster whirling through my head.

I squeeze my eyes shut as I tilt back on my heels. The skin around my ankle pulls, reminding me I still have Viper's cum on me.

Jesus.

My shoulders drop, and I rake a hand through my hair, trying to shove the memory of him away, but the heat behind his blue eyes as he looked up at me with a mixture of shock and...

Want.

As much as I've told myself we were all worked up, driven practically mad by need after our punishment, that I lost control and fucked any mouth that was near, I'm a liar and I know it. He knows it.

I don't know why I've denied this attraction for so long. It's not like I'd receive judgment from Reaper, or be less. I know I wouldn't. Even in my head, I know that what I feel, this craving for him, *them*, isn't something to be ashamed of.

I think, though, it's my heart that I'm too scared to lose.

I've already lost someone who held parts of my heart, and the thought of risking it further was too much. If I gave my body to Viper, he'd own more of me than I was willing to share. Reaper already holds all my delicate parts. If I give too many away, I'll have nothing left for myself.

The thought creates a sick feeling in my gut.

Isn't that what we're doing to her? Forcing Delilah to share pieces of herself with us until we own every acre of skin? Until her heart and mind are ours to use?

"Which one?" Reaper asks from behind me, snapping me back, the icy wind nearly carrying his voice away.

When I don't turn around or answer, he steps up to the ledge next to me. When he leans over, boots tipping on the edge, I resist the urge to pull him back as he peers at the rocks and crashing waves below.

Reaper leans back, his shoulder brushing mine, and stares out at the ocean with me for a while. "They're being weird," he says after a few minutes.

My eyes dart his way, my stomach hollowing out. "Weird?"

He smirks, gaze still floating over the sea. "Weirder than usual. Breaker looks irritated by Viper's existence, but he usually does. Viper looks a little subdued, and you're out here wallowing."

"I'm not wallowing," I snap. *Maybe I am a little.*

Reaper remains quiet, capturing his bottom lip in his teeth like it will hide his smirk.

Sometimes, I hate how good he is at reading people.

"Viper," I say in defeat, looking down at my boots. There's dirt scuffing the top, sending a rush of agitation through my chest.

Reaper shifts, turning to face me, but I grind my teeth, avoiding his penetrating, knowing eyes. "What did you do? Because he's quiet for once, so you should do it again."

Despite myself, I chuckle. "He'd probably let me."

From the corner of my eye, I see his brows raise, that shit-eating grin shifting until it's a little lopsided. Like he can't even hide his delight. "How bad?"

I wince, letting out a huff of air. "I pinned him against the wall and fucked his mouth." Saying it out loud makes it true, and it sounds brutal.

God, I'm an asshole.

He makes a half shocked, half knowing sound in his throat that sounds a lot like approval. "Serves him right." Then after a heartbeat Reaper asks, "Did he complain?"

"No."

"Did he try to stop you?"

"No."

Reap nods. "Did he *want* you to stop?"

I shoot him a look.

His lip curls with glee. "So you're out here mentally flogging yourself because you face-fucked the man you've wanted for years? I didn't think you had such a weak constitution, Strike." Reaper grips the back of my neck, turning me to face him, and it feels like a reward. Being touched by him. It always has, considering he won't let anyone touch him, and it feels so much like *his* hand on me. "It was bound to happen. I'm surprised it took you this long to face-fuck that crazy asshole into submission. He's practically been begging for it with the way he's been acting lately."

He squeezes my neck and then his hand drops. Digging into his pocket, he pulls out his phone, then hands it to me. I unlock the screen with my thumbprint and read the text that's already loaded. My hand falls to my side and I curse.

"Come on," he says. "We have to discuss this with the others."

STRIKER

***

"What the fuck do you mean, take her back?" Breaker yells, fists at his sides, his voice echoing around the empty room. He drops to the piano bench, laying his mask on his knee.

"We can't," Viper says as he crosses his arms, propping a hip on the side of the piano. "You saw her that day, what if..." He doesn't finish the sentence. He doesn't need to.

We all saw her that day she left Rune's office. It's the entire reason we became suspicious. Cora had left his office just a few weeks before we took them, with a bloody nose. We knew something was off, but had no proof. I think we all feared the worst. When we took her, it was confirmed.

Rune has been hurting her. More than likely in ways that make me want to kill him a thousand times over.

"You read the text," Reaper says from behind me. "We have orders to take her back."

"We stopped following orders the second we took Cora," Viper snaps. His eyes slide my way, then down to my crotch.

Fuck. I recognize that look. I give it to the girls anytime I'm within a few feet of them.

I glance at Breaker and catch his knitted brows. "Wait, wait, *wait*," he says, motioning between me and Viper at his side. "What the fuck is this?"

My stomach drops.

"What the fuck happened?" Breaker asks, his lip somehow managing to pull up into a smirk and down into a frown all at the same time.

Is he upset? Why am I worried? It's not like Breaker has any claim over Viper.

Shit. Why am I thinking like this?

"Not now," Viper growls, standing upright to walk further away from me. He stops next to Reaper in the center of the room, eyes dropping to his boots. "We have to decide how we're going to deal with this."

"There's nothing to decide. She goes back." Reaper rakes his fingers roughly through his hair. "You know damn well we have to. This isn't something we can ignore. They made a deal."

He's right. Even if we don't like it.

"And why the fuck should we care?" Breaker asks. "Too bad if Rune made a deal. We don't have to abide by it."

Reaper sighs. "But she does. Rune does. We all do, otherwise we'll start an all out war."

"We've already waged war the second we took his daughter," Viper reminds him.

"Against *Rune*," Reaper barks. He doesn't like this any more than the rest of us, but he's also not stupid. We were told to take Cora back. She's not ours to keep. She's already been promised to another. He gestures to the window and the black sky outside. "If we don't send her back, it'll be fucking World War Three out there."

"Does she even know?" Breaker asks.

"I doubt it," Viper says. "I doubt Rune would care enough to let her know she's been promised to Zane Devin."

My fists curl at my sides. Fucking Zane. He's a sick motherfucker, maybe even worse than Rune, and that's a hard task.

"Rune promised Zane a wife," Reaper says, looking down at his mask in his hands. He stretches it out, thumb sliding over the eyehole, then his shoulders drop. "You know how these families work. He didn't want to sentence Delilah to such a fate—"

"So he gave him Cora," Breaker says for him.

"Zane Devin is a powerful man with a powerful name. That's why he's Rune's right-hand man," Reaper says. "If he's been promised a pretty trophy, then that's what he's going to get."

"You know what he's like," I remind him. We all do. We have files, pages and pages detailing the level of depravity that lives under his skin.

"We don't have a *choice*," Reaper hisses. "If he doesn't get Cora as promised, Zane will make a move against Rune and all hell will break loose. The backlash will cause Rune to go into hiding. He'll be forced to clean up his act and we'll never be able to touch him."

He's right. Even if we hate it.

"I don't like this," Breaker says, eyes moving between all of us. His jaw pops and I wonder for a second if we can get away with defying these orders just so that tense look in his eyes leaves.

"I don't like it either," Reaper says, "but it has to be done."

"Fuck." Viper snatches his mask from the bench seat, stalking toward the door.

"No," I hear myself saying, thinking of the way Delilah holds her. We'll lose her if we send Cora back. "She can't go."

Reaper spins to look at me. It's like he can see what I'm thinking and his jaw tenses. I was right. Some part of him wanted Cora for Delilah and he knows the second she finds out we sent her best friend back, we're going to lose any chance we may have at making her ours. "It's already done."

Chapter 35

CORA

Delly isn't anywhere to be found. I've searched every unlocked room in the house and the back garden, and can't find her in the large ornate one out front either. I hope she's not trying something stupid. She won't tell me what happened between her and the men last night, but I know it must have been intense, considering they dragged me from the library and locked me in the fucking room. Not to mention the state she was in when they brought her to me. She was a mess. Her ass red and welted.

She finally calmed down after I sated her, and we both fell asleep. When I woke this morning to an empty bed, I scrambled up and went searching for her or one of the boys so I could find out what happened. But I can't find them, and now I can't find her either.

Delly's words ring in my head.

We aren't going home.

I know she's been hoping that Rune and Clyde were coming for us, but I've already figured it out. We weren't leaving. The four have something planned for us. What it is, I'm not sure, but I know men work differently than women. Women are cunning with their revenge. It's delivered with precision, making sure it cuts cleanly, deeply like a scalpel. Men, though, their cruelty is rough, with jagged edges delivered with brute force. I know because Rune took his hatred for my parents out on me.

Whatever revenge they have planned for Rune will be hard. Effective, and it won't just cut him, it will leave him with a jagged, open wound.

Like, say, taking his daughter and never bringing her back.

I can't say I'm upset at the idea of not returning. I like it here. Even if it's boring and we barely see the men, I like it just being Delly and me. I like getting my hands dirty and picking fresh herbs from the little garden. I like the domestic feel, the slowness of being cut off from the world. It's like we're living in a fairytale mansion, protected by four large guardians.

Even though we've barely seen them over the last two weeks, I know they're around and it provides a weird, reassuring tingle every time I think about them, I feel better knowing even if Rune tried to get us, they'd not let him have us. It sends a sliver of excitement through me that someone wants me so badly that they'd kill to have me. It's a crazy thought, but then all of this is crazy, so I embrace it.

The rumbling of a car engine snaps me back and I stop in the middle of the large garden, listening. We've been here just over three weeks and I've not once seen a car.

My heart hammers and I run toward the sound at the front of the estate, skidding to a stop, my boots slipping over the gravel walkway, when I see a shiny black unmarked van in the drive.

My chest tightens as I rush toward the vehicle, stopping to see if anyone's inside. I place both hands to the tinted window, but don't see anyone in the back, or the driver's seat as I walk around the van. My eyes move to the open front door. A shiver passes through me, settling grossly in my belly.

Hesitantly, I creep up the large stairs to the front door. Using just a finger, I push the door open and it swings, bright morning light spilling in from behind me, illuminating the dark foyer. I take a deep breath, my eyes moving to the doorway of the library, when I hear a deep rumbling voice I immediately recognize.

We've only seen them a handful of times over the last two weeks, and my stomach flips. Knowing they're just a few feet away suddenly feels more intimidating than comforting after whatever they did to Delly last night. Hearing his stern voice ring out again makes me question if I want to storm in there and demand answers.

"We fucking have to, Breaker," I hear Reaper grate, and the deadly tone makes me shoot forward, my eyes rolling.

He's just a man. A large, sexy man, a lethal looking one, but still just a man. I've dealt with far worse than the likes of him.

As I pass through the doorway, I see all their masked faces and large black-clad bodies sending heat to my core, remembering their heavy breathing and primal energy when they dropped Delly at my feet last night.

And there's a new face. An *actual* face.

I know right away he's a driver. Like the guys who deliver packages for people like Rune. Runners and delivery guys have a certain look about them and I wonder what the men had delivered.

When I step into the room, all eyes turn to me. A slippery sensation slides through my gut, the heated memory slipping away. "Have you seen Delly?"

Striker shakes his head and looks away. Reaper closes his eyes briefly, then glances over at Breaker sitting in the large wingback chair, tapping his foot on the floor, while Viper won't even meet my eyes.

"What's going on?" I ask, picking up on their body language. They're upset. Angry. Something has them on edge. "Is something wrong with Delly?"

"No, Baby Girl. Kitten is fine." Reaper holds his hand out for me to take, palm up, fingers beckoning me forward. I hesitate, the midnight hue of his eyes intimidating, even with the silvery light of morning reflecting brightly in them through the open curtains. But I take his gloved hand, letting him pull me forward. His arms wrap around me, hugging me to his massive chest like he would a child. It sends a calm wave through my middle, easing the tension in my shoulders. Inhaling, I take the deep woodsy scent of him into my lungs and I get why Delly felt that way with him that night. Maybe I should have spent more time with him. He's not as hard as he looks.

When I look up into his onyx eyes, what I see makes the tension in my jaw return. He pets my head, looking absently over at Breaker and Viper. I can't see his face, I can't see any of their faces, but Reaper's eyes tell me all I need to know.

They know.

I had hoped when I realized they had watched us long enough to stock up on our preferred supplies they hadn't figured out the relationship between Rune and I, but I was fooling myself. They've known all along.

My stomach churns, remembering how I called him Papa in front of them. They knew this entire time I was fucking Rune. They know he hurts me.

But that doesn't explain the driver.

"What's happening?" I ask, turning in Reaper's arms to look at the others.

Breaker's incessant foot tapping stops and he leans forward, resting his forearms on his thighs as he lowers his masked head to his hands.

He's wearing his gloves. They all are.

My teeth set on edge. They haven't worn their gloves in weeks. They've pushed up sleeves and I've caught glimpses of tattoos and scars. Pulled masks away to eat, revealing flashes of high cheekbones and tanned flesh. I've seen more than I did that night in the dim club. I could identify them by these things alone.

But today, they're covering everything up and that means only one thing.

We're being sent back.

"Where's Delly?" Even I hear the panic in my voice.

"She's upstairs," Striker says.

But then we all hear her say, "I'm right here."

I spin in Reaper's arms again and my gaze lands on her in the doorway, one hand on the doorframe, the other pressing to her belly, making me wonder if hers always flips and flutters around them like mine does. Her teeth sink into her bottom lip as her gaze bounces between the men. She still has that slightly feral look about her. Like she's about to come completely unhinged.

When her eyes land on the driver, she blanches. Blue eyes widen, darting to Reaper. "We're going back?"

I know they hear the same disbelief in her voice that I do.

"Not you, Princess," Striker says, reaching out to grasp her arm.

Not you...

Turning, I face Reaper, and grip the front of his shirt. He looks down at me and I think I see a flash of remorse in the black pools of his eyes as his jaw tics under his mask. "You're sending just *me* back?"

He nods. My hands tingle.

"Just me?"

"Yes, Baby Girl, we have orders," he tells me.

Orders. Like they *have* to, not because they want to.

Panic snakes its way up my throat, curling around my neck. My fingers dig into his shirt tighter, tugging it away from his chest until he's forced to make eye contact again.

I shake my head. "You can't send me back." Reaper blinks, then looks down at my hands on his shirt. His shoulders rise on an inhale as he cups my cheeks and he runs a gloved thumb over my bottom lip, the material so impersonal against my flesh.

Disbelief makes my fingers unfurl. *They're sending me back.* They know what Rune is like, what he's doing to me, and they're still sending me back to him.

Maybe they don't know all the details.

But they know enough.

My hands fist his shirt again and I tug, standing up on my tiptoes, pressing my chest to his, trying to force my words onto him so he can understand, "I *cannot* go back, Reaper."

His hands tighten on my cheeks briefly. "You have to, Baby Girl."

"No," I hiss, the sting of tears pissing me off as much as his words. His *stupidity* for not understanding that I can't go back. I tug harder, pulling his shirt down. "You know I *can't*."

Reaper's flinch mirrors my own as he tenses, his body turning to solid stone under my hands. His eyes dart to Delly behind me and then to the men around us.

My heart rattles when his muscles bunch and tighten more in his shoulders. "Please," I whisper. *God, I can't believe I'm begging him to keep me here.* "I can't go."

He closes his eyes and shakes his head. Then his gloved fingers clasp over mine and he rips my hands from his shirt.

"What are you doing?" Delly asks as he pulls me toward the doorway, shoving past her to the foyer. "Why is just Cora going back? Why aren't I going back?" Before we're halfway across the foyer, she marches forward, grabbing Reaper's arm. She grips my wrist and yanks me toward her, but he doesn't let me go. "I don't understand."

"You don't have to," Reaper snarls, shoving her away. She stumbles back into the railing. "We have orders to send Cora, *just* Cora, back to Gavin."

"*No,*" I whisper, my entire body melting in horror, like my bones may slip out of my skin. I jerk violently, a scream building in my throat as Reaper shoves me toward Striker, who grasps my arm and pulls me toward the door.

It feels like that day they took us all over again. When they were dragging me away from Delly. But that day I didn't know I was being saved. That day, I thought I was being taken somewhere to be hurt. Today, right now, I know what will happen to me when I return. Without Delly there, nothing will keep him from me. In his paranoia, he'll somehow blame me for Delly not being brought back and take it out on me.

I spin toward Striker, grabbing at his shirt. "You know what he'll do to me if I go back."

His eyes shift to Reaper.

"Striker, please." Tears burn my cheeks. "Please. You know he'll hurt me."

"Who?" Delly shouts, but Striker ignores her and grips my arm tighter, yanking harder when I dig my heels into the wood floor.

"Please!" I scream, dropping to my knees.

"*Fuck*," I hear Breaker yell behind me. "Reaper, I swear to fucking god."

I can barely hear past the thundering in my head, my heart beating wildly, making my entire body shake. The realization I'm going back alone, with no protection, with no Delly to counteract his cruelty, ripping terrified sobs from my throat.

"Reaper," Viper yells, but I can't see anything other than the front door Striker's dragging me toward, my legs flailing behind me, boots catching on the ragged grooves of the wood floor. But then suddenly he lets me go.

"Fuck!" Striker stalks forward and slams the front door, so hard the windows rattle, the sound echoing like a gunshot, but it pops back open like fate or the devil himself insists I leave this place.

"I fucking *know*, Strike," Reaper growls as he wraps an arm around my waist, pulling me to my feet, then bends over and tosses me over his shoulder, my scream catching in my throat.

"Stop!" Delly screams. "What do you mean?"

My trembling hands grip the back of his shirt, and I push up, trying to look at Delly. Striker grabs her arm as she lunges for me, but she hits him hard enough that he lets her go. The sight of her face, contorted with fear as she follows us outside, only intensifies my crying.

"Reaper, stop," Delly pleads as he places me down on the dirt drive next to the van. She shoves past him, eyes locked on me. Cupping my cheeks, she wipes the tears away and says, "Who will hurt you?"

My insides twist painfully. I want to wrap myself up in her, around her, protecting us both from him. I glance frantically at Reaper. He crosses his arms and takes a step back, like he's waiting. Like he's saying, *Go ahead, Baby Girl. Tell her. Tell your best friend you've allowed her father to fuck you so he won't hurt you anymore.*

My legs give, but Delly keeps me upright. She always has.

I can't tell her. It will destroy her. She'll never forgive me. She'll blame me. Why would she even believe her father, her doting, loving overprotective father, loves to bend me over his desk and slap the shit out of me afterwards? That he's cruel. That he turned on me before I even had the chance to fall in love or give myself to someone else. She'll never believe he stole my safety the day he killed my parents and forced himself on me all those years later.

"Tell her." Reaper's hard voice snaps me out of it, and I glance his way. Striker shifts at his side, his entire body tense, and Viper moves forward to stand on his other side. Reaper glances at both men, then says, "Tell her, Baby Girl. It's okay."

I shake my head. Delly grips my cheeks, fingers digging into my skin so tightly, I don't know how they'd manage to rip me away from her.

"Cora, my love," she whispers. I swear it's like she already knows. Her eyes frantic, brows knit, body vibrating with fear. Maybe she's not as blind and maybe I wasn't that good at hiding it.

I open my mouth and a sob escapes, creaking out of me, rusty and old. Useless because all the tears I've shed over the years never stopped bad things from happening. The only thing that can stop Rune is me.

By talking.

She wipes my cheeks again. "Cora," she whispers my name so gently, my heart feels like it's about to crack open. "Tell me."

I glance at Reaper. Those dark eyes wait. I swear it's like he wants me to tell her. Like he's just been waiting for me to say something. Part of me wonders if that was his plan all along. Force me to tell her the truth about her father, so she'd hate him as much as he hates Rune.

As much as I wish I could.

"Papa." The word has barely left my mouth when her hands drop. She backs away, shaking her head. I suck in a breath. "Papa will hurt me again."

Chapter 36

STRIKER

Fuck. Fuck. Fuck.

We've done terrible things, hurt people, killed people, all out of greed and some fucked up desperation that craves approval from a man who tortured us. But, I've never hated myself like this. Cora's screams make me want to rip myself apart. Tear Reaper's fucking face off.

We are monsters. She trusts us, and we're sending her away.

"Papa," Cora whispers, her face crumbling. I feel like I'm crumbling. "Papa will hurt me again. He has been for years."

Delilah shakes her head, backing away, until she crashes into Reaper. Turning, she swats him away when he tries to wrap an arm over her shoulders, but he grips her wrists and pins her to his chest.

The pain contorting her features makes my guts feel like they're being torn out.

"Stop," he growls. "Listen. Even if you don't like what she has to say. Listen."

My stomach roils. I don't think *I* want to listen.

"Papa." Cora shakes her head. "Rune isn't nice to me like he is with you. He..." She glances up at Reaper, almost for reassurance. "He's done bad things to me for years."

Delilah tries to break from Reaper's grasp, releasing an angry little snarl, but he forces her to remain still.

"You're a fucking—" she doesn't say it. She stops herself.

With an anguished cry, Delilah turns and presses her face to Reaper's chest, knees growing weak as a terrible, heart wrenching sob escapes her. He wraps an arm around her to keep her upright, but then she pushes him away, slapping his chest, hitting him over and over as his arms fall to his sides.

He just stands there, letting her hit him. Letting her take her anger out. Eating it up, absorbing each hit with an inhale like he's taking her rage into his lungs. My chest squeezes, wanting to stop her.

He doesn't deserve her anger.

None of this is his fault.

Not entirely.

Delilah hits his chest one more time so hard, he actually rocks back on his heels, then she spins to face Cora. She stalks forward, little hands balled into fists, then grips her by her chin.

"Why didn't you fucking *tell* me?" she grates, anguish and sorrow and pure rage coloring her voice. "You should have told me."

Cora wipes a tear, letting Delilah's rage sink into her as much as Reaper had. "Which time?"

Delilah shakes her head, backing away and before Reaper can grab her again, she runs, shoving past Breaker in the doorway, into the house.

I step forward to follow her, but Reaper says, "Give her a minute."

***

Breaker has refused to let Cora go ever since we returned to the library, sitting her on his lap as he rubs her back. Like if he keeps her attached to him, within arm's reach at all times, we can't take her from him.

The driver is out in the van on standby and Cora has just spent the last twenty minutes telling us, in horrific detail, why she can't return.

"We knew this was possible," Viper hisses, his eyes flashing dangerously. He glares at Reaper to my left before glancing over his shoulder to make sure Cora can't hear us. I can practically see the many ways he's envisioning killing Rune swirling in the blue of his eyes. "We aren't sending her back."

"Fuck." Reaper presses his gloved fingers to his eyes, but then pulls them away, glancing at the thick black fabric before ripping the gloves off and throwing them to the floor. Like he can't stand the sight of everything they represent.

The school.

The order we were given.

What we are.

"What the fuck am I supposed to do? Ignore his order?" he asks.

"Yes," I hiss. I pinch the bridge of my nose, trying to calm my thoughts.

A cracked noise, like a sob echoes from just beyond the doorway and Reaper's gaze snaps in that direction. I march forward, fear of what I'm going to find making me want to puke.

Please...

I step outside the door and she's there, crumbled on the bottom step, her face in her hands.

She heard everything.

"Princess," I whisper, moving toward her, but she turns, scrambling to stand. Before I can take another step, she bolts up the stairs.

Dammit. As much as we wanted her to know the truth about her father, seeing it, witnessing her devastation, is so much worse than I could ever have imagined. Cora didn't spare any details, and I can't decide if I'm going to vomit or jump in the van and drive hundreds of miles to kill Rune myself.

"Shit," Viper says behind me. I turn to face him in the doorway, gripping the frame so hard I don't know how it's not cracking. "She heard?"

I nod as I move past him to talk to Reaper. My body screams to run after Princess, but we have to figure out what to do about Cora. We have orders to take her back. We already know what will happen once Rune and Zane realize she's not being returned. Zane's family will start a war. But the thought of sending her back, of Rune getting his hands on her, and worse, Zane, makes me want to burn them alive.

We aren't supposed to care about their feelings, but we're watching them fall apart and it feels like we're being torn to pieces.

We have orders.

We have this mission. We were so close to having Princess, that I can still taste her. Now this.

And now...

Fuck.

Now the thought of being away from Cora actually makes my chest hurt. Seeing Delilah in pain just makes it all worse.

"We can't send her," Viper says from behind me. "You said she's ours."

Reaper's eyes darken. His gaze lifts to Cora clinging to Breaker like he's a life raft. And I think he is. "She is," he says, the strain of indecision making his voice thick. "But we also have orders."

"Fuck orders, Reap. She's *ours*," Viper hisses, like he's reminding Reaper what the single word means.

He doesn't need to be told.

When we claim something, we never let it go.

"He's hurting her," Viper says, voice turning so cold it sends a chill up my spine.

We suspected when we took her that Rune was abusive toward her, but we never once imagined this level of depravity. She was still just a girl, barely even of age, when he first attacked her. Knowing all she's endured, everything she went through in her childhood, on top of this? I refuse to send her back to that.

"She's not going," I tell Reaper. His eyes snap my way, narrowing. I can't tell them what she confided in me, but I will make it clear I'm not sending her back so she can marry that sack of shit. "I refuse to send a woman back into that." I point to her. "I refuse to send *her*, period."

Reaper fists his hands, staring at me for a second. I know what I'm asking brings up the past. That day when our lives changed forever. When Reaper decided he would not follow an order. It set into motion an entire series of events that has led us all here. I wonder if he sees the similarities like I do. I bet he does. The consequences of defying that single order have chased him for the last fifteen years. We've all suffered so much because of that one decision.

When I think he's about to argue, he just backs away and nods, eyes moving over to Cora and Breaker. "Then we'll deal with the consequences."

I can feel Viper's relief as if it were a living thing. "Shit," he breathes out, turning toward Cora. "I was really worried about you for a minute, Reap."

When Viper sits next to Breaker on the couch, he scoops her up, pulling her into his lap. The second she's situated, she presses her face to his chest.

How did this happen? We took them three weeks ago, and somehow in that time they've crawled under our skin. We're now defying orders, we're taking stupid chances by spending too much time with them, being too soft by allowing them to sass us at every turn, then to top it off, we started to fucking care about their wellbeing.

Then, when we tried to detach ourselves, take a step back, it just made the ache in my chest worse. It made being away from them so hard that I had to lock myself in my room most days and pray for sleep to consume me, so I'd stop thinking.

This isn't how it was supposed to be.

Now we're fucking *fucked*. And the worst part is we did it ourselves. We made the mistake of fucking them that first night. Of bringing Cora. Of letting them close to us. Talking to them. Watching them.

"The way you all doubt me is insulting," Reaper says, shoving his hands into his pockets as he watches Cora on Viper's lap.

My brows knit. It makes my mask pull uncomfortably around my eyes so I scratch my brow as I face him. "What do you mean?"

He shakes his head, not responding.

"What do we do when he demands we return her?" I ask. Viper says something to her, and she starts crying again, flinging her arms around his neck.

"Fuck if I know," Reaper says. He tries to run his hand through his hair, but it lands on his balaclava and he lowers it, shoving it back into his pocket in annoyance.

Breaker catches my eye and stands up to join Reaper and me by the door. "How did we miss this?"

"I don't think we wanted to see it," I say, but the way Reaper exhales tells me maybe he not only saw it, he weaponized the knowledge. That maybe this was his plan when he took her.

I cock my head to the side. "You knew it was this bad, didn't you?" I ask him, watching his reaction.

His black eyes meet mine and my heart crashes against my ribcage. I shake my head. *Asshole.* He *wanted* Delilah to know. And now? She'll never forgive her father.

"How?" I ask. "How did you know?"

"I watched her, Strike. If you watch people, they give away their secrets."

Breaker sighs. "I don't know why we listen to you. You're a fucking asshole."

"Because you know I'm always right." Reaper's eyes dart to the doorway and the dark foyer beyond. Even though he's a manipulative dick, I know he's worried about our Princess. He may do anything, regardless of who he hurts to achieve what he wants, he may be callous, and cold, and truly dark at times, but I also know him. He may have wanted her to know about Rune's relationship with Cora, but he doesn't want Delilah's pain. He's already experienced so much of it.

But he does want Rune's downfall.

I nudge his arm with my elbow, even though it earns me a deadly glare. "Go to her."

He shakes his head. "No."

We both look back at Cora. He rolls his shoulders, rocking his head from side to side. Reaper's shoulders ease, but I can still see the tension in his body.

"You go," Reaper says. Our eyes meet. "We all know it was going to be you who brought her to us."

Chapter 37

DELILAH

I CLUTCH THE EDGE of the toilet seat, stomach heaving again, but nothing comes up. I wish something would so I could expel this dark, putrid feeling. Expel her words from my mind. If I'd not gone back downstairs, scared they were really taking Cora back, I'd not have heard her. I'd not have heard the things Rune's done. Heard her sobs, begging them not to take her to my father.

Cora told them everything. These men who stole us, who've kept us captive. And she never once told me.

Probably because she was scared that I wouldn't believe her.

And I don't blame her. I almost called her a liar.

I almost told my best friend, my lifeline these last few weeks that she was lying to me about Rune. I sink to the floor and crawl out of the bathroom over to the window. Pressing my forehead to the glass, I close my eyes. Her face is all I can see.

She's not a liar. Part of me has known for a long time something was off. I saw it in the way he'd touch her. The way he'd say her name. *God.* How could he?

My mind whirls, flashes of him with her over the years, making me feel like I may actually be sick. The times he'd demand she be the one to bring reports. Demand she come to his office or to his house. He was hurting her while we lived at home with him, before we left for college. And all the times we came back to visit. My father's been hurting her... this girl who was supposed to be like his daughter.

Like me.

My stomach heaves again and I clutch my middle. *Clyde.* Does he know? There is no way that he would allow my father to brutalize Cora. But then again, I never thought my father could do the things I just heard Cora say.

"Princess?" When Striker enters the room, I don't look his way. They knew too and didn't tell me.

"Is this why you keep saying he's a bad man?" I ask. "You knew?"

"Yes, and no."

I stare blankly out the window, his words barely registering. My gaze lifts to the ocean. How many times did I stare out this window, wishing I could go home? That I could hug my father again. Now I never want to touch him again. Or see him. Speak to him. Work for him. He's not what I thought he was.

He's so much worse.

"We knew he was hurting her," Striker says. "But we didn't know to what degree."

I turn to face him, pressing my back against the window. "Does Clyde know?"

Striker shakes his head, eyes casting down to the floor, then back to me. "We don't know for certain, but I don't think so."

His response settles my stomach some. The idea Clyde was complacent to Cora being abused all these years may very well be what sends me over the edge.

"Is this why you took us?" I shake my head as the words are leaving my mouth. No. I always forget about the missing puzzle piece. I've racked my brain, attempting to piece together so many explanations for their thirst for revenge against my father, but none seem to fit or make sense. Power, money. These men don't need it. They've created their own. This mansion may be in ruin, but it's a statement to their wealth. I look up at Striker standing above me. "What did he take from you?"

His eyes close briefly, then he sinks to his knees in front of me. "It's more complicated than that."

"Uncomplicate it," I say quietly. His gold eyes look lost, like he's not even in the room. "Striker, tell me, please."

His gaze snaps to me, pupils dilating in and out as he regains focus. He sinks back on his heels and slowly lifts a hand. At first I think he's going to reach for me, pull me to him like he does when he wants me close, but doesn't want to admit it. They all do. Reaper, worst of all. They pretend they are big and mean and scary, using aggression to keep us from asking too many questions or from seeing that deep down, they just desperately want to be touched.

Striker lifts his hand to his head and I almost laugh, thinking he's once again trying to run his fingers through his hair like he does when he gets irritated. They don't realize that while they've been watching us, I've been watching them.

When his fingers curl into the top of his mask, my heart stutters. When he pulls and the thin fabric slides upward, my heart skips, once, twice, then pounds. At the first hint of his jawline, I nearly gasp. Even though I saw it before, saw the same full lips, and dark stubble, it's still a shock. I forgot how perfectly sculpted his jawline is.

As he continues to slide the mask up, I see high cheekbones and I remember yesterday in his room, and as it slips higher, his wolfish, gold eyes framed by those long lashes, come into view and then suddenly I'm staring at his face. At a thin, sculpted nose. An intensely cut brow line. At warm, dark brown hair that falls around his eyes, frames his ears. A thick, masculine neck.

My first instinct is to shut my eyes. "No," I whisper. "No." I choke on a sob. "No."

"Princess."

I shake my head. *No.*

"We took you—"

"No!" I scream, digging my fists into my eyes. I don't want to see him. If I see him, can fully identify him, it means only one thing. I'm never leaving. They'd never allow this unless they're planning on disposing of me, or worse.

Never letting me go.

My throat tightens with a clawing panic as the weight of it all hits me.

It all makes sense. I had thought at first they took us so my father would comply with their demands. Pay money. Make some business deal. I thought my father would do anything to get us back, thinking about how we may get abused. Raped. Tortured. But no.

I know now why my father never came. Why they said he doesn't know how to find me, or where to look. Why I'm so far away. Why Clyde hasn't brought an army here to kill them all and rescue us. Why they've kept us here, alone, then feeding me little tidbits of sweetness. Slowly giving me comforts. Touching me so gently at times that I waited with bated breath for the next bit of tenderness. Made it so I'm so starved for contact, so desperate for them, I'd accept a spanking with my face in the dirt. That I'd willingly spread my legs and beg for them. Why Cora was treated so differently. They guessed she would be relieved to be here. To be away from Rune's sickness.

I was right the second I woke up.

It's a complete mind fuck. But I wasn't their target. I never was. It was my father they were planning on ruining, not me.

They've been telling me over and over and I refused to listen.

He's not who you think he is. He's a bad man.

When they had me on that table, I could feel it. The possessiveness. They've been telling me for weeks and I wasn't accepting it.

I think I've known from the beginning. They claimed me—us—that night and I let them. They told me and I was too stupid to even hear it. Breaker told me in the club. I belong to Reaper. To them. They wanted me compliant. Submissive. And now they have me being all that for them without even having to try too hard.

I'm theirs. I belong to them. To punish. To please.

"You never planned to give us back," I whisper, my heart twinging with a strange sort of ache.

What's the worst type of pain you could inflict? Take something and never return it. Or worse. Take something from someone and turn it against them. And they've slowly been doing just that.

"No," Striker says. "We aren't."

His answer is so final that I know I'm never leaving them. My own mind wouldn't allow it when I had the opportunity.

A strangled sob escapes and I turn my face, burying it in my shoulder. The loss of everything I've ever had slams into me. My condo. My life and the dreams I had of taking over my father's company. The silly dream of someday settling down with someone who actually loves me, not for my name or money, but because I'm me.

My father.

God. I've lost my father in a far worse way than I lost my mother. I'd rather have watched him die like I did her than have the truth ripping me apart.

But all of my love for him, my future with him, is lost anyway. Because it was all a lie. My father is a brutal man, but he always seemed to love Cora and me so much. Yet, he didn't love her. You can't hurt someone like that and love them. Love isn't cruel. It's supposed to protect and nurture. Now all my memories of him are stained. I want nothing from him again. And the worst part is they didn't even have to convince me. Cora did it for them.

"Was this the plan the whole time?" I open my eyes and stare at him, drinking in his features. I've spent weeks with him. Shared moments that have been more intimate than that night in the club and I'm finally seeing his face. He's beautiful. Sculpted full lips, hard jaw, stern but soft eyes. He's a contradiction of himself. Soft lines and jagged edges. My heart hammers painfully. "Why? Why like this? What did he take from you?"

"You've been asking the wrong question," Striker says, and I can't seem to look away, completely mesmerized, like I've never seen a human man's face before.

His words slam into me and I blink, scrambling to stand upright. He stays kneeling in front of me and part of me is glad. He's too big. Too male. Too real. Before he was a mask. Faceless. Now he's this man with expressions and sadness in his eyes.

I clench my jaw. I want to scream at him so that vulnerable expression is removed from his face.

"Who," he whispers. "Not what, Princess, but who."

I remember the lock screen.

There were five of them. Now there's just four.

"Who?" I ask. "Who did my father take from you?"

Striker sucks in a breath, and for the first time I can see how his jaw tightens. See how his brows furrow, like he's remembering something he doesn't want to. His eyes meet mine and I press my hand to my chest to keep my heart in place because it feels like it's shattering into a million pieces.

"Our brother," he says. "Rune Gavin killed our brother."

A thousand questions run through my head, but I just say, "Why?"

"Revenge."

"I don't understand."

He shakes his head. "That part will come later. All you need to know right now is that he brutally murdered our brother. He held him for weeks. Tortured him in ways even we can't fathom."

I know my father has killed people, ordered people to be killed. Rivals or anyone who threatens his family or finances, or his role of political and business mogul favorite. But what Striker just said means my father is far worse than some business tycoon who craves power and money. He's cruel. For fun.

Cora. He is cruel to her. He gets off on it.

Panic slams into me, making my heart race. I knew when I spent that night with these men that he could never find out. He'd go crazy and want them killed for touching me. What will he do now if he actually gets his hands on them?

Striker must see the fear in my expression because he grips my hips, pulling me forward. His face, his beautiful, perfect face, presses to my belly and my hands fall to his hair. I curl my fingers into the soft strands, marveling at how silky it feels, raking it back from his forehead as he looks up at me.

I don't know what they did to me, but the thought of something happening to him, of my father taking Striker, any of them, somewhere and hurting them, of him ever getting his hands on Cora again sends fire and anger and terror crashing through me until I feel like I can't breathe.

Striker lowers his face and presses his forehead to my belly. He pulls me to him tighter, turning his face, rubbing his cheek on the front of my dress. I'm reminded of that day in the garden. How he seemed so hungry to feel his skin next to mine and I can't help but wonder what made him this way. So starved for touch. What life he lived that he seems so desperate to feel every inch of my skin. I think of all of them. How they all seem so hard and soft at the same time.

And god. I want all those soft edges and cutting hard lines. From all of them.

From Striker right now.

I want the too rough touch of Viper that forces me to give him parts of myself, the man who armed me when he knew I was scared, simply because he wanted me to feel safe. And that single act made me feel secure. That one gesture of trust on his part, that I wouldn't use it against him, gave us our own little secret that I've carried around, reminding me they may keep me here, but I had the roughest, loudest one at my back.

My body craves the silent man who forced me to be close to him, touching me so gently that I felt secure, even though the world around me was uncertain.

My mind, parts of my heart, wants that darkness that lives in the man who even though his body tenses with some old need to seek revenge on Rune, he can't help but crave me the same way I crave him.

I crave that softness from the man who could barely contain himself that day in the garden. Who wanted me so badly he couldn't keep his hands off me. Not because of my father's name. My father's name made them all hate me.

It is me they want. Me, they desire.

Me, Striker's showing his face to right now.

Like he can sense my need climbing, his grip turns harder, edged with desperation and then suddenly his hands aren't gripping my hips, they're sliding down my legs, gathering my dress and pushing it up. His nose digs into the underwear over me, and my back hits the cold glass. Shoving my dress up higher, he breathes in. The guttural groan he emits makes me throb. My fingers tighten in his hair as his hot breath fans over me, and I grip it at the roots, nails clawing into his scalp. Striker makes another sound, like a gravelly moan, and with one hand, he grips my underwear and drags them down my thighs. I step out of them.

Striker grips my thigh and hooks it over his shoulder, and I groan in anticipation. Before I can tilt my hips to meet him, before I can even think, his mouth is on me. His tongue swirls over my clit, then lower to my opening. My head falls back to the glass and I move my hips in little circles as he devours me, completely mindless, the scrape of stubble on my skin sending me higher and higher. I'm still so keyed up, every nerve cracking with desire from last night, that it doesn't take me long to crash over. I cry out at the sudden orgasm crashing through me, faintly aware of his moans against my flesh, and how my hands hold him tightly to me.

Still coming down, my eyes barely focused, I let out a gasp as his tongue travels up higher, over my stomach, then even higher as he stands, pushing my dress up. When the material catches under my breasts, he takes his free hand and grips the little row of buttons over my chest and rips it open. I gasp, my back thudding against the window. An animalistic desire pours through me, and I reach for his belt, the same belt that I got just last night, as he leans down and tugs my cotton bra aside and takes my nipple into his mouth.

The sound of the metal clanking sends a weird shiver through me, remembering the cutting pain as he cracked it over my ass. Striker grips my thighs and lifts me up, sliding my body up on the glass, the wood of the panes digging into my back as his mouth drags up my neck to my jaw. I turn my head, feeling the heated trail he leaves as he moves to my mouth. We crash together, so desperate that I moan, parting my lips for him to sweep his tongue past my lips. I taste myself, my desire, on his tongue and it sends me higher.

My fingers weave into his soft hair, and I use it to tug his mouth to me harder. He breaks the kiss long enough to free himself, and then the heat of his dick is pressing into me. Even though I'm ready, already wet and needy, when he pushes into me barely an inch, I bite my lip at the sting.

Nothing he's doing to me right now is gentle. There's a carnal, starved edge to his movements, and as he pulls back, I suck in a breath, waiting for it. He slams forward so hard I cry out, squeezing my eyes shut, the burning pain mixing with the blinding sensation of being so full.

"Oh, fuck," he hisses, pressing his open mouth to mine, holding still deep between my thighs. He adjusts his grip, bringing me up higher on the window, giving me a second to adjust to him, but then he pulls back and does it again. I whimper, my hands falling to his shoulders. "You feel so good."

I nod, my head hitting the window, watching his face as he slips out. My eyes flutter when he drives in again and his brows furrow like he's in pain. Then he drives in again and again, and all I can do is hold on as he fucks me. Feel him moving in and out. Feel his desperation mixing with my own. The intense way he's watching me, thrusting in so deeply, placing hungry kisses on my parted lips, makes me crave more. Harder. Faster. Until this cutting desire is released.

The force of his movements feels like the window should be shattering behind me. And there's a part of me that wants to break through, shards of glass cutting me, stripping everything away. Tearing into my skin, bleeding me dry until I'm no longer me. Until I'm no longer Rune's daughter. Until all that's left of me are the pieces they've created and formed into this new woman. The feral woman who spreads her legs on the forest floor. Who arched into the belt.

Right at this moment, I don't mind being his. Theirs. I want them all here. Touching me again. Claiming me again. Like they did last night. Like they did in the woods. Like they did in the club.

Teeth scrape over my collar bone hard enough that I cry out, but it just adds to the intense swirling fire burning through me, building low in my belly.

"Come for me, Princess," he grates. "I want my name spilling from your lips as I fill you up."

I nod, ready to obey. Ready to please him. To let him have me.

"Come on, beautiful," he grates out. "Give me another one."

Like his words bring it forth, I cry out as another orgasm crashes through me, my walls clenching down on him. Striker's groan scrapes out of his throat, and his movements become jerky as heat floods between my thighs and he's fucking his cum deep into me with sloppy, desperate sounds, as curses and praises tumble from his lips.

So perfect.

So beautiful when you fall apart.

And then it's just silence except for our heavy breathing and the distant sound of crashing waves. He buries his face in my neck, and we stay like that, breathing, his face hidden as the world comes back around.

When it does, my mind flies in a million different directions and he must feel me tense, because he lets me go, sliding out, his cum slipping down my thigh, making my fingers tighten on his shoulders. My feet hit the floor, and he whispers, "It's okay," and then his mouth covers mine again. But it's softer this time, that feral edge gone with our release.

He stands to his full height and lets me go so he can swipe at my cheek. More tears break free, but I don't even know what they are for. Maybe for me. For him. Maybe for his brother my father killed. For Cora and everything she's never had.

Tears for everything I've lost and all the things I can't recover.

"I know." Striker scoops me up, carrying me to the bed. He pulls my dress off, then removes his shirt and pants, and lays me down, moving between my thighs. The tears won't stop, but he leans forward and kisses my cheeks until I can breathe again. As he hitches my thigh up and moves over me, I tilt my hips to accept him, my nails scraping down his back as he slips into me gently.

Everything, all my anger and pain, releases on an exhale.

Striker's lips press to mine as he says, "I'm sorry," and drives forward, hitting that aching place deep within me.

I want to ask him for which part, but I already know, deep in my gut, from the way he's kissing me, the way he's rocking into me, I know he's sorry not just for everything they've done, but everything they're about to do.

Chapter 38

STRIKER

5 years ago, July, Age 25

I ADJUST MY SCOPE, making sure I have the large wooden door centered in the crosshairs.

"Where the fuck is he?" Hunter asks in my ear. I shift just enough to tap the earpiece, adjusting the volume.

"He's probably just late," Viper says, his voice tinny through the earpiece.

"He's never late," Breaker says.

"Just sit tight," Reaper says.

I wince at how loud it seems, his voice coming from next to me and through the earbud. I swing the rifle, focusing on where I know Hunter, Viper, and Breaker wait.

I wanted to be the one down there, in the middle of it, see his face when he realizes why we are here. Sometimes I hate that this was my skill. Killing without ever touching my victim. These missions are hard on my body. Over the years I've spent more time crawling and slinking through mud and bushes, getting bitten by god only knows what bugs, as I try to piss while laying on my side. While I should feel good about being their cover, or being able to hit a mark, then protect my brothers while they exit a target area, I don't like the looks I get when others learn my skill.

They give me that flickering, judgmental look, like they can see skewed morals or some dark layer that hangs over me like a veil. Because what kind of person can kill so impersonally? As if killing someone in cold blood while they can see your face is somehow superior and less immoral than being a sniper.

But, I'm good at it. Compartmentalizing. Sitting for hours almost completely still, ignoring any pain as it laces up my spine and stiffens my shoulders. Shutting my mind down to the extreme cold or heat, or fatigue. Sleeping in bursts. Ignoring the world around me, my mind and my body, any pangs of hunger, until I'm suspended in a single mindset that allows me to focus on the task at hand.

At least my mother gave me something. Thanks to her, I learned how to survive. It's the only gift she's ever given me, and it came at the expense of her life.

Ironic that I use it to take others.

This is why I'm up here. I'm the best shot and am needed to cover them in case things go wrong.

And the possibility of that happening is high.

We got our orders two days ago, and barely have had enough time to plan, much less learn the layout of the lodge. But, we have orders and if there's one thing we all do, and do well, is kill.

Reaper sweeps his scope to the left and freezes as Hunter raises a fist, telling us to hold and wait. We decided that having Breaker and Viper on the ground with Hunter was best. They are fast, and can sweep in, take out our targets, then fall out before any of them can escape.

Right as Hunter lowers his hand, a loud clack rings out and smoke curls around my brothers, and my sight's filled with gray. My blood turns to ice as I watch the porch on the lodge holding my brother's swarm with Rune's men, smoke curling around them like vines. Suddenly there's screaming and *pops* of gunfire and all the blood in my head drains out.

Someone betrayed us.

For a split second, neither one of us moves, too shocked at the sight before us, then we're up, running through the short grass, toward the lodge, using the dark tree line as cover. I spot several men sweeping the place, with rifles raised, no doubt looking for us, and I take them out. They fall quietly to the ground. Reaper takes out two more while I shoot three in the back of the head, standing where my brothers should be.

Someone screams. The smoke clears some and then I see Breaker on the ground, a pool of blood under his thigh. I shoot the man holding a gun to his head and the soldier crumbles. Viper's scream makes us both pivot, and I shoot the second my eyes land on the man next to my brother, but Viper's already slashing his throat. Blood splatters his face, both from his knife and the bullet I put through the soldier's head.

"You tell that sack of shit he's going to fucking pay!" Rune screams.

I spin, rifle raised, and I see him.

Hunter's on the ground at Rune's feet, legs sprawled out, blood pooling under his leg. I aim, swinging my rifle up to Rune's face, but men swarm in front of him, blocking him and Hunter from my view.

There's static and noise in my head. Voices. Reaper cursing, telling me to *move in*. Viper next to me, telling me to *move, move* but I can't seem to drag my feet from where they are planted.

We have to get him.

We have to get our brother.

I have to get to Hunter.

My feet unfreeze and I bolt forward, weapon aimed, following Reaper's dark form, keeping Rune and his men in my sights.

"Stay back!" Rune screams, and we all freeze. My blood chills.

"Fuck," Reaper grates from my left and in my earpiece.

"Which one of you fuckers was it?" Rune screams and my stomach bottoms out. Between the press of bodies and guns surrounding Rune and Hunter, I catch the glimpse of a Glock pressed to Hunter's temple.

"It was me," Reaper calls out.

Liar, I think just as Hunter screams, "It was me!"

An angry snarl roars from behind the line of soldiers. I aim, considering taking out each one until I can get a clear shot at Rune, but know the second he realizes what I'm doing, he'll shoot.

God. Please.

I move my finger off the trigger, sweat beading my brow, soaking my mask. I've never hesitated before.

But then I've never had something I was scared to lose.

"Was it him?" Rune asks. "Did *he* give the order to have her killed?"

I shift, trying to get a clear shot and one soldier suddenly shifts, aims, fires.

Pain explodes through my chest as the air punches from my lungs. I hear Hunter's animalistic scream as I stumble back, landing on my ass.

Fuck. My hand flies up to my chest, sliding over my vest to my shoulder. My pulse quickens as I sit stunned, trying to determine if the pain in my chest is fatal. If I'm about to bleed out.

My finger hits a spot just above my vest and agony shoots through my nerve endings into my brain like an electric bolt.

Reaper appears next to me, and I hear more movement. Shouting. The *pop, pop, pop* of guns firing. His arm laces around my shoulders and I'm pressed back against his chest.

When did I lie down?

"Fuck, fuck, fuck," Reaper rasps, pulling me up, each curse scraping out of him like it's painful.

"He shot with a hell of a curve," I say, reaching for my chest again, but my arm feels heavy. "That asshole was a good shot."

"Almost as good as you," Reaper says, and I realize I'm sprawled across his lap.

"Get back!" Rune screams. "I'll fucking shoot him right now!"

"I'll cut your fucking throat," Viper screams. "You kill him and I'll gut you."

Reaper sits me upright. I grit my teeth, fire shooting through me. I don't know how the fuck I was hit at that angle, but it's not clean.

"Asshole got me," I say as my eyes move over to Rune. A break between the bodies gives me a glimpse of Hunter. His mask has been torn away and, like he can feel me looking, his dark eyes meet mine. They grow large and he jerks in Rune's grasp.

"Get him out of here!" Hunter screams. "Reaper, I swear to god, get him out of here!"

Reaper curses, looking from me to Hunter. He shakes his head. "No."

"Do not let him die!" Hunter screams. My vision swirls in and out of focus, but I keep my eyes locked on Hunter. His face contorts and my insides feel like they're contorting, stretching, and twisting too.

"No." I shove Reaper away. Pain lances down my arm. "Go. Go get him, Reap. *Please.*"

"Fuck." Reaper's shaking hand lands on his helmet and he hits. Once. Twice. "*Fuck.*"

I suck in a shaky breath, and my gaze falls to my weapon laying across my lap. That's when I notice the blood. It pools in my lap, coats my glove, thumps between my ears, making my head swim.

Breaker's face appears and then I'm hauled up, one arm holding me up from either side. Dammit, I'm tired. I wish they'd just let me lie back down. I just want to go to sleep. Like in the darkness, when I went to sleep and there wasn't pain anymore.

The thumping in my ears slowly gets louder, the wind picks up. Leaves and dirt hit my mask. I glance up at the starless night and make out the black chopper swooping in low.

I don't realize I'm screaming until my throat grows raw.

We can't leave him.

Please, we can't leave him.

Please.

"Please." My begs are ignored as they drag me forward. "Reap. You know we can't leave him. He's my—"

My vision blacks out before I can finish, cutting my words off.

The world comes back around as well as the pain in my chest, but it's not the bullet wound that's making me feel like I'm being shredded alive.

"We'll get him," Reaper says over the roar of blades as the chopper lands. "We'll come back and get him. Do not fucking die on me, Strike. Do not fucking die. He'll never forgive me."

CHAPTER 39

CORA

When I open the bedroom door, finally having worked up enough nerve to face Delly, I see a naked man standing by the bed. Well, not entirely naked. He's currently bent over, hiking his pants up over his hips, tucking his dick into his fatigues. My gaze snags on a large tattoo of five skulls across his back, one marked with a red gash. He turns toward the sound of my gasp, warm honey eyes moving up from Delly's sleeping form on the bed to me.

Holy shit.

I open my mouth, but he slides over, pressing a finger to my lips, and I'm so stunned at the sight of Striker's face that all I can do is huff out a breath. He grips my waist, hoisting me up, and I wrap my legs around his hips as he carries me to the bathroom.

After he sets me on the counter, he shuts the door quietly and turns the light on. The room floods with pale yellow light, and I grip the edge of the counter, trying to control my breathing. Forcing myself to remember I'm upset with them as much as I'm relieved. They intended to send me back. Even if they didn't know the details, they still knew something.

"Striker?" I don't know why I say his name. It's obviously him, but without the mask hiding his face, my mind can't piece together the skull mask with the scar over the eye he always wears with the man standing in front of me with smooth flesh and a sculpted chest that begs to be touched.

No, not completely smooth. My eyes fall to the circular wound just above his heart. "It missed your heart by an inch," I say.

His head drops, looking down at his chest, and his hand moves to the scar, his finger lightly grazing over the raised skin. That's when I see more scars on his forearms.

"Your heart would have exploded if that bullet went any lower," I say, unable to keep my mouth shut as I watch his brows knit and his jaw harden. Maybe his heart did explode that day.

It must be shock. From the last few weeks, the remnants of spilling my guts to my kidnappers, telling Delly about Rune, and seeing his insanely handsome face for the first time. The tanned skin and abs that lead to the chevron of muscles dipping below his still open pants, the top of his dick peeking out.

"As you can see, it didn't miss," Striker says, pulling me out of my head long enough to focus on evening out my breathing. "He was just a shit shot."

My eyes fly up to meet his.

"Who?"

He shakes his head, and a lock of hair falls around his eyes.

"You're beautiful," I say, because I have zero control over my mouth right now.

The corner of his full lips curl up, making my belly dip. I'd probably be sleeping with him too, if I wasn't so busy having an existential crisis downstairs. I can see why Delly was a bit overcome and—

I press the back of my hands to my eyes, sucking in a breath, trying desperately to get my thoughts under control. My head spins, emotions flinging every direction at once, so it feels like I'm spiraling downward. So much has changed in just twenty-four hours. I know my brain's still playing catch up.

I'm mortified they know the details of Rune, humiliated that I allowed it to happen for so long, and relieved someone knows. I don't have to carry the burden of hiding it anymore.

A part of me always wanted to scream from the top of my lungs until my throat was raw and he was exposed, but I was scared. Too scared of Delly finding out. Too scared I'd be seen as weak for allowing it. Worried I'd not be believed.

Terrified, Delly would think I did something to warrant his sick attention.

Deep down, I know it's just fear and my own warped thinking that kept me silent. But I don't have to worry anymore. She knows. *They* know.

"Pretty Little Flower," Strikers says, cupping my cheeks.

Shit. I can't even think straight when he pulls my hands down and kisses the tears away from the back of my fingers.

"No more tears," Striker says, and I nod, eating up every detail of his face, his neck, the white scars on his forearms.

Scars. Like his mask. "What are those from?" I ask.

He releases me, crossing his arms over his chest, gripping each forearm. His eyes drop to my mouth. In this light, they're a dark amber, flecked with a deep brown.

"I did it when I was locked in the cold room," he says quietly, the words slipping out like a secret. "I was trying to keep myself from falling asleep like I did before when my mother left me in darkness."

My fingers splay out with the memory of my own fingers raking down the wood door. He told me about being left in a closet like me, but I don't know what he means by the cold room, so I ask, "Was the cold room different from the darkness?"

A small smile, more a grimace than anything, tugs at the corner of his mouth. My heart actually flutters at the sight. "They were similar, but I came out of the cold room a different person."

I want to ask more, but I don't think I want to know. The way his brows knit and his eyes lose focus tells me he doesn't want to remember. Lifting my hand, I run a finger along one of the thicker scars, thinking about a boy so scared of dying that he tore himself apart to stay alive.

"I have scars too," I whisper. Striker unfolds his arms, letting them drop to his side. "Mine are all inside my head."

"They leak out when you dream," he says, reaching for my hand. "But you don't have to be scared anymore."

"Viper told me I'm staying." I drag my gaze all over him again. I wonder if the other men are this beautiful. This damaged, carrying scars under their clothes and inside their heads like we do.

"You're safe here." Cupping my jaw, his thumb grazes my bottom lip as he leans in and presses a gentle kiss to my mouth. The soft kiss burns, making me lean into him, pressing his mouth to me harder, trying to ease this fire flaming across my skin.

God, this is all so insane. He was obviously just fucking Delly. I've been fucking Delly. We all fucked just weeks ago. They kidnapped us. We are supposed to be scared, and hate them, and here we are sitting in a bathroom, the man responsible for stealing and saving me, peppering me with soft kisses and all I want to do is wrap myself around him so he doesn't stop.

"You both need rest," Striker says when he backs away. "And I need to talk to the others."

I nod, watching his lips form the words.

"Little Flower?"

I glance up at his eyes. I *knew* they weren't bad. I know evil men, and I felt with every fiber of my being, they weren't the same.

"Are you okay?"

I lick my lips, tasting his kiss, wondering if his mouth had been on Delly. If he just kissed her or if he licked her cunt like I did just last night.

"Why was I going back?" I ask.

He blinks and looks away. When he steps back, I watch his hands, the cords of muscles in his forearms and the scars his life has left on him, as he pulls his pants away from his body and tugs up the zipper. The urge to stop him, move his hand and reach into his pants and free him is so strong that I grip the edge of the counter to stop myself.

"It doesn't matter now," he says, adjusting the waistband of his pants and stepping in closer.

Releasing the counter, I trail my finger up his abs, the muscles rippling like he's ticklish, then drag it up the center of his chest. Stopping at the scar above his heart, I lean in and place a kiss on the raised skin. His breath hitches and fingers weave into my hair, tilting my head back to look in his eyes. Up this close, I can smell his maleness and the hint of sweat and sex.

"You're too sweet for this world," he whispers, pressing his lips to mine. "I don't know how it's not ruined you."

"It didn't ruin you," I say back, keeping my voice just as low. His breath fans over my cheek when he places another kiss on my lips, then backs up enough so I can look at his face fully.

He's so beautiful it hurts to look at him. I almost want to tell him to put his mask back on, so he's a little less real. So he can remain the man who killed people and stole us, and not this soft face that so obviously isn't the hardened killer he wants us to believe he is.

He's just a man. Just that boy who was trapped like I was. But we both made it out.

"Father ruined me, not the world." Striker grips my waist, once again lifting me.

I wrap my legs around him, resting my arms on his shoulders as he walks us to the door. He reaches around me and opens the door, his biceps straining as he carries me quietly to the bed. I slip down his body, eating up the sight of his sculpted muscles in his chest, then the skull tattoos between his shoulder blades as he turns and reaches for his shirt, then tugs it over his head. He places another chaste kiss on my lips before grabbing his mask and backing away.

When the door clicks shut quietly, I turn and find Delly watching me, her blue eyes red rimmed.

"I'm sorry," I whisper. So, so sorry her father is who he is, and that she found out this way.

A tear slips out and hits the pillow under her head. "Me too," she whispers back, but then her face crumbles, and I feel like Rune's ripping me apart all over again. Hitting me over and over as I watch her cry, powerless to make it stop. He made me feel so helpless, like I am now, unable to take her pain away. His lies and betrayal battering her, cutting so deep she's going to have scars.

"Do we have to talk about it?" I ask, my stomach flipping as I sit on the edge of the bed. She drags a finger down my arm, watching as goosebumps form on my skin. "I'm so tired of talking about it."

Delly shakes her head, drawing her hand back, wiping under her nose.

"Was his dick as good the second time around?"

Her blue eyes snap up to mine, and she breathes out a laugh, squeezing her eyes shut. "Better."

"Helps, he's not a butter-face." When she smirks, my chest warms. *We're okay.* "Do I get to fuck him too?"

The smirk falls and she grimaces.

"Too soon?" I ask, capturing my bottom lip with my teeth. *Yeah. Too soon.* "Why'd he take off his mask?"

"Because we aren't going home," she says, throwing the blankets back and holding them up for me to join her.

I crawl forward, drinking in the sight of her pale flesh and hard nipples. The dark mole on her thin collarbone. Even with red, puffy eyes, hair a tangled mess spread out behind her, she's still so beautiful. It makes me want to press my lips to every inch of her flesh.

"I know," I tell her, slipping under the blankets, but my heart hammers as I look up into her eyes, placing my head on the pillow. "Do you want to?"

Her features harden, gaze drifting to my mouth. "No." She gathers me up, pulling me close and tossing her leg over my hip until we're pressed together so tightly I feel every breath she inhales. Feel every exhale like it's mine and for the first time in my life, I know I'm truly safe. Her lips press to my forehead. "Does Clyde know about Rune?"

I shake my head, burying my face in her sticky neck, breathing in the salty sweat on her skin, and the faint scent of soap and sex. She's always been my safe place. My beacon. Now she's something else.

Her entire body relaxes. "Good. I'd hate to have to kill him."

A chuckle slips out and I glance back up at her, placing a kiss to her jaw, but then catch the murderous gleam in her eyes.

Sometimes I forget she's Rune's daughter.

He's going to regret creating her.

Chapter 40

DELILAH

I wake up to an empty bed. My hand sweeps over the rumpled sheets, seeking her.

Him.

I flash on the last several hours: Him in bed with me, retaking me but slower, his full lips pressed to my slick flesh as he moved deeply with such gentle strokes I felt all the darkness, all the terrible things I overheard leaving me.

My belly flutters, skin warming as if he was touching me again. I curl onto my side, drawing my knees up to my chest. I'm not sure what to think about the fact I slept with one of my kidnappers. If that's even what I could call them anymore. I can't deny the dark, dangerous attraction that has led us here. To this place where they've gone from our kidnappers to the men

I—we—crave. Men who protect Cora from evil. From men like my father.

Like them.

They aren't all bad.

No. Not like them.

No. These men are nothing like Rune.

She'd never have trusted them enough to beg them to stay if they were.

After Striker left, I held Cora for a long time. There was no need to talk anymore. She must have slipped away when I fell asleep, and I wonder where she is now. If she found Striker or if she's with Viper or Breaker. I wonder, too, what they are telling her about their brother.

If Striker's kissing her again.

I like the thought of him kissing her. Of him gifting her with the same heated passion he's given me.

Closing my eyes, I press my face into my pillow, trying to put my thoughts back in order. I don't know what any of it means. I have no idea what happens from here. A huge shift happened between us all, leaving me hanging on to my sanity by a thread.

The thought of going home makes my stomach churn. There's no way I can face Rune any time soon. I also know that I can't stay here forever. Rune Corporations may be the company my father built, but it's mine. I've spent my entire life learning, preparing myself for the day I took it over. And I'm not going to let that go.

The men's words ring in my head.

I'm theirs. To do with as they please.

I just wish they'd tell me what it is they have planned.

Sitting upright, I lean over to turn on the lamp in case Cora comes back when my eyes land on the dark figure in the doorway. My fingers curl into the bedding, recognizing the cut of his body. I bring my knees up to my naked chest, dumb considering he's seen every inch of my skin.

"You were going to send her to him, knowing he was hurting her." It's not a question.

"We had orders," Reaper says.

"That you aren't following now."

"No." Reaper moves forward and holds out his hand. Disappointment floods me when I see he's still wearing his mask.

"Why?" I ask, but I know he doesn't need me to explain what I'm asking. *Why were they going to send her back?*

I can feel his indecision like a thorn. He doesn't want to tell me, but he needs me to understand. "There would have been, there will be, dire consequences. One's far worse than defying an order."

I don't know what he means and when I open my mouth to ask; I close it, not wanting to push too far too soon. Not sure if I really want to know.

"She's not leaving," he says as I take his hand and place my feet on the cold floor. I can't see his black eyes in the dark room, but I feel them on me, moving up and down my naked body the same way his hands did. Slightly invasive. Possessive.

"Where is she?" I ask.

"With Viper."

I jerk at the feeling of his warm hand on my bare thigh. Heat surges through me, as he trails it up higher and grips my waist like he can't stop himself from touching me.

From the way they talk, they seem to share everything, so the possessive grip he has on me is confusing, since he doesn't seem to mind that Striker was inside me. If anything, I think he *likes* the idea. He did that night in the club. That alone should have been a clear sign that these men clearly share women often and enjoy it.

Women.

Cora and me.

My chest constricts at the thought of them with *other* women. With someone else besides us and I exhale slowly, not sure how to digest the thought.

I glance back up at his face, but it's just darkness.

"He told me," I say, my voice barely a whisper.

I feel his body go completely still.

"About your brother."

His fingers flex on my hip.

"Striker told me my father killed your brother. That's what you call each other? Brothers? That's why you want revenge. That's what—who—Rune took."

"Rune killed a piece of us," Reaper says. "Viper, Striker, Breaker. They are the only brothers I have left."

His family. The one he created.

I keep silent, hoping he'll reveal more. Reaper has been so vague, they all have, and to possess this little piece of information makes me feel privileged he's allowed me to hold one of his many secrets.

The feeling spreads in my chest, loosening that tightness. I want more. Of their secrets. Of him. Of them.

When he doesn't explain further, I say, "I'm sorry."

"Don't be," Reaper says. "He was justified in killing him."

My brows knit. "Justified?" I ask, moving closer to him, wishing I could see his face. I remember every bit of skin he's let me see. The shape of his lips and the scars across them are burned into my memory like a brand. "Justified like you were in taking Cora and me?"

His grip tightens on my hip before he drops it and steps away, turning toward the door. "Get dressed."

"Why?"

Reaper stops midway and turns around. "As much as I'd like to watch your ass bounce as you walk down the stairs, I have a feeling you'd prefer to be dressed for what I'm about to show you."

My heart does this weird flip before it hammers. "What are you going to show me?"

Neither one of us is going back, but I'm smart enough to know that they didn't do all this so we could stay in a crumbling mansion in the middle of nowhere forever. They have a plan, and it involves Cora and me.

"Get dressed, Kitten." Reaper walks through the open door and says over his shoulder, "It's time you learn what your father truly is."

***

As we walk into the dining room, I wrap my sweater around me tightly, but the chill seems to have settled in my bones, refusing to leave, nerves jittering with dread. I've waited weeks for answers and now I'm not so sure I want them. The things I've already learned are bad enough.

I stop in the doorway, surprised to find the room empty. I glance at Reaper's back, then to a large box, like the ones that hold files, sitting on one of the dining room chairs.

"Sit down." Reaper points to the table as he removes the lid from the box.

"I don't want to," I say, my nerves jumping higher.

"Trust me, Kitten, you're going to need to be sitting for this." Reaper pulls out a file, but keeps it to his chest until I pull out a chair and sit. On instinct, I place my hands on the table, palms down, waiting. When I realize what I've done, I jerk them away and set them in my lap, focusing on my fingers as I curl them into the thick fabric of my sweater.

It appears they trained me well.

Taking a deep breath, I look up at Reaper's masked face. "What's in the file?" I ask as he opens it.

"Your father's sins." Reaper lifts the corner of a piece of paper, then glances at me. I could swear it's like he doesn't want to show me the contents, but that would be a foolish thought. I'm here because of whatever that file contains.

"Sins that can be linked to him?" I ask. My father is good at covering his tracks. Hell, I'm good at covering his tracks.

Reaper doesn't answer. He picks up a thick sheet from the file and lays it on the table, sliding it in front of me.

I lean over to examine the picture. A large wooden lodge with a green metal roof, massive sheets of glass for windows, and thick pillars framing carved wooden doors take up the entire image.

My brows knit. "That's my father's lodge." Even though I've never been, he has enough pictures of him and his friends on this same front porch that I recognize it. Although after Cora's parents died, he removed all the framed photographs of them from the walls.

"It is," Reaper says and sets down a picture of my father next to a large buck hanging upside down from a pole. "His members only lodge."

That unease I felt walking down here roils in my stomach. "Why are you showing me these?"

Reaper places another image in front of me. "Our father used the land for the final test when he started the school."

My head jerks up to him. *Father? School?*

"The final test," Reaper says. "The wilderness, Father called it. It was how we proved ourselves. How we showed our father we were ready."

"Ready for what?" I ask. But I take in his uniform and his mask and I already know. Ready to be killers. Guns for hire. Trained to kidnap, kill, do whatever. I've heard of men like them, mercenaries that will take any job that pays high enough, not caring about politics or justice.

Not caring about fairness or morals.

Money. That was it. Money and power.

But the one lesson my father taught me that sticks more than the others was once you accepted money for doing a job, a part of you was always in debt. Rune always said just because you were paid for it doesn't mean things are settled. Someone still knows what you did for money. Or worse, what you paid someone else to do.

My gaze slips down to the images, my head whirling with questions. "So Rune knew about this..." My mind trips over the word. "This school and..."

"The wilderness," he says for me. "We would complete our final task of surviving on our own, with no weapons, nothing but the few clothes on our backs for a week. We would have to..." his voice trails off, but then he says, "Father would use the land and Rune would turn a blind eye, promising no interference."

I shake my head, none of his words settling. "I don't understand."

"Rune and our father used to be close," Reaper says, laying down another image.

This one looks different from the others, so I lean over, trying to make out what I'm seeing. At first, it's just shades of black and cream and slashes of rusty red. Placing my hands back on the table, I stand, leaning over the image, trying to make sense of it. Then I see it.

My hand flies to my mouth, and I stumble back, my legs hitting the chair.

He catches it before it falls over. "Sick, yes?"

My gaze snaps to Reaper. Bile rises in my throat and for a second I think I might vomit, so I sit back down, inhaling slowly through my nose.

Reaper places another image next to the first. Like I can't control my eyes, they move to it and I regret it immediately, but I can't look away.

"You said they were close?" I ask, my gaze snapping to him, his words finally breaking through.

"Yes. Past tense." Reaper lays out another picture, and this one is worse than the others. I grip the table, trying to keep focused on his words.

"Friends?" I say, my eyes bouncing from the images to Reaper, trying to sort through my memories but coming up blank. I know all my father's friends and associates. "You said *used* to be."

Reaper's eyes seem to darken, like they're suddenly full of shadows. "Close friends until our father took a job he would later regret."

Reaper slips another image onto the table and I can't look at anymore, so I focus on Reaper's mocking skull mask and black eyes.

"Then," his eyes flicker away and I swear I see something flash in them, but he lays another image down. "Rune had an idea." He slides another picture toward me and I suck in a breath. "He thought of a way to make the wilderness a little more exciting."

Bile stings my throat. He places another and another until I squeeze my eyes shut, but it doesn't help. They are all I can see. Pieces. Fragments. Bits of people chopped up, limbs torn from carcasses. Bodies riddled with bullets. Pretty floral nightgowns soaked in blood, molded to small breasts and creamy thighs.

How many times has Zane invited me to my father's lodge? How many times has Clyde kept me from going? How much money have I hid over the years, as membership fees, enormous sums of money being handed over to my father out of nowhere for no reason?

"Rune liked the idea of a hunt," Reaper says. "He wanted the excitement. So he decided to change the rules."

Another picture lands before me, but I turn away.

"He didn't want to sit back and watch us in the wilderness. Rune wanted to be out there, in the heat and mud himself. He wanted to be the one tracking for his food. Surviving off the land and his skills."

My father always got excited in the fall. When it was time to go to his lodge and meet his friends. They'd spend a week there every year and when he'd come back, he'd be different. Changed in a way I didn't understand. Somehow more excitable, but calm too. Like something within him was placated.

Reaper places another image, but I bolt up from the chair, bending over, trying to control my breathing and the swirling in my head. I stumble away, bracing my hands on the wall, bile churning, threatening to come up.

"Others loved the idea too. Going out to the wilderness, tapping into their baser instincts. Feeling the excitement, feeling the adrenaline. But he didn't want to send multimillionaires out in the wilderness to snare rabbits and shoot squirrels."

"What do you mean?" I hear myself saying, but it's like I'm not even in the room anymore.

"What's the best way to make the wilderness feel a tad more brutal?" Reaper asks.

My stomach sinks.

"Rune decided to add prey to the hunt."

Chapter 41

DELILAH

I don't know what a nervous breakdown is supposed to feel like, but I think I'm having one.

The thought that my father was doing all this, is too much to absorb. He's been using his company—my future company—to funnel money, what I can only assume are *payments* for what he's doing at the lodge. He is granted so much money every year, but then he pays out so much too. And He's been using Cora and me to help him hide his sick, evil games.

The last few hours spin in my head and I can't seem to focus on anything. All I can see are the images of bodies. Blood and gore that would make horror movie directors grimace.

And it was all my father's doing.

And me too.

I hid the money he was collecting.

Cora too.

What will she do if she ever finds out? She can't know.

Reaper spent the last few hours showing me the information they acquired, but refused to tell me the source. Files upon files with my signature, my numbers, my fucking contracts hiding his actions in membership fees, or fake sales. I knew he was doing bad things, but not this.

Never this.

Glancing around the room, my eyes land on the box and my head falls to the table. I squeeze my eyes shut, trying to focus my whirling thoughts.

I didn't know.

Any of it.

There's a part of me that's so angry at them. Instead of kidnapping me, scaring Cora and me, they could have just told me. Shown me the files. But even as the thought springs to my mind, I know it's not true. I never would have believed them. I was so blinded by my father's drive to make me like him, by my craving to have his approval, I would have thought all this evidence was fabricated to take my father down.

Who would believe their parent was capable of the level of depravity I saw in those pictures?

No one.

Certainly not from a loving father who protected me to the point of imprisoning me. Reaper and the others needed me to see that they were more than just mean men hired to kidnap me. I needed to see them be kind to Cora. I needed Cora to tell me about my father and *then* and only then would I be ready to believe them when they showed me.

I have a feeling this was all planned. Every minute detail to get me on their side.

But to do what?

I don't know because Reaper left me here over an hour ago and I can't even think straight to guess at what they want. Because they want something. There's a reason they did all this.

Revenge.

Maybe.

My heart picks up pace, imagining Cora's face when she thought she was going back.

Blood is thicker than water.

My mother was wrong.

Rune may be my father, but Cora is *mine*.

"Tiny Thing."

I jerk at the sound of Breaker's voice behind me, but don't turn around. When I don't move, I hear him walk up, then feel his large hand land on my shoulder.

"You're not screaming," he says. "Or cursing or crying."

I shake my head.

"You're processing."

"Screaming and crying won't change what—" I swallow around the bile rising in my throat. "Reaper showed me. I heard Cora."

It's not like I don't want to scream and cry. Tear at my hair and skin. But I shed enough tears hours ago and Rune doesn't deserve any more of my tears. And I don't want to cry anymore for Cora. She'd hate to see me crying, and besides, tears won't change what happened. She doesn't need my sadness. Cora needs my anger. My fucking *rage*. Cora needs my thirst for vengeance.

For the first time, I truly understand Reaper. Viper. Breaker. Striker. My father killed their brother.

They want revenge. They want Rune to pay for taking something from them. Something valuable that they loved.

I want to hurt him for hurting Cora. For destroying my trust and cutting away at my best friend and my life support after my mother was killed.

For hurting the woman I love.

My father....

No. The man I *called* my father, the man he pretended to be, would never do this.

Rune is a liar and thief. He's lied to me most of my life. He stole Cora's innocence. The same man who would come tuck me in at night, kiss my cheeks, and whisper promises to always protect me, was murdering people for sport. Then, after promising to protect Cora, was forcing her to fuck him. Forcing an innocent woman to bend to his will, all while keeping me trapped so that no man would do to me what he was doing to her.

The man who hunted those people? He doesn't deserve any tears.

That man deserves....

My breaths seize.

I sit upright, running my fingers through my hair, squeezing at the roots. My mind flashes on all the meetings we attended. The chain of hotels along the west coast we just purchased and all the money Cora and I hid. My stomach twists.

Cora and I have always known we were hiding criminal activity, but I justified it, telling myself Rune wasn't that bad. Not like the gangsters in movies. He was my father. He had a good heart even if it was broken after my mother died.

I convinced myself Rune was a good man, deep down, despite knowing he wasn't.

I'm no better than him.

The images Reaper showed me flood my mind again.

He made me a part of this and I let him. It doesn't matter that I didn't know.

"You're spiraling." Breaker's voice centers my thoughts and I suck in a breath. The chair to my left scoots out, legs grating across the floor. From the corner of my eye, I see his massive frame sit next to me. "Come here."

Breaker pats his thick thigh. During those days of feeding me, I'd sat on his lap so many times that the thought right now shouldn't flood me with heat. My eyes fly up to his face and his mask. That first night, I thought they were wearing costumes. Just four men out for a raunchy night and Cora and I were the lucky girls they had in their sights.

But they lied to and manipulated us.

"Come sit, pretty thing," he says. "Talk to me."

"So you can lie to me some more?"

His fingers curl into his pants, but he pats again. "When did I lie?"

My brows furrow. "Asks the man who wears a mask to hide his identity and kidnaps and murders people."

"If you are trying to tell me that withholding information is the same as lying, you wouldn't be entirely incorrect," he says and pats his leg again. "But we never looked you in the face and lied. We withheld information until you were able to handle the truth. That's protecting, not lying."

My shoulders droop. They lied by omission. They fed me information slowly. Giving me tidbits because they knew the scope of this would ruin me. If anything, I'm the liar. I've lied to myself my entire life. I worked for a ruthless man and was letting him mold me into a version of himself. I watched him grow powerful and rich and wanted the same things.

I told myself I did. I don't want that now. All the things I wanted in life feel so unimportant now. The only thing that matters is keeping Cora safe.

And stopping Rune.

Breaker grips my wrist. I'm pulled forward, slightly too rough, and he places me on his lap. I settle down, expecting his erection, but just feel his thick thigh and him pressing his mask to my shoulder. He takes a long, slow breath. These men and the whole smelling thing.

I don't hate it.

I don't hate any of them.

I don't think I ever did.

"You can't tell Cora," I whisper, my eyes gravitating back to the box. "It'll kill her to know. She's not ready."

"I won't," Breaker says, running a hand up my back, his fingers moving over the dips in my spine. "None of us will until you give us the okay."

I nod, relaxing under his soft touch.

When did this happen? That first week after they took us, I was so alone, so starved for any interaction. Then I had their attention on me so much for those few days that I liked being with them. Then they left us alone after I got Cora back and I wanted them around.

Now...

Now I have it and I want even more.

"You were supposed to be a mission," he whispers. "A job. We weren't supposed to care if you were scared or confused." He breathes out a heavy sigh, warming my shoulder through my sweater.

"You took me, intending to turn me against my father," I say for him.

I feel him nod.

"Yes. We were to take you, manipulate you, fuck with your head a little, force you to help us by any means, and that was it. You were supposed to be nothing. Just a hot cunt to have some fun with and convince to follow along with everything we said. But we fucked up."

I try to shift to face him, but he doesn't let me. He presses his cheek to my back. Out of all of them, Breaker has seemed the kindest. Not quick-tempered. He laughs. He takes part in whatever Reaper asks him to do, but he's not cruel. If anything he's felt the safest out of all of them.

"By fucking us?" I guess.

He chuckles. "By caring that you cried."

It seems insane, but I get what he's saying. I was supposed to be their target. They were supposed to be my captors, and instead they saved my best friend from a sick, cruel man. They manipulated my affection, yes, but they ended up earning my trust.

If someone took Cora, hurt her in anyway, I'd want to kill them, too. Those first few days, I was too scared to be furious with them. Then, when I knew she was safe, I was just angry that we were apart.

But I understand now why they wanted to steal me, and hurt Rune by never giving me back. By turning me against him.

Now, the fact that they are going against whoever hired them to begin with means everything they've said is true.

They want me. Us.

They didn't want to force me. They wanted to earn me the way they did Cora.

I flash on Reaper's dark glare. His hands on me edged with violence but turning tender at the strangest moments. He hated me that night in the club. He hated me when he took us.

But I didn't feel that hate when he came barging into the room and I haven't felt it since. I wonder at what point he stopped despising my existence. Maybe he never really did. Maybe none of them did.

"Breaker," I whisper, looking over my shoulder and meeting his pale eyes.

I wish I could see his face. I cup his jaw, feeling the hard curve under his mask. The urge to lean in and kiss him until that dark expression leaves his ice-blue eyes makes me want to rip his mask off so I can taste his lips. But I don't because I understand why he's still wearing it.

I'm not ready to show him everything there is to know about me, either.

His hand lands on top of mine and I say the one thing I know will break away those shadows in his eyes, "I'm hungry."

He leans back, gaze dropping to my mouth, and I swear, one day I'm going to see that smile under his mask and I know, deep in the pit of me, it's going to shatter my heart.

FANNY LEE SAVAGE

"Then let's get my pretty, Tiny Thing, something to eat."

Chapter 42

CORA

Moonlight slants across the herb garden, making the frost on the mint leaves shine like crystalline stars. I pluck a half-dead leaf from the stem and bring it to my nose, crushing it to make the scent bloom between my fingers.

A light gust of wind sends a shiver through my shoulders. I tug Breaker's black peacoat closed, and I'm glad he never took it back. He's let me wear it every day since he first put it over my shoulders.

I think that small gesture solidified what I had already guessed. They took us, intending to keep us. But they were prepared to send me away, like all the threats of being owned by them, all the sweetness that bled out of them when they pretended to be mean, meant nothing.

Because of a fucking *order*.

While I understand being forced to do things you don't want to, I can't help the anger rippling through me now that my mind has settled.

Reaper was going to send me back. The other men I know didn't want to. I could tell by the way they acted when they told me. But Reaper was prepared to follow orders, knowing what I was returning to.

They've been saying this entire time, Rune is bad, evil, sick. I already know just how evil he is. Seems they know too, and it's something worse than getting his kicks from hurting me. There's something else. Something darker.

He *knew*. And still...

God. What would Delly have done without me? She'd have lost her mind being here by herself.

And yet, he was still going to send me back and keep her.

He's weirdly obsessed with her. All of them are, and I can't wrap my head around why they'd send me, knowing she'd be so upset. I can't help but think—part of me hates the thought—that they didn't send me back solely because she'd be upset.

They took her, after all.

They wanted Delly. Not me.

I was just a bonus.

The reality of that slams into my gut, making my eyes sting.

Maybe I'm thinking too much.

Breaker's deadly glare and Viper's whispers, telling me I was safe, that I wasn't returning, that no one could hurt me now, crash through my thoughts.

Maybe I'm important too.

No. That line of thinking will get me in trouble.

Stupid girl and her stupid thoughts. Always pretending to be more important than she really is.

My mother's words cut through me. My stomach roils, hating that her voice still lingers in my head all these years later.

You're a terrible little girl who can't listen. An obedient daughter wouldn't defy her mommy, would she? I was cursed with a bad daughter.

She's right. I was a bad daughter. I was glad she died and even happier to know that she was murdered.

The crunch of boots on the gravel behind me sends a jolt down my spine, and I'm brought from my memories. I drop the leaf and gather the black jacket around my shoulders.

"It's cold out here," Viper says, his voice making lights spark in my veins. "Come inside."

We spent two weeks barely seeing them, and suddenly they're everywhere. All muscles and power and Striker's handsome face. I have yet to decide how I feel about the drastic change that's just occurred between us all, but it seems my body already has with the way heat builds in my core from Viper just being close.

"I like the cold," I say, turning my head slightly to look at him over my shoulder. His eyes glow eerily from the little light by the back door. "It makes the bad stuff harder to feel."

He doesn't respond as I turn back around, picking another mint leaf. The poor plant is mostly stems now. I've spent so many days out here replanting the sprigs of herbs, trying to get them to grow again, but I always pick the mint leaves. Like it's the one thing I'm willing to sacrifice simply because I like the way it reminds me of things that are clean.

Unlike me.

I've fucked Rune *and* his daughter.

Gravel crunches, and his leather boots come into view. I look up from my seat on the edge of the planter box. He's so big. Somehow, with not seeing him up close every day, I forgot his intimidating size. How broad his chest and thick his thighs.

"Why Striker and not you?" I ask, pressing the tips of my fingers to my lips. Viper watches my tongue dart out to taste my skin. "How come you're still wearing a mask?"

When he doesn't answer, my eyes fall back to his boots.

"You don't trust me," I say for him.

"Why should I?"

"Why should I trust you guys?" I ask. "You were sending me back."

"We had orders."

"So I've heard." Shifting, I pluck another leaf. I feel him watching me like he did those weeks I spent with them. I can't say

I don't like it. In fact, I like it too much. I like him. Them. I like the idea that they were somewhere in this mansion looking over us. Keeping us tucked away from bad things. Watching Delly and I fuck. Maybe they got so turned on, Breaker shoved his huge dick in Viper's mouth again.

I wonder if they do that a lot.

"What's with you and Breaker?" I ask, tearing the little leaf apart. I pop the mint into my mouth, liking the way Viper tracks each of my movements. How his eyes gleam beautifully, the color washed out. I wonder what he looks like. I bet he's pretty. Or maybe his features are as sharp and brutal as his personality.

"He's my brother," he says.

My nose scrunches. "Brother seems like a strange word choice since you suck his dick."

He sucks in a deep breath, letting me know I've riled him. Strange how he's not necessarily protective of their sexual encounter that night, but... uncomfortable? It makes me think maybe they don't fuck one another like they made us believe.

"We're all brothers," he says quietly.

My gaze slides down his black shirt, the black pants, the military look, and feel of him. Yeah. Okay. Brothers in arms, I suppose. I know so little about him. So little in general.

"Tell me a secret and I'll tell you one," I say, offering him the tiny pinch of green leaf remaining. His eyes snap down to my fingers and he takes it. He's removed his gloves, and I'm glad. He may not let me see his face, but at least he's not covering every inch of skin like I don't know his touch.

He holds the leaf to his masked nose. "I have a name."

My brows knit, unsure what he means. But I remember him saying he got his name because he was fast and mean. The way his confession leaves his chest makes my fingers curl into fists. Like he's handing me something heavy I need to hold on to.

"Other than Viper?" I guess.

"Yes."

I lick my lips, tasting mint and the cool night air, silently wishing it was his taste on my tongue. "Do the others not have...." I sit upright, suddenly fully aware that he's telling me something important. My heart hammers as pieces knit together with the snippets I've learned over the last few weeks. "You're the only one with an actual name?"

"I'm the only one who was old enough to remember before I was Viper. Except Reaper. But I think he's always been Death trapped in a man's body."

I nod, like I understand, which I don't, my blood zinging with an electric current. "And your names were given?"

"At the school."

My stomach drops. Images of a military style boarding school flood my mind and I wonder how far off I am. "School?"

"No," he says, the single word a command. A period. An end to this conversation and my questions.

"Then tell me why," I ask. "Why us? Why all of this? Why do you hate Rune?"

"Rune killed our brother."

I nod. I think I already knew it was something like this. Men seek revenge for damaged pride or because they thirst to make someone hurt as much as they do. It's rarely ever as simple or as meaningless as money.

"He didn't want to send you away," Viper says suddenly.

"But you were prepared to," I remind him, knowing he means Reaper. Knowing too that they all seem to follow his orders. "You *all* were."

Bending down, he places his large hands on his thighs, looking me in the eye. "We're defying an order right now to keep you from him."

I swallow.

Viper grabs my hand and pulls me up. My jacket slips down my back, but he snatches it before it can fall to the ground. Dipping low, he hooks an arm under my butt, around my thighs, and he hoists me up with one arm like I'm a defiant child. A harsh gasp slips from me as he adjusts my weight and I grip around his neck to keep from slipping down his chest.

"What are you doing?" I ask, feeling small and mildly alarmed, but kind of liking it. His brutish behavior isn't coated with violence. It never has been. But he doesn't hold back or treat me delicately either. Like he knows I can handle him.

Not bothering to answer, he carries me into the house as I cling to him, my fingers slipping under his balaclava, feeling his warm skin at the back of his neck. Using his boot, he slams the back door shut, then strides to the counter and places me on top, but doesn't back away. He stays right there, between my thighs, glaring at me from behind his fanged-skull mask as the tips of my fingers draw little circles on his skin.

"I said I liked it outside," I say. "I don't want to be in here."

"And I said it's too cold outside," Viper says, his arm still around my waist. "Our little Vixen needs to learn to behave."

Ours.

They've said this since we woke up. Ours. Our girls.

Maybe they wanted me too.

His breath kisses my face, so hot through the mask I don't know how he can stand wearing it. "Are you going to be a good girl and listen to us?" Viper says, still inches away.

My breath comes out shaky and my thighs squeeze involuntarily around his hips. "I've always been told I'm not good at listening."

He makes a seductive rumbling sound in his throat. It reverberates through his body, so I feel it between my legs. "Maybe I should show you how to be a good girl for us."

"And how does one go about that?" I ask, too breathless. Too aware of him.

His hand slips up my thigh, inching up my dress. As his fingers move higher and higher, he watches my face, waiting for my reaction. To see if I'm going to stop him.

I wonder if he even would.

Part of me thinks Viper wouldn't. He's the type to force you to admit you want something rather than wait for you to decide.

My fingers dig into his skin. His eyes darken to the color of a stormy sea.

This is why I like him. Them.

They listened to me tell them what I've allowed Rune to do, and he's not treating me differently. He's not shying away from this animalistic attraction. Viper's not treating me like I'm damaged or broken, or worse, dirty from the things that have been done to me.

Things I've done to survive a dirty man.

He's still touching me, wanting me.

Like I'm clean and pretty and desirable.

When his fingers slip under the seam of my panties, my head falls back and hits the cabinets. Dishes and glasses rattle from the impact.

I spread my legs for him.

"Seems you already want to be my good girl," he whispers. A finger flicks on my clit and I arch into him.

"I like being a good girl," I say, but am reminded of Rune and I look away, my chest squeezing.

"Then be my sweet little girl and let me see your pretty eyes as I make you come." Viper grips my chin, forcing me to look at him. My eyes meet his, then he drives two fingers into me so hard, I gasp, my legs stiffening. Then they move, dragging my slickness in and out and my lips part, fingernails clawing into his skin at his neck.

Viper angles his head, studying my mouth as I breathe out harshly. My hand slips around to the side of his neck, still under his mask, feeling stubble. I stop when my fingers are wrapped around his throat like he did with me that day in my old room, my thumb skimming along his pulse. His eyes snap from my mouth up to mine, waiting to see what I'm going to do.

When he doesn't stop, when he doesn't remove my hand, I shift my grip, fingers sliding up under his mask, feeling his strong jaw, his thick neck, letting my fingers stroke the skin behind his ear. His eyes dip to my mouth as my hips tilt, meeting his hand, a desperate hunger gnawing at my belly, wanting more. He angles his palm up, hooking his fingers so they hit that place that makes my thighs tighten around his hips. He leans forward, pressing his masked mouth to my neck as I throw my head back, rocking into his rough touch.

"Please," I whisper, desperate to go over the edge. Desperate for him. To be wanted.

I've wanted him to touch me again for weeks, been so starved for him, for all of them, I can't care about what happened earlier. I can't care about anything other than his hand driving me closer and closer.

"Come for me, Vixen," he whispers against my pulse. "Come all over my fingers."

When he takes a deep breath, I slide my hand at his neck up, dragging his mask upward until his mouth is exposed. I press my fingers to his lips. He sucks them in, teeth nipping.

Faintly, I'm aware he's letting me lead this. Take control of my pleasure in this moment until I'm the one with the power. He's handing me his control, his everything, letting me know I am safe to seek this comfort.

That clawing hunger grows more starved at the thought, and I hook my fingers into his mouth and drag him to meet mine. My lips enclose over his. I breathe out into his parted lips, slipping my tongue in, savoring his familiar feel and taste.

"Deeper," I rasp, mindless with need. My chest feels tight. I keep trying to be angry at them and I can't. Not him. Not Breaker.

Not Striker. His darkness smiles at the demons living in my head. We're drawn together, all our darkness seeking the other out, needing to feel seen and heard.

Viper gave me a secret to hold and Breaker's given me a gentleness I've never felt before.

"*Madadh-ruadh,*" Viper purrs against my lips. "Pretty red fox, come for me, please."

The beg makes my breath hitch. His fingers drive in hard as he swipes his thumb over my clit.

My release bursts out of me like an exploding star, all brilliant light and blinding darkness. Viper sucks my bottom lip between his teeth, biting down on the flesh as the world shatters. The rough bite adds to the pleasure, a cry scraping up my throat.

"So fucking beautiful." His words settle as I come down, collapsing forward. "I want to watch you come over and over, whimpering my name until it's all you can taste."

My forehead hits his shoulder as he slips his fingers from between my thighs. Leaning up, I watch as he brings his fingers covered in my slickness to his lips, painting them with my essence before sucking them hungrily into his mouth.

They *pop* out with a slick sound as he sucks them clean, his gaze never leaving my face. "Next time you'll come on my cock as you're choking on my brother's cock, so deep in your throat you'll never again forget you're ours." He pulls his mask down and backs away.

I slip off the counter, landing on shaky legs as he steps back lazily, dragging his feet. Even though I can't see his mouth anymore, I can picture his satisfied smirk.

"Next time?" I ask. My hands tremble as I adjust my dress.

He stops in the doorway. "Next time." Viper grips his hard dick through his fatigues. "You've only had a taste of us, *Madadh-ruadh*. And now you're ours. So *next time* will be the time you finally accept that you will never escape us."

Chapter 93

STRIKER

"I'M NOT FUCKING HUNGRY!"

With my hand hovering on the railing, foot on the first step, I pause and look toward the library. I glance up the stairs, knowing I need to talk to Delilah after I left her and Cora last night, after Reaper showed her the truth about her father, but Reaper's muffled response to Cora's scream sends a shiver down my spine. I don't have to see him to know he's furious. That deadly, low voice tells me maybe I should intervene.

God, it's only been twenty-four hours since we sent the driver away and Reap may already regret it.

I backtrack, spotting Viper and Breaker coming from the direction of the dining room.

"What's going on?" I ask as they approach, ignoring the way my cock thickens as Viper stalks forward. Ignoring how his large muscles ripple under his tight shirt and how his fatigues tug at his dick, his thick thighs pulling the material tightly around him. I rub my temple, averting my gaze and look at Breaker.

It doesn't help. If anything, it makes it worse. He's just as breathtaking.

I need to get a grip on myself.

"She's refusing to eat," Breaker says, stalking past me. He must have heard Reap's tone too.

When we enter the library, my eyes immediately land on Cora's smaller frame, caged in by Reaper's massive body. I'm struck by how small she is next to him. Her head doesn't even reach his shoulder, but that's not deterring her. She glares up at him with such defiance, I can't help but wonder how this woman was ever so submissive that night in the club. She looks prepared to scratch his eyes out.

Reaper points toward the doorway we're all occupying and says with a low growl, "Go back and eat your food."

She crosses her arms, unaffected by his deadly tone, his proximity, his clear anger, and shakes her head. "No."

"Don't make me put you over my knee," Reaper grates, pointed finger curling into a fist. Fuck, he's so tense, so riled. She has no idea how much he's restraining himself right now.

"Go for it," she says, narrowing her green eyes. "Rune did far worse."

His arm drops and I swear he melts back like her words slapped him across the face.

"But what do you care?" she snaps. "You were going to send me back to him, knowing what he's like. Knowing—" her voice cracks and she angrily wipes at her eyes before looking at the three of us in the doorway. My insides twist when she juts her chin out as she returns her glare to him and says, "*You* didn't *care*. You know what he's like, know what he would do to me, and you didn't *care*."

A knife in my heart would be better than this slicing pain shooting through my chest. She's right. We suspected he was hurting her and were prepared to send her right back into hell.

I can't even defend our actions by saying we didn't know the extent, but we know everything he's capable of. We have a box full of evidence that paints a perfect picture of Rune's sickness. It took us years to compile enough evidence and, thanks to our source, we gained enough to help convince not only Delilah but a handful of others to help us stop him.

A part of me is glad Delilah decided to keep Rune's secret hunts to herself for now. I couldn't imagine what Cora would feel like knowing the hands that killed those people so brutally, touched her too.

And we were going to send her to him.

To fucking Zane Devin, who may very well be worse than Rune. We haven't even told Delilah about Zane yet. I think we all worry about how she'll react after we do.

Reaper's growl of fury snaps me from my thoughts. He glares down at Cora, who shoves his chest again.

"Oh fuck," Breaker whispers as Viper lets out a low whistle.

My brows raise, glancing over at Breaker. He shakes his head.

Yeah, Little Flower is going to regret that. No one shoves Reaper around.

To my surprise, instead of reacting to her, his fingers flex at his sides, shoulders going stiff. Reaper is a man of pure control until, like me, he loses the battle.

"You know we had order—" he starts, but is cut off when she shoves him again.

"Fuck you and your fucking orders," Cora snarls back, her entire body vibrating with anger. Getting up on her tiptoes, she points at his mask. "That's just a coward's excuse to avoid using your own judgment and—"

Reaper's hand slams over her mouth, and her eyes grow wide. Gripping her arm, he tugs her toward the couch. She stumbles, grabbing the front of his shirt and the hand over her mouth as he sits and tugs her forward. She lands at an awkward angle over his lap.

An enraged cry breaks the silence when he releases her mouth and yanks her further up his thighs. Using one hand to hold her in place, he takes the other and hikes up her dress, revealing thin pink panties.

I have to admit that Viper's fetish is rubbing off on me.

"What the fuck are you doing?" she screams, trying to push herself upright, but he grips her by her hair and shoves her face to the couch cushion.

"Adjusting your attitude," Reaper growls, struggling to keep her still.

Her indignant snarl makes me smile. She's like a feral cat, squirming, reaching around to slap at his hand, her other clawing at the one pinning her cheek to the cushion, legs flailing wildly.

"Hold still, Little Red," Breaker says, and I can hear the grin in his voice. "Reaper only gets more excited when you try to escape."

"Fucking freak!" she screams.

Next to me, Viper crosses his arms, but when she manages to break free from Reaper's grasp, he darts forward, snatching her wrists, dragging her back over Reap's lap, and stretching her arms out so he can pin them to the couch.

"Not even tiny Delilah was this hard to hold still," Breaker says, shaking his head as he steps forward and grips Cora's ankle before she can kick Reaper in the face.

Once she's secured, Reaper adjusts her on his lap, and tugs her underwear down to reveal her creamy, round ass. My cock thickens at the sight. My hunger for them may have been sated briefly last night, but I can't wait to get my hands on our Little Flower.

"You wouldn't dare," she seethes when she realizes what Reaper intends, but her next few words are cut off with the sharp slap of flesh meeting flesh. It's so loud that she sucks in a breath and goes completely rigid. He lands five more in rapid fire succession and she holds her breath, not moving an inch.

I expect her to curse and struggle again, but she remains completely still. My jaw tenses, worry flooding my chest. Scared she's having some sort of trauma response and Reaper never should have put her over his knee, but then she laughs and his hand pauses mid air.

"Your kinky ass can do better than that," she says, *still* defiant with her cheek squished to the cushion. "If you're trying to make a point, you have to make it *burn*."

My brows knit. Viper's eyes meet mine. Breaker shakes his head but chuckles. I hope they're prepared to grab her before Reaper loses control and really lets them land hard, but the hand hovering over her ass darts to her shoulder and he tugs her upright, shifting her to her knees. She scrambles to pull her underwear back up. He rises from the seat, adjusting his grip until his long fingers weave into the hair at the top of her head, snapping her head back.

She makes a small, angry little sound in her throat, one hand shooting up to grip his in her hair, the other landing on his thigh, but she pulls it away quickly.

Then I see why.

The long, thick outline of his cock trapped in his fatigues makes my heart stutter. Fuck. I know his frustration. I'd love to fuck her into submission. Into believing we didn't want to send her away. The very last thing any of us want is for her to be hurt. She's even snuck under Reaper's skin, and he'll never say it, but he'd rather endure punishment than have her hurt again.

And we're definitely going to pay for keeping her.

"You think we wanted to send you away?" he says, his tone edged with violence. Reaper's anger and frustration leak out of him, turning his grip hard. "You're mistaken, Baby Girl, if you think we ever *wanted* to let you go."

Furious emerald eyes glare up at him, her hands falling to her sides, fisting into little balls. Anger radiates from her, making her shoulders tense, her jaw set hard. I wonder if this is the first time she's really let herself feel anger. Real true rage for the shit life she's endured. Maybe she's never felt safe enough before to do so.

Her chin quivers, making me want to gather her up and kiss away her sadness.

Reaper must feel it too because he crouches down in front of her, releasing his grip on her hair, letting his hand trail over the curls down to her shoulder.

"Baby Girl," Reaper whispers so gently, my chest tightens. "You're ours, do you understand? I don't let go of anything once I claim it as mine. Even if I had to send you away, I'd always come to get you." Reaper grips her chin, forcing her to look at him. Even crouched, he's still so much bigger than her. "If you ran, we'd hunt you down and drag you back to us. You have no say in the matter."

She uses the sleeve of her sweater to wipe her cheek, but I see her jaw pop and her eyes glitter with defiance. "Maybe I don't want to belong to all you freaks. You kidnapped me, remember?"

"We just took what was already ours," Reaper says.

What was already ours.

Maybe Reaper isn't such a liar after all.

These two women have been ours longer than they realize. Maybe even longer than we realize.

"You've wanted to be ours since the night we fucked you on that leather couch," Viper says. He steps forward, glancing at me, then down to Reaper and Cora before him. "And you certainly wanted to be ours when you were coming all over my hand last night, pretty Vixen."

Reaper chuckles, slipping back on to the couch behind him.

"I'm not some toy that can be claimed." She attempts to stand, but Viper keeps her on her knees by placing a hand on her shoulder. A fiery spark ignites behind her eyes. "I won't be owned. I'm so sick of *men* thinking they can fucking *own* me and *use* me."

"You can use my cock whenever you want, Little Red." Breaker leans down, hooking a finger under her chin to tilt her head back. "I'd love to have you spread open for us again."

Her chest rises on a shaky inhale. He drops his hand, standing upright.

"I'm thinking our girl forgot how your cock felt," I say, adjusting my stance to lean against the doorframe, crossing my arms. Breaker looks my way. "Maybe she needs a reminder of how good we can make her feel until she's begging to be ours."

I can practically see Reaper's smirk forming. His gaze shifts to me and that familiar, dark gleam in his eyes tells me this night's about to get interesting.

Reaper removes a hand from the couch back and turns his palm up. It's then I notice his black eyes are focused on the doorway behind me. He crooks one finger in a beckoning motion and says, "Come here, Kitten, and play with us."

Chapter 44

STRIKER

I TURN JUST AS Delilah walks into the room. Her eyes flicker from Reaper over to me and her steps falter, breaths hitching. The immediate, heated look that sparks in her eyes gives me a sick sense of satisfaction. Blue eyes drink in my features, as if she forgot what I looked like in less than twenty-four hours.

Breaker steps back to let her pass. As she does, she trails her fingers over Cora's hair with a gesture that tells me they are both okay after the emotional reveal last night.

Delilah spins, sitting obediently on Reaper's lap. His hand flattens to her stomach, dragging her back so she's pressed against him.

"You'd track us down?" she asks. Her gaze flickers to Cora, then back to me. "And force us back to you if we tried to run?"

Reaper's fingers snake up between her breasts, grasping her throat as he pulls her against his chest. He dips his nose to the side of her neck, whispering, "You know we would, Kitten. Do you really need a reminder of just how much we love the chase?"

Her teeth sink into her bottom lip, but she shakes her head. "You planned to get her," she says, turning toward Reaper. It's not a question. It's a realization.

Reaper brushes his masked nose to her temple, but doesn't respond. My chest squeezes at the way his eyes close, breathing her in.

Cora's shoulders relax, and she sits back on her heels. Her pretty features seem to turn lighter, brighter when Reaper doesn't deny he'd have stolen her once again.

I think even I'm relieved, though not surprised he was going to follow orders, then defy them. Reaper is possessive and overly protective. He also doesn't like us upset. I just wish he'd have shared his plan with us, because dragging her toward that door was the worst I'd ever felt. But then again, he rarely does.

"Pretty, Little Red." Breaker leans down, running a finger along Cora's jaw. "Such big tears you have."

Her eyes flicker up to his mask.

"Such scared eyes you have," he whispers. "Does my girl need a reminder of how hungry we are for you?"

Her chest heaves as he stands up.

"Breaker," Viper says, watching as Cora's eyes drag down Breaker's body to the bulge in his pants. "I think Vixen here wants a reminder of how good your cock felt buried in her throat."

"I bet she's already dripping wet at just the thought of your dick in her mouth," Reaper says. He lifts his chin slightly at Viper.

Viper drops to his knees behind her. Cora's head snaps over to Reaper, like she knows he's the one silently commanding this.

He always does.

"Are you?" Viper brushes a fiery curl back. She turns her head to the side to look at him over her shoulder. He grips the back of her neck, then slides his finger down her spine. A shiver ripples down my back, remembering how he touched me like that just a day ago. "Lift your pretty dress and let me feel under those pink panties. Let me feel how wet you are for us."

Even as her jaw clenches, she grips her dress and pulls up. I smile at Reaper when he looks my way.

Maybe fucking them in the club wasn't so much about fucking with Rune as it was about making sure our girls remembered all the ways they already gave themselves to us.

Viper slides his hand around her stomach and down into the front of her panties. She arches back into him as he drives into her.

"God, I fucking love those," Breaker says, eating up the sight of Viper's large hand moving underneath the thin material. "They're so thin, you can see how wet she is from that spanking."

Delilah quirks a brow, eyes trained on Viper's hand. "Spanking?" She squirms in Reaper's lap. *I bet her pussy is just as drenched.*

Cora's response gets distorted with a gasp as Viper drives into her again, burying his masked face in her red waves, his chest expanding on an inhale. My heart stutters when his eyes dart up and meet mine. The way he's savoring her scent reminds me of how he breathed me in before I shoved my cock into his mouth. His blue-green eyes move down to my crotch, darkening, like he is remembering the taste of me. It makes my cock so hard, I have to shift to keep it from pressing brutally into my zipper. Breaker must notice because I feel his gaze and clench my jaw, avoiding eye contact.

Cora groans, lashes fluttering. Viper breathes her in again, fingers still thrusting wetly into her heat. Delilah removes Reaper's hand from her neck and leans forward, cupping Cora's flushed cheeks, swallowing our Little Flower's delicate groan with a sloppy kiss, then sucking her tongue into her mouth.

"Oh shit," Viper hisses.

I wonder if he's jerked off to the memory of them as much as I have.

Reaper gathers Delilah's hair so he can see and says, "That's my good girls. You've tempted us for so long. Let us see how sweetly you kiss."

Both women melt at his words, breathing becoming heavy, kiss growing heated. Cora whimpers, one hand gripping Viper's wrist, the other squeezing Delilah's thigh like she's using her to keep grounded.

They break their kiss, chests heaving, eyes sparking with desire. Delilah's gaze meets mine and I can see the shift. Even when I moved inside her last night, she was guarded. Now all her walls are down, knowing we'll do anything within our power to keep our girls from being hurt.

"Our girls like performing for us," Reaper says, motioning for Breaker to step closer as he pulls Princess back. "Show us how much you've craved us."

Over her head, my eyes meet Reaper's and he lifts a finger from the back of the couch, signaling me to come over.

I push off the door and step forward, my heart thundering. Breaker's heated gaze turns to me when I stop next to him, his pale eyes smoldering with anticipation, something flaring behind them when they land on my unmasked face. A metallic clink echoes in the nearly silent room as he undoes his belt buckle. I watch his long fingers gracefully slide the belt open, and he's so hard already that when he pops the button of his pants, he has to tug them away just to pull the zipper down. The grating sound of the metal teeth opening sends a surge of desire straight to my cock.

This wild, lustful sensation snaking through me as I watch his movements is new. I've never been quite so affected by his nearness before. The sensual way he moves. It feels like I can't get enough air in my lungs. Even though my breathing is heavy, it's shallow, my pulse thumping so quickly, so loudly, it's not letting me take in a full breath.

Cora's little whimper when his long, hard cock springs free, cuts through the room.

She certainly didn't forget what he was like.

"Just the sight of your cock got her pussy fluttering," Viper says, his voice laced with satisfaction.

She exhales sharply. "I bet the sight of his perfect dick got yours hard, didn't it?"

Viper's eyes fly up to me, then over to Breaker. "The need to tame you makes my cock hard, little Vixen."

"What a shame," she breathes. "I was hoping to share Breaker's dick with you again."

Reaper leans back again, and his eyes move from me to Viper. "Viper, help our pretty girl."

Immediately Viper reaches for Breaker's dick with his free hand. The second it fists around him, Breaker groans, hips jerking into Viper's grasp.

"That's so insanely hot," Cora whispers.

"Tongue out," Breaker says. She obeys, pink tongue offered up, green eyes locked on his mask. Breaker wraps his hand around Viper's and guides his dick to her parted lips. She swirls her tongue around the head and my cock jerks, like it was her mouth on me. Breaker throws his head back, releasing a groan. "Oh, fuck."

"That's it, Baby Girl," Reaper says, his voice husky. "All the way until he hits your throat."

She makes a sound, like a little purr of excitement, and Breaker drops his head to his chest and jerks forward, gripping the back of her neck to keep her still. She chokes, and he releases her, but she sucks him in again with wet, sloppy sounds.

Delilah leans forward and tucks several red curls behind Cora's ear. "You're so beautiful," she whispers, sending a surge of desire straight to my dick. "You suck his cock so good, just like you did my pussy."

"Fuck me," Breaker rasps. "Tiny Thing has a dirty mouth."

She grins up at him. "Bet you can't wait to fuck it."

His hips punch forward, making Cora choke.

"Striker." Reaper's coarse voice shoots down my spine, drawing my focus to him. His black eyes meet mine and I see the question in them. *How far are you willing to go?*

I glance at Viper, intently watching Cora take Breaker back into her mouth, then back to Reaper.

How far? Do I want Breaker to know?

Who the fuck am I kidding? They *all* already know.

I nod, my heart stampeding wildly in my chest.

Reaper grips Delilah by the back of her neck and squeezes. She cocks her head to the side as his thumb skates over her pulse. I want to lean down and kiss where his finger was. Her lashes flutter, making me think of how she looked when I slammed into her last night. How her eyes glazed over like they are now. Her gaze moves up to me as he gathers her hair and holds it in a fist, but he turns his focus back on me.

"Let Baby Girl taste your cock," Reaper tells me, then says, "Viper, help our girl suck him in deep."

Viper freezes. Breaker stills. Reaper waits.

Cora releases Breaker's dick with a slick *pop* and shifts my way, eyes darting up to my face, tongue already out and ready. Delilah scoots closer, biting her lip, blue eyes clouding with lust as she looks up at me, reaching for Cora again, obviously planning on joining even without Reaper's command.

My heart hammers and I realize they don't know. Our girls have no idea the change happening because, for all they know, we do this. Fuck each other. Neither one detects how we've all paused, waiting for the other's reaction. Like the entire planet didn't just slip off its axis, and my life hasn't suddenly changed with this one command.

Breaker's hand lands on my shoulder and electric bolts shoot through my head. Suddenly, I can't remember if he's ever touched my shoulder. I can barely breathe as I try to work through the noise in my head.

He's touched me. Plenty of times. Our dicks have even touched, slipping into a waiting cunt on more than one occasion. But somehow, his fingers on my shoulder right now, makes the room feel like it's tilted sideways.

My gaze flickers over to him and I catch his pale blue eyes watching me, like he's silently checking in with me. I wish I could see his face. See if his lips have turned up at the corner with a small, knowing grin or if they tugged into a frown like they do when he's concerned.

I wonder what that frown tastes like.

Reaper's voice breaks through the static in my head, thick with lust. "Kitten, help them get Striker's cock in our girl's mouth."

Delilah reaches for my belt. Viper's gaze drops to the bulge in my pants. The sound of my zipper being pulled down snaps through me, and it's like the entire world's moving again.

Delilah's warm hand reaches into my pants, wrapping around me and I hiss out a breath. She frees my dick and my hand lands on Cora's head, trying to keep myself upright. Excitement, adrenaline, lust, all course in my veins, making my head spin.

"Even his cock is gorgeous," Cora whispers, and I'm slammed back to reality.

Before I can change my mind, Princess's and then Viper's large, thick fingers wrap around my base. My hips jerk involuntarily at the contact. Viper's other hand weaves into Cora's hair at the back of her head, guiding her to me and our finger's brush. I squeeze my eyes shut, clenching my jaw. The feeling of all of them, all those fingers, *his* hand on me, makes me feel unsteady, so I dig my fingers into Cora's red hair as she leans in and sucks me into her mouth.

My eyes flutter, fire sparking down my spine.

"That's my good boy," Breaker says and his words crash through my head, making my eyes pop open. Cora chooses that moment to suck my tip hard and I gasp as Breaker's gaze shifts to me. Am I the good boy or Viper? Do I want it to be me? Then Breaker says, "I knew you wanted to be Strike's good boy too, Viper."

All the blood drains from my head to my cock. Viper's grip tightens around my shaft. Breaker squeezes my shoulder and I'm grateful for it. It feels like permission. Like reassurance that this is all okay. Our girls don't know, but they do. *He* does. Viper hasn't always sucked his dick. They haven't always touched when we've taken a woman. What I'm doing right now, changing how we interact during these moments, is altering not just my life, my mental and emotional state, but theirs too.

Cora releases me with a slick pop, sending a surge of heat through my gut. "He's huge," she says, completely unaware of the dynamics being established. I drop my gaze to find her looking up at me with an open, satisfied expression. Her eyes flicker to Delilah. "I bet he felt good stretching you open."

Princess makes a sound in her throat, her thumb slicking over Cora's wet lips and the saliva dripping down her chin. I try to focus on her face as Cora sucks me in deep, but I can barely think straight as she swirls her tongue around the head of my dick, and Viper tugs my shaft, forcing Delilah's hand to slip lower. She trails her fingers over Cora's cheeks as they hollow out and the sight's so erotic, so sensual and loving that my balls draw up tight.

"Viper," Reaper says, and I snap my focus to him, trying to keep from exploding into her mouth. "Take our Baby Girl while she sucks Striker's cock." He pets Delilah's head, making her grip on my cock tighten. Black eyes move from my cock to my face before moving over to Breaker. "Breaker, come take care of our pretty Kitten."

Next to me, Breaker lowers himself to his knees, placing one hand on the cushion next to Reaper, his other sliding her dress up. She releases me and now it's just Viper's hand on my dick.

"Lift your hips, Kitten," Reaper says as he tugs her dress up and hooks his thumbs in her underwear, slipping them down her thighs. Breaker removes them all the way, then undoes the buttons of her dress, pulling it over her head until she's just in her white bra.

The sight of her pink nipples under the thin material makes my fingers tighten in Cora's hair, and I thrust forward roughly into her mouth. Cora chokes as I hold her head still, feeling her throat constrict, and I realize she's trying to swallow me down.

"Shit," I hiss and ease up, letting her breathe. I look down at her satisfied smirk. "You're a dirty little girl. You like choking on cock."

She wipes spit from her chin. "I like dicks."

"Our dicks," Viper growls. Gripping my dick so hard, I bend forward slightly, trying to keep from spilling over as he forces her mouth back onto me. "Just *our* cocks, Vixen. Suck this dick right here and show Striker how much you want his cum while I fuck you."

My vision blurs. He slips his hand up and down my length, gripping me firmly.

"Shit," I rasp out, barely able to hang on to my sanity. If he keeps stroking me like that, I'm going to come before he can even get inside her. After a second, he lets me go and I suck in air, pulling back so Cora's forced to suck just the head, but it doesn't help.

Viper pulls her off me. I lick my lips, trying to refocus as he unties the wraparound dress and it falls open, revealing her pink panties and bra.

I grip my cock as she leans in to take me again. Faintly aware of Breaker next to me, positioning Delilah on Reaper's lap, but I can't focus on much beyond Cora's wet mouth.

Viper unhooks the bra, and it falls away. Rosy nipples on large breasts, covered in smooth, fair skin dotted with freckles, are now my new favorite thing.

Viper reaches around and pinches her nipple and the sound she makes reverberates through my dick.

"I told you next time you'll be choking on cock," Viper says to Cora.

Her hands land on my ass and she sucks me in, so roughly it feels like she's trying to suck my fucking soul from my body.

"Fuck," I groan, my eyes falling to her pretty face. Saliva spills down her chin, eyes watering, but she does it again, and I snap my hips forward, shoving deeper into her mouth.

"Come here, Vixen." Viper doesn't bother removing her underwear. He tugs them down her thighs, pressing on her lower back, leaning her forward slightly as he frees himself. The sight of his cock makes my balls tighten. His sea-blue eyes move from my dick, barely over a foot away from his face, and lock onto mine as he thrusts into her. The movement drives my cock deeper into her mouth and she releases another groan that shoots up my spine.

"Oh fuck," Viper grates. "She's already so wet."

I hiss out a breath. She must feel so tight like that, her legs restricted by her underwear halfway down her thighs. He threads his fingers around her throat and I eat up the sight of him on his knees again before me, thrusting into her, holding her still as I hit her throat.

"She loves sucking your cock, Strike," Viper rasps. "Her pussy tightens on me so hard when you fuck her mouth."

I lick my lips, mouth dry, and release her head to touch the top of his mask. "You like my cock in your mouth too."

Reaper's dark chuckle is drowned out by the slick slapping of Viper thrusting against her ass.

"You bet I do," he says, driving into her. "I loved feeling your thick cock hitting my throat."

She groans again and I clench my jaw, my fingers tightening on his head. I want to rip his mask off and shove my dick down his throat, but I'm not sure he's ready. Not for his mask to be removed or for us to go that far again in front of everyone.

The sweet cry from next to me snaps my attention away from him and Cora. Delilah's legs are hooked over Reaper's thighs, his hand at her throat as Breaker kneels before her, his mask up just high enough so that his mouth is exposed. His tongue slips over her pink clit, then swirls just the way we know she likes it. The way he groans, sucking her into his mouth, makes me wonder how many times he jerked off to the memory of her too.

Reaper's hand at her throat drags down between her breasts and Delilah arches into his touch, like she's starved for him. When he lifts his mask to press his lips to her neck, she gasps, her legs widening.

"Striker, come take this pussy," Reaper says, tongue gliding over his scarred lip. "Show our Kitten who owns her."

Chapter 95

STRIKER

Breaker lets her go and sits up. I catch sight of his wet mouth before the mask slips down and I wonder how his lips would feel wrapped around my cock.

The thought nearly sends me over. I slide my hand from the top of Viper's head to hold Cora's jaw with both hands. She sucks me in hard, then I pop out of her mouth. Viper's brutal thrusts force her to her hands and knees, but Breaker quietly takes my place, lifting her upright, before slipping his hard cock past her lips, drowning out her whimpers.

Gripping my dick, I drop to my knees between Delilah's thighs and lean down to press a soft kiss to her folds, flicking my tongue to taste her sweetness. Knowing Breaker was just eating her out makes me suck in the mess, lapping up every ounce of where he's been. Now that I've admitted to myself, my desire for Viper and yeah, Breaker, too, I don't know how I've lived so long with this heated blood and desperation without combusting.

"Striker, please," she begs so sweetly that I release her and sit up, guiding my dick toward her entrance. Her back arches off Reaper's lap as I slip in an inch, biting my lip at the intensity of her clenching down around me.

"Fuck," I grate between teeth. "Our dirty little Princess begs so sweetly for my cum. I think she needs all of us to fill her up."

"You want that, Kitten?" Reaper asks, dragging his lips across the delicate skin below her ear, as his hand digs into her skin, fingers clawing at her like he wants to rip through her. "You want all of us to fill you up?"

I slip into her, hissing out in pure bliss as I seat myself, her pussy fluttering at the intrusion. The soft greedy groan and the way she tilts her hips to take me deeper, makes me drive in harder.

"Answer him, Princess," I rasp, my breaths ragged from being on the edge for too long.

The way her mouth falls open, a low cry slipping past with no response, makes me wish I had her bent over so I could take my belt to her ass as I fucked her.

Reaper's hand shoots up to her throat. "Answer when we speak to you."

"Yes," she whispers, lip lifting in the corner like a fucking brat. "I want all of you."

"Naughty Princess." I slap her clit as I pull out, loving her gasp and the way she tries to widen her legs, but they're hooked over Reaper's thigh, restricting her movements. "Our greedy Princess wants all of our cum."

The sounds from behind me as Cora whimpers around Breaker's cock, as Viper slams into her, sets my blood on fire. I grip Delilah's hips and thrust in deep, over and over, her breaths hitching, pleasure shooting through my middle.

Reaper keeps his hand at her throat, pinning her to his chest as I fuck her, his other gliding down, backs of his fingers trailing along her curves until he's cupping her breast and pinching a hard nipple. She releases a throaty groan at his touch, gripping my forearms. His massive fingers and the black lines of the tattoo inked into his warm flesh on the back of his hands contrast beautifully against her unmarred pale flesh. Unable to resist, I grip her breast, cupping his hand under mine, and his gaze darts to me.

Blood surges to my cock, making her walls flutter and her hips tilt. Reaper feels her movements, and instead of pulling his hand from under mine, he drops his other down from her throat, and trails it to her lower belly, pressing down, feeling my cock hitting deep within her.

"Oh shit," she cries out, squeezing me so tightly I bite out a curse. "That's so good. I can't. It's too good."

Reaper keeps his hand pressed down and the sensation, the *knowing* he can feel me like this, *wants* to feel me inside her, makes my grip tighten on both of them.

"I'm going to come," she breathes. "Oh, my god. Fu—" A shiver cuts off her words, her walls fluttering.

"She feels good, doesn't she?" Reaper places another kiss on her neck. "Tight, and hot, and wet."

"She's heaven," I grate out, working up speed, thrusting forward hard enough that my hip hits Reaper's inner thigh, shoving her back into his chest.

Someone's hand lands on my hip, tugging at my waistband until my ass is half exposed, but I don't care whose it is. We're all doing this together, so it doesn't matter if it's Viper's or Cora's because I want them all.

Sliding my hand from her hip, I grip her shoulder, driving in harder. Her delicate groan quickly turns into a feral moan.

Reaper's gaze lifts from where I'm driving into Delilah to mine, but they dart over to the others behind me. "Save your cum for Kitten. We're going to claim her tonight."

My balls tighten. The thought of Viper fucking my cum deep into her sends a primal need through me. Her eyes flash, feeling me thicken, that dark animalistic desire to claim her making my movements sloppy. I grind my teeth trying to draw this out, but she's already falling apart around me, her pussy clenching down.

"Oh god, *yes*," she breathes. "Fuck me harder."

"Oh, fuck. That's right, Princess. Milk my cock with that tight cunt."

"Striker," she breathes, still clenching around me, head thrown back, the thin column of her neck exposed. "Oh, *god*. Fill me up. You feel so good."

Every part of me draws up tight, and then my vision blacks out, my release shooting heat down my spine. I spill over, throwing my head back as I pump into her, my chest expanding, my bones, joints, my fucking skin nearly melting in pleasure. Then I feel my body curling in on itself, my hands gripping flesh, hanging on for dear life as I'm torn apart. I hear Reaper mumbling something, curses or maybe praises, my dick hitting hard into the pressure of his hand at her belly. I hear her cry out again, but it's cut off on a whimper.

I fall forward, all of my torn parts, snapping back into the room as the world returns, my heart hammering so hard as my hips still rock, and my eyes lock on my hand tightly gripping Reaper's wrist as he rolls her nipple between his fingers. She continues to writhe, hips moving as she rides out her orgasm, her arms thrown up and over Reaper's shoulder, gripping the back of the couch.

"Fuck," Reaper breathes, barely loud enough for anyone to hear, and my focus shifts from where I'm holding on to him, to his black eyes. They gleam, fire flaming behind them so brightly they look filled with sparking embers. His chest heaves. I drop my hand, but not my gaze.

"Viper, fuck our girl harder," he orders, eyes still locked with mine. "I want to hear her scream as she comes all over you."

Whatever string drawing us together snaps as Delilah sits upright and I slip out, the head of my dick hitting her clit, making me wince. She falls forward, resting her head on my chest, and I wrap my arms around her, pressing her close. Reaper's black eyes track her hands as she slides them over my shoulders, then hooks her arms around my neck, burying her face against my shirt. He pulls the mask back down over his full lips, but I catch the way he licks them before he does. Like he can't wait to taste her.

I wonder why he denies himself.

He rips his eyes from her and looks back at me. The wild, slightly unhinged gleam lingers. I get it now. Reaper hides it from us, but sometimes he has no control over it and it pours out of him. Like right now.

He's so reserved all the time, keeping himself closed off. Nothing and no one can touch him. But in these moments, he lets himself free. I realize this is the only way he'll ever allow himself to be close to us. By directing us, asking us to follow him, allowing for these few primal driven moments to be touched by us. Even if it's just thighs brushing, or hands landing on the same sweat slick waist. Dicks moving into the same wet cunt.

We can't touch him. Not physically and not emotionally. This is the only time he's intimate with us. Not because he craves us how Viper craves Breaker or even I find myself craving the two of them. Not how he wants our Princess and maybe Cora, but intimate in the way of letting himself be vulnerable and exposed.

Except, I just saw it.

Reaper's desire. His need.

Maybe this is how he eases that pain living in his chest that misses *him*.

Hunter loved us. *Me*. We never came together, not the way he wanted to, but I felt it all the same. Hunter loved me differently than he loved the others.

I wonder if maybe Reaper thinks by getting this close to us, closer to *me* in this way, he's somehow filling that black, empty space Hunter left behind. We're what Hunter loved. He never hid how much he cherished us all. Never denied his desire for me.

Never once tried to hide his love or affection or his lust.

Like Reaper does.

But I just fucking *saw* it.

Felt it.

Reaper loved Hunter so much. They had a connection that none of us could ever comprehend.

And I'm the only thing left in this world that Hunter craved, loved, cherished, desired.

I'm everything Hunter wanted. Something he loved so desperately, he sacrificed his life to save mine.

Chapter 46

Delilah

"Turn around, Kitten," Reaper says. "Let me look at your face. I want to see those pretty blue eyes when you come this time."

Pretty.

That single word slips through my veins like lava, igniting my flesh. Reaper's not said one sweet thing to me until this very moment.

Unraveling myself from Striker, I pull back, but he grips my chin, holding it between his thumb and forefinger before he captures my mouth. His hand slips between my thighs, feeling the mess he left. I melt into him, weaving my fingers into his soft hair, then rake my nails down his scruffy cheeks as his finger dips inside me.

"You like my cum in you," he says as he breaks the kiss, dragging the wetness up over my clit. "Such a filthy little Princess. You're going to look so beautiful, dripping with the mess we make of you."

He slips his hand up over my belly, dragging his cum up between my breasts, then to my mouth. I open for him, letting him slip two fingers covered with our release past my lips, tasting us together. He moves them in and out, fucking my mouth with his fingers before he pulls them out, and his mouth crashes to mine again.

I break the kiss first, drinking in his features as he shifts to help Viper move Cora to her feet. I twist, still on my knees to face Reaper, laying my hands on his thighs. He tenses under my touch but relaxes when I don't move them.

The soft giggle from Cora beside me drags my attention back to her. Striker towers over her, pressing a light kiss to her lips. She groans, moving to her tiptoes as she kicks her underwear off and wraps her arms around his neck, angling her head to deepen the kiss. His strong fingers slip around her bare ass and knead the soft flesh.

I drink in the sight, loving how small she looks next to him. I love how delicately he kisses her, knowing exactly how it feels—how they both feel.

"Breaker, come fuck this pretty mouth," Reaper says. "I love hearing her slutty little moans."

I feel a sharp slap to my ass. Viper kneels next to me, helping Striker position Cora on his lap as he sits down next to Reaper on the small couch. Viper angles his dick, bringing it to her entrance, and drives into Cora. Striker's large hand slips under her chin, tilting her head back so he can take her mouth, hands slipping greedily all over her flesh.

"Come here, Tiny Thing," Breaker says, dragging my attention from the three to him, where he stands next to me. His hand cups my jaw as I look up at him, and he slips his thumb into my mouth. "Open for me."

I open obediently, a thrill running through me at the sight of him. With his pants undone, his dick hard, aching for us, he's the perfect picture of masculinity. All hard lines and smooth abs under his perfect, deeply toned flesh. I've wanted this for weeks, all of them like this again, and to have them sends a shiver of excitement through me.

Wrapping my hand around him, I slide my tongue over his slit, gathering his salty pre-cum, then sucking him clean before running my tongue along his length. The gravelly groans he emits makes me want to do it again and again until he explodes on my tongue.

"That's it. Get my cock wet. Good girl," he grates, grip tightening on my jaw. "Suck the tip, that's it. Really hard. I like it rough, just like my girls."

Hollowing out my cheeks, I suck him hard, letting his tip pop out of my mouth lewdly. When I lick the slit again, he groans, grasping my hair with an edge of roughness.

From behind me, I hear Viper groan, then a hand lands on my ass cheek. "Arch your back for me, Sweetheart so I can see your pretty pussy."

Tilting my hips, I feel Viper's rough grip on my ass cheek, spreading me open. His growl of approval shoots through me, making my hips tilt even further, desperate for more of his praises.

"Don't stop," Breaker rasps. "Keep sucking, Tiny Thing."

"God, you have a sexy ass," Viper grates. "Fuck. You're both so perfect."

Reaper tucks a strand of hair behind my ear, letting his finger trail to my chin as I suck the head of Breaker's dick back into my mouth. "You're the perfect, sexy little slut swallowing his cock."

My fingers curl into Reaper's thigh at his gentle touch, his filthy praise, but he grips both hands, bringing them together, clamping them with one hand. His other weaves into my hair, holding me still. As Breaker drives forward, I gag, saliva spilling down my chin, my jaw open as far as it can go. I wonder how the fuck Cora took him so deeply. He's enormous, girthy.

"Oh fuck," Breaker groans. I want to hear that desperate, reedy sound again, so I open my throat. "That's it. Take me deep. *Fuck*," he breathes out the curse word, hips jerking as he hits my throat.

Cora makes a whimpering sound, but it's drowned out, and I don't have to see her to know Striker's kissing her again. I want to turn to watch, but Reaper's holding my head still, not letting me move as Breaker drives in again.

"Tongue out. Good girl. Relax your throat, Tiny Thing. I want to feel you swallow me." Breaker hits deep, and I choke on the intrusion, but he doesn't let me go.

"Fuck, *yeah,*" he moans as Reaper twists my hair in a fist, holding me still. "Just like that. Let me feel those teeth. Oh *fuck,*" he hisses, hips jerking when I let my teeth slide along his dick. "A little bite, pretty girl. *Fu-ck*. Just a little rough."

His hand lands on my head along with Reapers, his other wrapped around my throat. I gag, eyes tearing, heart hammering from the power he has over me in this moment. My pussy throbs, wanting more. He finally pulls out, and I cough, saliva slipping down my jaw, but I don't care. I open my mouth, showing my tongue, silently begging for more.

"Perfect, greedy little whore," Breaker says and drives back in. My pussy clenches around nothing when he hits deep again and I hear Cora make a desperate, animalistic sound. She's close to coming. I recognize the sound.

Breaker pulls out, and Reaper lets me go.

"Claim that pussy as ours," Reaper says to me, reaching over to brush strands of hair off Cora's face. His hand slips around the back of her head. I wait for that slithering sensation in my gut, but it doesn't come. I wonder if that night in the club I didn't want him touching her because he felt too ruthless to touch something I secretly craved. Scared his hard edges would spoil her sweetness, not knowing it had already been used against her.

Right now, with how he's gently weaving his fingers through her hair, like he's cherishing just how delicate she is, I want him to touch her. Fill her up with every ounce of his niceness, even if it leaves none for me.

"I've been dying to watch you eat her out," Viper grates, snapping my focus to how he's driving into her.

My pussy throbs. I've not done that. Not yet. I shift between Reaper's thighs, leaning over to take her mouth when Striker breaks their kiss. She groans, her body moving with Viper's hard thrusts. Drifting lower, I shift again, nibbling at her salty, sweaty skin, until I'm bent over Reaper's thigh, and my mouth skims her lower belly.

"Eat that pretty pussy, Sweetheart," Viper says, slowing his movements. His hand lands on the back of my head as I lean over further.

Up this close, I see the thick veins in his dick, how hard he is. How he glistens with her wetness as he slips out further. I slide my tongue over her clit as Viper's dick slips back in. Sweetness and musk hit my tongue, filling my bones with a primal craving. I do it again, letting my tongue drag slowly over the little nub, loving his earthy taste. Her tangy sweetness. When I lick her again, I let my tongue slip lower, the tip slicking over Viper's dick as he slides out of her.

A throaty moan breaks free of his chest when he feels my tongue as he moves into her. "Jesus, fuck," he breathes. "Again, Sweetheart."

Viper pulls out of her and his wet dick hits my lips. I suck in the head, running my tongue over the slit, loving the male musky taste and his carnal groan that sends shimmering need through my blood faster, and I suck her swollen clit into my mouth.

"Oh, shit!" Cora's hips tilt. "Oh, baby, fuck yes. "

Viper drives back in as Striker says, "That's right, Princess." I feel his hand land on my back, feather light strokes flittering along my spine. "Suck her pretty little clit."

"Oh shit," Cora says as my tongue flicks over her again, trying to angle herself so I can easily reach her. "I dreamed of this."

I squirm, my pussy clenching. Like Breaker knows how desperate I am, I sense him lean over before he drives two fingers into me, gathering Striker's cum and dragging it over my clit. I exhale heavily, making Cora whimper and Viper groan.

"I love the sight of Strike's cum running out of you," Breaker says, then I feel the scrape of teeth before they sink into my ass cheek as I continue to lick her clit.

Beneath me, I feel Reaper's cock pressed to my chest and how his hand slips around my throat, fingers tightening at the pulse like he's feeling for the excitement coursing through me. How my body and pulse race from tasting her, from them.

Suddenly, Cora shatters with a scream, her palm flattening to my cheek, shoving me away. My tongue runs over my bottom lip, tasting them, watching her face as her mouth falls open with a quiet, gravelly cry, breasts heaving as she comes down. The sight saturates my blood with a primal desire, making me want to hear that throaty scream again, but she pushes my head away when I lean back down to taste her.

"Jesus. That's too much," she breathes. "I need a minute."

"Viper, come claim this pussy. Breaker, I want to hear Baby Girl whimper as your cock spreads her open," Reaper commands and pulls me up to face him. To me he says, "Hands and knees."

Repositioning myself, I fall to my hands between his thighs as he brushes a finger along my mouth, wet from Cora's release.

Large hands land on my ass, then Viper's finger glides over the tight hole at my rear. "Soon, we're going to claim this perfect ass and fill you up here," he says as he leans over to press a kiss to my shoulder. Behind me, I see him shift, sliding a finger roughly over Cora's clit as Breaker positions himself between her splayed thighs. "And then we're going to fuck your pretty ass until you can't breathe without saying our names in worship."

There's so much happening. So many hands and groans. Every sound and sharp flavor, every sensation skating over my skin so vivid it feels like I'm living in a fever dream. Brilliant colors and rough fingers making me want to drown in this moment. Stay here forever with them.

"Spread wider for me, Little Red," Breaker says, angling his dick to her entrance.

Cora's still spread out, legs held open over Striker's thick thighs. Reaper's knee hits Striker's thigh, and I notice how he shifts, pressing it harder to him as Striker widens his legs, making room for Breaker to inch closer. When he presses in, she arches her back and opens her legs wider. Striker lowers his face and presses it into her hair, his thumb slipping over her clit.

"Oh shit," she whimpers.

Reaper grips my cheeks, forcing my attention back to him. Black eyes flicker up to Viper behind me. "I want her begging."

His dick slips over my clit. I suck in a breath, focusing on Reaper's mask. The melting jaw doesn't look like it mocks me anymore. It looks like it's screaming.

My lips part, the thought of how I can't wait to hear him scream in pleasure nearly spilling out, when Viper slams forward and my teeth clack together from the force. If I wasn't already slick and ready from Striker, so horribly turned on and desperate after Breaker's dick was in my mouth, from tasting Cora and him, the pinch of pain of him moving into me so fast would burn far worse. Instead, it's edged with pleasure. I groan at the feeling, stars shooting through me.

Reaper slips his thumb into my mouth and I suck, greedily tasting his skin. Salt and musk and so perfectly him. Some carnal part wants to bite him so I can taste the metal tang of his blood again. I swirl my tongue around his thumb, biting down lightly, loving how his black eyes seem to grow even darker as he watches my mouth. How when he moves his gaze to Viper, pounding into me from behind, he looks like he's teetering on the edge. Like he's the one driving into me so hard he's having to hold me in place.

Viper's hand slips down my back until he's cupping my ass, his thumb sliding down to press into my tight hole. "Oh fuck, Sweetheart. You're so perfect. That's it. You take me so good. So deep."

My arms give a little as he presses into my hole. I've never had anyone take me there, never even a finger, and I suddenly want his thumb in me, moving in and out just as roughly as his dick in my pussy.

"She's close. Fuck her harder," Reaper demands, voice raspy. My lashes flutter. "Press into her ass. She's about to fucking lose it."

I hear Viper spit, then warm wetness lands in my ass crack. His thumb swipes over it and he brings it to my hole, running it around the opening in little circles. When he presses in suddenly, there's a sting of pain but it shoots to my pussy and I bite into Reaper's thumb.

"Oh shit," Reaper grates, eyes going feral. "Keep going. She's fucking going wild."

"Her ass is so tight. I can't wait to take you here, Sweetheart."

"Harder," Reaper says, watching me as my eyes lose focus.

Viper slams in again, his thumb moving slightly deeper too, and I jerk forward, releasing a gasp around Reaper's thumb. He hooks my cheek, turning my head to the side, letting me see

Breaker fucking Cora in Striker's lap. Watching him moving into her, knowing I get him next, slick and desperate from fucking her, ignites something primitive in my brain.

I tilt my ass, giving Viper better access, loving his approving moan.

My entire life, I've been this controlled woman who plans everything in advance. Every detail is controlled. But they're stripping it away. Flaying my skin from my bones. Separating the person I was from the woman right now, getting fucked so hard her knees scrape into the worn wood floor. Stripping away my inhibitions, hollowing me out. Making room for that feral woman living under my skin. Letting her come to the surface and live openly. Freely.

And god, I want her to.

"Please, please," Cora whimpers. The familiar beg sends me higher, and I'm only faintly aware of the three just inches away. Breaker driving into Cora, Striker holding her close, wrapping her in his warmth like he did me, whispering in her ear as she clings to his forearms around her, his sweet words slipping out like they're meant for me too.

So beautiful.
Pretty Little Flower.
Sweet, perfect girl.
Come all over him like our good girl.

Then he looks my way and says, "You take Viper's cock so beautifully. It makes me hard all over again, seeing you wrapped around him."

"She loves it when you talk sweetly to her," Viper rasps. "Her pussy is pulsing around me so hard, I'm going to fucking come soon."

"My pretty, pretty, Princess," Striker says, the corner of his full lips lifting, making me want to sink my teeth into his smile. "You're such a good girl, taking our cocks so well." He looks at Viper. "Be my good boy and fuck my cum deep into her."

"Fuck." Viper's harsh grunt echoes in the nearly silent room and he drives in even harder. "Come on, *mo leannan*, come for me sweet girl, I'm not going to last."

A whimper escapes me when Striker reaches over to touch my cheek. My eyes lock on Cora, but she's lost, drowning in pleasure. I want to reach for her, cling to her, and give myself and her, something to hold on to as these men chisel us down to fragments only they can put back together.

And that's what it feels like. Like I'm just pieces. Shards of who I used to be, all that's left of who I was, just broken up shadows. Long slanting lines of dusty gray. There's darkness in me, parts of me that woke up that night in the woods, then sparked alive again when Striker took his belt to me in his room. But there are light spaces, too. My love for Cora, my need for them. The need to protect her, and this new blooming craving to protect them too.

Pressure builds low in my belly. Viper's slamming into me so hard, I feel him deep enough to hurt, but when he angles himself just slightly downward, his dick sliding against that perfect spot, thumb driving in further, it's like the gates are kicked open, and I'm screaming through my release, pleasure cutting the world away brutally, until it's just blackness.

"You're fucking perfect, *mo leannan*. Your pussy is squeezing me so tight." Viper's choked groan as he leans over my back, brings me back into focus. Not knowing or caring what *mo leannan* means, but it sounds like a sliver of sweetness, so I drink it up, tilting my hips responding to the way it slips past his lips like a praise. Like I'm something to be cherished. Worshiped.

Heat floods my pussy as his movements slow. Teeth bite into the skin on my back, then he rests his forehead to my spine, thumb slipping out. Then his fingers dig into my hips with a gentle squeeze before he pulls out.

I sag into Reaper's lap but then he says, "Breaker, come claim our girl."

Chapter 47

Delilah

My mind and my body feel separated. Like I'm floating between two different realities. One where I'm Delilah Gavin, cold, controlled, and controlling. The other I'm his Princess. His Sweetheart. Reaper's Kitten. Breaker's...

"Come here, Tiny Thing," he says, his large hands sliding over me. "Let me feel you."

I press my cheek to Reaper's thigh as Breaker kneels behind me, feeling his dick slip over my opening, making me tense. I'm already a little sore after just the two of them and as I settle back down from my high, I wonder how I'm going to take him.

Neither Viper nor Striker were gentle with me. As he pushes in, I whimper, the pleasure and stretching sting making me want to tilt my hips higher and pull away at the same time. Under my cheek, I feel Reaper's hard length, the promise of him next, as I try to focus on the sensations of Breaker pushing into me.

Reaper's fingers weave gently into my hair, and I want to weep at the soft touch. "Relax, Kitten, I know you can take him."

"Give her a minute, she's never had so many at once," Striker says and I feel his—god I know they are his hands now—slip under my stomach and he lifts me until I can rest my hands on Reaper's thighs. His thumb skates over my lips and I melt. "You're so beautiful with Viper's cum dripping from your pussy. Let me see how Breaker fills you."

Reaper's grip turns hard in my hair, yanking my head back. "I know you love the feel of our cocks stretching you, pretty Kitten. Tell me how much you want it."

I nod as much as I can with his hand gripping me so tightly, wanting to please them, needing to please them. Next to me I hear Cora scream out another release and I blink my eyes open to catch Viper between her legs, thrusting two fingers into her, his mask pulled up just enough so he can suck her clit. Reaper and Striker release me and Breaker's warm breath fans over my back.

"Tell me, Tiny Thing. I want to hear you say it."

"Yes," is all I manage as Breaker nudges at my entrance again, wrapping an arm around my shoulders and drawing me up so my back's pressed to his front, the warmth of his chest securing me to him. "I want you inside me."

"That's my girl," he breathes into my ear. "You ready to be my sweet little whore?"

Nodding, I slowly breathe out, my mind centering, but my body still existing in the space that belongs to them as he slips in gently.

"Oh fuck," I hiss. The feeling of being so full makes my pussy throb and I hear him groan in my ear.

His masked mouth presses to the skin of my ear. "Are you okay?" When I nod, lashes fluttering closed, he whispers, "I'm going to give you a little more, Tiny Thing, you ready?"

"Yes," I breathe, already trying to move my hips to create some friction. He's so big, I'm stretched open so much, it feels like the only way to deal with the sting is to ride it out and move.

"She's already close," Breaker says, using his free hand to angle my head back so he can capture my mouth. I groan, grateful he's pulled his mask up so I can have his mouth, his familiar taste that makes my belly dip, my chest expand. "She won't last long."

My pussy clenches down on him when he moves again, and he grates out a raspy moan.

"*Fuck.* She's squeezing me so tight, *I'm* not going to fucking last," Breaker breathes out, sliding his other hand down from my jaw to between my breasts. With one arm over my shoulders and his other snaked up my middle, I'm caged in, tucked against his warm chest as he slips in and out with slow, delicious strokes. At this angle, he can't go too deep and it doesn't feel so overwhelming, but then he bends us over, his palms sliding over my shoulders then down my spine until I'm back on my hands and knees, my head back in Reaper's lap, and I whimper at the way he drives in deeper. "Hold on, Tiny Girl."

Then he pounds into me. Cora screams out another release, but it breaks on a sob, and it feels like it's coming out of me. I bite my lip, trying to hold back, trying to hold it in.

"Oh fuck. Let it out," Breaker rasps. "Don't hold it in. Scream for me."

Reaper grips my cheeks, forcing me to look up into his eyes. His skull mask smirks at me as Breaker slams into me from behind, forcing me to rock forward. My eyes lose focus as he drives in again, hitting that place that makes my fingers dig into the wood floor, as a tightness coils in my belly. Reaper leans down, placing a soft kiss to my lips through his mask, making my eyes sting. I gasp, feeling like that one masked kiss is tearing me in two as much as Breaker's brutal thrusts.

"Say it," Reaper whispers, breath still lingering on my lips. "Tell us, Kitten."

Breaker slams forward again, then slips out slowly so I feel every thick inch. Then he does it again.

"Yours," I grate, trying to hang on to the world around me.

"Ours," Breaker rasps the same moment I sense Striker lean over and skim his thumb over my lip and the world breaks away.

Faintly I'm aware of Breaker's groan. Of his heat filling me. His hands sliding up my back and how he says my pet name over and over as he comes. I hear my whimpering cry, my voice begging for more, for it to stop because I can't take anymore, but please don't stop. Please give me more, but the voice doesn't belong to me.

It's the voice of the woman who belongs to them.

I belong to them.

My head falls to Reaper's lap and I breathe, my cheeks wet, hair sticking to my face and sweaty shoulders. Reaper slips his hands under my arms and lifts. With shaky legs, I crawl until I'm straddling his thighs. My head falls to his chest, my fingers curling into his thick shoulders.

In all these weeks, I've been this close to him a handful of times and each of those times his touch was harsh, with tiny bits of sweetness bleeding through, leaving me wanting more. Right now, his fingers trail down my bare back, sliding with a featherlike touch over the curve of my hip until he's gripping my rear. I suck in a breath, closing my eyes, absorbing the smell and feel of him.

Reaper's lips press to my ear, his breath heating my skin through the mask. "Do you feel it?" he whispers.

I try to sit upright so I can see his eyes, but he keeps me pressed to his neck so I take what I can get, wrapping my arms around his neck, and breathe him in. Musk and male and darkness.

"How your body belongs to us," he says, shifting to press his masked lips to my jaw. "Like you were made for us."

The hand cupping my ass slips over my thigh to between my legs. On instinct, I lift myself slightly so he can angle his hand between us. A finger slips over my opening and I clench my teeth as he slides it over my too sensitive clit. His finger slips inside me and I feel his groan under my cheek.

"Filthy girl, you begged for their cum and look at the mess they made," he grates. His finger slides out. He grips the back of my neck and pulls me upright. Blackness stares back at me, but his eyes aren't just dark pools. They reflect the dim light in the room, making the midnight color look like they're filled with stars. "You want my cum too, pretty Kitten, don't you?"

God, yes. My teeth sink into my bottom lip. His eyes snap to my mouth. Leaning forward to press my lips to the side of his masked face, I whisper so only he can hear, "I want you to fuck me like you've wanted to do for weeks."

The hand on the back of my neck tightens. Reaper's fingers weave into my hair and he tugs roughly, forcing me to arch my back, my neck exposed. My hands fall from his shoulders to my sides, waiting. I may be on top, but I'm certainly not in control.

"Oh god, you're going to kill me," Cora whimpers from next to us and I want to turn to see who's got her at their mercy, but Reaper's gripping me too tight to do anything but wait for what he does next.

"Such a fucking brat," he grates, running his finger up my stomach to between my breasts. "You don't know what you're asking for, naughty girl. I don't think you can take what I've wanted to do to you."

"I've taken everything you've given me," I say, my eyes falling closed. I like his roughness, but I don't tell him that. I like it because every time I've felt it, I'm left feeling a little softer.

"Greedy, greedy, girl." My eyes pop open from his familiar voice to find Striker towering over me, his lip curled into a grin. He steps in close, gripping my throat under my jaw. My head hits his chest and I focus on his upside-down face. It's still shocking to look at him. He's so unbelievably beautiful. He slides his hands over my shoulders to my breasts, cupping each one in his hands. "We knew you could handle us. We knew you'd be our perfect Princess, begging for us and spreading your legs so sweetly."

Still holding me tilted back, so I'm arched backward slightly looking up at Striker, Reaper reaches between us and I hear the grate of a zipper. That sound fires through me and I tilt up so he can free himself. When his hard dick hits my inner thigh, I can't help the moan that slips out.

Striker leans forward and captures my mouth, his tongue slipping in with a long, sloppy stroke against mine. My hands slide up his forearms and I grip the back of his neck, forcing his mouth down on me harder.

He breaks the kiss and backs away. Viper leans over, blocking Striker's face, and he lifts his mask to reveal his perfect lush lips before they enclose over mine, taking, possessing in that way he did before. Like he can't help but greedily drink in every ounce I give over to him until he's sucking on my tongue. Reaper's cock slips over my cum soaked opening and a shiver racks my body.

"I'm going to fuck all our cum so deep into you," Reaper growls, releasing my hair as Viper breaks the kiss. I sag down against him. Reaper grips my jaw, forcing me to look at him. "You'll not be able to take a single step without remembering you belong to us."

His hand glides down from my jaw to my waist, making my blood sing with anticipation. I'm sore, but already so wet, so filled and slick, and I want more. I want him.

Keeping our eyes locked, I reach between us, sliding the tips of my fingers along his shaft, feeling his silky flesh before I slip my fingers around him and guide him to my opening. He slicks over the mess and his eyes go feral.

Angling my hips, he slips into me just barely. I lick my bottom lip, capturing it between my teeth. His fingers tighten, nails digging into my flesh like he wants to rip me apart. I lean forward and he slips in even more. Reaper's breath rushes from him, when I press my cheek to his mask and whisper in his ear, "Make me beg."

I expect him to slam me down onto him, take me roughly, like he did in the club, but he yanks my head back pulling me away. He keeps his eyes locked on mine as he grips both my hips and eases me down so gently that a whimper slips past my lips.

"Fucking *brat*," he groans, his voice seductively low, making me tighten down around him. "*Fuck*. Your pussy remembers me, doesn't she?"

I nod, biting my lip, keeping the whimper sealed behind my lips. I've remembered him, every moment, unwillingly. My body craved him again, and even though I didn't want to, I've wanted this since that night with him. All of them using me. Reaper's harsh edges outlined with this gentleness I've felt since he took us.

"*Shhh.* Give it to me," he whispers when I flinch as he hits in so deep it hurts. Lifting me slightly, he pulls me back onto him somehow going even deeper. "Let me in."

My chest tightens as he eases me up again, then pulls me gently down onto his hard length, grating out an approval as I grind down, circling my hips. My breath hitches as he jerks his hips, my nipples pebbling, goosebumps breaking out all over. They all feel so different. So good, and at this angle, I'm forced to take Reaper all the way. Feel every inch of him, even more than the others.

When he leans back some, repositioning us, I keep my legs locked around his thighs. He lifts me, his dark eyes colliding with mine, and I suck in a breath, recognizing that dangerous gleam.

My chest tightens, my pussy clenching.

"There's my dirty girl," he grates. "You ready for me, Kitten?"

As I place my hands on his shoulders, and look down to where our bodies join, I suck in a breath, drinking in the sight of him. His shirts pulled up, fatigues open and pulled down some, showing off toned abs covered with ink. Roses and black vines, curled around skulls and bones. The outline of that chevron of muscle leading to his dick makes me crave him in a wild, animalistic way that feels like insanity. He's so perfectly built, with smooth, tanned skin. His thick cock slips out as he lifts me higher and I wish I could see him fully as he enters me again, but he shifts, changing the angle.

"Hold on, Kitten," he grates, his grip tightening as he leans back. "And keep your eyes on me. I want to see you come apart."

I cry out when he slams up into me. My fingers curl into the muscles of his shoulders and he does it again and again, building up a steady pace until he's fucking me so hard and fast, the tightness in my chest feels like it's breaking apart each time he drives in.

My mouth falls open in a silent whimper.

"Keep them open," he rasps, slamming up into me harder. My eyes pop open. His hands slide up from my hips and he holds my waist, keeping me still as he pistons in and out. I want to meet him, force him to fuck me even harder, but all I can do is hold on.

"Oh fuck, oh fuck," I cry, my words spilling from me the same moment I hear Striker say, "Play with her pussy, Little Flower."

My eyes meet hers next to us, the vivid green somehow dazed and bright at the same time. She slides over, reaching for me. Reaper's eyes flash to her briefly as she scoots in next to him, her arm sliding under his to reach for me. She's so small next to him, soft compared to his hard planes. Fiery hair next to his black mask, falling over her creamy shoulder as she reaches for me.

I let go of his shoulder and meet her hand, guiding her to my clit. She angles her hand up, letting Reaper's dick slip between the V of her fingers as her thumb glides over me. The feeling of her hand at my pussy as he slides in, of her thumb rubbing little circles over my clit, sends a jolt up my spine.

"That's it," Reaper grates. "You feel how tightly she's gripping me, Baby Girl?"

"She's got a tight little cunt," Cora says and I clench around him at her dirty words. She leans over, her mouth pressing to Reaper's arm, as she slides in closer, dragging her other hand up my spine. "Come for him like you do on my hand, baby. I want them all to see how pretty you are when you fall over the edge."

"Oh fuck, Kitten," he grates, jaw moving under his mask.

"Harder," I whimper. "Fuck me harder, please."

Reaper makes a sound in his throat, and his fingers tighten, digging harshly into my flesh. He drives up harder. Then even harder.

"Please."

"Beg for it. Beg for my cum," he grates. "Beg to be *mine*."

My lips part. He trusts upward so hard the beg catches in my throat. Then I hear myself whimper. Hear his growling groans responding to my quiet begs as I hang on, only faintly aware of the other's around us.

Please. Please don't stop. Please. Please.

His eyes darken, head tilting back slightly, and just the sight of him starting to unravel sends me over. My cry cuts through the room as the world shatters around me, all my shadows spilling out, but then as my walls pulse, his hips snap up, once, twice, then he buries himself so deep, Cora's hand gets smashed between us as heat floods me.

I fall forward, curling into myself. My whimpers don't even sound like they're mine as I bite down on his collarbone, teeth scraping over his shirt.

"*Fu-uck*," he grates, again pumping in and out, riding out the last dregs of his release, hands sliding up from my waist to my back and into my hair.

Cora stops the little circling motions on my clit, but she keeps her fingers between us as he continues to pump with little jerky movements, then suddenly stills, his fingers loosening in my hair.

I breathe. He sucks in a labored breath. I open my eyes and find Reaper, mask askew, his chest heaving, onyx eyes watching my face. He's still buried deep, his cum throbbing and pulsing inside me.

Cora pulls her hand away, using it to brush damp hair away from my sweaty forehead. "Holy shit," she whispers. "That was intense."

Reaper keeps me locked in place with his gaze, but sits upright, lifting me enough that he slips out, heat sliding down my thigh. He reaches between my legs and drives two fingers deep into me, dark eyes moving to my lips as I gasp. I'm so sore from them all. But then he gently slips his fingers in and out and my shoulders ease, liking how he's giving me even more of his flesh. When he pulls his hand back, his fingers glisten with my release, his cum, Breaker's, Viper's, Striker's, and he holds them up.

"Open," he tells Cora, and her mouth falls open obediently. He slips his drenched fingers into her mouth and she sucks them in, enclosing her lips around them. "You taste us all, Baby Girl?"

She nods, looking up at him through her long, thick lashes. She's so pretty that I run my thumb over her cheek, tucking her red hair behind her ear, unable to stop myself from touching her.

"Kitten is yours too," Reaper says. "This pussy is yours. All of us are yours."

She sucks his fingers harder as he hooks her chin between the fingers buried in her mouth and his thumb, pulling her close.

"Next time you think we're going to send you away," Reaper says, jerking her head slightly. Her lips tighten around his fingers. "You remember you are ours and we will never let you go."

My heart hammers, bright light filling up my chest. Reaper pulls his fingers free and slides them into me again, meeting my gaze as he curls his fingers deep into me. When he slides them out, my lips part, ready for him, and he makes a sound of approval that shoots straight through my veins like liquid gold. His fingers slip in, and the musky tang of us all hits my tongue.

"Good girl," he says, his voice barely audible. "The next time you think you're going back to Rune, you remember we killed to make you ours."

Chapter 48

DELILAH

Cora's scream wakes me from a dreamless sleep. I bolt upright, reaching for her. My hand lands on her bare breast.

"You can't do *that*," Cora breathes out.

I pull my hand away, brows knitting. She sure hasn't minded before. Blinking my vision clear, I prop myself on my elbow to look at her face. Her eyes focus on the end of the bed as she sucks in one lungful after another, her hand moving over her heart.

"Good morning," Striker says, his voice making me jolt. I shift to look toward the end of the bed. He's sitting in the chair by the window, legs sprawled out, hands resting on the arms, the early morning light leaking in through the drapes, highlighting his features. The grin he gives us makes my breathing shallow, and between my legs throbs, like my body's remembering all the places he's been.

Where they were.

I'm not sure how we got upstairs. I vaguely remember Striker carrying me to bed and tucking me in, while Breaker laid Cora next to me before I passed out.

Getting fucked by four men, one right after another, really wears a woman out.

Cora pushes the hair back from her face, glancing at me as she lies back against the headboard, not bothering to cover up. If the state of her is any sign of what I look like, we need a shower and a brush. Her red curls stick out from having so many hands running through it. Her cheeks are flushed red, no doubt from remembering last night too, and several bite marks travel down from her breast to her belly.

Shit. Was that me?

Last night was so intense, I don't doubt I bit into her flesh like an animal. I wanted to devour her. Be devoured by them as well.

"How are you feeling?" he asks, leaning forward in the seat, resting his forearms on his thighs.

Striker's wearing jeans.

I sit upright, to better look at him, the blanket falling away. His focus shifts to me, gaze traveling silkily over my body. I've never seen him in any other clothes besides their uniforms. I really,

really like the jeans. He's still wearing a tight black long-sleeved shirt and his boots, but the jeans are new and...

Shit. He's incredibly sexy.

"Sore," Cora says. "My cunt feels like I got thoroughly fucked."

Striker's lip curls up. "Because you did." His eyes slide my way and he lifts one of those perfect brows.

I bite my lip. He knows damn well I'm sore.

"Breakfast?" Cora asks, tossing the blankets back. Striker's gaze drags down her naked body, raking over her pebbled nipples and her bare pussy as she stands. My gaze slides over her pretty flesh too. "I'm famished."

"Get cleaned up and we'll head downstairs to eat." He leans back again, propping his ankle on a knee, eyes tracking her as she walks toward him.

"You mean we get company for breakfast again? You're not going to disappear for another two weeks, then pop back up when you want to get your dick wet?"

The smirk he gives her is so devilish it makes his entire face look almost boyish. "I plan on getting my dick wet again, as you so eloquently put it, after you both eat."

Now my cheeks heat. I shift, sitting upright to lean against the cold metal headboard. Striker's eyes move from Cora to me and his brows knit when he sees me wince.

"Or maybe after dinner," he says.

"So we get you for dinner too?" Cora asks, slinking over to him, hips swaying. When she stops in front of him, he grips her waist and brings her down onto his lap.

"And lunch," he says, nestling his face into her messy hair. Her eyes move to me, like she's checking my reaction. I smile, lifting a brow. "And breakfast tomorrow too, if you can handle my company for that long."

My belly dips. That sounds...

I'm not sure how that sounds.

Oddly *domestic*?

I sink back down into the bed, heart thundering as what he's saying cuts through my mind, fragmenting into a million different thoughts. Splinters of all the information I've nearly drowned in slice into my lungs, air suddenly hard to suck in.

"What next?" I ask Striker, inhaling deeply to center my racing thoughts. He lifts his head from Cora's hair, a strange expression passing over his features.

It feels odd knowing him, being familiar with him in so many intimate ways, but not knowing how to read his expressions.

"We have breakfast." He smiles, biting his lip. My body aches, but I want to take that lip between my teeth as I sink down onto him again.

I shake the thought from my head. It would be easy to stay here. Live in whatever it is we've just created, pretend bad things don't exist beyond these walls, but I want to know their plans.

"So we aren't going to deal with this?" I ask.

STRIKER

Striker helps Cora to her feet, tapping her bare ass as she walks toward the armoire. "Right now, we're going to have breakfast."

I nod, pulling the covers up around my chin. It's obvious we can't go back, at least not yet, but we have to at some point. I have to deal with this. With my father and all this knowledge living in my head.

I need to deal with Clyde.

There's no way he doesn't know about my father's.... *Hunts*. He's been with my father since he began Rune Corporations, helping guide him. Clyde *has* to know about the lodge. That has to be why he always told me I would be bored or hate to be stuck out in the middle of nowhere with zero cell reception.

Zane.

Fucking Zane. He has to know, too.

My stomach churns.

"—if you want to," Cora's saying.

My gaze snaps up to her. Her brows raise like she's waiting for an answer.

"Sure," I say, not even caring what I've just agreed to. Anything would be a nice distraction from the chaos in my head.

Cora grabs a dress, then pulls one of mine out of the armoire. "What's for breakfast?" she asks, sauntering over to the bathroom, Striker tracking her every move.

Last night, he barely touched her. I think I'd like to watch him fuck her.

"Reaper made pancakes," he says, rising from the chair.

"Reaper?" Cora and I say at the same time.

The one and only time I caught Reaper in the kitchen over the last few weeks, he was making a sandwich. He dropped everything, knife clattering to the plate, and left the room, leaving it and everything else on the counter when he stalked out. Like my presence was enough to disgust him to the point he lost his appetite.

Now, I know that's not true. Not with how he fucked me last night. He's craved me as desperately as I craved him.

A chuckle breaks free as the image of him standing over the stove, flipping pancakes wearing his mask, fills my head.

They both look my way.

I slip back under the sheets.

"Get cleaned up," Striker says, stalking across the room toward the bed. I eat up the strong hard planes of his body, the way the jeans hug his dick and how muscles move in his arms.

I wonder, watching his eyes darken as he moves forward, dragging me from the bed, and pushing me toward the bathroom, if what Reaper said is true.

If we belong to them and they'll never let us go, I wonder if that means they're ours too.

Because I think I like the idea of them belonging to me.

Think I really, really like the idea of these four men belonging to Cora, who needs someone strong, someone dangerous and edged with violence to keep her safe.

Chapter 49

BREAKER

The red flowers in the cracked pottery gleam in the early morning light, the dew slightly frozen on the petals glistening like drops of blood. Winter sunlight creates deep shadows and brilliant highlights in the garden below. The entire world looks overly saturated this morning, last night's rainstorm washing away the dirt and dry leaves, leaving the world brighter. Crisp with a frigid chill that makes the air taste clean.

Fitting after last night. It's like the sun rose on this day, knowing we needed a fresh canvas. Knowing that after all the dark days and uncertainty about what we set out to do would work, after all the terrible things revealed, we needed this brilliant morning to remind us that the years we planned for this were worth it.

Last night proved it was.

"No!" Cora's shriek of laughter brings me back to center, and I lean over the balcony peering down to where she's standing with Delilah and Striker in the center of the front garden. He grips her arm, pulling her to his chest, his mouth descending on her like he's done this a million times. Like it's the most natural thing in the world to kiss her. Like we didn't keep them locked away for weeks, forcing them to bond with us.

"Do you think they wanted this?" Viper asks from behind me. I grip the railing as he steps up next to me, my chest constricting. It always does when he's close. It tightens, making it hard to breathe. "Do you think it actually worked and we Jedi mind-fucked them into wanting us?"

I asked myself that same question over and over last night after I carried Cora and Striker carried Delilah upstairs. In the darkness of my room, I laid in my empty bed, wondering if they gave themselves over to us so easily because they had wanted us all along or if we really succeeded with our mission and molded Delilah, and Cora too, into wanting us, believing us, needing us.

"I don't know," I tell him. I don't admit I'm not sure I care. We have them both, and that's all that matters.

He steps up close, letting his arm brush mine. He always does this, touches me, and I've learned over the years he doesn't even realize he's doing it. It's like some unconscious thing where his body wants to be connected to mine in any way possible.

Viper pulls at his mask, adjusting it around his neck, then crosses his arms as his hip hits the railing. My eyes fall to his hands clasped over his massive biceps.

Fuck. He's so fucking sexy and he has no idea.

"I would like to think that they made this choice of their own free will and not because we did that captive syndrome thing with them," he says. "Last night sure felt real."

Last night was amazing. It would have only been better if we didn't have to wear these masks anymore, but I don't know if we're ready just yet. Striker may trust that the girls will remain loyal to us, but I'm unsure. Even after last night.

"Stockholm," I say, my eyes gravitating back to the garden below. "It's called Stockholm Syndrome after that bank heist in Sweden."

"Whatever it's called, do you think that's what it is?" Viper asks, clearly distressed at the idea we coerced the girls. What he doesn't realize is that all we did is show them the truth. What he cannot see is that we saved Cora from Rune without even knowing it, and when Delilah discovered we would rather break orders to keep her best friend turned lover safe, we earned her trust.

"No," I say. "I think what happened is exactly what Reaper had planned. We showed them the truth, and they made a choice."

What I don't say is that I had seriously doubted Reaper in the beginning. That I had thought his hatred for Rune was clouding his judgment and he was determined to make someone, anyone, pay, even if it was a small woman with red hair who had nothing to do with Hunter's death. Or that he was so hellbent on revenge he was blinded, unable to see his own lust for Delilah, that it turned into something dark and depraved.

What I don't say is that I should have trusted him, like we've all trusted Reaper our entire lives, because he knew what he was doing. He was freeing Cora and convincing Delilah.

The asshole knew too that if he let Cora sit in her fear for a tad too long, I'd snap, break his order for him so he didn't have to admit he hated seeing her scared as much as the rest of us, and I'd do what I wanted.

Because I always, always do, consequences be damned.

He knows us all a little too well.

But that's how Reap works. He takes charge, forms a plan, and enacts it. He doesn't care who he walks over in the process as long as the job is done.

He didn't used to be like this. Reap used to be a little nicer.

"I hope so," Viper says, making me turn to look at him.

I almost laugh at how his voice turns gentle. He's erratic, driven by his emotions, and fucking nuts sometimes, but his heart is soft. The little knife he gave Delilah in secret showed everyone what he only ever lets me see.

Viper glances my way, and I avert my gaze back to Striker with the girls in the garden below. Cora laughs again as he pulls Delilah to him and gives her a light kiss. I envy him. Striker's ability to trust after all he's been through. I want to trust them. That they will be true to their word and remain with us after this short a time. I'm envious he's no longer wearing his mask and doesn't feel like he needs to hide anymore.

I wish I could feel that secure. But Fallon fucked us all up so much I don't think we know how to trust completely. Trust each other, yes. Trust outsiders? No.

Delilah is loyal to Cora. Cora is loyal to Delilah. But are they loyal to us? We'll see once things are set into motion.

Viper scoots a little closer, turning to face me. I keep my hands on the rail, my focus on Striker. His boots hit mine and awareness jolts straight to my dick.

Fuck.

Last night, I was surprised when he didn't come to me after we fucked the girls. He usually does, but maybe he was feeling as out of sorts as I was. We'd fucked them to the point we were mindless, instead of the other way around. If only these women knew what they'd done to us.

Maybe it's good they don't.

Stupid things like feelings can be used against us, and I know for a fact this constricting feeling, like a wire wrapped around my lungs, cutting through me every time they're this close, is the dreaded feelings we all avoid. The only people we have ever let close are one another, and even that was nearly broken after Hunter.

God. Hunter.

What would he think of this? Of them? Of Striker down in the gardens with them now, kissing their pretty pink mouths and smiling at their light laughter.

He'd love it. He'd fucking *love* to see Striker's smile and how just looking at them eases the tightness in his shoulders. Lightens the darkness behind his eyes.

He'd tell us to cherish Cora. Because it's rare to find someone who can see your darkness and match it with their own, all while showing you the light that lies beyond. Hunter would love that Striker had someone who knew about the darkness he carried because she had lived with it too.

I wasn't supposed to hear, but I did. That day, he sat with Cora in her room and she told him about her mother. I had come back in, unable to stay away, and found the camera room empty. Then I noticed Striker in the room with her. Of course, I sat and watched, wondering what the fuck he was up to. To say their conversation was shocking is an understatement.

We researched her past, discovered so much. And we watched them for so long, knew so much about them before we set out on this mission, but that part never, never came to light.

Cora's mother was truly an evil person.

She got what she deserved.

"Are you jealous?" Viper asks.

My eyes snap to his. It takes a minute for the meaning behind his words to sink in.

Not jealous of Striker with the girls…

Of Striker with *him*.

Something flashes behind the sea green color, telling me he'd like it a little if I was.

Am I jealous? I don't know exactly what happened between him and Striker, but it's about time. I think Striker is the only one who didn't see what he wanted for years. But am I jealous Striker obviously fucked the mouth of the man I've coveted for most of my life?

No. I like the idea of Striker using Viper the way he likes. Just as I enjoy watching Viper lick and suck and fuck our girls. So no, not jealous. Turned on? Fuck yes.

"That you sucked him off?" I ask, shifting so we're standing face to face. "Should I be?"

His beautiful eyes narrow.

Yeah. He wants me to be jealous. Okay. I can't deny this man anything. If he wants me jealous that he wants Striker's cock as bad as he wants mine, then that's what he'll get. I wonder, though, what he'll do if I let Striker face fuck me. Or if I fuck him. The thought sends blood rushing to my cock, making it press against my zipper painfully.

Damn. I glance back down at the girls. My blood heats.

Viper didn't get jealous when I fucked Cora and now Delilah, but more than likely will if I do Striker. Because Viper *will* get jealous if I *touch* Striker.

I shouldn't like that thought so much.

The only man I've ever fucked was Viper, and that was just once. When he was overcome with so much darkness that he let me bend him over and take what I needed. What we both did. I know Reaper and Striker think we have often, but after that first time, it's only ever been Viper's warm mouth after a night with a woman, and my hand on his dick.

That one time in his room only happened after that first night we all shared a cunt. We were both so aroused, driven nearly mad by too many emotions we didn't know how to express and too much sadness we couldn't let go of.

It wasn't like I didn't notice him before then. If anything, I noticed him too much as we grew up. He did too, but I don't think he knew how to name what it was we shared. I didn't either until I felt it for the first time with that girl from the village.

Viper moves closer, invading my space. He's built like a fucking tank, stocky and tall, muscles and thick thighs that make me want to sink my teeth into them. Fuck. I've held on to this secret attraction to him for so long, it's spilling over. It doesn't help that Cora and Delilah love to see him sucking my dick. That they got so turned on that night with them, and seem to crave us even though we don't fit into conventional molds that little girls are taught to want.

I lean down, inhaling his clean scent. My mouth waters, remembering the night in my room just weeks ago when he nearly had me on my knees, ready to let him fuck my throat. Then his fucking mouth got in the way and we ended up arguing as usual.

I've never taken him in my mouth, but the thought of sucking him until he explodes makes my balls tighten.

He widens his stance, ready for a fight.

"I think next time you want to be used like a slutty boy, then you should come to me." I lower my voice, trailing my finger along his shoulder to his thick neck, loving how heat sparks in his eyes. "That pretty mouth of yours belongs to me."

"Maybe it belongs to Striker too," he says, stepping even closer, challenging me.

This fucking man. He's never going to learn. Then again, I think he likes the lesson as much as he likes defying a command.

Before he can react, I grip his throat, pulling him onto his tiptoes. His eyes drop to where my mouth hides behind my mask. I'd give anything right now to see his lips. Have him sink to his knees, sucking me into his warm mouth, and feel his greedy groan around my cock.

His breath rattles out of him, and I press my cock to his stomach. A promise and a threat. "Be a good boy, Vipe, and don't test me. You know I'd love the chance to fuck your tight ass again."

His eyes brighten.

I knew it. Crazy, sexy man. He loves when I get dominant with him. Maybe, with this new day, this shift in the air, we can all embrace what we've wanted. We have the girls now, their presence giving us the courage to express what we've wanted. I know being this close to them for weeks has made us all crazy with desire, but if last night proved anything, our girls are more than willing to please. More than willing and ready to let us do whatever we want, whether it be Viper sucking my dick, or Striker, and gladly join in.

"Are you two finished rubbing your dicks together?" Reaper's voice breaks through the chaos in my head and I step back, my hands falling away like we're caught doing something illegal. My eyes shift from Viper to Reaper and find him standing just inside the doorway, his mask in his hand.

Pain clutches at my heart like it always does when I see his face.

"I take it neither of you have your phone?" he asks, pulling his mask over his head as he steps onto the balcony.

Viper casts me a strange look as I back away further and say to Reap, "No, we don't. What's going on?"

Reaper braces his hands on the balcony, leaning over to watch Striker loop an arm around each woman's shoulders as he guides them back into the house.

Yeah. I am jealous.

I want that too. That freedom to kiss them whenever I want. For them to look up into my face with their gorgeous smiles. Maybe it's really that simple. Remove the mask and simply trust.

After the front door shuts behind them, Reaper pushes off the balcony railing and stalks past us, back into the hall.

"What's the fucking message, Reap," Viper calls after him. His gaze darts to me and I see the same nervous tension stiffening his shoulders that's settling in my gut.

STRIKER

Looking back over his shoulder, he says, "We defied his order. And he's on his way to teach us a lesson."

Chapter 50

DELILAH

As my feet hit the bottom step, I'm greeted by a blast of cold air from the open front door. I pause, irritation heating my neck. It's so careless, but then I have to remember they are just men with emotions and bad habits, like everyone else.

I shift the stack of Cora's books in my arms, debating crossing the foyer to shut and lock it, but a stern voice from the library snags my attention. My stomach flutters. I've not seen any of them since last night, except for Striker this morning, and the thought of walking in there sends desire crashing through my belly.

When I woke up in that room just over three weeks ago, I never could have imagined how my life would change so drastically. Instead of fearing the men who took me, my pulse thunders, my body sore, yet electrified at just the thought of being in the same room as them.

Another grating command echoes through the house. I adjust the stack of books and take the last step off the stairwell, unease making my jaw tighten. They sound like they're arguing.

As I enter the library, my gaze lands on the four men standing in a row, their backs to me. They all seem to tense, sensing my presence. The four step aside, parting to reveal an unfamiliar face in the center of the room.

My heart skips, my gaze instinctively falling on Reaper, then Striker next to him. My stomach drops as I notice the mask covering Striker's face. Uncertainty gnaws at me as I hesitantly take a step forward, searching for any signs from Reaper that I should be concerned.

His black eyes tell me nothing. His tense shoulders and fisted gloved hands tell me I need to tread lightly.

The man's polished shoes click against the wood floor as he steps forward, drawing my eyes. "Delilah Gavin," the man says, voice like velvet. "What a pleasure to finally meet you in person."

In person.

My grip tightens on the books and I hug them to my chest, heart hammering so hard it's making it difficult to focus. I tilt my ankle in my boot, but remember my knife is gone. Viper never gave it back to me. As he steps closer, my eyes dart up his body, from his shiny black shoes to his face.

It's so strange to see a face after so many weeks of just seeing my own and Cora's, and Striker's barely two days ago, that I stare at him, taking in his features. He's tall—almost as tall as Reaper—lithe, dressed in a charcoal three-piece suit that accentuates his lean, athletic build. Silver hair, styled elegantly, long on top, but shaved on the sides. High cheekbones and a sharp jawline chiseled to perfection.

He's striking in a way that's intimidating, but it's his eyes that make my skin prick with alarm. Piercingly clear, cold. Like ice, reminding me of Breaker, but lacking in depth or emotion. Like all color bled from the iris, leaving them empty.

"Who are you?" I ask before I can clamp my mouth shut, years of training on how to interact with cold, calculating men fleeing my body in this man's presence.

This. *This* is a predator.

His lip curls, revealing a flash of white teeth, as his smirk cuts through me. "How impolite," he says, his voice smooth and controlled. The instinct to back away is so strong I nearly do it, but I plant my boots on the hardwood floor and set my jaw, tracking his movements as he takes another step toward me. "No tact, but beautiful. I can see why my sons have become so enchanted with you." He offers a large hand with thin fingers. "I'm Fallon Byrns. Their father."

His words crash through my head, paralyzing me.

Sons.

Father.

"You're their father?" I ask, my brows knitting. I glance at Reaper. When he spoke of their father, I'm not sure what, if anything, I pictured, but I certainly couldn't imagine the man before me. The four men flanking either side of him are all of a different ethnicity from what little I've seen of them, and maybe in some remote part of my mind I knew they were adopted after Reaper said they were all brothers, but I never would have pictured this man before me as their father. Or anyone's, for that matter. My gaze moves back to the man Reaper said used to be friends with Rune. "How do you know Rune?"

His perfect silver brow arches. "I see Reaper has told you."

I swallow the unease trying to choke all the air from my lungs. "He's told me some, but I would still like to know why I'm here."

Fallon turns his head to the side, looking over at Reaper. His profile is something an artist would weep over. He's older than my father, but so handsome, so stoic and cold, that he looks years younger.

"She knows," Reaper says, and his deep voice makes my nipples pebble.

"I'm aware of what Rune is doing," I say, gathering all my courage to keep my voice from trembling. I refuse to show any weakness around this man. He is someone to fear. Someone to watch carefully. My instincts scream, telling me to be wary. This man, their father, is here for a reason after all these weeks.

Their father who lost a son.

The son Rune killed.

I guessed from the moment I woke up, my father knew who was taking us. He said as much when the four stormed into the lobby. That means he's known all along who's had us.

Did he send you?

He's doing this...

He's come to collect.

He's known, this entire time, that this man in front of me took Cora and me, and Rune's known this entire time *why* we were taken.

And he didn't try to get us.

Fallon is the reason I'm here. He has to be the one who told these men to take us. Even though they explained, even though I know why they did what they did, having the man responsible for giving the order to use me standing before me, sends sparks of rage through my head.

I know why they did it. And I also know they were incapable of going through with whatever their father ordered them to do. I'm not angry with them. I understand them now.

But this man ordered them to manipulate me, and do god only knows what in order to get my cooperation. This cold, calculating man standing before me.

"Why am I here?" I ask, leaning over to place the books on the sofa I was fucked on last night. I push the thought away and meet Fallon's cold eyes. Part of me wonders if he told them to fuck us that night in the club or if they did that on their own.

Does it matter? I was willing every single time.

I certainly was last night.

"Revenge," he says, tucking his hands into the pocket of his slacks.

"Not good enough," I snap, irritation clawing up my back. "I'm aware of your thirst for revenge. Kindly explain what it is you want me to do. It's my understanding you need my cooperation."

Fallon's lip curls again, and it reminds me of Reaper's smirking mask. He's got that same slightly arrogant, wholly brutal air about him that puts me on alert. "It's a bit more complicated than that, Delilah."

Goosebumps prick the back of my neck the second my name slips past his lips. Dread snakes up my arms, slithering around my neck. The way he says my name is too familiar. Too sweet, like candy coated violence. Like he knows a secret about me, but will never tell.

"You collected all that evidence against Rune," I say, glancing briefly at Reaper. "It's safe to say that you plan to use it."

"Indeed," Fallon says, rocking back on his heels, cocking his head to the side as he eyes me. The man tries to have a casual air about him, but he's too.... hard and polished to pull it off. "Our source has provided us with years of evidence. Enough to take it to the right people and have him removed."

"This is the second time I've heard about a source. Is it someone close to Rune? On the inside?" I ask. Reaper mentioned this when he showed me the files, but it didn't register. When

Fallon smiles coldly, I know he's not going to answer, not that I expected him to, so I say, "If you take this evidence to the authorities, they'll cover it up for Rune. He pays too well and knows too many people for them not to."

"Which is why we haven't," he says. Fallon backs away, passing between the four men. He stops by the large windows overlooking the lawn at the front of the house. Pulling a black phone from inside his jacket pocket, he glances at the screen, then tucks it back.

"What do you want us to do?" I ask, growing impatient. I've waited weeks for answers and they are finally in front of me, yet I'm still being denied. "We're here, willing to listen. Willing to help. Now, what do you want us to do?"

Fallon raises his brow. "We?" He turns to face me fully, eyes boring under my skin, to my bones. It feels like he's seeing all the way down to the blood in my veins, and the unease curling around my ribs. "There is no *we*. I just want you, Delilah."

My stomach twists.

"It's a shame," their father says. "But we must abide by the code."

"Father," Viper breathes and I glance over to find his pretty blue eyes gleaming with... Fear? Dread?

God, I want to see their faces so I can read them better. Learn their tells.

Fallon spins on his heel to face Viper. "I heard you, my son, but I'm not sure if it was a question or a defiance."

Viper's eyes drop and my stomach hits the ground with a sparking crash. My fingers curl into my dress at my sides, gathering it in fists as Viper takes a step back.

Jesus.

"Why are you here?" I ask, my guts churning with rage. How dare this man come in here and make Viper... make him *retreat*.

Fallon looks over his shoulder at me. "My sons have defied an order. I'm here to correct this."

"What order?" I snap. "I said I was willing to help. I said I was will—"

That's when I hear it.

It's distant at first, just a faint *thump, thump, thumping* pulse like a heartbeat, but as it moves closer, I know exactly what it is.

No.

My fingers unfurl. My heart slams into my chest. I slide my foot back, shaking my head, and I turn, running for the foyer, fear ripping at my throat. I skid to a stop, frantically scanning the entry like she'll suddenly appear and I can wrap my arms around her, when my eyes land on the partially open front door. I stumble forward, my legs weak with panic.

"Where is she?" I scream, the pulsing of the chopper blades growing louder and louder. My chest squeezes, like someone's reached into my chest and has my heart, my lungs, my soul in a death grip, ready to rip them all from my body.

My boots hit the hardwood with loud thuds, and I reach for the door. But before I can fling it all the way open and run to her, a strong arm wraps around my waist and pulls me back into a solid chest. My fingers slip off the rough wood and it swings open.

A black mass, like swirling shadows, descends from above and the chopper lands on the lawn. Several men rush from the side of the house just as two more jump from the helicopter, their black uniforms blending into the night.

Suddenly, a dark figure materializes from the left side of the mansion. In the corner of my eye, I catch a glimpse of a white dress and flowing dark red hair.

I kick back, connecting with a shin, a feral scream ripping from my throat.

"I'm sorry," Striker grates, trying to keep me still, but I claw at his gloved hand, kicking out wildly. "I'm so sorry."

But I don't care about his apologies. Nothing matters but getting to her.

Cora jerks in the soldier's grasp, her hair wild around her face from the chaotic wind of the helicopter. She kicks the black-clad soldier, but he flings her forward and she falls to her knees.

"Cora!" My scream tears from my throat. I kick back again, but Striker shifts, and we both fall to the ground. "Cora!"

She must hear me over the roar of the blades because she looks back over her shoulder, scrambling to stand as she tries to crawl away. Tries to run. But he grips her by her waist and shoves her through the black mouth of the chopper. The two men follow her and the door slides closed. It isn't until the whipping noise of the chopper blades begins to fade that I can hear it.

My screams.

No. No. No.

You promised.

"I'm so sorry. We'll get her. I'm *so sorry.*" Striker chokes on the last few words, like they're ripping his throat to shreds. He lets me go and I wrap my arms around myself, rocking forward. My fingers furl into my chest, clutching at the open wound where my heart was just ripped out.

They promised.

I feel someone drop next to me, then large hands pull me to his chest. I slap him away because he's a liar. He promised her. She was his. She's ours and he just let her go. They all did. They stood by and did nothing as she was taken from me.

They did *nothing*, knowing what she was being sent back to.

I hit him again and again, my cries growing more hysterical. But he refuses to let me go. Reaper grips my shoulders, pulling me against him. I crash into his chest, burying my face in his shirt.

Cupping my cheeks, Reaper pulls me up to look in his eyes and leans in, whispering in my ear, "Don't worry, Kitten. We'll get her back. I never let go of what's mine."

Next to him, Breaker crouches, brushing hair from my face, his light eyes watching the sky. I grip Reaper's shirt, barely able to breathe around the agony in my chest.

"No one takes what's ours," Breaker says, and his winter eyes meet mine. They swirl, icy with something I've never seen in them before. Utter violence.

The story continues with

BREAKER

Cast of Characters

Delilah Gavin – 26, Virgo
Cora Julian – 25, Cancer
Reaper – 35, Virgo
Striker – 30, Gemini
Breaker – 28, Taurus
Viper – 32, Sagittarius
Rune Gavin – 53, Scorpio
Clyde Harlow, 55, Gemini
Zane Devin, 40, Libra
Fallon Byrns, 59, Aries
Commander Maxim, 51, Scorpio
Cook, 50, Sagittarius
Teacher, 46, Libra
~~Hunter~~
~~Raid~~
~~Sniper~~
~~Seeker~~
~~Caroline Julian~~
~~Drake Julian~~

Acknowledgements

Striker is the hardest book I've written to date. His character is complex, his story is dark. He's good and not so good. Sweet and not so sweet. Passionate but oh so cold if you cross him.

As a panster/discovery writer, I know little about the books I write other than the characters, the general plotline, and the end. The story unfolds for me the same way it does a reader most days.

Striker is close to me because I really had to tap into some dark themes to get this book out. I triggered myself constantly, but pushed through out of sheer insanity. I lived and breathed this book. It consumed me night and day, even when I wasn't at my desk writing, my mind was a mess, thinking about this book and the characters.

There are a few people I want to thank for their amazing support.

My partner, my rock, my person, played a huge part in these first two books being put to page.

Scott, you've listened to me rant about these books for *months*, knowing there are four more to go and will be listening to me talk for endless more. You helped me plot. Endured hours upon hours of me talking about these characters, the story. The dreaded lodge. Striker. I asked you endless questions about weapons, which you patiently answered. Thank you for putting up with me.

Thank you for not being offended that I spent our days off together consumed with these books even when I wasn't writing.

My beta readers. You are the backbone of this story. I dribbled this book out to you, and more times than not it was a mess of half ideas, and you ate it up. Thank you for your patience and understanding.

Sam. Thank you for reminding me it's okay for Striker to be sad and sensitive and angry and an asshole at times.

TK... You are my biggest fan and its hard to take anything you say seriously because you always, *always* love it. But, you also told me to remember that men are animals and need to be fed.

And they love to hunt pretty girls who refuse to be tamed, most of all.

Clary. I can't thank you enough. You told me you loved this book because of the emotional depth. It reminded me that people love complex characters as much as the spice. Your input and the detailed feedback on so many different aspects helped tremendously. If it wasn't for you, we'd not have such a clear picture of Viper, or have learned a little more about what drives Reaper.

Thank you all.

This book wouldn't be what it was without you.

Oh...

And Striker.

Thank you for this book. I you will always live rent free in my head.

Note to Readers

Thank you for taking the time to read this book!
If you enjoyed, please consider leaving a review.

Reviews help readers find new books!

About the Author

Finding Strength in Love

Steamy romantic suspense author and lover of all things romance.

MEET FANNY LEE SAVAGE, the bestselling romance author known for her suspenseful and steamy stories of characters overcoming trauma and hardships. In her novels, she explores the resilience of the human spirit and the power of love to heal even the deepest wounds.

In the *Guardian Series*, a paranormal romance set in modern times, Ms. Savage combines her love of ancient history and folklore to create a dark new world. Her action-packed *Playhouse Series* immerses readers into the underworld of Miami and the inner workings of the modern-day mob. Her novels are full of sensual romance, dark humor, and edge of your seat suspense.

If you're looking for a romantic read that will make you laugh, cry, and fall in love, Ms. Savages' books are for you. Every story is full of sensual (steamy) romance, and characters that struggle with finding the courage to move forward and fight for themselves. With her powerful storytelling, she'll take you on an emotional journey that will stay with you long after you've turned the last page.

Also By...
Contemporary Romance
The Fake Series

Fake Hearts and Kisses

Fake Coral and Keys

Fake Whiskey and Words

Fake Enemies and Allies

Fake Book 5 — COMING SOON

Fake Book 6 — COMING SOON

Taboo/Forbidden Love Series—Standalone Novelettes

One Night—A Taboo Stepbrother Romance

Mr. Dylan—A Boss Romance

Romantic Suspense
The Playhouse Series

Seven Days

Four Days

Seven Weeks

Paranormal Romance (Modern Fantasy)
The Guardian Series

In the Shadow of Angels

In the Shadow of Monsters

In the Shadow of Demons – COMING SOON

Printed in Great Britain
by Amazon